Heidi Swain

'Sweet and lovely. I guarantee you will fall in love with Heidi's wonderful world' **Milly Johnson**

'Wise, warm and wonderful – a real summer treat!' ***Heat***

'Sparkling and romantic' ***My Weekly***

'The queen of feel-good' ***Woman & Home***

'A fabulous feel good read – a ray of reading sunshine!' **Laura Kemp**

'The most delicious slice of festive fiction: a true comfort read and the perfect treat to alleviate all the stress!' **Veronica Henry**

'Sprinkled with Christmas sparkle' **Trisha Ashley**

'A story that captures your heart' **Chrissie Barlow**

'Fans of Carole Matthews will enjoy this heartfelt novel' **Katie Oliver**

Heidi Swain lives in Norfolk with her family and a mischievous black cat called Storm. She is passionate about gardening, the countryside and collects vintage paraphernalia. *A Taste of Home* is her twelfth novel. You can follow Heidi on Twitter @Heidi_Swain or visit her website: heidiswain.co.uk

Also by Heidi Swain

The Cherry Tree Café
Summer at Skylark Farm
Mince Pies and Mistletoe at the Christmas Market
Coming Home to Cuckoo Cottage
Sleigh Rides and Silver Bells at the Christmas Fair
Sunshine and Sweet Peas in Nightingale Square
Snowflakes and Cinnamon Swirls
at the Winter Wonderland
Poppy's Recipe for Life
The Christmas Wish List
The Secret Seaside Escape
The Winter Garden

Heidi Swain

A Taste of Home

SIMON & SCHUSTER

London · New York · Sydney · Toronto · New Delhi

First published in Great Britain by Simon & Schuster UK Ltd, 2021

1 3 5 7 9 10 8 6 4 2

Simon & Schuster UK Ltd
1st Floor
222 Gray's Inn Road
London WC1X 8HB

Simon & Schuster Australia, Sydney

Simon & Schuster India, New Delhi

www.simonandschuster.co.uk
www.simonandschuster.com.au
www.simonandschuster.co.in

A CIP catalogue record for this book is available from the British Library

Paperback ISBN: 978-1-4711-9582-2
eBook ISBN: 978-1-4711-9583-9
Audio ISBN: 978-1-3985-0059-4

Typeset in the UK by M Rules
Printed and bound in Great Britain by CPI Group (UK) Ltd, Croydon, CR0 4YY

To

My warm, wise, wonderful friend

Jenni Keer

I'm blessed to have you in my life

Chapter 1

The sun had long since set over the Italian horizon before the last of the mourners finally headed back to their homes, leaving behind a mountain of food and a silence in the farm-house kitchen that neither the Rossi family nor I could bear to acknowledge.

No one's eyes strayed to Mum's much-loved patterned Moroccan shawl draped over the chair next to the stove, or to her collection of thin gold and silver bangles bundled together in a box on the table amid the crockery and cutlery. Early that morning, I had thought I might wear them to her funeral, but when it came to it, I couldn't.

'I don't think I can do this,' I had sobbed, pulling them off again when it was time to leave for the church, but I wasn't talking about wearing her jewellery. 'I'm not ready.'

I had watched Mum's last breath leave her body and yet somehow, I still couldn't believe that she was gone. I didn't want to believe that she was gone. We might have spent more time apart than together, more hours sparring than hugging, but the thought of never seeing her again, never having another spirited cross word, wrenched my heart in two.

I had tried to make myself believe that she was travelling again, off on one of her adventures, but the image of her final moments was imprinted on the inside of my eyelids and that made the pretence impossible.

'You will never be ready, darling Fliss,' Nonna had said, her eyes as swollen from crying as mine as she gently took my hand and guided me out the door into the spring sunshine and then to the waiting car. 'Not for this.'

Nonna's diminutive figure had been by my side all day. She had led me through the service, walked me to the graveside, and afterwards found me a seat and another plate of food back in the kitchen which had bulged with Rossi relatives all wanting to pay their respects. She was watching me even now, from the far side of the room. I quickly got up and began covering dishes and rearranging chairs, not wanting to worry her further.

'Fliss,' said Alessandro, Nonna's son, the dear man who considered Mum his sister even though they hadn't shared a single drop of blood. 'Leave that.'

'But it needs doing,' I replied, my voice every bit as hoarse as his. 'The food needs to be put away, at least.'

There were no dishes to wash. The many friends and relatives had made sure of that. Practically nothing had been left for the family to do aside from grieve for my mother, the woman who had arrived at their door, a pregnant teenager, all alone in the world, almost three decades ago. Without question they had welcomed her in, given her a home and taken her to their hearts and now they mourned her passing every bit as gravely as if she had been one of their very own.

'It can wait,' Alessandro kindly said. 'I need to give you this.'

'What is it?' I asked, turning to face him.

'*Una lettera*,' he said, holding out a white envelope.

'A letter?' I swallowed. 'For me?'

I never got mail at the farm. I had no one to write to me in Puglia. Everyone in the world I loved was right here. Except for Mum. I swallowed hard, pushing the thought of her final destination away.

'It's from your mother.'

My eyes flicked from the envelope to Alessandro's care-worn face and I bit my bottom lip to stop it trembling. I couldn't have more tears to shed. It surely wasn't possible for my body to produce another single one.

'She wrote me a letter?' I croaked.

'You know your mamma,' he shrugged, the tiniest smile on his lips. 'She always liked to have the last word.'

I slid the envelope into my skirt pocket and minutes later, having grabbed a coat and lantern from the porch and made sure Nonna was looking the other way, I slipped out of the house and made my way down to the cherry orchard. It was chilly, even for April, and I turned up the collar of the coat and walked a little faster.

The letter sat heavy in my pocket, almost as heavy as the weight which had settled on my chest the moment Mum had returned to the farm after cutting her last trip short. Footloose and fancy free, there were few corners of the globe she hadn't visited and she had planned to be away for months. When she turned up again, just a few weeks later, we knew something was wrong. Just one glimpse at her unusually pale and painfully thin face told us something was seriously amiss. The doctor confirmed our fears and the cancer rampaging through her system had claimed her before any of us had even started to take the diagnosis in.

'Oh, Mum,' I sobbed as I came to a stop at the foot of one of the oldest cherry trees on the farm. I rested my back against the trunk and slid down, coming to a bump on the hard ground.

I tugged the envelope out of my pocket and arranged the lantern so I could read what was inside. The writing didn't look much like Mum's. It was spidery, obviously scribbled before her strength had left her and she couldn't even hold up her head, let alone control a pen. I pushed the image away. I didn't want to think of her like that. She had always been so vibrant and full of energy, that was what I needed to remember.

Even though the words didn't look like hers, the tone was unmistakably Mum's; I could imagine her standing over me and I could hear her voice in my head.

'This can't be true,' I whispered into the evening air as I scanned the page. 'I can't believe it.'

'It is,' came her swift response, clear as the night sky and carried on the chilly breeze. 'You must.'

I looked at the letter again.

Fliss, I have something to tell you, something I should have told you years ago but I could never find the words. I know it will come as a shock and I hope you can forgive me.

I could tell the letter had been hastily written, as if she wanted to commit her confession to paper before she changed her mind . . . or ran out of time.

Do you remember when you told me you didn't want to travel with me anymore? That you'd seen enough of the world, and that you wanted to stay at the farm because it was where your roots were planted?

I did remember saying that, and mostly because of her reaction. Rather than laugh my words off, as I had expected her to in her free-spirited I-refuse-to-be-tethered kind of way, she had been upset. I had always assumed she was disappointed that I wasn't going to carry on following in her flighty footsteps, but apparently not.

The truth is, I stayed away for so long after that because I was feeling guilty. I know you will roll your eyes at that because you've always said I'm too self-absorbed to feel bad about anything . . .

I wasn't rolling my eyes. Far from it.

. . . but I did feel awful and that's because I have kept something from you Fliss. I have kept something important from you and the Rossis. Your roots shouldn't be planted here in Puglia because you have family elsewhere. I know I've always maintained it's just the two of us in the world, but it isn't. It never has been.

When I left the UK in search of your father, I left my family behind. I never got on with my dad, but I think you might. I think you might be a better fit for the family farm than I was too. I think your roots should be there, Fliss, buried in the British Fenland soil, not planted here in Italy where I put them.

I know I'm not in a position to make demands, but I think you should go to the farm and see it for yourself. It's called Fenview Farm, and it's near a town called Wynbridge. Go and find it before you finally settle on your place in the world.

I'm sorry I never told you any of this before and I'm sorry there's no time now to tell you more. I hope you can forgive me. I'm not sure I can forgive myself.

With all my love, Mum xxx

I stared at the letter, my hands shaking with more than the cold. Countless times both Mum and Nonna had recounted how she had arrived at the farm pregnant and looking for the boy she had had a holiday romance with. The address he had given her didn't exist, but the Rossis did and they had taken her in. Their farm became ours. It was where I belonged.

Or at least it was where I had always believed I belonged. I had never given a thought to what Mum's life had been before Puglia, but now I knew she had grown up on a farm in England that bore the Brown name and she had left it behind, along with her family, and I felt shocked to my very core. She must have fled under one hell of a cloud if it had stopped her going back.

'Fliss!'

The sudden voice, cutting through the silence, made me jump. I almost dropped the letter and pulled in a lungful of air. I hadn't realised I was holding my breath.

'Fliss!' bawled the voice again.

It was Marco, Alessandro's son, Nonna's handsome grandson. The man I thought of as my brother. We had grown up on the farm together. I had been there for him when he lost his mamma and now, he was here for me as I tried to navigate my way through saying goodbye to mine.

'I'm here!' I shouted back, making the dogs in the yard bark.

'*Sbrigati*!'

'I'll be there in a minute.'

'It's time to eat!'

The long day had been punctuated by nothing but crying

and eating. In fact, the whole of the last few days had been an exhausting mix of the two. I really didn't think I could manage to do more of either.

'*Sbrigati*,' came Marco's demand again.

'I am hurrying,' I muttered, trying to slip the letter back into my pocket and only then realising that there was another, slightly smaller, envelope inside the first.

'What are you doing out here?' Marco asked, his voice closer as he negotiated the path I had taken through the trees, aided by the torch on his phone. 'It's too cold.'

'I just wanted a minute,' I sniffed, my eyes quickly scanning the second envelope which had the request 'please pass on when you arrive' scribbled on the back.

Mum obviously expected me to deliver her missive, but that wasn't going to happen. I wouldn't be going to Fenview Farm or to Wynbridge. I had no need of another family, even if they were my flesh and blood. My home and my heart were here in Puglia with Nonna, Alessandro and Marco.

'What have you got there?' Marco asked.

I shook my head.

'Sorry,' he said. 'It's none of my business.'

'It's fine,' I told him, pushing the letter further into my pocket, but not wanting to shut him out. 'It's a letter. From Mum.'

'What does it say?'

'Nothing important,' I lied, holding out my hand so he could pull me up.

He stared down at me, his eyes searching mine.

'It really is nothing,' I swallowed.

Arm-in-arm, we set off back towards the house.

Even though we were all used to Mum being away for months at a time, there was no deluding ourselves that she was coming back. As much as I would have loved to, I couldn't erase the memory of the last couple of months any more than I could pretend that her letter wasn't sitting on the nightstand next to my bed.

I felt her absence everywhere. It was the last thing I thought of before I tried to sleep and the first thing I remembered when I woke from the hours spent tossing, turning and dreaming. As the days slowly passed, and even though I tried not to because my life really didn't need further disruption, I began to think more about the words she had left behind and the implications they could have if I acted on them.

The internet at the farm was intermittent at best which was frustrating because, as my thoughts strayed more and more often to what this Fenview Farm and Wynbridge looked like, it couldn't maintain a consistent enough connection to satisfy my curiosity.

I had been adamant the day of Mum's funeral that the Rossis were all the family I needed, and that I wasn't going to share with them what she had revealed, but my inquisitiveness had slowly got the better of me. Just as Mum had known it would. What sort of farm was it, I wondered, and more to the point, why did she think that I would be a better fit for it, and her father, than she had been?

Within a fortnight I was fit to burst and couldn't keep the details of the letter secret any longer. I had made up my mind that I would go. I would take a flight to the UK and find the previously unheard of family and farm for myself. If nothing else, the trip would take me to a place where I wouldn't constantly be reminded that Mum had left me for good.

'So,' I said, carefully laying the letter on the kitchen table after supper one evening. 'I need to talk to you all. I have something to tell you.'

Grandmother, son and grandson sat in silence but each became increasingly wide-eyed as I read what Mum had written. Their expressions told me that they had absolutely no idea there was a Brown family back in England missing their daughter. When I had finished, I slowly drank my coffee, letting the words settle and sink in.

I knew it would have pained Mum to know that I would have to share her secret. To the Rossis, nothing was more important than family; they were the classic Italian *famiglia* and she would have worried about lowering herself in their adoring estimation. But she needn't have. They were shocked, but not unkind.

'Almost thirty years,' Alessandro quietly said. 'She left England almost thirty years ago and she never breathed a word about growing up on a farm or about her family.'

'I know,' I nodded.

'I suppose we all just assumed that she had no one,' he said, shaking his head. 'No one who would miss her anyway, but this,' he said pointing at the letter, 'suggests otherwise, doesn't it?'

'Yes,' I agreed. 'I think it does.'

'Has she been in touch with them at all in all that time?'

'I don't think so,' I swallowed. 'I don't even know if she told them she was pregnant before she left, so they might not even know I exist.'

Alessandro ran a hand through his thick salt-and-pepper curls. Marco chewed his thumb-nail and Nonna stared at the letter.

'How old would that make your grandparents, Fliss?' Alessandro frowned.

'Pretty old,' Marco haphazardly calculated before I could answer. 'Perhaps as old as Nonna. What are you going to do, Fliss?'

'She's going to go, of course,' Nonna firmly answered, finally finding her voice.

'Yes,' Alessandro added. 'Fliss, you must.'

They sounded as though they were all set to try and convince me, but I'd already decided.

'But we're Fliss's family,' Marco cut in. 'What was Jennifer thinking, dropping this bombshell from beyond the grave? Why did she wait?'

'Probably so she didn't have to deal with all this,' I answered, with a wry smile.

Marco reached across the table for my hand and squeezed it tight.

'She shouldn't have said anything at all,' he frowned.

'Yes,' said Nonna. 'She should.'

'I'll come with you then,' Marco added, having taken a moment to absorb Nonna's pronouncement.

'No,' I said. 'You're needed here. And besides, this is one journey I really feel as though I need to make on my own.'

Alessandro and Nonna exchanged a look, clearly relieved that I didn't need talking around.

'Are you going to contact your grandparents before you go?' Marco asked.

'I wouldn't know what to say,' I shrugged, my heart fluttering at the thought of having to find the words.

'I suppose it would be difficult to explain in a letter or on the telephone,' said Alessandro, sucking his bottom lip as he looked down at Mum's spidery words.

'And I don't want to overthink it,' I told them. 'Now I've made up my mind, I just want to go. I'll think about what I'm going to say when I get there. It's the only way to make sure I don't talk myself out of doing it. One step at a time, you know?'

'One step at a time,' Marco repeated.

'When will you leave?' Nonna asked, her eyes filled with tears.

'At the end of the week,' I told her. 'I'll book a flight for Friday.'

She nodded and reached for my other hand, and just like that the course of my life completely changed direction.

Chapter 2

My worldly goods didn't amount to all that much and when I sorted through Mum's things it transpired that she had amassed even less. Aside from her bangles, her other possessions were staying at the farm and I packed the little I needed to take with me into my capacious rucksack and carry-on bag. Materially, I didn't have a lot to show for twenty-eight years of living, but my heart had always been full and that was all that mattered to me.

'I don't understand why you're taking so much,' Marco sulked the morning I was set to leave, even though he could clearly see I was taking very little. 'It's not as if you won't be coming back, is it?'

'Don't worry,' I said, pulling him into a hug. 'You're not getting rid of me for good.'

'I should hope not,' he said, squeezing me tight. 'The season starts soon and you need to be here to organise the troops. That's still your job, you know?'

Inspired by how Mum had worked on various farms

around the world to fund her happy-go-lucky lifestyle, the Rossi farm was set up to welcome travellers who wanted to stay and immerse themselves in local life for a while, rather than whizz through, barely taking in the sights before moving on.

Everyone worked and lived together over the summer months and even though each year welcomed a different mix of people, the atmosphere was always the same – inclusive and a lot of fun. From mid-May to late October the farm buzzed and we all preferred it to the quieter months of winter.

'I know it is,' I smiled, amused that Marco was using my role at the farm to mask how much he was going to miss me. 'And I'll probably be back even before the first lot arrive.'

'Probably?' he asked, pulling away, his eyebrows raised.

'Stop pressuring her, Marco,' said Alessandro. 'She'll be as long as it takes. Fliss, we need to go.'

He took my bags out to the truck and I swallowed down the lump in my throat. I wasn't sure I could handle saying goodbye to Nonna.

'Here,' she said, holding out a sheet of paper. 'This is for you.'

'What is it?' I asked.

'Read it and see.'

I only took in the four words written at the top before my throat closed up and my vision blurred. Copied straight out of her ancient handwritten family cookbook it was the Rossi cherry and almond tart recipe. I had been asking her for it for years, but she had always refused to give me the exact details. The particulars were a closely guarded family secret, not even Alessandro and Marco were privy to the extra ingredient which she only ever added when no one else was in the kitchen.

'Wherever you end up,' she shakily said, 'this will always give you a taste of home.'

I let out a steadying breath and nodded.

'I'll keep it safe,' I huskily promised, carefully folding and tucking it into the breast pocket of my shirt alongside Mum's two letters.

Together they felt like a protective talisman close to my heart and I was in no doubt of the honour Nonna had bestowed upon me by handing the treasured recipe over.

'And you only add the last ingredient when no one is watching,' she sternly reminded me.

'Of course,' I smiled, bending to give her one last hug.

This departure from the farm felt very different to when Mum was dragging me off somewhere. It felt unsettlingly final. Not as though I would *never* be coming back, rather that when I did things would be altered for good.

The journey from Puglia to Peterborough wasn't all that long but by the time I checked into the hotel where I was staying for my first night on UK soil, I felt exhausted. I briefly video called the farm to let everyone know I was safe and then, refusing to give in to the bout of homesickness the sight of the familiar kitchen aroused, I indulged in a long, hot bath.

Still with no real idea of where I was going to end up the next day, but knowing I had come far enough not to change my mind, I snuggled down in the comfortable double bed and began to google.

'Fenview Farm,' I said aloud as I typed the name into the search bar. 'Wynbridge.'

There was no website for the farm, or social media presence, and Google Street View offered up little more than a view of a Fenland drove road, flat and far reaching, but the land on either side of it appeared to be full of orchards. I hadn't given much thought to what sort of farm Fenview might be, but looking at the landscape, a fruit farm felt likely. My heart skittered at the thought. The acres of trees would provide a setting I could relate to and there was some comfort in that. Perhaps that was why Mum considered it a match for me, but why hadn't it been for her?

I could see that most of the trees looked to be well-tended, but there were a couple of areas which were either neglected, or altogether abandoned. The exact spot on the road where the farm was located was obscured by a row of silver birches so I couldn't see much, but from what I could make out it looked to be a proper working farm.

It pained me to think that Mum had never once mentioned it. She had worked her way around numerous farms over the years, but she had never shared a single detail about the one which was owned by her family. Why exactly was that? My mind started to race again in spite of my efforts to stop it before and, knowing I was in danger of undoing all the good my relaxing bath had done, I quickly put my phone down and turned off the light before I worked my way up to a panic.

Saturday was a warm, soft, spring day and practically as soon as the bus left Peterborough I became mesmerised by the landscape. Parts of Puglia were flat, but nothing like the Fens. The vast fields stretched all the way to the horizon, occasionally interrupted by a distant copse, or boundary defining ditch, but beyond that there appeared to be nothing. Or there was nothing until we reached the outskirts of Wynbridge. Then the orchards began.

Acre upon acre of rows of flat-topped trees, many laden with frothy bursting blossom, were planted along both sides of the road, just as I had seen on Google. My heart soared at the sight and I wondered if there would be as much of a spectacle waiting to welcome me to Fenview Farm. I hoped the discarded orchards I had seen online didn't belong to the place. That really would be too sad.

But more to the point, would there be a welcome for *me* at Fenview Farm? For the first time since I had decided to come, I felt a real rush of nerves. It was more intense than what I had felt the night before and it stamped all over practically every other emotion I had recently experienced. I began to feel nauseous.

Was I making a mistake? Why did Mum think that me coming here was so important when she herself had left almost thirty years ago without a backwards glance? She had written that I would be a better fit for the place, but were she and I really so different?

'This is as far as I go,' said the bus driver, as he twisted round to look at me from his seat and pulled me out of my reverie. 'Are you getting off or going back?'

He didn't know it of course, but that was actually a huge question.

'Getting off,' I said, grabbing my bags and rushing along the aisle and down the steps before I bolted back to Peterborough.

'Town square's that way,' he called after me, pointing along the road.

Clearly, I didn't look like someone who knew where they were going.

'Will I be able to find a taxi there?'

'Shouldn't be a problem,' he said, before closing the doors and swinging the bus round to face the way we'd just come.

I hoisted my pack on to my back and headed in the direction he had indicated. The little town looked lovely in the sunshine, almost idyllic. There was a busy market in the centre of the square and an interesting variety of shops around the edges. There was a pretty café set behind a cherry tree, with some sort of gallery next door, and a pub with an impressive array of spring flowering containers.

The friendly chatter and busyness reminded me of where I shopped in Italy and I tried to marry my initial impression of the place with a vision of Mum. This must have been where she visited and hung out when she was growing up, but I couldn't picture her anywhere. 'Work hard, play hard' was the ethos she had lived by. The second she'd earned enough in the country she was off to the bright lights and big cities to spend it and immerse herself in new experiences, but there didn't look to be those sorts of opportunities here.

Wynbridge looked too restrained for her taste, altogether too small, but I was charmed. That said, the town was no doubt a very different place all those years ago, and Mum a different person. Perhaps it had satisfied her until she fell pregnant with me and her life had inevitably changed.

'Can you take me to Fenview Farm, please?' I asked the only cab driver who was parked in a bay marked out for taxis.

'Do you have a postcode?'

I couldn't place his accent.

'Yes,' I said, pulling a scrap of paper out of my jeans pocket and handing it over. 'It's on Lady's Drove, if that's any help.'

'Yes,' he said, as I stuffed my bags into the back of the car. 'I know that road. It's the fruit farm you want.'

The journey only took a few minutes but in that time my heart started to canter again and as we came to a stop and I took in more of the landmark orchards, I thought it was going to make a bid for freedom and burst right out of my chest.

'This is it,' said the driver. 'That's four pounds, please.'

'Keep the change,' I said, the words sticking in my throat as I handed him a five-pound note.

'Thanks. Do you need a receipt?'

'No. No, thank you.'

I took in the peeling farm sign which was leaning drunkenly towards the road. This didn't look like the Fenview Farm that I had spent the long watches of the previous night building up in my mind. I wondered if the rosy-cheeked Nonna and big-hearted Nonno I had imagined were going to be missing too. There was a small red car parked in the yard, so clearly someone was home.

The taxi driver cleared his throat, making me jump.

'Sorry,' I said. 'I'll get out.'

I still didn't move.

'Do you need a hand?'

'No,' I said. 'It's all right. I can manage.'

I had barely closed the door before he pulled away, leaving me in a cloud of dust. I watched until he was out of sight, then took a tentative step into the yard.

'Eliot!' shouted a voice from the house. 'Is that you? You've taken your time, haven't you?'

The voice didn't sound old enough to belong to my grandmother and obviously I had no idea who Eliot was, so I felt on the back foot even before I'd knocked on the door.

'Come on!' called the voice again. 'Hurry up. I have to go.'

I took a deep breath, walked briskly to the open door and knocked loudly on the frame in the hope that whoever was inside would realise I wasn't who they were expecting.

'Stop buggering about and give me a hand, would you? I need to get to Mrs Simpkins. Her stats were ridiculously low first thing, and I . . .'

The words trailed off as the owner of the voice glared up

from the pile of paper she was rifling through and saw me hovering in the doorway.

'Oh,' she frowned. 'Not Eliot then.'

'Afraid not,' I smiled, apologetically.

'And not the doctor either.'

'Definitely not the doctor.'

The young woman, dressed in a blue healthcare tunic, her hair pulled back in a tight ponytail, looked me up and down and then dumped the papers back on the table. She couldn't have looked more annoyed if she tried.

'So, who are you then?' she frowned.

I cleared my throat. I really didn't want to tell her. She was obviously neither of my grandparents and I had planned to announce myself to them before anyone else.

'Do you not know?' she snapped.

'Fliss,' I swallowed. 'Felicity Brown.'

I knew instantly that I should have just said my first name, but her waspish manner had thrown me and I found myself in an even more heightened state of tension than I had been when I climbed out of the taxi.

'Brown?'

'Yes,' I swallowed.

There was no point retracting it now.

'You're a relative?' she asked, sounding slightly less peeved.

'Granddaughter,' I told her, my voice barely louder than a whisper.

There. I'd said it. The cat was definitely out of the bag.

'Granddaughter?' she repeated.

I wanted to ask her to lower her voice, but daren't. She still looked irritated and I found her a bit intimidating, even though she was only a tiny little thing.

'That's right,' I confirmed.

It was a less than satisfactory start and I felt my shoulders sag. In my head, I'd imagined finding my grandparents sitting together, perhaps enjoying a mid-morning coffee and looking through the newspaper when I rocked up, presented myself and made their day. Facing a harassed care worker before I'd even properly crossed the threshold hadn't been part of any of the fantasies I'd indulged in. I wondered which of my two grandparents required the assistance of the aggravated carer.

'Well, come in properly then,' she said, looking me over again.

I shuffled into the cool kitchen and rested my rucksack against the table while my gaze flicked around the room. It was practical with a few homely touches, but not particularly tidy. I wasn't sure exactly what I had been expecting, but this place didn't match the comforting rustic Rossi space that I associated with country kitchens.

'You don't look much like a Brown,' said the carer, narrowing her eyes. 'And Bill's never mentioned family to me, but then he is quite a private person, isn't he?'

Bill was my grandfather's name then. I wondered if it might be short for William. Mum really should have added her parents' names to her letter, but then given the little energy she'd had when she wrote it, it was a miracle she'd got down as much as she had.

'Mm,' I tentatively agreed, guessing that it was most likely him who was under the weather. 'And I've not been around,' I added. 'I've been abroad.'

It wasn't quite a lie.

'Been travelling, have you?' she asked, sounding envious.

'I've been in Italy,' I said, my cheeks colouring.

'Lucky you,' she sniffed, thankfully distracted from my family connection. 'The furthest I've been in the last couple of years is the other side of Peterborough and that was only for a weekend and it chucked it down the whole time. I'm Vicky, by the way.'

'Nice to meet you, Vicky.'

'I shouldn't still be here,' she then impatiently added, before checking her watch. 'I was only supposed to get his meal sorted, but he's not right, so I thought I'd better hang on. I called the doctor ages ago and Eliot's supposed to be on his way too.'

I still had no idea who Eliot was but didn't want to raise her suspicions by asking. The way she casually dropped his name into the conversation suggested that if I knew my grandfather, then I should know Eliot too.

'What's wrong with him?' I asked, now completely certain it was my grandfather who was unwell.

'Water infection, I reckon.'

Thankfully that didn't sound too serious.

'He's got a bit of a temperature and he can't stop peeing.

He's confused too. He keeps asking for Felicity, your grandmother.' Vicky shook her head and let out a long breath. 'The poor love.'

My head began to spin and I gripped the edge of the table. I had my grandmother's name. Mum had given me her mother's name. How could she never have mentioned that in the years since I'd been born?

'I see,' I swallowed.

'I haven't got the heart to keep telling him she's been dead for the last thirty plus years every time he starts shouting for her. It's nice that you're named after her though. You all right? You've gone a bit pale.'

I clung tighter to the table, my knuckles turning white, and nodded.

'Yes,' I said, my voice an octave too high. 'I'm okay. Just a bit tired after my journey.'

But of course, that wasn't it. I'd had no idea that my grandmother wasn't alive. I'd been expecting to find both her and my grandfather at the farm. My cosy Nonna and Nonno dream was evaporating before my eyes. What else had I mistakenly assumed?

'Thankfully his scar is healing up nicely,' Vicky carried on, blissfully unaware of the blow she had just delivered. 'So that's something, but he's going to be stiff when he starts the exercises again. But it can't be helped. He's certainly not steady enough on that new hip to carry on with them at the moment.'

'Right.'

A water infection *and* a new hip. Definitely not a quick fix. My timing really couldn't have been worse.

'But thank goodness you're here now,' Vicky rushed on, smiling for the first time since I'd arrived. 'You'll be able to manage until the doctor gets here, won't you?'

'Oh no,' I quickly shot back. 'I'm not staying. I can't.'

Vicky looked shocked, but not as shocked as I felt.

'Well, I can't either,' she said, fiddling with the papers again. 'I've got to get to Mrs Simpkins. I told her I'd be there almost an hour ago.'

'But I don't know what to do to help him . . .' I protested.

I didn't add that I didn't know him either.

'You won't have to do anything,' said Vicky, who was already halfway out the door. 'The doctor will be here any second and she'll sort him out. Just go and sit with him. Tell him about your holiday in Italy. That'll distract him.'

I didn't know about distracting him, I thought the shock of my unexpected arrival was more likely to finish him off completely.

Chapter 3

I watched with a sinking heart as Vicky speedily completed a neat three-point turn, pulled out of the yard and drove off in the same direction as the taxi had gone without a backwards glance. She hadn't even said goodbye to my grandfather and now he was left in my care and I had absolutely no idea what to do with him.

With one ear still on the road and desperately hoping to hear the cavalry, I turned back to the kitchen and took the room in, in more detail, all the while trying to assimilate the wealth of new information I had just been given.

Looking beyond the piles of newspapers, dirty laundry in the basket and unwashed dishes crowding the sink, I could see there were the foundations of what had once been a lovely room. Whether it was no longer fulfilling its potential because my grandfather couldn't manage to keep on top of it, or because he didn't care whether it looked lovely or not, I had no idea, but it wouldn't take much to get it back to its former glory.

I ran my fingers along the edge of the battered pine table which stood in the middle of the floor and wondered if this was where Mum had sat and eaten when she was growing up. Had she been responsible for any of the dents and scuffs which marked the wood? Had she sat and lamented the loss of her mother here, like I had so recently mourned for her around the Rossi table?

'Vicky!'

My hand flew to my chest and my heart thrummed. If that was how my grandfather usually sounded, then I could appreciate some of the reason why Mum had distanced herself from him. He sounded terrifying.

'Vicky!' he belligerently bellowed again. 'Where are you? I need you!'

The gruff demand hadn't come from upstairs, but from somewhere on the ground floor. There was no longed-for timely arrival of a car on the drive and I knew I was going to have to make my presence known, but what was I going to say?

Bill Brown sounded extremely agitated and the sudden appearance of a complete stranger, when he was already in such a vulnerable state, was hardly going to endear me to him or form an instant bond, was it?

'Right, I'll do it myself!' he yelled.

That sounded serious. What if he was trying to get off his chair, or out of his bed and took a tumble? That wouldn't help embed a recently replaced hip. I took another deep breath and quickly headed towards the room I could hear him calling from.

There was no time to process my emotions as I laid eyes on my grandfather for the very first time because he was, just as I had feared, trying to get himself out of the bed which had been shoehorned into what looked like the dining room. I dithered for a fraction of a second, then rushed forward to stop him toppling over.

'About bloody time,' he muttered, leaning his full weight against me.

He was heavier than I expected and it took all of my strength to support him and stop my knees from buckling.

'Who the hell are you?' he wheezed when he realised, I wasn't Vicky. 'What are you doing in my house?'

It was exactly what I had feared. He was going to have a coronary and it was all my fault.

'I'm Vicky's helper,' I told him, in what I hoped was a placatory tone as I eased him carefully back on to the bed.

'I don't want you,' he said, looking over my shoulder to the door. 'I want Vicky.'

I wanted Vicky too.

'She'll be back in a minute,' I told him, 'and the doctor will be here too.'

I was feeling well out of my depth and more than a little afraid.

'I don't want that quack,' he shouted. 'There's nothing wrong with me.'

I begged to differ, but was in no position to say as much. With him leant back against his pillows, I could see his face properly. His glasses were a little skew-whiff and I automatically reached out to straighten them, but he batted my hand away and did it himself. His hair was white, and his face, hands and forearms were deeply tanned. It wasn't the sort of tan you got from a holiday, rather one that you developed as a result of a lifetime working outdoors. He looked older than his years, but then having recently undergone surgery and with a water infection brewing, that was little wonder.

'Who are you?' he wheezily demanded.

'I'm Felicity,' I said, my name escaping before I had the sense to check myself.

'Who?'

'Felicity,' I said again, though this time more quietly.

His frown disappeared and his eyes were filled with wonder and then, to my horror, they were awash with tears.

'I've been calling for you,' he said, his lip trembling.

Oh god, now he thought I was his wife.

'No!' he suddenly yelled, making me jump back. His expression transformed into one of pure fury as he realised I wasn't the Felicity he wanted. 'You're not my wife! You're not my Felicity. What are you doing here? Get out!'

I took another step away, my mouth opening and closing like a trapdoor, but no more words fell out. Which was probably just as well, because I'd already said too much. I should never have come here. As soon as the doctor arrived, I would head back to town and get the bus to Peterborough and then book a flight back to Puglia.

This whole debacle was a disaster, I'd made a huge mistake

and so had Mum in thinking that I'd fit in here. It was foolish of her *and* me to think it was necessary for me to come. A lot had happened in the time since she'd left and neither of us had had the sense to realise that.

'Get out!' he shouted again, making me flinch.

'Now then Bill,' said a calm voice behind me. 'What's all the fuss? I can hear you out on the road.'

I spun round.

'She's not my wife,' he said again. 'She's not my Felicity.'

'I'm Doctor Clarke,' said the woman who had slipped in unheard, thanks to the furore. 'I'm here so see Mr Brown. Who are you?'

'She's not my wife!' my grandfather persisted, his words accompanied by an accusatory finger. 'She's not my wife.'

'Would you mind waiting outside please?'

I couldn't get back to the kitchen and outside fast enough.

My hands were shaking as I reached for my rucksack. I couldn't believe I'd made such a mess of everything. I hadn't been so naive as to think my turning up would go without a hitch, but I hadn't for a single second thought it would all go so spectacularly wrong either. Twice I'd stupidly blurted out my name, and in the process, ruined everything. Right on cue, Mum's letter, safe and snug with Nonna's recipe, rustled against the fabric of my shirt. Should I leave it, I wondered?

My fingers hovered over the pocket for the briefest moment and then retracted. No, I'd keep it with me and dis-appear again without a trace. With any luck, my grandfather's delirium would stop him from remembering the ugly little scene that had just played out once he'd recovered. Assuming he did. And with even more luck, the doctor wouldn't mention me, Vicky would be too busy and stressed to remember our brief exchange, and it would be as if I'd never existed.

'Blast,' I muttered, as I pulled out my phone and tried to ring for a taxi.

Not a single bar of signal was filled. I hoisted my pack higher and stepped out of the door. Hopefully I wouldn't have to walk too far along the drove before I hit, if not a signal hotspot, then perhaps a lukewarm one.

The distant drone of an engine met my ears as I reached the farm gate and I swallowed down the lump in my throat which had grown even bigger because of it. It was a Ducati motorbike engine, there was no mistaking it.

Alessandro had strictly forbidden his son from buying a motorbike, but that hadn't stopped Marco firing up YouTube and watching *endless* videos of the powerful machines going round and round the circuits at Mugello and Misano, or pointing out that with his famous surname, a bike should have been his birthright.

It used to drive both me and Nonna crackers, but in my heightened emotional state, it made me want to cry. In that moment I would have given anything to swap the dusty drove road in front of me for the equally dusty track which led to the Rossis' farm. This had to be a sign. I needed to get back to my haven in Puglia as soon as possible.

The bike was on me in a blink of an eye and turned smoothly into the farm gateway as I took a step out of the way. The person riding it was clearly a guy. Tall and well-built, easily filling the leathers which matched the machine's classic red livery. I turned back to the road and tried to decide which way to go.

'Wait up,' called the rider as he cut the engine.

I had no intention of 'waiting up'. I just wanted to get far away as quickly as possible.

'Don't take another step!' he crossly shouted, when I didn't stop.

Was he for real? Who the hell did he think he was?

'Are you talking to me?' I scowled, spinning back to face him and easily matching his aggression.

If he was looking for a row, he'd certainly picked the right moment and the right person come to that. I could feel all of my grief and frustration welling up. It really wouldn't take much for my volcano of emotions to erupt on an epic scale.

'I don't see anybody else here,' he shot back.

He unzipped the front of the all-in-one suit to reveal a broad chest encased in a plain dark T-shirt. His helmet and gloves were already balanced on the bike seat and I had to resist the urge to march over and knock them off. I also had to resist the flutter in my chest which occurred in response to the sudden and shocking spark of attraction which rushed through me as I took in his thick dark hair and handsome face.

What a ridiculous and inconvenient moment for me to fancy someone!

'What do you want?' I haughtily asked, struggling to

extinguish the growing flame as he ran his hands through his hair and readjusted his glasses.

The tough biker image, combined with the studious looking frames and glowering mood, was a total contradiction, but a very sexy one. I could almost feel Mum's elbow nudging me in the ribs and see the mischievous smile which would have lit up her beautiful face had she been standing next to me. She always had an eye for a handsome man. I ignored what I knew would have been her reaction to this guy's arrival and instead focused on snuffing out the flame of desire.

'What?' I shrugged.

The biker and I stood staring at each other for what must have been just a couple of seconds, but felt far longer. I couldn't be sure, but he seemed to be as taken aback by the sight of me as I was by the look of him.

'Who exactly are you?' he frowned.

'Who are you?' I quickly countered.

'I asked first.'

I shrugged and turned away again.

'I'm Eliot,' he said to my back. 'I'm a friend of Mr Brown's and currently one of his home carers.'

He couldn't have looked any less like what I assumed a home carer would look like if he tried. Not that I generally went in for stereotypes, but this guy was becoming more unfathomable by the second.

'Then it's a shame you weren't here earlier when Vicky needed you, wasn't it?' I snapped. 'She said you were really late and she had to leave, but the doctor's here now.'

'I couldn't be here earlier,' he told me, 'because one of the people I look after had a hypo and I had to stay with them until the ambulance arrived.'

'Oh.'

I supposed that sounded like an adequate excuse for his late arrival. It certainly took some of the gale force wind out of my inflated sails.

'But never mind that,' he continued. 'You still haven't told me who you are.'

'I'm no one,' I shrugged, turning away again and looking towards the road. I was determined not to give up my identity to another stranger. 'I was just passing and I heard someone shouting as I reached the gate so I stopped to check everything was okay.'

I knew that sounded unlikely, but I really didn't want this guy knowing my name. If he was as good a friend to my grandfather as he made out, then he would no doubt mention that he had bumped into someone claiming the family name, and that was the last thing I wanted. I needed to get out of Wynbridge without another soul sussing me out.

'But my colleague was here then, was she?'

'I've already told you she was.'

'And she left you with Mr Brown and headed off?' Eliot frowned as I risked another look at him. 'She just left you, a total stranger, in charge here and carried on with her day?'

'That's right.'

And it was right. I was a total stranger. Bill Brown and I might have shared blood, but we didn't know each other.

'Just like you, she had an emergency to get to,' I added for good measure. 'And I need to head off now as well, so if you don't mind.'

'I do mind actually,' he shot back. 'Because the way Vicky tells it, you told her that you were Mr Brown's granddaughter, called Felicity, and that's why she left you with him.'

Bugger.

Of course, she'd told him that. How could she not? She would have had to offer some justification for abandoning her post, and the presence of a family member would have been a more than adequate one, wouldn't it?

'Did she?' I asked, chewing my lip.

'She did.'

'Well, that's as maybe,' I said, aiming for distraction, 'but don't you think you ought to be going inside? The doctor might need some help.'

'I'm not going anywhere unless you come with me,' he said, pulling his arms completely out of the leather suit and pushing it down to his slim waist. 'I don't want to let you out of my sight.'

I wasn't sure how to read his tone but I knew I had no choice other than to begrudgingly follow him back inside.

The doctor entered the kitchen from the opposite direction just as we walked in and closed the door behind her.

'Ah, Eliot,' she smiled. 'You're a sight for sore eyes.'

'I'm sorry I couldn't get here sooner,' he apologised. 'I've just seen Joe off to hospital. The ambulance took an age to arrive, otherwise I would have been here a good hour ago.'

I rather wished he had been here then. I might not have been intimidated by Vicky and ended up revealing my true identity as a result. I could have scarpered without any of the intervening fiasco.

'What's the matter with them all?' Doctor Clarke tutted. 'They're dropping like flies today.' She eyed me curiously. 'You didn't get the chance to introduce yourself before,' she pointed out.

'Oh, I'm no one,' I told her. 'I just happened to be passing earlier, heard shouting and put my head in to see if everything was okay.'

I could feel Eliot's eyes fixed on me.

'Mr Brown was very upset when I arrived,' the doctor frowned.

'I don't suppose he was expecting to find a stranger in his house,' I smiled weakly. 'But I was only trying to help. He got more upset when I told him my name.'

'Ah,' she said as the pager in her hand began to bleep. 'Yes, Felicity. That'll account for some of his confusion then. That was his wife's name. She's been dead for quite some time.'

'Right,' I said, horribly aware that Eliot was still staring. 'I'm sorry to hear that.'

'Not to worry,' she said, thankfully distracted by the pager. 'You weren't to know. I've got his meds sorted now and he'll be right as rain in no time. Although Vicky shouldn't have left him here alone.'

'He wasn't alone,' I cut in, not wanting her to get in trouble. She might track me down and subject me to further intimidation. 'I was here and I said I'd wait because she was in a rush to get to someone else who was poorly.'

'I'll still have to talk to her,' said Doctor Clarke. 'It isn't usual practice to leave a patient with a stranger, under any circumstances.'

'Do I need to pick anything up for Bill today?' Eliot asked, thankfully not revealing to the doctor who Vicky had told him I was.

'No, I had everything I needed for today with me.'

'That's good,' said Eliot.

I thought his eyes were still tracking back to me, but I didn't dare check.

'Right, I have to go,' said Doctor Clarke, waving the pager about. 'Apparently, I'm needed back in town. Thank heavens this thing still works out here in the land of no mobile signal. You might need to pick up more meds for Bill next week, Eliot.'

'That's fine,' he said, moving aside. 'I'll see you out.'

'Nice to meet you Felicity,' she smiled. 'Why don't you get the kettle on before you go? I'm sure everyone would feel better after a nice cup of tea.'

'I'll do it in a minute,' said Eliot. 'And I'm going to stay here for the next couple of days too. Just to be on the safe side.'

That had to be service above and beyond the usual remit of home carer. Eliot had said that he was a friend of my grandfather's and that kind gesture proved it.

'That would be a great help if it isn't too much trouble,'

said Doctor Clarke. 'I had been wondering if it would be better to take him back into hospital.'

'Oh no,' said Eliot. 'Don't do that. You know how frustrated he was when they wouldn't let him home straight after surgery. I'm happy to be here and Vicky's already re-drafted the rota because I'm supposed to be on holiday.'

'Eliot, Eliot,' the doctor sighed. 'Where would we be without you?'

He ducked his head, but didn't answer and I began to feel guilty for biting his head off when he turned up. I supposed my unexpected arrival and claim to the Brown name did, in some way, justify him ordering me back into the house, and now I hadn't fessed up to the doctor about who I was, his continued suspicious stare was nothing more than I deserved.

'I'll put the kettle on,' I offered, trying to make amends.

Given the circumstances, it was the least I could do.

'Excellent,' nodded Doctor Clarke before rushing out.

By the time Eliot had seen her off, pulled off his boots and leather suit and checked on my grandfather who had fallen asleep, I had made a pot of tea and rinsed out a mug.

'Who isn't having any?' he frowned.

'Me,' I told him. 'I think it would be best if I left, don't you?'

'But you've only just arrived.'

'I know,' I said. 'But my timing's not ideal, is it? I'll go.'

Eliot looked at me again, this time his head was cocked as if he was trying to weigh me up. He was probably wondering if I was the real deal or a possible impostor.

'Look,' he said, as I fiddled with the straps on my rucksack. 'I know you probably think I was out of order for snapping at you before.'

'No, I don't,' I quickly interrupted, though just a few minutes ago I'd been fizzing. 'You're just looking out for my grandfather. I get that. And someone turning up out of the blue and claiming to be a relative isn't a usual Saturday morning occurrence, is it?'

'No, it isn't,' he said, clearly relieved that I'd accepted his previously harsh tone. 'And you don't look like a Brown. Not that I'm suggesting you're not who you say you are, but as far as I know, neither dark hair nor olive skin feature in the family tree.'

Definitely weighing up my credentials then.

'My dad was Italian,' I told him, giving up yet more information.

'Oh right.'

'I never knew him, but Mum left here to look for him when she found out she was pregnant with me. She didn't find him though.'

I didn't seem able to stop myself from blurting stuff out. It was definitely time to head back to town.

'And she's never come back here in all that time, has she?' Eliot mused.

'No.'

'You know,' he pondered. 'I don't even think Bill knows she had a baby. He's certainly never mentioned a grandchild to me.'

That made me feel marginally better. At least my grandfather wasn't hankering for something he'd never had. Even if, thanks to Mum's letter, I had started to.

'How old are you?' Eliot asked.

'Twenty-eight.'

'I'm twenty-six, so only slightly younger.'

'Does he ever talk about her?' I couldn't resist asking.

'He used to, but not for years now. Not to me, anyway. That said, he hasn't talked about much at all recently. He's not had the best couple of years.'

'Oh.'

'He's not been well and not being able to properly look after the farm has only added to his problems. We're all hoping he's turned a corner now he's got this new hip. Hopefully he'll be up and running and back to his old self again soon. God knows, the farm needs him.'

Eliot was giving up information as readily as I was, and knowing my grandfather's life was on the up again did go some way to making me feel better about not hanging around. I knew Mum had wanted me to come and potentially stay, but her dad didn't need this sort of revelation at this point in his recuperation. Come to that, he probably never would.

'Finding out about you is going to come as a bit of a shock though,' Eliot then said.

'Well,' I said. 'I didn't tell him anything other than my name, and that could just be a coincidence like the doctor assumed, so if you and Vicky can keep it to yourselves, he won't find out, will he? I'll be out of sight in a minute and no one will be any the wiser.'

'Is that why you didn't tell Doctor Clarke who you are?'

'Yes,' I nodded. 'I'd already made up my mind to go again and so the fewer people who know about me, the better.'

And no one at all needed to know what had happened to Mum. No matter how she had left things here when she ran away, her premature demise would be the biggest shock of all. That was one thing I could stop myself revealing. Parents weren't supposed to outlive their children. It wasn't the natural order of things.

'But you'll come back at some point, won't you?' Eliot asked. 'Give it a few months and then come again?'

I shook my head.

'No,' I said. 'I won't do that. I shouldn't have come at all.'

'I'm not sure I can agree with you about that,' Eliot frowned.

'Well,' I said, pulling on my pack. 'I'm not asking you to agree with me, just forget you ever saw me.'

He scanned my face again and his flushed.

'I don't think I'll be able to do that either,' he smiled.

His face was completely transformed, the lines around his eyes crinkled in such a way that suggested he spent more time laughing than frowning and I found I was rather pleased about that. I broke eye contact first and looked away wondering if his libido had taken a hit like mine had.

'Does your mum know you're here?' he asked, clearing his throat.

I shook my head.

'What made you come now?' he carried on, determined to get more out of me before I left. 'No offence, but you've taken your time.'

I kept my lips tightly pressed together.

'Are you sure you're going to be okay?'

'I'll be fine,' I said, dashing for the door. 'It was nice to meet you, Eliot. Thank you for looking after my grandfather.'

Once I was back on the road, I sent up a silent apology to Mum. I was certain that she had written her letter with the best of intentions, with a view to making amends for all the years of holding back, but it was too late to try and squeeze myself into a shape that would fit Fenview Farm. Life there had moved on, her dad had the chance for the fresh start he obviously needed, and there was no way I was going to risk screwing it up for him. I was going to catch a plane back to Italy and my roots were staying put in Puglia.

Chapter 4

I had only walked about half a mile when I heard a car on the road behind me. My ears had been straining to hear the throaty rumble of the Ducati, but it hadn't come. For some strange reason, part of me had wanted Eliot to come after me, even though I knew my grandfather was in no fit state to be left alone.

I also knew that even though nothing could come of it, I had felt an almost magnetic pull towards Eliot, and the look he'd given me before I left made me think he'd felt it too. I didn't usually hanker for romantic gestures or grand 'at first sight' moments, but truth be told, I wouldn't have minded Eliot roaring up and sweeping me off my feet!

It was pure fantasy of course, because given his closeness to my grandfather, any sort of contact between us would have made keeping me a secret impossible, and besides, I was grieving and my life was in turmoil. A whirlwind romance should have been the last thing on my mind, shouldn't it? That said, I could have easily succumbed to a bit of nurturing, although I wasn't entirely sure that's where my thoughts about Eliot had been heading.

Feeling wrung out after the emotion of the morning and throwing caution to the wind, I stuck out my thumb. Hitchhiking was hardly the safest option, but thanks to the last dregs of adrenaline still coursing through my system, I knew I had just about enough physical strength in me to fight off even the most persistent assailant, should I need to.

Even so, it was still a heart-stopping moment when the car drove past and then bumped up on to the verge, effectively blocking my path.

The driver, a woman, leant across the seats and opened the passenger door.

'Hey!' she shouted. 'Are you Felicity Brown?'

So much for staying incognito. I wondered if it was Vicky or Eliot who had gone blabbing. I hoped it was Vicky. I'd felt pretty certain Eliot would manage to keep me to himself even if he hadn't been able to commit to forgetting he'd seen me.

'Can you give me a lift into Wynbridge?' I asked, ignoring the question and peering into the car to find a woman with wild, curly greying hair and a tentative smile. She looked to be about Mum's age.

'Later perhaps,' she said, her smile slipping a little as her eyes met mine, 'but for now I'd like you to come back to the farm with me.'

'What? The farm back along the drove?' I asked, feigning ignorance.

'Yes.'

'Why on earth would I want to do that?'

'Because you are Felicity Brown, aren't you?'

She was like a dog with a bone and I didn't know how to shake her off. If I carried on walking, she'd doubtless follow me all the way to Wynbridge.

'Yes,' I sighed. 'I am, but I'm not going back to the farm.'

'Please,' she pleaded.

'Who even are you?' I asked, letting my rucksack slip off my shoulders.

I was sure it felt heavier than when I'd left Italy.

'I'm Eliot's mum.'

I hung my head and let out a long breath.

'He just rang to ask me to take some stuff to the farm and mentioned that you'd turned up.'

I nodded.

'He went nuts when I said I was going to come and find you.'

That was probably because mentioning me had just slipped out and given the bout of blabbermouth I'd experienced at the farm, I could hardly hold it against him.

'And why would my turning up be of such interest to you?' I asked.

'Because I'm an old friend of your mum's.' The woman explained, her voice catching. 'My name's Louise Randall. Your mum wrote to me a couple of months ago and told me all about you. I hadn't heard from her in almost thirty years. She said you might turn up.'

She knew then. She knew what had happened to Mum.

'Right,' I said, swallowing down the lump which had lodged itself in my throat again. 'I see.'

In Italy, no one had mentioned another letter, but someone must have sent it on Mum's behalf. I didn't think it could have been Alessandro, Marco or Nonna, because they would have said about it when I read them mine. Perhaps Mum had coerced one of the nurses who came to visit into helping, or the doctor perhaps. I wondered if any more revelatory letters were waiting to be revealed.

'Come on,' Louise encouraged. 'Come back to the farm and we'll have a proper chat.'

'But what about my grandfather?'

'Don't worry,' she said, unable to keep the wobble out of her voice. 'William doesn't know anything. Not about you or your mum.'

'And I want to keep it that way,' I said, sounding fiercer than I perhaps intended to.

'That's your call,' she nodded. 'I just want to talk to you for a few minutes.'

'And then you'll drive me to Wynbridge?'

'If that's what you want.'

'It is.'

'All right then. We'll have some lunch and a chat and then I'll take you to town.'

Back at the farm, Eliot had set out more mugs, refreshed the pot and made a plateful of chunky cheese and ham sandwiches.

'I'm so sorry,' he said to me while glaring at his mum the second we walked back into the kitchen. 'It just sort of . . .'

'Slipped out?'

'Yeah,' he said, running a hand through his already mussed up hair.

'It's okay,' I shrugged. 'No harm done, I suppose.'

'What with that and pointing out that you don't look like a Brown,' he said, evidently still feeling bad, 'you must have a pretty low opinion of me, right now.'

'What on earth made you say that?' Louise tutted at him.

Eliot and I looked at each other and exchanged a smile. Surely it was more than obvious?

'I think it was something to do with the fact that I look more Italian than East Anglian,' I told Louise, pulling my thick, dark ponytail over my shoulder.

'But your father was Italian,' she said, then clapped her hand over her mouth.

This inability to keep quiet was catching. Everyone seemed to have a dose.

'You knew Jennifer was pregnant when she ran off?' Eliot glowered.

Louise pulled out a chair and sat down heavily on it.

'Yes,' she said, as her face and neck flushed scarlet. 'Yes, I did.'

'Why didn't you tell Bill?'

'And further add to his misery?' Louise shot back without hesitation. 'Not likely.'

I joined her at the table wondering what else she knew that my grandfather and I didn't.

'Was this letter you received from Mum a few weeks ago a one-off?' I asked her. 'Or had she been in touch before?'

'And she wrote to you?' Eliot flared again.

'Keep your voice down,' Louise said, jerking her head towards the door which led to the room where my grandfather was sleeping. Eliot rushed to close it. 'Apart from the brief note she left when she ran away, it was a one-off,' she then said to me. 'And it was a shock to get it, I can tell you.'

Given what it no doubt said, I'm sure it was. 'I can imagine,' I breathed, feeling another rush of grief.

Eliot stopped in his tracks, but this time didn't say anything.

'She told me she had cancer and that she hadn't long to live,' Louise softly said. 'She also said that she'd left you a letter about this place, that she felt ashamed for not telling you about it before and that you might make up your mind to come here when you read it after . . .'

She pulled a tissue out from her sleeve and wiped her eyes.

'So, your being here,' she asked between sobs, 'means she's gone, doesn't it?'

'Yes,' I said, as tears slid down my face. 'She's gone.'

Eliot passed me a box of tissues from the dresser.

'I'm so sorry,' he said. 'I didn't realise.'

'I didn't tell you,' I told him, 'because I didn't want to burden you with knowing about that as well as me and not being able to say anything.'

'You don't have to explain,' he kindly said.

'And I didn't tell you about the letter for the same reason,' Louise told her son. 'You're so close to Bill, it wouldn't have been fair. I thought it best to bide my time and see if Felicity turned up and then decide what to do.'

'And here she is,' Eliot smiled down at me. 'I wish it was under different circumstances, but I'm glad you came.'

'I'm not sure I am,' I sniffed. 'I don't know what to do now.'

We all sat together and, over the tea and sandwiches, I told them about the colourful and often nomadic life Mum had lived. About the travelling and the adventures and how even though she'd been let down by my father, she'd found a refuge at the Rossis' and established a base with them in Puglia.

'We did come to the UK sometimes,' I explained. 'But never near here.'

'You travelled with her?' Eliot asked.

'Not so much recently, but when I was growing up, she took me everywhere with her then.'

Eliot was agog.

'She sounds amazing,' he dreamily said.

'She had her moments,' I smiled, this time through happier tears.

'But she never mentioned the farm or her father?' Louise wanted to know. 'Or the fact that she'd named you after her very own mother?'

'Never.'

'She might have been amazing, but that sounds like her too,' Louise sniffed. 'I don't mean to speak ill, but even as a young woman, she had a tendency to live her life exactly how she wanted to.'

I couldn't deny that she was right about that but given that it had been a life cut so short, I felt happy that Mum had pleased herself when it came to living it. Although not that she had left her father to endure a lifetime of worry about what had happened to her when she took off, of course.

'And you never thought to ask about what her life was like before you were born?' Eliot asked.

'No,' I flushed. 'I didn't. I know that was stupid now, but I never had any reason to give it a thought.'

'It wasn't stupid,' said Louise, reaching for my hand. 'You no doubt trusted her. Even though you weren't consciously aware of it, deep down you probably thought that if there was anything worth knowing then she would have told you about it.'

'Perhaps.'

'You must have been very happy living with this family to think of them as your own,' she added.

'I was,' I said. 'I am.'

'And besides, we all have our secrets, don't we?'

'Some more than others,' Eliot remarked.

He was obviously still smarting over the fact that his mum had known my mum was pregnant when she disappeared and never said anything, but I could completely understand Louise's reasoning for keeping it to herself. My grandfather certainly wouldn't have felt any better knowing he had lost his daughter *and* a grandchild.

'And what about your father?' she asked me, picking up on what Eliot was getting at. 'Did she tell you anything about him?'

'Only that he was a holiday fling and very good looking.'

'Oh, he was,' Louise nodded.

'You knew him?' I gasped.

'Not *knew* exactly,' she said, allowing herself a wistful smile at the memory. 'We weren't with him long enough for that, but I did see him. Your mum and I were holidaying together. It was our first trip abroad. Your grandfather didn't want us to go on our own, but I convinced him it would be all right. I was always the sensible one and I promised him I'd keep Jennifer out of mischief.'

'You didn't do a very good job,' said Eliot, looking pointedly at me.

'Thanks,' I swallowed.

'Eliot,' Louise quickly stepped in.

'Sorry,' he said, shaking his head. 'That didn't sound how I meant it to.'

'And you'll never know the depth of the guilt I've carried for all these years for not keeping a closer eye on her,' Louise then said, making me feel a hundred times worse.

'Oh, and thank you too,' I said, pushing back my chair.

'Oh love,' she said, 'I don't mean . . .'

'No matter,' I said cutting her off and walking to the back door. 'I'm just going to get some fresh air.'

There wasn't much of a garden attached to the side of the house, but I found some shade from the spring sunshine under an ancient apple tree which was in the middle of an overgrown lawn around the side furthest from the yard. I sat down and looked back at the house and outbuildings, determined to phase the conversation out for a few minutes and take my surroundings in.

I knew Eliot and Louise hadn't meant any harm, but I was feeling tired and emotional and it had been easy for me to take offence at their poor choice of words. Best to have some time out, before I said something I'd regret, especially as I was relying on Louise to run me back to town. I rested my back against the tree and looked about me.

From what I could see of Fenview Farm, it was all a little rough around the edges but homely enough, and there was no doubt in my mind that I would have found the day so much harder to cope with had it not been happening on a farm. The setting was comfortingly familiar, even if the events and revelations that were unfolding were completely alien.

'I'm sorry about our inability to turn a phrase,' said Louise, when she came out to join me a few minutes later. 'This has all been such a shock.'

'For all of us,' I pointed out.

'Yes,' she said, sitting on the grass next to me. 'For all of us and I don't want you to misconstrue or take anything that Eliot might foolishly say to heart. It's really not personal or aimed at upsetting you, he's just very protective of Bill.'

'I can see that,' I conceded. 'My grandfather is very lucky to have Eliot in his corner.'

'Their relationship works both ways, Felicity,' she smiled.

'What does that mean?' I asked. 'And it's Fliss. No offence, but everyone calls me Fliss, not Felicity.'

'Fliss then,' she nodded.

'What do you mean about things working both ways?' I prompted.

As one we looked towards the house where Eliot had just come out with a basket of laundry which he then started to peg out on the old-fashioned washing line.

'He's very fond of your grandfather,' Louise quietly said, still watching her son.

'That much is more than obvious,' I smiled. 'You'd have to be an idiot not to realise it. Not everyone would give up their holiday to look after a grumpy old man.'

'He's not really a grumpy old man,' Louise smiled back. 'From what Eliot told me the doctor said, you just caught him at the wrong moment.'

'That's good to know,' I said. 'I'd hate to think that bad-tempered was his go-to.'

'It's really not,' she carried on. 'He was a saviour to my son when he was a teenager.'

'How so?' I asked, turning from staring at Eliot to look at her.

She took a deep breath and a moment to compose herself.

'As you've no doubt worked out, I had Eliot quite soon after your mum had you. I had fallen in love and married a local lad but he tragically died young and Eliot went off the rails quite badly until Bill took him under his wing. Your grandfather helped him find a purpose again. He kept him busy here on the farm, out of the bad company he'd fallen into and consequently out of further mischief.'

The way Louise spoke so fondly about my grandfather and the protective feelings Eliot obviously had for him, made me wonder what had been the problem between him and Mum. From what I'd just heard, he didn't sound like a man who was difficult to get along with. What had happened between my two relatives that caused a rift that lasted, in Mum's case, a lifetime?

Then I remembered some of the fallings out Mum and I had gone through when I hit my teens. I supposed other people's family were quite often easier to get on with than your own, weren't they?

'I'm so sorry,' I said to Louise. 'About your husband I mean.'

It must have been so hard for her, struggling with her loss and an angry teenager.

'Thank you. It was a difficult time, but we eventually moved on.'

'That's good.'

'It is,' she agreed, then sagely added, 'but you can't rush grief. You have to let it run its own course if you're going to deal with it properly and you must accept that it never leaves you. It becomes a part of you and you learn to live with it.'

I didn't much like the thought of carrying the way I was feeling now around with me for ever.

'It will get easier,' Louise then added, gently resting a hand on my shoulder. 'In time it won't be as all consuming as it is now.'

I nodded, not trusting myself to speak for fear of crying again. I'd naively thought I was all cried out after Mum's funeral but the well was still far from dry. A day hadn't yet passed when I hadn't succumbed to tears at some point. So much for assuming that coming here would take some of the edge off how much I missed her.

We let the silence settle around us for a while, but I eventually broke it. I needed to move the day on.

'Thank you for fetching me back,' I said. 'I'm pleased we've had this chance to talk.'

'So am I,' she smiled. 'I can't tell you how lovely it is to meet you. I wish it had happened twenty-eight years ago, but there we are.'

'At least it's happened now,' I said, standing up and brushing the grass off my legs.

'Exactly,' she agreed.

'I asked Eliot not to say anything about me to my grandfather and I still stand by that, Louise.' She looked aghast, but I pressed on. 'Like Eliot pointed out, this new hip marks a return to health for him and he doesn't need to have his fresh start hindered by my arrival and news of what's happened to Mum. He's lived without her for almost thirty years and, given the circumstances, I think it would be best if he continued to do so.'

Louise shook her head and I walked back over to the house before she launched her counter-argument. I knew she was going to try and make me change my mind and given the emotional low ebb I was at, I had a feeling I might just relent and that wouldn't be any help to my grandfather's new beginning at all.

'It was nice to meet you, Eliot,' I said, picking up my rucksack again.

'You're not leaving?' he asked, looking up from the magazine he was reading.

'As soon as your mum starts her car.'

'But you can't . . .'

'I must,' I said over him.

'Are you sure, Fliss? Is that really what you want?'

'It doesn't matter what Felicity wants,' said Louise, who had followed me inside. 'There's only one person whose opinion really matters in all of this, and that's Bill's.'

'But his fresh start,' I reminded her. 'We agreed nothing should jeopardise that. Didn't we? Eliot?' I said, turning and appealing directly to him.

He looked at his mum and puffed out his cheeks. I knew in an instant that he'd swapped sides, the traitor.

'Finding out that Mum's gone will be the worst news he *ever* hears,' I told the two of them. 'And he didn't even know Mum was pregnant, so I'm no loss to him at all.' Mother and son looked at each other and then at me. 'You're both mad,' I told them. 'This is wrong.'

'More wrong than the two of us knowing about Jennifer and you and keeping it from him?' Eliot questioned.

'I don't think I could live with myself,' said Louise, shaking her head. 'Especially now I've met you, my love.'

This was all wrong. We were supposed to just be having a

chat and then I was going to leave. Earlier on the road, that was what we'd agreed.

'I should never have come,' I muttered again, more to myself than them. 'And now I'm thinking I shouldn't have let you bring me back.'

'Yes,' said Louise, her tone full of certainty and a determination I knew I couldn't beat, 'you should. Your mum wanted you to come here for a reason, Felicity, and I think you should stay.'

I wanted to remind her that I was Fliss, not Felicity, but for the moment had more pressing concerns.

'So do I now,' said Eliot, backing her up. 'I know I let you go before, but that was a mistake.'

Louise looked delighted, but then she would, she was winning.

'Don't overthink it,' she said, reaching for my hand. 'And don't think too far ahead. Just take one step at a time.'

Her choice of words pulled me up short. That was exactly what I'd told the Rossis I was going to do.

'For now,' Louise carried on when I didn't protest, 'let's just say you're staying until Bill's recovered from his infection.'

Eliot nodded in agreement. 'Give him a day or so to get back to his old self, and in that time, you can think about whether you want to talk to him or not.'

'But he's already seen me,' I reminded her. 'And I've told him my name. It's already a total mess.'

'Nothing we can't fix,' she briskly said, her tone victorious. 'Right, Eliot?'

'Right,' he said, backing her up. 'We'll work something out. It'll all come good in the end.'

I wasn't sure it would, but looking between the two of them, I had no choice but to accept that the next few steps I took would be walked in the Fens.

Chapter 5

When Louise had reassured me that she and Eliot would find a way to sort out the muddle surrounding my arrival, I had assumed that she meant by offering me a bed at their place, with a trip or two back to the farm when my grandfather was recovered from his infection. However, it turned out that wasn't any part of her plan.

'Oh Mum!' Eliot protested, when she explained what she did have in mind. 'That's a ludicrous idea.'

'No, it's not,' she responded, every bit as determinedly as her son. 'This is the Brown family home and I think it's important that Felicity stays here. It's the ideal opportunity for her to get to know the house and the farm where her mother grew up.'

There was no way I was going to agree to that. 'That's impossible,' I told her. 'I'll book into somewhere in town. I'm not risking bumping into my grandfather before he's completely recovered again. I couldn't bear another awkward encounter. I've already lied about who I am once, I'm certainly not going to put myself in a position where I have to do it again.'

Eliot nodded his approval but Louise waved my concerns away.

'Bill's so out of it, he won't remember that,' she airily said.

'Well, that's good then,' I readily agreed. 'And while we're waiting for his meds to kick in, I'll bide my time in town and come back again when Eliot says he's all better. That way it'll be like starting from scratch. We can pretend that my arrival at the farm then, is my first.'

There was so much of this ill-fated day that I already wanted to forget and I hoped that some time on neutral territory would help me do that. The town had looked warm and welcoming so I'd take on the role of tourist and hang out in the pretty café and shops and explore the market. Wynbridge had reminded me of the town I knew in Puglia the second I stepped off the bus, so the familiarity would be bound to settle my nerves and make me feel more at home. I wouldn't need to tell anyone who I was. I could take a leaf out of my mum's book and play the part of the mysterious traveller. Only she genuinely had been that person.

'Sounds good to me,' said Eliot, coming to stand next to me in a show of solidarity and treating me to a waft of his wonderful aftershave.

I flashed him a grateful smile. For taking my side, not for his heady scent. I didn't want him getting wind that I appreciated that.

Unfortunately, Louise was far from convinced of the merits of my plan.

'Can I have a word please, Eliot?' she said to her son. 'Excuse us for a minute, will you, love?'

She led Eliot outside and even though I couldn't hear what was being said, their body language suggested if not an argument, then a heated discussion was taking place. It didn't look as flamboyant as the arm raising Marco and Alessandro sometimes went in for, or sound as dramatic as their rapid-fire Italian, but it wasn't far off.

I dodged out of sight of the door when they turned to come back in, hoping Louise hadn't somehow got her son on her side again but he'd already come around to her way of thinking once.

'I've changed my mind,' Eliot sheepishly said, rubbing a hand around the back of his neck. The gesture told me immediately that he'd been coerced and cajoled. 'I think you should stay here. Get to know the place, like Mum said. Settle in a bit while Bill gets better.'

His face was bright red by this point and I wondered what Louise had said to make him change his mind. There was very little conviction behind his words. He clearly wasn't convinced his mother's idea was the right one and neither was I.

'If you're all the way back in town, it'll be awkward fetching you in and out,' said Louise, adding weight to Eliot's poor performance, but I could tell that wasn't anything to do with her real desire to keep me on site.

I didn't know what her real desire was, but it wasn't the inconvenience of having to drive me about.

'I'll be working,' she further said, 'and Eliot only has the bike so it won't be easy for either of us.'

'That's no problem, I can use the taxi,' I shrugged. 'That was how I got here and it was cheap enough. I wouldn't want to put you out, although I wouldn't mind riding pillion if push came to shove.'

Marco would be green with envy and Eliot looked momentarily thrilled but then caught sight of Louise's arched eyebrows.

'I won't be able to leave Bill,' he muttered, avoiding my eye.

Credit where it was due, Louise had done an extremely good job convincing him to agree with her mad plan.

'But where will I sleep?' I said, clutching at the very last straw I could think of. 'I'm not taking my grandparents' bed and I certainly wouldn't sleep in Mum's old room.'

'There's a spare,' Eliot huskily said.

'But you'll want that.'

'No, I won't,' he said, his tone apologetic. 'I'm going to sleep in the room with Bill. I can't risk being anywhere else in case he decides to go for a wander and falls. Doctor Clarke will zip him straight back into hospital if there's even the slightest hiccup and I'm not going to be the one responsible for putting him, or the nursing staff, through that trauma again.'

'That's settled then,' said Louise, bringing the conversation to a close that satisfied her but no one else. 'You're staying here. Eliot can go on the floor in the room where Bill is and you'll be in the spare room. Oh, and here's Rebecca,' she added, looking to the door as a car pulled into the yard.

'Who's Rebecca?' I asked Eliot as she rushed outside.

'My little sister.'

Not another one! I didn't think I could cope with more of the Randall clan and the sigh which spontaneously escaped my lips let him know it.

'Don't worry,' Eliot smiled, picking up on my reluctance to become acquainted with more of his relatives. 'You'll like her. She's fun.'

Thankfully, he was right.

Rebecca was a sparky young woman, with her mother's head full of curls, only hers were dark blonde and long, rather than greying and she was dressed in bright, floaty clothes. She was only a year younger than Eliot, but she had a kind of youthful exuberance whereas her brother and I perhaps came across as a bit more world weary. He was right about her being fun. The atmosphere in the kitchen had become rather oppressive but it lifted and lit up the moment she walked in.

'I'm really sorry about your mum,' she sincerely said, after Louise had introduced us and explained who I was but how, for now, my identity had to be kept a secret. 'But how amazing is it that you've found your way here?'

I wasn't sure it was amazing yet, but her bright smile certainly made me feel a bit better about life.

'You mustn't say anything to anyone,' Eliot sternly told her. 'That's *really* important.'

'I won't,' she pouted, before turning her sparkling eyes back to me. 'And you must call me Bec, not Rebecca.'

'And I'm Fliss,' I smiled back. 'Not Felicity.'

Louise had introduced us using our full first names, but we obviously both preferred the abbreviated versions.

'Fliss,' Bec grinned, side eyeing her mother. 'Cool.'

'I don't understand you girls.' Louise tutted. 'You've both got beautiful names and yet you refuse to use them.'

Bec ignored this and I got the distinct impression that it was a comment she'd heard many times before.

'I'm going to head into town for supplies for Eliot,' she told me. 'Is there anything I can pick up for you? Or would you rather come with me?'

'I'll come with you,' I hastily said. 'I could do with a couple of things now I know I'm going to be staying for a day or two.'

I didn't really need anything, but I wasn't going to pass up the opportunity to get away from the farm, and Louise's well-meant bossiness for a little while. The last few hours had been intense and some time out would give me the chance to draw breath, think things through and get my head around everything.

'I'll just grab my purse and phone,' I said, rifling through my rucksack.

There was no chance to think anything through en route however, because Bec talked all the way into town and by the time she parked her battered bright yellow 2CV next to the market which was packing up for the day, she had given me a potted history of her entire life. Even though my head was spinning, her monologue had been an entertaining distraction and I was surprised to find myself feeling calmer.

She was an artist, recently graduated from Norwich University of the Arts, and in the process of setting up her own studio at home. She was currently specialising in abstract paintings. Huge canvases full of colour were what she loved most and given her outfit and sunny disposition they sounded very 'Bec' to me.

She was happily single, straight and hoping to travel the world, when she could afford to, to further fuel her inspiration. She was as free flowing as the river running under the bridge we'd driven over and she really reminded me of Mum.

Bec hadn't shied away from talking about what I was going through and readily told me what she'd felt and experienced when her dad died. And, not that I was looking to form any hasty attachments to the place, but I loved her already.

'You can tell me about yourself on the drive back,' she grinned, when she realised, she hadn't given me the chance to say a word.

'There's nothing much to tell,' I shrugged.

'Rubbish,' she said, locking her car. 'I don't believe that for a second. Mum said you grew up in Italy. How can you have nothing to say about yourself with a start in life like that?'

I laughed and shook my head. Bec was obviously a glass half-full kind of girl, but she was right. I had had an unusual start in life, what with growing up with the Rossis and joining Mum on many of her adventures before I decided to settle, and now of course, it was about to become even more intriguing.

The plan for the trip to town was for us to stock the farm fridge, take books back to the library and pick up a takeaway for dinner, but it was still a bit early for the takeaway part.

'How about I cook instead?' I offered, when I spotted a smart looking deli at the opposite end of the square.

Eliot had told Bec not to be too long and if we didn't have to wait for the takeaways to open, then we'd be back all the sooner and to be honest, I didn't much fancy fish and chips or a kebab. I was craving a taste of home, but not Nonna's tart. I was going to save that for a special occasion. Unbidden, my hand checked that the recipe and Mum's letter were safe where they should be.

'Could you?' Bec asked, wide-eyed. 'Could you cook?'

'Yes,' I said. 'If you think it will be okay and as long as everyone likes Italian food?'

'What like proper Italian, rather than greasy take-away pizza?'

'Yes,' I said, eyeing the stalls on the market.

'Yeah,' she nodded. 'Okay. Great!'

Bec left me to source the ingredients for dinner while she went to sort everything else. I soon found that the market was local foodie heaven and as there was a fabulous fish stall, I decided to make a creamy lemon and shrimp risotto and an accompanying seafood salad.

Everyone was very friendly and I ended up buying far more than I needed, but I knew that a taste of Puglia and a few sessions at the stove would help me zen out and stop me stressing about staying at the farm. I thanked my lucky stars that Eliot was going to be there too, although I didn't like to think how I'd react if I bumped into him half dressed in the middle of the night, especially if he was still wearing that wonderful woody aftershave. Or was it just eau de Eliot that had set my pulse racing?

I was weighed down even before I reached the deli to pick up the risotto rice and cheese and components for antipasto, but there was such a great array of ingredients on offer, including freshly made grissini and locally cured meats, that I couldn't resist piling my basket high in there too. The olives weren't quite up to Rossi standards, but they would do.

'I wasn't expecting to find such a well-stocked deli in such a small town,' I told Thomas, the manager and owner, according to his name badge. 'This place is a real find.'

'We're new,' he told me, slipping a leaflet into a reusable bag bearing the shop logo. 'We've only been open a few weeks. But business has been brisk, so far.'

'How exciting,' I nodded, looking around. 'Sorry,' I said, squeezing closer to the counter when I realised there was someone trying to get by.

'You look as though you've got the ingredients for a great dinner there,' said the other customer, flashing me a smile as he looked over my shoulder.

'I certainly hope so,' I said, feeling my face colour a little as he handed a bottle of olive oil to a woman who was also serving.

'Those grissini are delicious,' he grinned. 'I tried some last week.'

'Excellent,' I smiled back, taking in his blonde hair and deep blue eyes. 'Nothing beats a personal recommendation.'

'That's very true,' he agreed.

We ended up leaving at the same time and as I was so weighed down with bags, he opened the door for me.

'Thanks,' I said, trying to evenly distribute everything.

I'd definitely got far too much. I could probably cook Italian dishes for at least a fortnight, rather than the few days I was imagining I was going to be at Fenview Farm.

'Can you manage?' the guy asked.

'Not really,' I admitted. 'But I'm only going over there,' I added, with a nod to where Bec had parked.

'In that case,' he said, holding out his hands. 'Let me help. I'm heading that way too.'

He slipped his bottle of olive oil into one of the bags and we split the haul between us. Our fingers became entwined during the sorting and he gave me an even wider smile.

'Thanks,' I swallowed. 'This is very kind of you.'

'It's no problem.'

We crossed the road together and I came to a stop behind Bec's dazzling ray of motorised sunshine.

'Nice car,' laughed the guy who I'd named in my head, Mr Helpful.

'Thanks,' said Bec, suddenly appearing. 'I've had it since I passed my test years ago. Striking, isn't she?'

'Just a bit.'

'I call her the Banana-mobile.'

'Well,' he said, putting down the bags. 'I'll certainly keep an eye out for her from now on.'

I thanked him again and then he climbed into the sporty Audi next to us, waved and drove off. He'd forgotten to take his olive oil.

'Who was that?' Bec wistfully asked, looking after him with a soppy expression on her face.

'No idea,' I told her. 'He was in the deli and offered to help carry the shopping.'

'Manners and beguiling good looks,' she dreamily sighed, giving me a nudge. 'What a thrilling combo.'

'If you say so,' I laughed.

Personally, I thought her big brother had the edge on that particular pairing, but obviously I wasn't going to tell her that.

'What's all this then?' Bec asked, taking in the many bags around my feet. 'I thought you were cooking dinner for five, not feeding the five thousand!'

'I'm used to Italian portion control,' I told her, pulling my phone out of my pocket.

'Or lack of it,' she giggled.

While Bec loaded the boot, I took advantage of the fact that my phone had enough signal for me to message Marco and give him an update on how the day had gone. I didn't go into detail, or brag to him about Eliot's bike, but I knew Alessandro and Nonna would take comfort in knowing that I was staying at the farm. It would suggest to them that all was well and, for now, that was the impression I was keen to convey. They didn't need to know about the muddle I'd made of my arrival.

When we arrived back at the farm, Louise had gone home and Eliot was washing up. I wanted to ask him what his mum had said to make him change his mind about me staying at the farm, but he seemed a bit distracted and I hoped they hadn't had words. The last thing I wanted was to be a burden.

'I thought we were having fish and chips,' he commented, as Bec and I finished decanting the contents of the bags on to the kitchen table.

'Fliss's going to cook for us instead,' Bec told him. 'That's why she picked up all this lot.'

'Oh,' he said. 'Right.'

'And this wasn't the only thing you picked up, was it Fliss?' she said with a much-exaggerated wink.

'I don't know what you're talking about,' I tutted as I carefully set the bottle of olive oil Mr Helpful had left behind to one side.

'Yes, you do,' she persisted. 'A side order of handsome and helpful isn't forgotten that quickly.'

I shook my head, hoping she'd shut up because I was pretty certain the spark I'd felt when I first set eyes on Eliot was mutual and, even if nothing was going to come of it, I didn't want him thinking that I went through life flirting with every man who crossed my path. Mr Helpful might have been attractive but in a completely different way to Eliot.

'So,' said Eliot, thankfully ignoring his sister's silliness. 'What are you going to make?'

I reeled off the evening's menu, embellishing with a few words of Italian. Saying it out loud made my tummy rumble and even just the thought of time spent stirring the creamy risotto soothed my soul.

'But Bill won't eat any of that,' was Eliot's reaction and it well and truly burst my bubble.

'Oh,' I swallowed, my face flushed with embarrassment.

So keen to comfort myself, I'd got carried away and only factored my tastes and preferences into the evening's dishes.

'I didn't think,' I apologised. 'I'm sorry.'

'Don't get me wrong,' said Eliot. 'It all sounds great, but your grandfather has a rather less sophisticated palate. He's more a meat and two veg kind of guy.'

I felt a total fool.

'Which is why,' said Bec, coming to my rescue and shooting her brother an accusatory look. 'I picked up some eggs and Skylark Farm bacon from the butcher. Bill will be happy with that.'

'Yes, that's more like it,' Eliot agreed. 'Though he's not got much of an appetite and the meds are making him drowsy, so he probably won't want to eat anything anyway.'

'So why make me feel bad about choosing the wrong thing?' I snapped.

'I didn't mean to,' Eliot said.

He looked shocked by my outburst and I was mortified

to find myself instantly on the verge of tears. Bec looked daggers at her brother again.

'Sorry,' I said. 'I didn't mean to bite your head off.'

'It's all right,' he said. 'It's been one hell of a day. I'm feeling it myself.' That no doubt accounted for the change in his mood too. 'You must be exhausted and I could have put that better. I'm the one who should be apologising. I seem to have a habit of putting my foot in it today.'

As relieved as I was that he hadn't meant to make me feel bad, at the same time, I wanted to tell him not to be nice to me either. Kindness and understanding would tip me completely over the edge, but because I didn't trust myself not to blub, I didn't.

'I think I'll just freshen up,' I sniffed. 'Do I need to go upstairs?'

Eliot succinctly explained that there were four rooms upstairs – three bedrooms and a bathroom – and I rushed off, keen to have a minute to myself. I could hear Eliot and Bec talking in the kitchen below and made a mental note to talk in whispers whenever possible for the next few days in case my grandfather caught the sound of my voice.

The doors to two of the bedrooms were closed but the spare was open and the bed was made with my rucksack sitting next to it. Thanks to the open window, the room was filled with warm spring air and I pushed the curtains further back to take in the far-reaching Fenland view. I pulled out my phone and took a photo. The Rossis would love that. I would send it next time I had enough signal.

I wasn't sure what I was expecting of Fenview Farm, but from what I could make out, it looked to be nowhere as big as the Rossis' plot. There were a couple of fields full of blossom-heavy trees and I could see a few large cages filled with soft fruit bushes as well as rows and rows of strawberry plants. There was no straw on any of them yet, but I knew that would have to go down soon.

The season would be starting in just a few weeks, sooner if it stayed warm, and if the berries weren't going to be spoiled, then they'd need that straw buffer between them and the earth. Modern, commercial farms grew the berries off the ground and under cover, but Fenview Farm looked distinctly old-school and I felt my back groan at the thought of bending and filling punnets. I would no doubt be long gone before they ripened, but it didn't stop my body reacting to the thought of the back-breaking work. I wondered who my grandfather would get to pick them. That was one job his new hip wouldn't be up to so soon.

I looked back to the orchards. Even from this distance I could make out that they weren't quite so tidily kept as some I'd seen on my journey from Peterborough, but they weren't in as poor a state as others I'd glimpsed courtesy of Google. Was it really only a few hours since I'd been in the hotel and looking at these views online? It felt like a lifetime ago.

My stomach growled again and after freshening up I pulled myself together, took a deep breath and went back downstairs to set about preparing my Italian feast.

*

'That,' said Bec, as she wiped her mouth on her napkin, 'was the best meal I've eaten in *for ever.*'

I was delighted she had enjoyed it. I had soon found my way around the Brown kitchen and had loved preparing the food as much as eating it. Losing myself in the familiarity of it all was exactly what I needed after a stress-filled few hours and insisting that we eat outside on our laps as the weather was so wonderful, had made it all the better.

'I have to agree with you sis,' said Eliot, stretching back in his chair and rubbing his hands over his tummy which still looked washboard flat, in spite of all the carbs he'd crammed in. 'That was phenomenal, Fliss. Where did you learn to cook like that?'

I flushed at the compliment which found its way straight to my heart. I was never happier than when folk were enjoying my food and I knew Nonna would have been proud.

'Not from her mother, that's for sure,' Louise, who had come back to join us, laughed. 'From what I can remember from cooking at school, Jennifer was as good at burning toast then as I am now.'

Mum and Louise really had gone a long way back then.

'You've got a lot more going for you than being able to find your away around a kitchen, Mum,' said Eliot, closing his eyes.

'Just as well,' she laughed, 'because I can't!'

'And before you think it, Fliss,' Eliot quickly said, opening his eyes again. 'That wasn't me saying that's all you've got going for you. Although even if it was, that'd be no bad thing because that meal was amazing. I mean . . . I know you can do more than cook . . . not that it would matter if you . . .'

'Eliot,' Bec squawked.

'What?'

'For pity's sake, shut up.'

'I learned to cook in Italy,' I said, answering Bec's question and pretending I hadn't noticed that Eliot had got himself in a muddle again, 'and I had the most amazing teacher.'

A vision of me wearing one of Nonna's aprons, standing next to her at the old stove and stirring a vast pot of rich tomato sauce, popped into my head and yet another prickle of tears accompanied it. When I'd decided to come and find the farm, I hadn't taken into account that as well as still missing Mum, I'd be bereft without the Rossis too.

'Tell us about them,' said Louise, settling back in her chair.

'Another day,' I sniffed, standing up. 'I'd best get tidied up.'

'Oh, no you don't,' said Bec. 'You cooked this feast, *we'll* tidy up.'

'I better check on Bill first,' said Eliot. 'And I need to get the bike undercover.'

'Any excuse to get out of the washing up,' tutted his sister.

'I really don't mind helping,' I said.

'You stay where you are,' said Louise. 'Sit back down, have another glass of wine and enjoy the sunset.'

The Fenland spring sunset really was a sight to behold. The cloud streaked sky turned gold and then orange as the great orb slipped gently towards the horizon and then slowly sank below it. I closed my eyes, listening to the chatter of a robin which was swiftly followed by a blackbird. He sounded keen to announce the farm as his own.

It was all every bit as tranquil as Puglia and for the first time since I'd arrived, I thought about how there might be a possibility of my roots working their way into the soft, dark earth beneath my feet. It was probably down to the wine, but it was a settling sensation nonetheless.

'I'm not asking you to pay for it. I'm giving it to you for free.'

My eyes snapped open. There was a chill in the air but someone had laid a blanket over me, so I hadn't felt it. The dishes had all been cleared away, along with my empty wine glass and I could see the drive was empty. Eliot must have put his bike away and Bec and Louise had gone home. I was sorry not to have said goodbye, but I hadn't heard a thing. I must have been out for the count.

'Yes, mate. I know, and believe me, I was looking forward to it too, but it can't be helped.'

I wondered who Eliot was talking to.

'I've asked Bec to forward you the booking email and I'll let the organiser know you're taking my spot. You'll need your insurance documents. Okay, well, have fun and do not even think about stopping by here on the way back to tell me how it went.'

He ended the conversation and I called over to him, momentarily forgetting I was supposed to be keeping quiet.

'Everything all right?'

'Yeah,' he said, wandering over with the phone from the kitchen still in his hand. 'Just a change of plan for tomorrow.'

'Oh,' I yawned. 'What were you supposed to be doing?'

'A track day on the bike. It's been in the diary for months.'

'I'm sorry you've had to cancel,' I said. 'You must be really disappointed.'

'Yeah, well,' he shrugged. 'There'll be other days, but there's only one Bill.'

I smiled, but didn't know what to say to that.

'What about you?' he asked. 'Had you got anything planned you need to call off now you're staying?'

'No,' I said. 'I came to England with the sole purpose of doing this. Not that I expected it to work out the way it has so far.'

'It must have been quite a shock, finding out about this place.'

'Yes,' I said. 'It was. Come to that, it still is and I'd no idea it was going to be just my grandfather here on his own.'

'And I daresay you're going to be in for a few more surprises given that you still know so little,' Eliot pointed out.

'Thanks for that,' I said, giving him a rueful smile.

'Sorry,' he smiled back. 'I don't know what it is about you Fliss, but you do seem to get me tongue-tied in double-quick time. Nothing I've said to you today has come out right, has it?'

'No,' I sighed, trying not to think of his tongue. 'Not really.'

'Come on,' he said, holding out his hand. 'You go up to bed and I'll lock up.'

I rested my hand in his and as he pulled me to my feet, an explosion of fireworks coursed through my system and turned my knees to jelly.

'Are you all right?' he asked, resting his other hand under my elbow to steady me.

'Too much wine and not enough sleep,' I bluffed, taking a step away. 'Night Eliot.'

'Night, Fliss,' he huskily replied. 'Sleep well.'

Chapter 6

I had no idea whether it was the wine, the emotion of the day or Eliot's warm night-time wishes, but I slept surprisingly well. The unfamiliar mattress and inner turmoil didn't impact at all, and I was up with the lark and feeling refreshed early the next morning. I was grateful for the early start too because the Fenland sunrise was every bit as spectacular as the sunset.

I quietly made myself a coffee and, wrapped in the blanket from the night before, crept outside to enjoy a calm, slow and steady start to the day. I was feeling wonderfully relaxed after some mindful meditation and ready to face whatever the day threw at me, but when I went back inside my tranquil state immediately took flight.

'Oh, for fuck's sake!' gulped Eliot, who was filling the kettle at the sink and wearing nothing but his boxers. 'Where did you spring from? I thought you were still asleep.'

'I've been outside,' I said, trying to keep my eyes on his face and stop myself from laughing because he had jumped almost as high as the ceiling. 'I wanted to see the sunrise. How did you sleep?'

'Badly,' he muttered, thumping down the kettle and flicking it on. 'Bill was awake all night and now he's out for the count.'

'Oh,' I said. I don't suppose it mattered when my grandfather slept, but it was tough on Eliot. He had dark circles under his eyes and his hair was even more mussed up after the night spent tossing and turning than it had been when he'd worn his bike helmet. 'That's not great then, but do you think he's getting any better?'

'Maybe,' he yawned, rubbing his eyes. 'Perhaps. I dunno.'

'Look,' I gently said, wishing he'd at least sit down so I couldn't see quite so much of him. 'You're exhausted, why don't you go back to bed for a bit?'

'No,' he said, running a hand up and down his bare chest before arching his back. 'I'll be all right. Besides, the floor isn't all that comfy.'

'Then take your sleeping bag and lie on the bed I slept in,' I suggested. 'And I'll listen out for my grandfather.'

'No,' he said, more firmly. 'You're all right. I'll be fine when I've had a coffee.'

'A shower then?' I brightly proposed. 'That, combined with the caffeine, might make you feel a bit brighter?'

'Are you insinuating that I'm not my usual sunny self this morning?' he asked, one eyebrow cocked.

'Not at all,' I said, looking away. 'Well, a bit. But then if I'd spent the night on the floor, I'd probably be feeling a bit jaded too.'

What I wouldn't be though, was walking about the house half-dressed. Eliot didn't seem in the slightest bit bothered that the one item of clothing he was wearing left very little to the imagination, but then with a body like that . . .

'All right,' he relented. 'I'll go and shower. You keep an ear out for Bill, but whatever you do, do not disturb him, okay?'

What did he think I was going to do, rush in and shake him awake? I might have wanted to be useful, but after what had happened the day before, I would most definitely be avoiding implementing the element of surprise.

In the few minutes it took Eliot to get showered and dressed, and with one eye on my slumbering relative I made a list of all the dishes I could cook with the leftover ingredients from my culinary shopping spree the day before and got some breakfast on the go. Eliot reappeared smelling and looking great and the smile that lit up his face when he saw I had buttered bread, made more coffee, had bacon sizzling on the grill and the biggest eggs frying on the hob, made me feel as smug as Nigella.

'I thought you might like some breakfast,' I said, setting out the plates which had been warming on the stove. 'And I know my grandfather didn't eat last night, so he might fancy something too.'

'I'll have some,' he said, 'but Bill's going to be asleep for a good while yet.'

I looked back at the hob. There was definitely too much food for two.

'But don't worry,' Eliot said, rising to the challenge. 'I'll make short work of it.'

Where on earth did he put it all, I wondered, then hastily decided not to ponder.

'Are you cooking bacon in there?' My grandfather suddenly called out, making us jump. 'I could go for a bit of that and an egg or two if there are any.'

'Sounds like you won't get the chance,' I whispered with a smile on my lips.

I turned my attention back to the pan and competently flipped the eggs, feeling thankful for Nonna Rossi's 'the bigger the better' opinion on portion size.

'He's demolished the lot,' Eliot told me, when he came back in carrying a tray bearing two empty plates and mugs a little while later. 'And he's had all the tea, too.'

I was pleased to note that he hadn't left a scrap of anything either.

'Well, that's good,' I said, feeling well satisfied. Nonna's cookery lessons had not only equipped me with the knowledge to fill plates with delicious food, but also to feel the satisfaction of seeing them empty too. 'He must be feeling more like himself, if he's eating and drinking so much.'

'It's a definite improvement, that's for sure,' Eliot agreed.

'And has he mentioned anything about yesterday?' I steeled myself to ask.

'About you, you mean?'

'Yes,'

'No, not a word. I reckon you've got away with it.'

'Thank goodness for that,' I sighed, feeling relieved.

'You'll be able to introduce yourself in no time,' Eliot then said, pushing my nervousness back up the scale again. 'Don't look so worried. He's a really great guy.'

If he was that great, then why had Mum left him all those years ago? I didn't think there was much point asking Eliot. Louise was more likely to have the answer, although she hadn't offered it up yesterday. Not that it had been the day for further revelations and explanations. My turning up had been more than enough to contend with. For all of us.

'Doctor Clarke rang earlier to say she's coming out again later,'

'On a Sunday?' I asked.

Given what he'd said yesterday, I didn't think my grandfather would be particularly pleased to see her again so soon.

'She's on call and said she might as well pop in as she's bound to be passing. She'll take another look at Bill and then we can decide how to take things after that.'

'All right,' I agreed. I supposed that did sound like small enough steps for me to be able to manage. 'That's a good idea.'

'Maybe you could go and take a walk around the farm for a bit while she's here?'

That was another good idea.

'I guess that would save any awkward questions, wouldn't it?' I nodded. 'She'd probably want to know why the stranger from yesterday is still hanging about, wouldn't she?'

'Definitely,' Eliot nodded. 'Nothing gets past Doctor Clarke.'

'In that case,' I said, squirting washing up liquid into the sink, 'I'll get this lot sorted and head straight out.'

'Great,' said Eliot, making to walk out.

'Tea-towel is right there, Eliot,' I said nodding to the hook where it hung.

'Right,' he grinned, giving me a nudge. 'I'll dry up then, shall I?'

I made sure I was well out of the way by the time Doctor Clarke's car turned into the yard and I was careful not to walk anywhere near where I guessed the dining room window was too. Having managed to find a spot where my phone picked up an iota of signal, I typed out another message for Marco to relay to Nonna and Alessandro and attached the photo I'd taken the day before. I would have liked to hear their voices, but neither my Italian family nor I had WhatsApp downloaded and unsure of the cost of a call, decided not to risk it.

Before I started pining for them too much, or letting the sharp pain of missing Mum get the better of me again, I reminded myself why I was here and strode out to what I thought was the furthest point of the farm boundary and looked about me properly.

'Right,' I said to Mum, as I patted the pocket which had her letter and Nonna's recipe in. 'Let's see why you thought I might like this place, shall we?'

It didn't take long to work out. I knew it wouldn't be the

same as it had been thirty years ago, but I could see there was plenty of work to be done, which backed up what Eliot had said about my grandfather having not been able to keep on top of it for the last couple of years. That said, it was a lovely spot and potentially very productive.

As I walked about, I imagined myself getting stuck into what needed doing. I had worked on fruit farms across Europe and in the UK and there didn't appear to be anything beyond my skillset, but would my grandfather want me helping out if I did decide to stay on for a while? The evening before I had imagined potential tender new roots anchoring me to this place, but should I allow them to sink down if there was a chance that my grandfather might slice straight through them when he found out who I was?

I slowed my breathing and reminded myself about those tiny steps I was supposed to be taking. There was no point in trying to look too far ahead, because I couldn't see that far. No one could.

'You must remember to live in the moment, Fliss,' I heard Mum dreamily say as she drifted through my mind reclined on a patchouli-scented cloud. 'Just go with the flow.'

'Yes,' I said, out loud. 'Well, I'll try.'

As I'd surmised from the bedroom window, the farm wasn't at its best, but there was nothing that couldn't be fixed with hard work and commitment. In the right hands, the neglect could be turned around in no time. Everything was salvageable and it was a credit to my grandfather that it was only at this point after a couple of slack years. I could tell that everything would have been perfect before his hip gave up on him, because had it not been, the state of things would have been far worse.

I inspected the rows of trees in the orchards, admiring the light as it filtered through those in blossom. The apple, pear, plum and few cherry trees would produce a decent enough harvest, even though the apples and pears were in need of some pruning. I soon discovered the soft fruit would be fine too, as long as the holes in the cages were repaired before the birds found their way in and stripped the lot.

On closer inspection, I could see that the netting needed completely replacing. Some areas were definitely more hole than net, but that was a job for later in the year. Completely removing the covers when the harvest was over would make weeding easier and also encourage the birds to pick off any bugs and clear up any rotting fruit.

There was a healthy abundance of raspberry canes, as well as gooseberry, black and redcurrant bushes. There were blackberries outside of the cages too, along with the long rows of established strawberry plants. Second to the cage repairs, they needed the most urgent attention. It was important to get the straw on as soon as possible and I wondered where that was usually sourced.

Even though it wasn't my place to, I automatically made mental notes of everything as I walked back to the yard and pondered over how farming in the area had changed in recent years and how the place could financially stay afloat in the future.

I was aware that in the fairly recent past, a farm the size of Fenview would have been a common sight as well as a competitive and profitable prospect. The Fens had been dotted with dozens of places of similar acreage who all took their harvests to the local auction houses to sell on a daily or weekly basis, depending on the crop and the season, but those days were long gone.

Even using 'locally sourced and grown' as a USP was no longer entirely enough for a small farm to compete in the large commercial market. My grandfather must have been horribly aware of that and, assuming that he kept tabs on his finances, known that the farm income was feeling the pinch.

What, realistically, was the future of this place going to be? As a small-scale farm, it wasn't likely to still be turning a profit, not enough of one to comfortably live off anyway. If Fenview Farm was going to keep afloat then it was going to need to do more than just sell fruit. Did my grandfather have long-term plans for it or hadn't he thought that far ahead?

'Well, hello puss,' I said, bending to stroke a rather thin ginger and white cat who ran towards me with its tail standing to attention. 'Where did you spring from?'

I hadn't seen the ragged little scrap before and wondered if it was a stray. It clearly wasn't feral because it would have pelted in the opposite direction when it spotted me.

'Who do you belong to then?'

It decided it'd had enough of me and trotted jauntily over to the brick-built barn which sat at the far side of the drive. I watched in amusement as the cat walked through a hole in the bottom of the door which had obviously been sawn there for that purpose.

'What's in here then?' I mused, following the cat, sliding the bolt and trying the handle on the huge arched wooden door which, to my surprise, was unlocked.

I tugged the door open and slipped inside.

'Wow.'

The barn was bigger inside than I expected, with beautiful wooden beams and it was currently being used as a storage space. Intrigued, I pulled the doors further back, coughing as dust motes filled the air and my eyes adjusted to the change in light level. The cat looked at me accusingly from its perch atop some straw bales. It clearly wasn't impressed about having its home invaded.

Along with the bales, there were old bits of machinery, a few ancient tools and half a dozen or so tea-chests and larger boxes. They were filled with what looked like old Fenland paraphernalia. I had researched the history of the Fens a little, as well as fruit farming, when I had been on the coach from the airport to Peterborough and could therefore recognise the willow woven eel traps and a few of the tools, and it was obvious what the ice skates were.

I wondered if they had been used for competing when the winters had been cold enough for the flooded meadows to freeze. They certainly looked old enough, but what were they doing in the barn? What was any of this stuff doing here?

'Fliss!'

Eliot's voice rang out across the yard. So much for keeping

my presence under wraps. If he carried on bellowing, my grandfather wouldn't be in any doubt that the impostor who had upset him was still in the vicinity. Assuming he could remember. Eliot had suggested he wouldn't and I really hoped he was right. It was far better for my nerves if I agreed with him about that.

'Coming,' I shouted back, although not quite so loudly.

I pushed the barn doors closed again and went back to the house.

'Whose is the cat?' I asked, when I was close enough to not have to shout.

'The mangy ginger and white thing?'

'It's not mangy, it's sweet.'

'It's Bill's,' he said. 'But it's not a house cat. It lives outdoors and you might not think it, but it's a great ratter.'

My body emitted an involuntary shudder.

'She's not afraid of taking down a rat, even though they're bigger than she is.'

'Oh crikey,' I said. 'I would be, I hate them.'

'Yes,' said Eliot, matching my shudder with one of his own. 'Me too. It's the naked tails that make my flesh crawl.'

'And mine. So, what did the doctor have to say?' I quickly asked, keen to change the subject. 'Could she see any improvement?'

'Definitely. She's told Bill to take the whole week's worth of antibiotics to be sure the infection goes, and now he's not so confused I'll be able to get him out of bed and doing his exercises again soon.'

'Can you manage to do that on your own?'

'Yes, no problem.'

I was relieved about that.

'But even though he's well on the mend,' Eliot carried on, 'I still think it would be best to give him another day or so before you introduce yourself.'

I was relieved about that too.

The rest of Sunday ticked slowly by and by mid-afternoon, thoughts of Mum's last few days and of what the Rossis were doing, were beginning to plague me as they always did when I had nothing to do.

I'd cooked as much as I could, but I hadn't felt the usual unadulterated pleasure I generally derived from time at the stove because I had to be careful about staying quiet and out of view as Eliot flitted in and out. I'd had to try and contain the delicious smells too. None of that had been an issue the evening before because my grandfather had been fast asleep, but now caution was the watchword and I was feeling tense.

Rather than give in to my anxiety, I took a notepad I'd found on the kitchen dresser and began to doodle and jot a few things down. I made detailed lists of all the jobs around the farm that needed doing, prioritising those such as strawing the strawberries and fixing the fruit cages, which were most urgent.

Then, having filled one side of the A4 sheet and decorated it around the edges with a border of roughly sketched strawberries and leaves, I then began to scribble down ideas which could help the farm turn more of a profit. Obviously, it was only for fun, but it helped pass more time and occupied my mind.

Increasing yields or growing different crops wasn't an option because, as far as I had seen, the farm didn't have space to expand. I would have to ask Eliot if there was more land attached to the place than that which surrounded the house though, just to be sure.

I thought again of the barn, with its mellow bricks, attractively arched doors and lofty interior as well as the collection of vintage paraphernalia someone had squirrelled away inside. Was there any value in any of that I wondered? Not in selling it necessarily, but in finding a way to utilise it?

I wrote down 'venue' in large capitals and then listed what was currently fashionable in alternative uses for farm buildings, assuming you could secure the official change to its use, and any subsequent planning permission of course. Weddings were the obvious choice, but the Fenview barn wasn't big enough to make it worthwhile and there was no space for decent parking. A dozen vehicles max and the yard would be rammed. And more to the point, I couldn't imagine my grandfather in the role of wedding planner.

Hiring the space out to another farmer, or even a landscaper looking for machinery storage might be an easier option and then there were the residential conversion opportunities, as long as you didn't mind someone living practically on your doorstep. That would most likely mean selling it, but I added it anyway.

I did another quick doodle then added farm shop to the list along with Fenland museum. I was scraping the barrel a bit by then, but the unusual collection had stuck in my head. It was obviously there for a reason and meant something to someone.

'What's this?' asked Eliot, leaning over my shoulder and making me jump. 'Possible diversification ideas?'

'It's nothing,' I said, turning the paper over. 'I was just thinking about things that could help get the farm back on its feet.'

'What makes you think it needs any help?' he said, sounding a little defensive.

'Well, I've seen a few things about the place that need attention so I've written them down.'

'What sort of things?'

'Well, the fruit cages for a start,' I told him, feeling my temperature rise under his inquisition. 'A couple of them are torn and if the birds get in, then the protection might as well not be there.'

'What else?'

'The strawberry rows need strawing to stop the fruit from resting on the soil and getting spoiled in the rain,' I said, referring to the second thing on my list.

'And how do you know about any of this stuff?' he asked, nodding at the notes I'd made. 'What do you know about running a fruit farm?'

There was a definite narky edge to his tone and I thought it had more bite behind it than just being nudged to the fore by a sleepless night.

'You'd be surprised,' I found myself snapping back.

'And what's all this?' he asked, taking up the paper and turning it over. 'Wedding venue, barn conversion, farm shop,' he reeled off. 'Got plans of your own for Fenview Farm, have you?'

'No,' I said, further taken aback by the unkind accusation. 'Of course not.'

I hoped he didn't think that I had travelled to Wynbridge with a potential inheritance in mind. That's not what I had come to Fenview for at all.

'I was just doing it to fill the time, that's all.' I quickly explained. 'This,' I said, pointing at the paper he still held, 'is just my way of letting my mind wander. I need to keep busy. It stops me thinking—'

'About what?' he cut in.

'My mother's last moments,' I choked. 'Watching her last breath leave her body. Seeing the light leave her eyes. Walking to the grave behind her coffin.'

'Shit,' Eliot swore, dropping the paper back on the table.

'Knowing I'll never feel her arms around me again.'

'Stop,' he said, pulling out the chair next to mine and sitting on it. 'Please, Fliss.'

'Well you asked. You clearly wanted me to justify the silly scribbles, didn't you? You wanted me to prove that I haven't rocked up here with a view to trying to secure myself a Fenland future.'

'No,' he said, hanging his head. 'No, of course not.'

'Well, that's what it sounded like to me.'

'Fuck,' he said, and then he was back on his feet and pulling me along with him. 'Come here.'

He wrapped his arms tight around me and my body melded to his in spite of my vain attempt to resist. I was too wound up to cry and too shocked by his proximity to feel anything other than annoyance. If there had been a spark between us the day before, then, for the time being at least, he had succeeded in snuffing it out.

'I'm sorry,' he said, his breath close to my ear. 'I just worry about Bill. He's so vulnerable right now and I just want to . . .'

'Protect him,' I said, pulling away. 'I know, but you really don't need to protect him from me.'

We looked at each other, as an uncomfortable awkwardness filled the space between us.

'I'm going for a run,' I said. 'Maybe you should think about taking a nap.'

It was a good couple of miles before I had even started to work my way out of the upset Eliot's reaction to my note-making had shoved me into and even then, it still stung. I could appreciate the second part of my list could have been open to misinterpretation, but it was the fact that he had reacted with such instant suspicion which had taken me aback.

Granted he didn't know me yet, but he could have framed his curiosity about what I had been scribbling so much better. He might have looked buff in boxers, but thinking so badly of me had turned me off him a bit.

I picked up the pace again and turned back towards the farm, smashing my PB as the farmhouse came into view. My heart was hammering and my breath was sharp in my chest by the time I drew level with the gate.

'Hey!' called a voice as I began to stretch out my muscles. 'Where's the fire?'

I pulled out my earbuds and spun round, abandoning the series of extra-long stretches I always did after a really hard run. Mr Helpful and his sleek Audi had crept up behind me and I hadn't heard a thing. I never usually played my music so loud for fear of not hearing traffic but Eliot had got me so fired up I'd shot the volume up as soon as I set off.

'Oh hey,' I puffed, still breathing hard.

'That was some serious speed you gathered back there,' he beamed, taking off his sunglasses and unashamedly looking at my legs.

I didn't usually run in shorts, but they were the only thing remotely suitable for exercise that I had with me. That and the halter neck top I had teamed them with. Fortunately, I'd got my running shoes because I never went anywhere without those.

'I thought I'd better make the effort to burn off all those calories I'd ingested after my spree in the deli,' I said, making a joke even though I still didn't feel much in the mood for a laugh.

'You look just fine to me,' he said seriously.

I knew my face was already flushed and was pleased he couldn't see that I was blushing.

'You left your olive oil in my bag,' I said, neatly side stepping his comment. 'You can come and get it if you like.'

I wasn't sure what Eliot would make of me inviting a stranger in, but given that I was still smarting over our almost argument, I wasn't all that concerned.

'What from here?' asked Mr Helpful, looking at the farm.

'Yes.'

'Are you staying here?'

'Sort of,' I said, wrinkling my nose as I realised that I'd put my foot in it again and let another local know I had a connection to the place too soon.

'Either you are or you aren't,' he laughed. 'Unless of course you're squatting. Is that what you're doing?'

It did feel a bit like that.

'In a roundabout sort of way,' I sighed, as I looked along the road and spotted the Banana-mobile heading in our direction, 'I suppose I am.'

He noticed my gaze had shifted and checked his mirror.

'Oh crikey,' he grinned. 'You can't miss that thing, can you?'

'Absolutely not,' I smiled, this time the reaction felt far more genuine. 'I wouldn't be surprised if it glowed in the dark. So, do you want to come in and get this oil?'

'It'll have to be another day, I'm afraid.'

'If you're sure?'

'Absolutely. It'll be a good excuse to bump into you again.'

'Do you need one?' I laughed.

I realised with a jolt that I was flirting. So out of practice, I thought I'd lost the ability, and I had no idea why I was doing it. Perhaps it was some sort of reflex to Eliot's meanness.

'I guess not,' he grinned. 'I'll see you around.'

He put the car into gear and smoothly pulled away.

'Yes,' I called after him. 'I'll see you around.' It was only then that I realised that I still hadn't found out who he was.

Chapter 7

It didn't make any difference to me, but Monday was a bank holiday, and that did have an impact on Eliot.

'I have to go out,' he told me, when I eventually went down to the kitchen, dressed and stiff legged, to seek out some coffee.

I'd avoided spending time with him the afternoon and evening before. He'd apologised profusely for his suspicious snappiness more than once and I had accepted it, but I didn't much like the change in atmosphere the misunderstanding had left behind, so I absented myself from it and stayed upstairs on the excuse of being tired. Which wasn't an excuse really because the previous day's events had been exhausting.

'Oh,' I said, my nerves instantly jangling at the thought of being left home alone, in case my grandfather needed anything while he was gone. 'Right.'

'I'm not going to be long.' Eliot elaborated, picking up on my apprehension. 'So, don't worry. I just need to collect some meds for Bill that I hadn't realised he was running low on, and as it's a bank holiday the pharmacy in town is shut so I've got to go to the one in the big Waitrose in Peterborough.'

'All right,' I nodded, trying to look more in control than I felt, as he pulled on his leather suit. 'Here's hoping you won't be needed before you get back.'

'I promise I'll be as quick as I can.'

I didn't much want him to ride fast but a speedy turn-around would be appreciated.

'You're going to be hot wearing that,' I said, with a nod to the suit.

For a British bank holiday, the weather felt unseasonably warm and that was inside the house.

'That's as maybe,' he said, wriggling his shoulders to get the suit to slide more comfortably into place before offering me a cheeky smile, 'but I don't ride without protection.'

I couldn't help but laugh.

'Honestly Eliot,' I said primly, but with a smile. 'Well, that's good to know.'

He laughed back and even though I was nervous about him leaving, I was relieved that the awkward feeling between us had been banished. I busied myself making coffee and toast while he pulled on the cumbersome boots which filled the space by the back door.

'I won't be long,' he said again, reaching for his helmet and gloves. 'Bill's asleep and fingers crossed he'll stay that way. I'll push the bike down the road a bit before I start it, and the window in his room is shut, so he shouldn't hear it.'

He was going to great lengths to ensure everything should run like clockwork and I appreciated that.

'All right,' I said. 'And don't worry about how long it takes, just ride safe. The roads are bound to be extra busy today and not all car drivers have their minds on bikes when they're in a rush, do they?'

'Unfortunately not,' he agreed. 'I've had my share of near misses.'

I didn't like the thought of him having to take evasive action as he sped along the poker-straight A47. It seemed to me to be just the sort of road that could easily catch you out if you didn't have your wits about you.

'See you later then,' he smiled, ducking out the door.

Even though he pushed the heavy bike a good way along the road before he started it, it was still loud and barely out of earshot before I heard my grandfather moving about. I crossed my fingers and sent up a quick prayer in the hope that I wasn't in for a repeat of what happened when Vicky left on Saturday.

'I know you're still here!' he called, making my feet leave the floor before I'd even uttered an amen. 'So, you might as well come in.'

I stood stock still, barely daring to breathe and wishing I'd prayed faster. That said, maybe it was Eliot that he was referring to.

'Come on, young woman! Show yourself.'

Or maybe not. Eliot was as far from womanly as it was possible to get.

'Quick now,' came the voice again. 'Or am I going to have to come and find you myself?'

I dithered for a second and then, knowing I couldn't risk him getting out of bed unaided, popped my head into the room.

'Good morning,' he said. 'The enigma reveals itself at last.'

'Good morning,' I blurted out, my voice ridiculously squeaky and high. 'I'm here to help Eliot, Mr Brown. I'm a trainee. He's gone to get you some tablets, but he'll be back in a minute. Why don't you just go to sleep?'

I don't think I'd ever spoken so fast.

'I know exactly when he'll be back,' he calmly told me. 'I'm capable of working out how long it takes him to get to Peterborough and back on that death trap he rides. I've been waiting for him to go. Just because my eyes are closed, neither of you should assume I'm asleep, you know.'

He'd obviously overheard mine and Eliot's every word. I wondered what else he'd been privy to. At least he wasn't shouting anymore though.

'If you're serious about pursuing a career in caring,' he added, his eyes twinkling, 'then you should remember that.'

'I will,' I nodded, playing along. 'That's good to know. Thank you. Duly noted.'

'And you should always have the kettle on the boil too,' he said with a sniff. 'I generally have a cup of tea about now and I wouldn't mind something to eat to go with it, if that's all right with you?'

As I boiled a couple of eggs and buttered bread, I tried

not to think about what was going to happen next. I was in no way prepared to keep telling lies because that would only cause more problems in the long run, but I wasn't ready for the conversation about my true identity which seemed to be nudging closer either.

I had no idea what Eliot was going to say when he got back and found I'd been playing out the caring role, but I could hardly have ignored my grandfather's calls, could I? Eliot would have been far unhappier if I'd left him to find me and he'd taken a tumble.

'Here we go then, Mr Brown,' I said, trying to smile as I wobbled my way back into the room with the breakfast tray. 'How about some boiled eggs to kick your day off?'

I was probably overdoing the upbeat tone, but I was nervous. I hoped I didn't sound patronising. If I was, my grandfather was thankfully willing to let it pass.

'Perfect,' he said, grimacing a little as he shifted himself further up the bed. 'Just the thing. Thank you very much.'

'I'll leave you to it then,' I said, hastily turning away.

'No, don't go,' he said, deftly slicing the tops off the eggs. 'Stay and talk. I could do with a bit of different conversation.'

'I'll just grab my coffee then,' I said, my breath tight in my chest.

I took a moment to compose myself and when I went back in, I noticed how stuffy the room felt. With the curtains closed it was dull too. It reflected nothing of the bright and sunny May bank holiday morning that was unfolding outside, and with the added smell of the eggs it made my nose wrinkle.

'Mr Brown,' I said. 'Would you mind if I opened the curtains?'

'Not at all,' he keenly replied. 'And some fresh air wouldn't hurt. I know Eliot's been keeping the curtains closed in case I spotted you walking about, and that the window has been shut this morning so I didn't hear his blasted bike, but as he's gone now and you're in here we don't have to worry about any of that, do we?'

He really did have it all sussed out. I tried not to think about what else he already knew, or at least suspected.

'I take it you're not a fan of the Ducati then?' I said, putting down my mug.

He sounded even more scathing than Alessandro who appreciated the power and beauty of the machine, but was also adamant that Marco would never ride one. Conversely, my grandfather didn't sound at all in awe of the bike's esteemed credentials. His tone was a much better match for Nonna's.

'No,' he bluntly said. 'I'm not.'

I rattled the curtains back along the pole and threw the window open.

'Ah,' he said, drawing in a breath of the sweetly fragrant air which rushed in. 'That's more like it.'

The atmosphere in the room instantly lifted. No longer a sick room, it felt light and fresh.

'Can I smell roses?' I asked, catching the heady scent as the sunlight streamed in.

'You can,' he proudly said. 'The back of the house is

covered with climbers and they flower early thanks to the sheltered spot. With the sun on them, they smell like that all day.'

I hadn't seen them when I made my tour of the farm because I'd avoided the back of the house.

'They smell wonderful,' I said, inhaling deeply as he smiled in approval. 'Oh,' I added, 'now we're in trouble.'

Having spotted an opportunity, the little cat had jumped nimbly through the window and straight up on to the bed.

'Eliot told me she's not a house cat,' I frowned, wondering how she would react if I tried to lift her off the bed or shoo her out. 'Shall I try and put her out again?'

'No,' my grandfather said. 'She won't do any harm and to tell you the truth, I've missed seeing her. But the lad's right, she's not usually one for coming in, so I guess she must have been missing me too.'

It didn't take him long to finish his breakfast and by the time I returned from clearing up and making more drinks, the cat was curled up on his lap, purring away and looking every bit like the feline who'd got the cream. Louise had told me my grandfather wasn't really a grumpy old man and the way he fussed and tenderly coddled the cat suggested she was right.

'Do you think she's hungry?' I asked, as he stroked her back, covering the pristine bed linen with a fine layer of cat hair.

'No,' he said. 'I wouldn't have thought so. She's pretty self-sufficient.'

I shuddered at the thought of her rat-catching capabilities.

'What about you?' I asked, keen to dismiss the image as I sat in the chair next to the bed. 'Can I get you anything else, Mr Brown?'

'No, thank you,' he said. 'I'm fine. In fact, this is the first time in a while that I've felt properly like myself.'

Thankfully he bore absolutely no resemblance to the confused old man I'd seen, shouting and flailing about, the day I arrived. His brow was smooth, his manner relaxed and there was even some colour in his cheeks.

'You aren't feeling the cold, are you?' I asked, worried that the rosiness could be the result of the air which might have felt fresh to someone who had been indoors for a while.

'No,' he said. 'I'm cosy enough with all these blankets. Although, I still can't get properly comfortable. What I wouldn't give for a night in my own bed, and how Eliot has stuck it on the floor, I'll never know.'

'He's a saint, isn't he?'

'He is that,' my grandfather agreed. 'And then some.'

'I did suggest he could nap on the spare bed where I've been sleeping.'

His gaze shifted from the cat to my face. 'Staying in the house, are you?'

Damn. My nerves had started to dissipate and in their place my ability to blurt had popped back up again.

'Well, yes,' I said, quickly composing myself. 'Just to make sure Eliot had some back-up until you were over the worst. You've been very poorly you know.'

I was quite proud of the speedy justification for my sleepover, and reminding my grandfather that he'd been properly poorly might make him think that what occurred on Saturday was just a dream. Assuming he could remember any of it, that is.

'Well, that's very kind,' he nodded, taking a moment to gauge my expression, which I kept as neutral as I could. 'Clearly you've both gone above and beyond. Are you and Eliot an item, by any chance?'

My face flushed brightly enough to more than match his and my regained composure and impartial appearance flew straight out the open window.

'Why on earth would you think that?' I stuttered.

'I thought I heard you having words yesterday,' he smiled. 'And wondered if perhaps it was a lovers' tiff, but given the look on your face,' he added with a chuckle, 'perhaps not.'

'Absolutely not,' I firmly said. 'Our relationship is purely professional. We did have a slight disagreement about something yesterday and I'm very sorry if it disturbed you.'

'No harm done,' he shrugged, clearly amused by my reaction.

I mentally crossed my fingers and toes hoping he hadn't heard the cause of our raised voices.

'That's very generous of you,' I said, standing up again, 'but I am sorry we bothered you. I think it would be best if I left you in peace now. Eliot and I won't disturb you again, Mr Brown and he'll be back to take over soon.'

My grandfather looked at me and shook his head.

'I think we can drop the title, don't you? Mr Brown is a little on the formal side.'

'William, then,' I smiled, thinking I'd got away with it. 'That's right, isn't it? I'll call you William or Bill.'

'Not Grandad?'

For a second or two the world seemed to stop turning, then it started up again like a super slow-motion sequence beloved by movie-makers, before finally coming back into focus. I groped for the chair behind me and sank into it.

'Grandad,' I swallowed. 'Why would I call you that?'

'Because you're my granddaughter, aren't you?'

He sounded completely unfazed by the pronouncement he had just made, but I was floundering. Should I deny who I was, or confirm it? Was this the moment I had been waiting for? It didn't feel like the moment I had been waiting for. That moment was supposed to be decided upon by me, Eliot and Louise. They were supposed to be holding my hands and helping me take those teeny tiny steps we'd talked about and yet, here I was with my grandfather, the very person we were trying to protect and *he* was pulling *me* along the path and telling me to get a wriggle on and take bigger strides!

'I've often wondered if Jennifer had a girl or a boy,' he further shocked me by saying. 'If I had a granddaughter or a grandson somewhere in the world.'

Tears prickled my eyes and I looked down at the floor, unable to meet his gaze.

'You knew she was pregnant?' I whispered.

'I had a pretty good idea,' he quietly said.

I couldn't bring myself to look at him.

'I knew she'd had a holiday romance,' he carried on. 'And you look to be about the right age, and then of course there was your name. You told me Saturday that it's Felicity, didn't you? Same as my dear wife's. That's a bit of a coincidence, isn't it?'

'I didn't think you'd remember that,' I said, my voice constrained as I had to force the words over the lump in my throat. 'I'm so sorry.'

'What are you apologising for?'

I shrugged, unable to say that I was sorry his daughter, my mother, was dead and that it had taken the acknowledgement of her impending demise for her to finally tell me that he existed. That could all come later.

'You've got nothing to apologise for,' he said. 'She was the one who ran away. I just want to know, are you my granddaughter, Felicity?'

'Yes,' I said, looking up at him through my tears. 'Yes, I am. I am your granddaughter.'

Chapter 8

'What do you mean, he knows?' Eliot frowned as I relayed the details of what had happened in his absence.

The supermarket pharmacy hadn't got the prescription ready when he had finally arrived, having weaved his way through the bank holiday traffic, and then there had been some mix-up which meant he'd had to call Doctor Clarke, so he'd been gone ages and arrived back in a far less happy mood than the one he'd left in.

My grandfather and I, or Grandad, as he was now insisting that I called him, hadn't got any further than establishing our relationship to one another but that was more than enough for either of us to get our heads around and looking at the expression on Eliot's face and the colour that had flooded it as I explained what had happened, I realised that it was a shock for him too, coming straight on the back of his hot and tiresome trip out.

'I can't believe it,' he grimaced as he tried to shrug himself out of his leather suit.

His hair was plastered to his head and his T-shirt clung to his chest. The outfit obviously wasn't easy to get off when he was so hot. As in temperature, I reminded myself as I looked anywhere but at his taut muscles straining to free themselves from their leather confines.

'Me neither,' I told him. 'It turns out we hadn't been quite as clever, or as quiet, as we thought we had over the last couple of days.'

I didn't mention that Grandad had heard us arguing because I didn't want to bring that particular topic back up again, but I did rush to grab the pile of papers, including my list, which the air blowing through the house had whipped up.

'And he'd worked out why the curtains were being kept shut,' I added, thinking of the other clever deductions Grandad had made which would have rivalled Hercule Poirot himself.

'The canny old bugger,' Eliot tutted. 'And why is it so breezy in here?'

'Because I've opened some windows,' I told him, securing the papers with an empty mug.

'Bill won't be used to this sudden change in temperature,' Eliot pointed out, making my desire to freshen things up a bit feel rather reckless. 'It was hot in the hospital and I've tried to replicate that here and bring it down gradually.'

'Damn. I'm so sorry,' I said. 'I didn't think about that.'

I really needed to leave the caring side of things to Eliot. He was the expert, after all.

'I take it you're another fresh air fiend?' he asked.

'Yes,' I admitted. 'I suppose I am a bit. Though not at the cost of Grandad's health of course.'

Eliot looked at me and smiled. It wasn't quite the reaction I expected, given how hot and bothered he was.

'What?' I asked.

'It's nice to hear you call him Grandad,' he softly said.

He was right. It was a little strange, but it felt good too.

'You aren't cross about what's happened then?' I asked him.

'Of course, I'm not,' he said, laying a hand on my shoulder and making my heart skip.

I wilted with relief. At least, I think it was relief.

'If anything,' he said, letting out a breath, 'it's a weight off my mind, and I bet you feel the same, don't you? Bill working it all out has saved us a whole lot of heartache.'

'Yes,' I said, lowering my voice to a barely audible whisper. 'It is a relief that he knows, but I'm still dreading telling him about Mum. That's going to have to happen sooner rather than later now, isn't it?'

Eliot gave my shoulder a squeeze.

'Yeah,' he said, running his other hand through his hair. 'I suppose it is. That's one conversation . . .'

'Eliot!' called Grandad, cutting him off.

'Yes, Bill,' Eliot called back.

'Can I have a word please lad?'

Eliot looked at me and grimaced.

'I'm going to be in the doghouse,' he said. 'I bet I'm going to get an earful for not letting on about you.'

'Shall I come in with you?' I offered.

The last thing I wanted was for Grandad to blame Eliot for anything. After all, I was a grown woman and had I really wanted to, I could have left on Saturday rather than given in to his and Louise's coaxing.

'Best not,' he said, standing tall. 'Better if I face the music alone.'

I paced about the kitchen, unable to listen in on what was being said because the doors were closed, but there were no raised voices. I was certain I would have been able to hear if either of them was shouting.

I kept purposefully busy and was hanging out the washing when Eliot came back out of the house. He was already wearing his leathers again and obviously in a hurry.

'Oh crikey,' I said, throwing the handful of pegs back into the basket. 'He hasn't banished you, has he?'

'No,' Eliot laughed. 'Nothing like that. And you can stop fretting because he didn't tell me off. Well, not quite. He was very understanding, given the circumstances. He's aware of how poorly he was and that if we'd said anything sooner, he wouldn't have been able to make head or tail of it.'

'That's a relief then, but where are you off to in such a rush?'

'Vicky just called. There's not enough staff to do the rounds today, so I'm going to help out.'

'But you're on holiday,' I pointed out.

'I'm not really though, am I?' he said, nodding back to the house. 'I was already looking after Bill.'

'But who's going to look after him now?' I panicked, thinking again of Saturday even though I knew Grandad was much better. 'I don't know what to do with him.'

'You'll be fine,' Eliot said, climbing astride the bike in one swift and smooth movement. It was rather arousing but I tried to focus on the matter in hand. 'Bill's well on the mend and you're my trainee remember,' he added, waggling his eyebrows.

'Don't tease,' I flushed. 'It's hardly the moment.'

'Well,' he mercilessly carried on, 'Bill did say that you were keen to point out that our relationship was purely professional.'

'Did he?' I said, turning red again.

'Which is a shame,' Eliot said, his eyes meeting mine and causing my heart to judder, 'because I thought there was a bit of a spark between us.'

'Did you?' I squeaked.

'I did,' he huskily said, making me tingle. 'I still do.'

I self-consciously scuffed at the ground with the toe of my plimsoll and felt about thirteen. I'd sensed he'd felt something that first time he'd clapped eyes on me and it was a thrill to know my spark was reciprocated. Perhaps we might, as Grandad had put it, become an item at some point in the future.

'But you were right, Fliss,' Eliot then burst my loved-up bubble by saying. 'Given the circumstances, what with me being Bill's carer and you having only just arrived, we should keep things on a professional footing. It wouldn't do any good to start something up when you've still got so much to discover and deal with, would it?'

'I suppose not,' I reluctantly agreed.

I imagined my fiery sparkler being shoved into a bucket of sand before I had even drawn so much as a love heart with it. Its sparkling charm was completely extinguished.

'You and Bill are going to be having some difficult conversations and working through some tricky times and what you'll both need more than anything is a friend, isn't it?' Eliot carried on. 'And I'd really like to be that person, Fliss. For you as well as him.'

It was an extremely kind offer and given the limited number of people I knew here in Wynbridge I considered myself most fortunate to have Eliot's wonderfully broad shoulders to cry on. I knew I could call the Rossis and tell them what was happening, but a proper hug and a sympathetic ear close by, was going to be much appreciated in the days to come.

'I'd like you to be that person, too,' I said, standing on tiptoe and kissing his cheek. 'Thank you, Eliot.'

We looked at each for a moment and then he pulled his helmet on and started the bike.

'I'll see you soon,' he said, his voice muffled. 'And don't worry about looking after Bill. Between you, you'll be just fine.'

I finished hanging out the washing, told myself I was fortunate to have Eliot as a friend, and that I must set my lustful feelings for him to one side. He was right, a new relationship would be an added complication neither of us needed right now. With a resigned sigh, I went back inside to check on Grandad.

'And what are you up to now?' I tutted, when I found him with the bed covers pushed back and his feet resting on the floor.

'Has Eliot gone?' he asked.

'Yes,' I said. 'The knight in shining armour has mounted his trusty metal steed and gone to rescue someone else. You didn't tell him off for not letting on about me, did you?' I asked, just to make sure.

'No,' he said. 'He's a good lad and I know he had my best interests at heart. He always does. And besides, I daresay, his mother had more to do with you staying on here than anyone else, didn't she?'

Nothing escaped this man's notice.

'Never mind that now,' I said, not wanting to dob Louise in. 'What exactly are you planning to do?'

'I just want to have a stretch,' he said. 'I've been in this blasted bed too damn long.'

'But I don't know what to do,' I said, feeling nervous.

'Do?' he chuckled. 'You haven't got to *do* anything. Other than make sure I don't end up on my backside!'

I had to laugh at that.

'Here,' I said, stepping forward. 'Let me just help you up.'

We took a couple of very slow turns around the room, as much for my confidence as Grandad's benefit, and then went into the kitchen.

'You've been tidying up,' he said, noticing the less cluttered dresser and the fresh flowers in jars along the windowsill.

'I hope that's all right? I'm not very good at twiddling my thumbs and I wanted to make myself useful.'

I didn't mention my list-making.

'Well, you've certainly done that,' he smiled approvingly. 'It all looks lovely. The place has missed having a woman's touch. Not,' he added with a wink, 'that we're supposed to say such things in these enlightened times.'

I thought I'd let him get away with it, just this once.

'Do you know,' he yawned. 'That's me done. It's been quite a morning, hasn't it?'

'It certainly has,' I agreed.

I was pretty tired out myself.

'Do you think it would be all right if I had an early nap?'

'I think it would be fine,' I told him. 'Let's get you back into bed.'

I had hoped that once Eliot had been to help whoever Vicky had drafted him in to take care of, he would come back and take over with Grandad again, but there was no Ducati rumble either nearby or in the distance and that was a shame, because there was something specific I wanted to do that went beyond doling out pills and straightening sheets. Something that I hoped we would be able to do for Grandad together.

Steeling myself to be brave and think positive, even though I was flying solo, I mentioned it to Grandad.

'I have a feeling Eliot isn't going to make it back today, and I don't know how we'll manage it between us,' I told him, 'but we're going to try and get you up those stairs and into your own bed tonight.'

There, I'd said it.

'There should be a set of instructions from the hospital physio about here somewhere,' Grandad immediately said. 'She printed them out to remind me how to go up and down stairs and steps safely.'

The fact that he hadn't said he'd manage another night in the single bed was proof enough that he really did want to be back in his own space and I resolved to do whatever was needed to make that happen.

'Your paperwork from the hospital is in a file in the kitchen,' I told him, remembering seeing Eliot look through it. 'I'll get it out and then we can read the instructions together and,' I added, 'as you'll be sleeping in there tonight, would you mind if I went into your room and gave it an airing?'

'Of course not,' he smiled. 'There are already clean sheets on the bed, but some more fresh air would be most welcome.'

'You can't beat it, can you?' I smiled back. 'I've always got the windows open. Mum moans about it all the time in the winter.'

'She was the same when she was growing up,' Grandad told me, thankfully not noticing the tears I tried to blink away as I realised not only what I'd said, but that I'd been struck by the realisation that Mum would never feel the cold again. 'Always moaning about being cold, right from autumn through to spring . . .' His words tailed off and then he added, 'You can air her room too, if you like. Have you looked in it yet?'

'No,' I said, fussing with the cushion on the chair, to avoid looking at him. 'I've only been in the spare room and the bathroom.'

'Well,' he said, his gaze returning to the window. 'Now we've finally established who you are, feel free to have a proper look about the place, won't you?'

'Thank you,' I said, pulling myself together and trying not to think how heartbreaking it was going to be to tell him what had happened to Mum. 'I will.'

I didn't mention that I'd looked over the farm, and in the barn, already and I didn't say that I'd leave exploring Mum's room for a bit longer either. I had no idea what I would find in there, but I certainly wasn't ready to face it yet.

'There is one thing I want to see,' I said, rushing back to the kitchen and drying my eyes before returning with some scissors and a jar filled with water.

I leant out of the open window and gasped at the sight of the roses which scaled the height of the house and were in full bloom. They were a riot of colour and the scent, intensified by the strengthening sunshine, was intoxicating.

'Wow,' I gasped.

The jars in the kitchen were full of flowers cut from the front of the house and they were lovely, but I knew another one filled with roses would look, and smell, even better.

'You like those, do you?' Grandad laughed.

'Just a bit! Did you plant them?'

'No,' he said. 'Not me. They were Felicity's passion. The whole garden was, not that there's much of it left. Whenever one of her roses has died off though, I've always replaced it like for like. It's been my way of keeping her floral legacy alive.'

I began to realise that every conversation we were destined to share was going to have an emotional undercurrent running through it. There was so much for me to learn and catch up on. Not least Grandad's explanation of the circumstances surrounding Mum's departure.

'Can I cut some of the roses?' I asked, again pushing the thought of the revelatory moments away. 'For you to have in here.'

'Of course,' Grandad keenly agreed. 'And we can take them upstairs tonight.'

Once I'd filled the jar with the yellow, red, pink and peach scented roses, and embellished it further with lime green Alchemilla mollis, I turned my attention to Grandad's bedroom. The décor was dated with lots of eighties pine furniture and floral sprigged Laura Ashley style prints, but I had expected that because it was similar to the spare room, but what I wasn't prepared for were the shelves full of framed photographs.

'Mum,' I murmured, picking up one of her in her late teens.

There were eighteen photos in total, one for each year of Mum's life before she left, I guessed. I lightly ran my fingers over the frame of the last one, wondering if she might have been pregnant with me when it was taken. The last three or four were classic moody teenage shots. She looked a bit begrudging to be facing the camera, unlike in the early ones where she was all smiles. What had changed? What was it that had turned her off the farm and indeed, away from her father?

'Hello!' called a voice up the stairs, making me jump. 'Are you there, Felicity?'

It was Louise.

'Yes,' I said. 'Yes, I'm here.'

As I reached the bottom of the stairs, she pulled me in for a hug.

'Have you seen Eliot?' I asked, blinking away the tears her kind gesture prompted, when she finally let me go.

'I haven't seen him,' she said, offering me a tissue. 'But he called to tell me that Bill had sussed out who you are and he wanted me to ring and check everything was okay. He's not going to be able to get back himself, so I decided to pop in in person.'

'That was kind of him,' I said. 'And you.'

'I'm not sure if he really is all that busy,' Louise admitted, biting her lip, 'or if he wanted to give you and Bill some space.'

Kinder still, but then I wouldn't have expected anything less of Eliot.

'So,' said Louise, studying my face. 'How's it going?'

I didn't get the chance to tell her that Grandad and I were

getting along wonderfully but that I still hadn't found the moment, or mustered the courage, to tell him about Mum.

'Are you two going to be out there whispering all day?' Grandad shouted from the dining room. 'Come in here. I want to talk to you.'

'Sorry, Bill,' said Louise. 'We're on our way.'

'What I'd really like to know,' Grandad said to me, once we, and the cat, were settled with tea and a slice of delicious shop-bought cake which Louise had arrived with, 'is why you've decided to come and find me now. Why didn't you come before?'

This was it then. This was the moment everything was going to be revealed. I was grateful for both Louise's kind and encouraging smile and the boost my blood sugar was receiving courtesy of the sweet slice of sponge. I pressed my hand against the pocket where Mum's letters and Nonna's recipe still rested, protecting my heart as best they could.

'Because,' I began, 'I didn't know about you before. I only found out about you and the farm very recently.'

Grandad nodded. 'Your mother didn't talk to you about me or this place or her mother while you were growing up then?'

'No,' I huskily said. 'I'm afraid not. If she had, I most likely would have come a long time ago.'

I couldn't promise that though, because when I'd first read Mum's letter, I'd been adamant that I wouldn't come, but then, it hadn't taken me long to change my mind, had it?

'So, where has she ended up then?' Grandad asked. 'With your father?'

I noticed Louise shift in her seat. Clearly, Grandad had known more than she thought.

'No,' I swallowed. 'Mum didn't find him. He'd given her a false Italian address when they parted after their holiday, so that turned out to be impossible.'

'And yet she still chose not to come home when she realised that,' he said. 'She preferred to make her life and yours elsewhere.'

He sounded incredibly sad and my heart broke for him.

'I'm ashamed to say, I was furious when I found out she was pregnant,' he carried on. 'I should have taken time to get used to the idea before I spoke to her about it, but I was so upset and scared. I'd struggled to cope with her wayward behaviour after Felicity died and I knew I'd let her get away with too much.'

'You can't blame yourself for her behaviour, Bill,' said Louise. 'She was a law unto herself. And I had no idea that you knew she was pregnant when she left.'

'Loving fathers don't miss much,' he sniffed. 'I also knew that you knew too Louise, but I appreciated that we never talked about it. It would have made it all so much harder if we had.'

'That's very generous of you,' said Louise, looking misty eyed.

'No point holding a grudge,' he shrugged. 'And like I said, our silence did make things a little easier.'

'Mum did settle in Italy,' I said, wanting him to know that she had made something of her life. 'Well, she had a base there. On a farm which belongs to the Rossi family. For the most part it was where I grew up. They mainly grow cherries and olives . . .'

'She settled on a farm?' Grandad gasped, his eyes wide. 'Well, I never. She always despised this place because it stopped us taking summer holidays and meant working long hours and yet she willingly settled on someone else's where it would have been just the same.'

I looked at Louise and bit my lip. Rather than make things better, I was just making them worse and the hardest part was still to come.

'You're forgetting how much she hated the British weather,' said Louise, trying to lighten the moment, but it didn't help.

'She didn't stay there all the time,' I rushed on, keen to make amends. 'As I said, it was more of a base. More often than not she was off travelling. It was her ambition to visit every country in the world. I used to go with her when I was younger, but then I began to work properly for the Rossis . . .'

'Fliss,' said Grandad, putting up a hand to stop me. 'Can I just ask you something?'

'Of course,' I swallowed.

I looked at Louise again. Her head was bowed and I realised I must have made another mistake.

'You just said this farm in Italy *was* a base for Jennifer and that it *was* her ambition to visit every country.'

'That's right,' I nodded.

'Why isn't it now?'

For the second time since I'd arrived, the world ground to a halt. Without realising, I'd been talking about Mum in the past tense.

'Because she's dead, Bill,' said Louise, reaching for my hand and saving me from having to say the words. 'She's not with us anymore.'

'Is this true?' Grandad asked, looking to me.

'Yes,' I nodded, my voice barely audible. 'It is. She died of cancer a few weeks ago and she left me a letter telling me the name of this place and where it was and that she wanted me to come and find you.'

A sob escaped Grandad's lips and I pulled my hand from Louise's grasp and rushed to his bedside.

'My girl has gone?' he choked.

'Yes,' I said again. 'She's gone. I'm so sorry.'

I don't know how long we sat, our hands tightly clasped together, but the sun had long since left the room by the time Grandad spoke again. Like mine and Louise's, his tears had flowed freely the whole time we were quiet and it was a relief to witness it.

The last thing he needed to do was bottle his grief up. He didn't strike me as the type to display his emotions, he was a proper old country boy, and even though it was tough to see his stiff upper lip disappear, it was a godsend too.

'I searched for her you know,' he eventually said, his voice raspy. 'And I never gave up hope that one day she'd come back. I hate the thought of her still hating me all the way to her grave.'

'I don't think she did, Grandad,' I said, pulling out and handing him Mum's letter. 'She left this for you. If it's anything like mine, it will hopefully explain a few things.'

He took it from me and I passed him the glasses on the little table next to his bed. It was too late for Mum to change anything inside the envelope now, but I hoped her letter answered Grandad's questions and gave him some of the peace and acceptance he so sorely needed.

'Another letter,' he swallowed. 'I hope it says more than the note she left when she disappeared.'

'We'll leave you to read it, Bill,' said Louise, standing up. 'Come on Fliss, love,' she added, holding out her hand.

'Before you go,' said Grandad just as we reached the door. 'Tell me Fliss, are you in a rush to get back to this farm in Italy?'

'That depends,' I told him.

'On what?'

'On whether or not you'd like me to stay here for a while.'

'I'd very much like you to stay,' he said, without a moment's hesitation. 'And for much longer than a while, if you'd like to.'

'I'd like that very much,' I said, crossing the room again and giving him another hug.

I know I'd promised Marco that I'd be back in time to work over the summer season, but that wasn't going to happen now and I hoped he wouldn't mind. I knew Nonna and Alessandro would be thrilled so hopefully they'd be able to talk him round.

'Good,' Grandad sniffed, as he patted my back. 'I'm pleased about that, because from what I've heard you saying to Eliot, there's plenty here to keep you occupied if you think you're up to it.'

'Oh, I am,' I told him, kissing his damp, whiskery cheek. 'I'm more than up to it.'

'Fancy yourself as a bit of a fruit farmer, do you?' he smiled through his tears.

'I do have a certain amount of experience in the field,' I smiled back.

'In that case,' he said, with a wobbly smile, 'I think both Fenview Farm and I are in very safe hands.'

Chapter 9

A downturn in the weather put the brakes on me starting any work on the farm for the next few days. Not that I had ever been a fair-weather worker, but according to the forecast it was going to be reasonably short-lived and wouldn't hamper me for too long, and therefore I took the opportunity to sort a few things in the house and spend some quality time with Grandad instead. We had soon got the measure of the stairs and having safely made the first ascent we were, if not quite zipping up and down, then gathering pace.

Grandad hadn't shared the details of what Mum had put in her letter and obviously I wasn't going to ask, but he seemed soothed by it and even though we both shed more tears after he had read it, they weren't as intense as those that had previously fallen.

Before I'd experienced it for myself, I had no idea that grief was so draining and all consuming, but I was beginning to understand what Louise had meant when she had told me it becomes a part of you. The pain of losing Mum was still prevalent, still very much in evidence, but the ache had dulled a little.

Grandad and I didn't go in for heart to heart conversations, but rather quietly felt our way, often focusing on the comfort of domestic tasks, eating the delicious Italian dishes I had already prepared and always with the windows thrown open. The gentle pitter patter of rain which formed the backdrop to the next few days was like a soothing ASMR soundtrack and I was comforted by it as I settled into the house.

The only thing missing was Eliot but he had telephoned, in lieu of not making it back to the farm thanks to the continuing staff shortage, which he assured me was genuine in spite of what Louise had said. He promised he would visit again soon and was happy that Grandad was in safe hands, even if he wasn't feeling quite so content about other things.

'I feel as though I'm failing you, Fliss,' was the first thing he said when Grandad handed the phone over one day. 'I told you I'd be there for you and Bill and now I'm not.'

'It's fine,' I told him and I meant it. 'I think it's good for Grandad and I to have this time to ourselves to readjust and now we've decided that I'm going to be here for a while, there's going to be plenty of time for you to be my friend in the weeks to come.'

He brightened at that and I found myself again wishing that we could be more than friends. That pesky spark refused to remain extinguished and I was constantly on the lookout for further distraction to stop it catching my eye.

'You know what,' Grandad said, after a few nights back in

his own bed. 'I feel like a new man. It's been weeks since I had such a good sleep. I know it's going to take me a while to get to grips with what's happened to my Jennifer, but at least now I know, don't I? There's no more wondering and wishing.'

'That's very true,' I agreed.

'And there was comfort in that letter she wrote,' he sniffed, confirming my thoughts. 'I thought she'd gone through life hating me, but she hadn't at all.'

I couldn't help wishing that Mum had had the sense to tell him that years ago, but there was no point in feeling bitter. It wouldn't change the past and we needed to focus on the future. It was reassuring to know that Grandad could move forward with his life with the blanks now filled in. It must have been so difficult to cope and carry on with that great big gap always nagging away in the background.

'I'm so pleased it's helped,' I said, looking at him properly and feeling relieved that I had decided to come to Fenview Farm, rather than pretend I'd never read any of what Mum had written to me.

He looked so much better for the combination of reading Mum's final words and the undisturbed rest. Nothing like the dazed and confused old man I had upset just a few days before, and I was feeling happier too. I had enjoyed putting the dining room back in order and getting to know the house. Although, that said, the brief peek I had taken into Mum's old room had come as a shock.

I hadn't gone right inside but I hadn't needed to to see that the place was a shrine. From the arrangement on the dressing table to the posters on the walls, I knew it was exactly as Mum had left it and a lump had formed in my throat as I thought of Grandad carefully tending and dusting, perhaps dreaming of her return to the fold. I knew we would need to talk about what to do with it at some point, but not yet.

'The forecast looks set to improve by the weekend,' Grandad said as I cleared our lunch dishes away.

I had been thrilled when he told me he was very much enjoying having his menu expanded and he certainly always looked replete. He had eagerly finished up every dish I had served as a result of my spree in the Wynbridge deli. I'd cooked spaghetti with rich tomato sauce that day and he'd mopped up every trace with a crust of garlic enhanced bread.

'Thank goodness for that,' I said, peering out the door. 'I'm getting desperate to know the outside of Fenview Farm as well as the inside.'

Grandad looked pleased.

'Good,' he smiled. 'Our little patch of the Fens needs you Fliss, and you do like it, don't you?'

I was touched that he had referred to the spot as 'ours' and I could feel those tender roots I'd imagined before, pushing their way further down.

'I'm completely smitten,' I told him. 'But to tell you the truth, I'm still struggling to come to terms with Mum leaving this place behind. It's absolutely idyllic in my eyes.'

Grandad was quiet for a moment and I hoped I hadn't upset him. I didn't want to have to spend my time here not talking about Mum. She had been as real to me as she had been to Grandad and even though our relationships with her had been very different, I felt it was important to keep her memory alive.

'Yes, well,' he sighed. 'You and your mum see things differently, don't you? And the pair of you are very different.'

'That's true,' I nodded. For a start, there was Mum's flighty spirit which was the polar opposite to my stay-at-home one. 'We never really were peas in a pod.'

Grandad readily agreed with that.

'So, tell me then, Fliss,' he further said. 'What exactly have you got planned to get done around here when this rain finally stops falling?'

I made us tea and we pored over the list I had made. I was a bit nervous about Grandad reading it. It felt like he was a prospective employer scanning my job application. What I'd written would demonstrate whether or not I knew my stuff and was up to taking on the role of caretaker of Fenview Farm. I hoped I passed the test.

'Looks to me like you've got everything covered,' he eventually said and I felt relieved. 'I've been meaning to wash and straighten the sign on the road and fix the cages since the end of last year, but what with the old trick hip, I didn't dare venture up the ladder.'

I was surprised Eliot hadn't stepped in and sorted the sign at least, but then he was always busy and I could tell Grandad was a proud man and as such, asking for help wouldn't have come naturally, even if he was surrounded by people who were willing.

'I would be out there now if it wasn't so wet underfoot,' I said, looking out of the window and Grandad nodded. 'When the harvest is over,' I carried on, 'replacing all of the nets will be a priority. It wouldn't hurt to leave the cages bare for a while either, so the birds can clear up anything that's left.'

'It's certainly been a while since they were done,' Grandad mused. 'And you're right, the soil could do with a good clearing and cleansing. We used to have a few chickens who were willing to help with that.'

'Perhaps you should think about getting some again?' I suggested.

'I might,' he smiled. 'If you were willing to help look after them.'

His comment seemed to me a way of finding out if I was planning on staying beyond the harvest without having to actually ask the question. I thought about my role with the Rossis; how I was accepted there and how I fitted in, and then my thoughts shifted and I realised that I now had the chance to create something as family orientated for myself.

I had always felt a part of the farm in Puglia, but at Fenview Farm my ties were that much stronger because they were bound by blood. It would be a wrench to leave my Italian home for good, but hadn't I felt, when I left for Wynbridge, that I might be going back there in a different guise and under changed circumstances?

'I haven't got much experience with poultry,' I therefore said to Grandad, feeling my attachment to the place and to him deepen, 'but I'm always willing to learn.'

'Explain to me what else you've got in mind to get on with then,' he grinned, giving me a nudge.

Clearly my answer was the one he wanted to hear and I knew I would soon have to break the news to Marco that I wouldn't be back to organise the season after all.

'The strawberries,' I said, tapping the paper and elaborating on the words I'd written. 'They're the priority. I'm worried they haven't got the straw on yet. They're going to need it soon, if they aren't going to spoil, especially after all this rain.'

Ideally it should have been down before the downturn in the weather.

'I'll give my friend Jake a ring,' said Grandad. 'He owns Skylark Farm and that's where the straw will come from. He helps sell the strawberries and he keeps a few hens too. He might even have a couple going spare and if we could patch up the old henhouse that would save us some money.'

'Sounds good to me.'

'So,' said Grandad, once we had finished going through the list and adding a few more jobs to it. 'How come you know so much about fruit farming? I know it's in your blood, but that doesn't account for your obvious knowledge and understanding. Your mother never showed much interest here, so you haven't picked it up from her.'

'She had skills though,' I told him. 'She used to work on farms to fund her travels.'

'They were just a means to end though, weren't they?' he sighed. 'Somewhere to tide her over, not somewhere to properly settle.'

'There was nowhere on earth capable of making her do that,' I truthfully told him.

'And don't I know it,' he tutted, before making us more tea while I gave him a potted history of my love affair with fruit farming.

'Obviously, it began for me with the cherry and olive harvest in Puglia, but my love for British fruit farming came from the pick-your-own places where Mum and I used to work when we were roaming about a bit.'

Grandad didn't look all that impressed with the idea of me missing out on my education, even if it was to pick fruit.

'There were a couple that we worked at fairly regularly,' I carried on, 'and I learned loads at those. Mum was happy just to do what was asked, but I used to trail around after the managers, asking questions and picking things up.'

Grandad's disapproval quickly changed to pride.

'You'll get far in life with an enquiring mind,' he told me.

Well,' I said. 'I loved learning how it all worked and I was never happier than when I was sunburnt or filthy, or both, and stuffed full of fresh fruit.'

Grandad laughed, his gaze drifting off as he pictured how I must have looked.

'What I remember most,' I carried on, 'is the taste of those first strawberries of the year, plucked fresh from the plant and greedily eaten before they made their way anywhere near the punnets I was supposed to be filling for the farm shop. They were so sweet and delicious and I always ate my fill before the end of the day.'

'There's nothing quite like fruit eaten straight from the plant, is there?' said Grandad. 'How anyone can enjoy stuff out of season that's been refrigerated and travelled halfway across the globe is beyond me.'

'I know,' I keenly agreed. 'But that's the way of the world now, isn't it? We expect to have access to anything and everything whenever we want it.'

'Yes,' he nodded. 'You're right. Did you do anything else on these farms besides eat the profits and ask questions?'

'Oh yes,' I said. 'I often helped with the orders and admin and things. As soon as I was old enough I was helping to run one of them throughout the summer so the owner could take some holiday and I loved it.'

'What did your mum make of that?'

'Oh, she wasn't with me by then. She'd found somewhere else to work by that point but I went back for a few years, before deciding to stay put in Puglia.'

'What prompted you to stay?'

'It was Mum, actually. She loved working on different farms, but she also enjoyed immersing herself in the life and culture of the places she visited and we decided to set something up at the Rossis' which would give travellers the opportunity to stop for a few weeks and have a similar experience.'

'Like a working holiday you mean?'

'Yes,' I said. 'Exactly that. The visitors work all day, then we eat together and, in the evenings and at weekends, I take them on organised trips to the less well-known sights in the area.'

'It sounds busy.'

'It is from May to December. The winter is very quiet. And cold too.'

'I'm not sure Fenview Farm can compete with all that,' Grandad sighed. 'There aren't many sights to see around here.'

'Oh yes it can,' I said reaching for his hand and giving it a squeeze. 'This place can definitely compete. It's got you for a start!'

Grandad laughed.

'And that's a good thing, is it?'

'It sure is.'

We were quiet for a moment, each lost in our own thoughts.

'So, if you're going to be staying here,' Grandad then asked, 'who will be doing your job in Puglia?'

'That's probably going to fall to Marco, the farm owner's grandson,' I explained. 'I'm not sure how he's going to feel about that, but I hope he'll cope. He lives with his nonna who owns the farm and his dad, Nonna's son, Alessandro.'

'They keep it in the family over there then?'

'Very much so and they always made me and Mum feel like family too.'

Grandad nodded.

'Mum never spoke ill of you to them, Grandad. I want you to know that.'

'She never spoke of me at all, did she?'

I couldn't deny that.

'You know,' I said, squeezing his hand again. 'They lost someone close to them too. Alessandro's wife died when Marco was just a boy. You should get to know them. I'm certain you'd get on well and they could tell you loads about Mum.'

'But I can't speak Italian,' he ruefully smiled.

'That's as maybe, but they can all speak English.'

'Well,' he said. 'I'll think about it.'

I don't know why I hadn't thought of it sooner. It would be wonderful to connect my two families.

'I don't suppose you have Wi-Fi here, do you Grandad?'

'Why, what?' he frowned.

'An internet connection?'

'No,' he said. 'I've never seen the point, although Eliot has mentioned it.'

'Not to worry,' I said, forcing myself not to linger over thoughts of our absent friend. 'I'll try the local library and see if I can send an email from there to Puglia explaining everything. Does Wynbridge have one?'

'Yes,' said Grandad. 'A very good one, but you'll need something with the farm as your address on if you want to register.'

'Of course,' I said, biting my lip. 'I hadn't thought of that.'

'Leave it with me,' Grandad smiled. 'I know the library manager. I'll see if she can help you at least access a computer to tide you over.'

'Thank you.' I said. 'That would be a big help.'

The lack of phone signal at the farm made messaging difficult enough, so sending emails and making video calls would be impossible and I didn't want to say I wouldn't be going back in a text. A lengthier explanation was definitely required.

'I have to say,' Grandad then said, 'it is a comfort to think that your mother did pick up something of the farming bug while she was living here. Not that she ever let me or her mother know it of course.'

'Was she really not a fan of this place?'

'Goodness me, no,' he vehemently said. 'By the time she hit her teens, she was a right sulky madam. She used to open her window to shout, or march downstairs to tell us how much she hated the farm because it stopped us taking holidays like all her friends. She said she couldn't wait to get away from this place and then she'd flounce off again or slam the window shut. I was grateful we didn't have near neighbours!'

'She sounds like hard work.'

'Oh, she was, but teenagers mostly are, aren't they?'

Thinking back, I knew I'd had my moments and Marco certainly had. There were a few months when he and Alessandro had done nothing but argue. I supposed he would have been about the age Mum was when she left the farm. It was awful to think of her leaving in a temper and never finding the courage or the ability to swallow her pride and come back. I wondered if her decision had impacted on her life and now, I'd never know. It was yet another of those questions that would forever be unanswered.

'Your grandmother and I could appreciate we were a bit

off the beaten track here,' Grandad continued, 'so we always offered to run her into town if she wanted to get a Saturday job, but Wynbridge wasn't good enough for her either she said. She had her sights set on bigger places with more thrilling opportunities.'

She always had.

'I suppose that's why I can't imagine her here,' I quietly said.

'What do you mean?'

'Ever since I arrived,' I explained, 'I've been trying to picture her here. First, I tried to imagine her at the market in Wynbridge and then sitting here at the table, but I haven't been able to conjure up anything. I just can't see her here at all.'

'I'm not surprised,' said Grandad. There was no malice in his tone, more resignation. 'She was never the right fit for this place and she went to great lengths to make sure everyone knew it.'

I wondered if those words had been flung about in an argument. It was ironic that Mum had chosen them when she had written about me being a better fit for the farm than she had been. Or was that more than a coincidence?

'And what about me?' I asked. 'Do I fit?'

'Oh, yes,' said Grandad, 'you fit Fenview Farm like a Savile Row suit, my love.'

Chapter 10

Having explained my fruit farming experience and listened to Grandad describe me as the perfect fit for Fenview Farm, I felt lighter and brighter than I had in ages and I was now entirely convinced that following Mum's instructions and turning up in Wynbridge had been the right thing to do. My life was set to change, and even though I still mourned her loss, I was grateful that she had gifted me this new opportunity.

I couldn't wait to make a start on all the work that needed doing and when the rain finally stopped, I was raring to go. However, a quick look through the storage sheds put paid to my plans and I inwardly cursed that I hadn't prioritised a stocktake as a wet weather essential.

'I can't find anything to repair the cages with,' I told Grandad. 'And the henhouse roof needs re-covering, but there's nothing for that either.'

Grandad looked up from the local newspaper he was reading, a frown etched across his forehead.

'I hadn't realised things had run so low,' he said, looking

concerned. 'I was sure I had an end of a roll of roofing felt kicking about here somewhere.'

'There is a bit,' I conceded, 'but only enough to patch it. Ideally the whole lot needs to come off and be redone, otherwise you're just throwing good money after bad.'

Grandad's frown cleared and he smiled.

'You like to do things properly, don't you, Fliss?'

'Of course,' I seriously said. 'If you don't do a job properly in the first place, you just end up doing it twice.'

Our conversation was interrupted by a strange honking on the drive which sent the cat, who had snuck in after me, scrabbling back outside.

'What on earth's that?' I asked.

'That'll be Bec,' Grandad grinned. 'Well, that car of hers anyway. It has the oddest horn.'

'That car has the oddest everything,' I giggled, peering out as she pulled on to the drive.

It was a bit early in the day for a social call, but as it turned out it wasn't one.

'I'm just off to work,' Bec told me after I'd greeted her, 'and wondered if you needed anything picking up in town.'

'We're running low on milk and bread,' I said, thinking of the depleted larder and fridge, as well as all the other things I now needed for the farm repairs. 'And quite a lot of other stuff actually,' I added, biting my lip.

'Do you want to make a list?' she asked, checking her watch. 'And I'll go and buy it all on my break and drop it off on my way home.'

'You are a love,' I told her. 'I don't suppose there's any chance you'd take me with you instead, is there? I can get a taxi back easily enough. If Grandad doesn't mind being left on his own for a bit, that is,' I hastily added.

'Grandad would love to be left on his own for a bit,' he said. 'No offence, but it's been a while since I had the place to myself and I promise I won't go doing anything I shouldn't.'

With that settled, I swapped the work boots I had borrowed from him for my own strappy sandals, grabbed my bag and jobs list and jumped in the passenger seat of the Banana-mobile. There was no time to get changed, so my messy bun, checked shirt and denim cut-offs would have to do. The outfit was a bit Daisy Duke, but the shorts weren't that short so I thought I'd get away with it.

'Are you sure you'll be all right?' I called to Grandad as Bec swung the car back round to face the road.

'I'll be fine,' he said, waving us off.

I had to admit, he did look rather happy at the prospect of some time alone. Privacy had no doubt been hard to come by since he'd been in hospital and now, with the added shock of what had happened to Mum to come to terms with, I didn't think a little solitude would do him any harm at all. I had tried to keep out of the way a bit, but it wasn't the same as being completely alone. I let out a long breath and watched the windswept verge whizz by.

'He'll be all right,' said Bec, sounding stoic. 'Now, tell me more of what's on your list and I'll drop you off closest to where you need to be.'

I quickly ran through everything and Bec suggested that Andersons, the timber yard and agricultural suppliers would be a good place to start. They opened early, and if the order was big enough, they'd deliver it straight to the farm. That was a blessing as I didn't fancy carrying a roll of roofing felt around town.

'And before you do your grocery shop,' Bec said, after she'd given me a few directions, 'come and find me in the Cherry Tree Café and I'll treat you to a slice of cake. It's on the square, so you won't miss it.'

I was almost certain I'd seen it already. It had to be the pretty place I'd spotted the day I arrived.

'I take it that's where you're working?' I asked her.

'Yes,' she said. 'I'm doing a bit of waitressing and helping out with some of the crafting sessions one of the co-owners organises. It's just until the Royal Academy accepts one of my paintings, of course,' she added with a mischievous smile. 'Then I'll be able to permanently swap cupcakes for canvases.'

She stopped to let me out and gave another blast on the goose-like horn as I pulled open the door to Andersons and stepped inside. Wandering around an agricultural supply store might not have been everyone's cup of tea, but I thoroughly enjoyed the time I spent seeking out all the things I needed for the farm, plus a couple of extra bits that caught my eye.

I negotiated a price for the end of a roll of roofing felt which had more than enough left on it for what I needed and then gave the address for where I wanted everything delivered.

'Fenview Farm on Lady's Drove?' questioned the elderly employee who had rung everything up on the till, his bushy grey eyebrows raised.

'That's right,' I nodded.

'What, where Bill Brown lives?' asked his younger colleague.

'That's the place,' I reiterated, rifling through my bag for my purse.

'I'm not sure his account is up to date,' said the chap at the till.

He looked embarrassed and I wondered if Grandad had a hefty bill to settle. I didn't ask, just in case. Thankfully, I could easily run to paying for the things I'd ordered.

'I don't want to put anything on account,' I smiled. 'I'll pay for my order and I'm guessing free delivery is all part of the wonderful Anderson service I've been hearing so much about, isn't it?'

'As you're paying today and the farm is only just out of our free drop off zone, then that will be fine,' said the younger man, sounding relieved. 'We can have it with you first thing Monday morning, if that suits.'

'That's perfect,' I told them. 'Thank you very much.'

I could tell they were gearing up to ask what my connection to the farm was and headed off before they had the chance.

The walk into town led me near the library and, as it was

open, I ducked inside, keen to find out exactly what ID and paperwork I would need to sign up.

'You wouldn't happen to be Bill Brown's granddaughter, would you?' asked the woman on the desk when I enquired.

'Yes,' I frowned. 'I am. How did you know that?'

'He phoned earlier,' she smiled. 'He said you might pop in and that even though you couldn't register with us yet, you'd appreciate access to a computer for a few minutes. Is that right?'

'It is,' I said. 'Is that going to be possible?'

'If I override the system,' she winked. 'I wouldn't usually but as you're a relative of Bill's, I'll make an exception.'

I thanked her profusely, then composed a lengthy email to the Rossi clan, explaining more about what had happened since my arrival, what Grandad was like, what the farm was like and finally, and with my breath held, that I wouldn't be back in Puglia for quite some time.

It made no sense to hold my breath, we weren't having a conversation and I wasn't going to see his reaction, but I had the image of Marco in my head from the day I had left, urging me to go back practically on the return flight. I hoped he would understand my decision to want to get to know Fenview Farm and Grandad better. I knew Nonna and Alessandro would, so if he was upset, they'd hopefully be able to appease him. I was relying on them to pave the way for me to break the news that I might well want to stay in the Fens for ever.

With the explanation re-read and finally sent, and my

heart rate steadying after the surprise of acknowledging the possibility of staying at the farm for good, I thanked the librarian again and carried on into the town centre. My stomach growled as soon as I caught sight of the Cherry Tree Café and I hoped the place had a good selection of cakes.

'How did you find Andersons?' Bec asked, almost before I was through the door.

'It was great,' I said, as my gaze swivelled around to take in the pastel spring themed interior and my nose picked up the sweet scent of warm pastries and hot coffee. 'Wow,' I grinned, 'this place is divine.'

'Wait until you taste one of Jemma's cakes,' said Bec. 'Then you really will be in seventh heaven. Did you get everything you needed?'

'Yes,' I said, still looking about me, 'and they're going to deliver it all free of charge, which is a bonus.'

'You must have charmed them with those long, tanned legs of yours,' she said, giving me a nudge.

'It wasn't my legs,' I whispered. 'They were so shocked when I gave them the farm address that I took advantage of the moment and kind of railroaded them into it.'

'Did you tell them who you are?' she asked, steering me to an empty seat and handing me a menu.

'No,' I said. 'I don't want to announce myself until I've had a chance to talk it all through with Grandad and we've decided what we're going to say. With what's happened to Mum it isn't going to be easy for him, so I'll be guided by what he wants.'

Even though he'd told his friend at the library about me, I still wanted to talk to him before I started saying anything.

'Right,' said Bec. 'Of course.'

I couldn't help noticing she'd turned a little pink.

'So,' she said, flicking open her order pad and pulling my thoughts back to my rumbling tum. 'What can I get you?'

I eventually settled on a trio of fruit and cream cheese breakfast pastries and strong coffee to accompany them. They were absolutely delicious. The pastry was crisp, the cheese was soft and the tang of the fruit cut through the sweetness, creating the perfect balance.

'What did you think?' asked the woman who cleared my empty plate, poured me more coffee and introduced herself as Jemma, the café owner.

'Scrumptious,' I told her. 'Delicious.'

She flushed with pride.

'They're a new addition,' she explained. 'And they're going down a storm.'

'I'm not surprised.'

'The only thing I'm not happy about is the fruit,' she quietly said. 'I'm trying to buy local, but the commercial farms all supply in such large quantities. They won't take smaller orders.'

She sat down in the chair opposite mine and her smile grew.

'I don't suppose you'd be able to help me out with that, would you? Bec mentioned that you've just moved to Fenview Farm. You're Bill's granddaughter, aren't you?'

I looked across to where Bec was standing. She looked even pinker than before and I guessed she'd let the cat out of the bag. She looked so upset that it felt impossible to be cross with her, especially as she might have found the farm some new business.

'To tell you the truth,' Jemma continued, 'I wasn't sure the farm was still trading, but Chris Dempster who sells fruit and veg on the market has told me its's still operational and that last year he and Jake at Skylark Farm took most of the crops to sell on your Grandad's behalf.'

'It certainly is still operational and we grow a whole range of fruit,' I told her. 'We've got apples, pears, plums, a few cherries, strawberries and a good range of other soft fruit.'

'That sounds perfect,' she said, her eyes sparkling. 'Just what I was hoping. I want to supply seasonal and local in here and I'm looking to forge permanent links with a reputable small-scale grower. I'm willing to adapt the menu to whatever's available and if that's only for a short while, then that's fine too, because it will make it even more special.'

'But what about things like the pastries I've just had?' I asked. 'Won't you want to sell those all year round?'

'Well yes,' she said. 'But I have enough freezer capacity to make that possible.'

She certainly sounded like she'd got it all worked out and it was obvious her business was thriving. In the time I'd been sitting there, the place had filled to capacity, as had the tables outside.

'So, what do you think?' she asked, her voice full of hope.

'Do you think we could strike a deal where Fenview Farm supplies the Cherry Tree Café fruit? It sounds like a winning combination to me.'

It sounded like a winning combination to me too. I was excited at the prospect of working with this clever and clearly competent business woman.

'I'll have to talk to my grandfather,' I told her, reining my feelings in and erring on the side of caution. It wasn't my place to sign the harvest away, even though I was tempted to. 'Just to be certain he hasn't got contracts lined up elsewhere, but I'm sure we could come to some arrangement.'

'Fantastic,' she smiled, as a woman with red curls came bouncing over the café threshold and set the bell above the door jangling wildly. 'And there's no real rush. As long as I can get my hands on some fresh, local strawberries, I'll be happy. They must be well on their way to ripening now.'

I smiled back, my heart skipping at the thought of what this opportunity could do for Fenview. If we could form a lasting collaboration with the café, then it could make a big difference to the farm and really raise its profile.

'Sorry I've taken so long,' said the curly haired woman, who was dressed in a pretty floral tea dress which clashed gloriously with her hair. 'I'm having a total mare this morning.'

'This is Lizzie,' Jemma said to me. 'My business partner and she isn't usually so flustered. Whatever's the matter?' she asked, turning to her friend.

Lizzie stood with her hands on her hips and explained. Her other half, Ben, had booked a table at a restaurant they had been trying to get into for months but the local taxi firm had let them down and they'd had to cancel because they had no transport. Their own car was in the garage awaiting repairs so they couldn't get there under their own steam.

'You didn't need to do that,' said Jemma. 'Tom would have driven you.'

'But you've got that event at school tonight,' said Lizzie. 'So that wouldn't have worked.'

'What about your dad?'

'It's too late now and besides, we wouldn't have wanted to eat knowing we were on a timer because he was waiting to ferry us home.'

'I suppose not,' said Jemma.

'What we need,' Lizzie pouted, 'is somewhere nice to eat around here in the evenings. The pub and other places are all well and good, but I want something a bit different every now and again. Something unique.'

'Well,' said Jemma, standing up. 'I'm not opening in the evenings. It's all I can do to drag myself home at the end of the day.'

'I wasn't meaning here,' said Lizzie. 'It would be nice to occasionally get out of town, wouldn't it? But not so far that it's a hassle to get back again.'

Having promised to talk to Grandad about the harvest, I left them dreaming about exclusive evening eateries. Jemma had refused to let me pay for either the pastries or the coffee.

'Consider it an incentive,' she had winked. 'A little sweetener.'

I thanked her, and feeling comfortably full, headed to the

supermarket to stock up on essentials and to the market for everything else. Just as had happened the weekend before, I was soon weighed down with bags and couldn't help wishing I had transport of my own.

There was no sign of the taxi in the designated bay and even though Bec had generously offered to run me home when she finished her shift, I didn't really want to have to wait that long. I had just decided to go back to the café and see if anyone had a number for the cab firm, when I felt a light tap on my shoulder.

'You're either running like the wind, or crawling at a glacial pace because you're weighed down with bags,' laughed Mr Helpful. 'I never know which version of you I'm going to run into. You're a woman of extremes.'

'What can I say,' I told him. 'At least I'm not predictable.'

'You're certainly not that. I don't suppose you fancy a drink?' he offered, nodding over to the pub.

'It's a bit early, isn't it?'

'A bite of lunch in the café then?'

'All right,' I said, resigned to the fact that I wasn't getting back to the farm anytime soon. 'Thank you. I was actually just heading over there to see my friend.'

'Yet again our planets seem to have aligned,' he said, flashing me a smile before taking some of the bags.

I didn't point out that he had suggested the pub, while I had been aiming for the café.

'Back again so soon,' Jemma said to me. 'There's a table just about to clear in the far corner, if you don't mind waiting.'

The place was still so busy, I thought we were lucky to get seated at all.

'Everything all right?' asked Bec as she rushed over. She was talking to me but very definitely looking at my companion. 'Do you want me to put your bags in the car?' she offered when she finally dragged her gaze back to me.

'I've got fridge stuff in this one,' I said, holding it up.

'I'll ask Jemma if there's room in the storeroom fridge. It isn't used for business supplies, so it should be all right.'

She disappeared with all of the bags and the guy I still only knew as Mr Helpful, and I, squeezed around the tiny table.

'I take it you've already been in here today?' he asked. 'Jemma obviously knows you.'

'I popped in earlier,' I told him. 'But I'm happy to be back again. The food was amazing.'

'It always is,' he said, handing me a lunch menu.

'You know, I still don't know your name,' I said, feeling suddenly self-conscious.

'It's Anthony,' he grinned. 'Anthony Judd.'

'Anthony,' I repeated. 'I'm pleased to meet you, properly at last, and I'm . . .'

'Fliss,' he interrupted. 'Felicity Brown.'

I couldn't ask immediately how he'd found that out, because an older lady, wearing a cupcake patterned apron, came over to take our order.

'So, how do you know my name?' I asked, the second she'd gone. 'I've hardly announced myself to the town. Was it Bec?'

I hardly thought it would have come from Grandad's friend at the library or the doctor or Vicky, and Eliot and Louise certainly wouldn't have said anything. Bec however, did have something of a track record now.

'You needn't sound so put out,' he laughed. 'There aren't any secrets around here and no, it wasn't your friend.'

I wondered if he'd heard anything else about me other than my name from whoever he'd talked to. With Grandad still coming to terms with what had happened to Mum, I didn't like the thought of her demise being town gossip. She might have left a long time ago, but there were bound to be people around who still remembered her as well as her dramatic exit.

'And you aren't squatting at Fenview Farm,' Anthony carried on. 'You're staying there with your grandfather, who you've only just met.'

I was flabbergasted.

'How do you know that?' I demanded, frustrated with trying to puzzle it out.

'I never reveal my sources,' he whispered, flashing me what he no doubt thought was another winning smile.

But it didn't win me.

'Oh dear,' he said, the smile vanishing, when he realised, I wasn't impressed. 'I've upset you.'

'No, you haven't,' I said. 'It's fine. I just don't like being the subject of gossip.'

'I didn't mean to speak out of turn,' he quickly said. 'And there was no gossiping. You are Fliss Brown, aren't you?'

'Yes.'

'So why the cloak and dagger? Don't you want anyone to know?'

'No,' I said. 'Not yet. As you pointed out, I've only just arrived and I was hoping to settle in and get to know Grandad and the farm before I was subjected to local scrutiny.'

As he hadn't mentioned Mum, I didn't either.

'In that case,' he said, 'I'm very sorry.'

'I don't suppose it really matters,' I told him, doing my best not to sound upset. 'You just took me by surprise, that's all.'

With a farm to run I knew it would have been impossible to stay under the radar and keep my identity a secret for long, and therefore there didn't seem to be much point in staying cross with Anthony, even though he had caught me off guard.

It had been just the same in the small town closest to the farm in Puglia. No one passed through there without being noticed and I guessed it was the same in Wynbridge. It wasn't necessarily a bad thing but it did make me feel a bit exposed, sitting in the busy café, eating lunch with a handsome stranger.

'Sure?' he asked, sounding genuinely concerned.

'Yes,' I sighed. 'I'm sure. Word was bound to get around, wasn't it?'

'Afraid so,' he agreed. 'But I won't tell anyone.'

'We'll just leave it to the Wynbridge grapevine, shall we?' I suggested.

'Exactly,' he smiled.

After lunch, he offered to drop me back at the farm so I wouldn't have to ring for a taxi or wait until Bec finished.

She gave me a knowing look as she handed me back my bags of shopping.

'I don't blame you swapping the Banana-mobile for Mr Helpful,' she grinned.

'It's not like that,' I tutted. 'He said he's heading that way anyway.'

'Yeah, right,' she snorted.

'And his name's Anthony.'

'Ooh,' she said. 'Progress.'

'Well I could hardly have lunch with him and not ask his name, could I?' I said, returning her reaction with an eye-roll.

'I suppose not,' she agreed.

'Thank you for the lift earlier and would you thank Jemma for me when you get a chance?'

'Oh yes,' said Bec. 'What were you two talking about earlier? I hope I didn't put my foot in it saying who you were.'

If supplying fruit for the café came off, then she would have definitely done the farm a favour, but I wasn't going to tell her what her boss had in mind. I needed to talk to Grandad first. It wouldn't be professional to go talking about the deal even before it was done.

'I meant, would you thank her for the pastries, that was all.'

'Yeah right,' Bec said again, though that time without the accompanying snort.

It was mid-afternoon when I arrived back at the farm and

I was worried I'd left Grandad for too long. If only I had my own transport, I would be able to make much shorter trips to town.

'Looks like you've got company,' said Anthony as he swung into the drive.

Eliot's Ducati was parked up and my heart skipped at the sight of it. Then I began to panic. Had he popped in to pay a random social visit, or had Grandad called him because he'd had a fall? My heart thrummed all the harder as I fumbled to get out of the car.

'Are you all right?' Anthony asked.

'Yes,' I nodded. 'Of course. Let's get the bags.'

I swiftly shifted them from the boot to the back door, said a speedy thank you and goodbye and rushed inside. Anthony looked rather taken aback by my hasty dismissal but didn't appear inclined to hang about either. In fact, he'd driven off almost before I'd crossed the kitchen.

The sound of laughter met my ears and I let out the breath I hadn't realised I'd been holding.

'Felicity,' smiled Grandad, when he looked up and saw me in the doorway. 'We've got company.'

'So I see,' I beamed, looking from him to Eliot.

My heart carried on thumping just as fast, but I tried to kid myself that was because I was relieved that Grandad was all right and not because Eliot looked and smelt even more delicious than I remembered.

'I've just given him a demo of how we've been negotiating the stairs,' said Grandad.

'Hello Fliss,' said Eliot, returning my smile with one of his own. 'I hear you've been doing brilliantly.'

'We've been managing,' I shyly said.

Crikey, at this rate I'd be swaying from side to side and batting my lashes. I had thought I'd begun to get the measure of my attraction for him, but that was obviously only because I hadn't seen him. Now faced with the handsome, and sensually scented reality, I had to acknowledge I had it every bit as bad as before. I'd just had lunch with a devastatingly good-looking, well turned out and intriguing man and yet my reaction to him hadn't been anything like the one induced by the sight of Eliot.

'More than managing,' he quickly said. 'Just as I knew you would.'

'I better get these bags unpacked,' I swallowed, not wanting to give my overwhelming feelings away. 'There's stuff that needs to go in the fridge.'

'How did you get on at Andersons?' Grandad called after me.

'Really well. Everything's coming on Monday. It's quite a place, isn't it?'

'It is. Did they let you put it all on the account?'

'Oh,' I fibbed. 'I didn't think to ask if you had one. I paid for it all there and then.'

'In that case, we'll settle up later.'

I went to mention Jemma's business proposition, but stopped myself. I really wanted to give it a bit more thought before I presented it. I should have picked up a notebook in town. Writing things down always helped me get a bit of perspective, as well as sparking off other ideas.

The rain clouds had gathered again and I was getting the washing in, when Eliot left.

'I hope you haven't stayed out of the way on my account,' he said, zipping himself into his suit.

'I thought it would be good for you and Grandad to have a bit of time,' I said, rather than admitting the truth, which was that I didn't trust my hormones whenever I was around him. 'He's really missed you.'

'I've missed him too,' he told me. 'And you, but I really have been busy with work.'

'So much for your holiday,' I said, trying not to get carried away with the thought of him missing me.

'I know,' he tutted, 'and my timing could have been better today because Bill said it was the first time he'd been alone in ages. I'm sure he had been enjoying the peace.'

'None the more for that, I bet he was thrilled to see you.' I said, picking up the washing basket. 'I know I am.'

'Are you now?' he grinned.

'Yes,' I swallowed.

'In that case,' he said, running a hand through his hair before pulling on his gloves, 'I'll try not to leave it so long before I come back again. Bill talked a bit about your mum earlier. He seems to be getting his head around it all. How are you doing?'

I loved that, like Bec, he didn't skirt around the issue as some people might.

'Not brilliant, but better than I was,' I told him, returning his frankness with my own. 'I appreciate you asking.'

'That's what friends are for.'

Friends, I reminded myself as I watched him pull on his helmet and start the bike. Eliot Randall and I were friends and destined to remain so. He turned in the seat and gave me a wave before he drove off. I nodded back because I was holding the laundry. What about friends with benefits? I wondered.

Chapter 11

Sunday was a gloriously sunny day so I took an early walk around the farm. The birds were singing away and the rain, which had fallen steadily over the previous few days, combined with the slowly rising temperature, had brought everything on a treat.

All the fruit looked as though it had the potential to ripen a little earlier than expected for the UK and Jemma's business proposition really couldn't have come at a better time. The previous evening I'd mulled it all over and I was planning to present it to Grandad over breakfast.

Having shooed a blackbird out of one of the fruit cages and tried to pull the holes in the net together, I walked back to the yard. I hoped the order from Andersons was going to come early the next day because I really did need to make the repairs, along with a proper start on preparing for the busy season ahead, as soon as possible.

With that in mind, I set about stripping the roof off the henhouse and gave it a thorough clean and airing. I was pleased to be doing something productive and having found a sanitising powder in Grandad's stores I also gave the whole structure a good dousing. It wasn't all that likely it still harboured any mites because it had been empty for so long, but I didn't think it would hurt to err on the side of caution.

'Are you ready for some breakfast?' Grandad shouted from the house.

'You're awake!' I called back, dusting myself down and walking over to the back door. 'And you're downstairs. You should have waited and I would have helped you.'

'I managed fine,' he told me, as the smell of bacon made my tummy rumble. 'I took my time and besides, you were nowhere to be seen.'

'I hadn't realised the time,' I said, glancing at the clock as I washed my hands. I was amazed to see that hours had passed since I'd headed out. I also felt surprised and a little guilty to realise that my thoughts hadn't strayed to Mum too. Perhaps the expression about time being a great healer wasn't a cliché after all. 'I had an early wander and then started sorting the henhouse.'

'Just as well,' Grandad smiled as he loaded our plates with bacon, scrambled eggs, grilled mushrooms and tomatoes, 'because I spoke to Jake at Skylark Farm earlier and as well as the straw, he's got three hens we can have. They're an ex-battery trio. Still a bit rough around the edges, but perfectly healthy and laying well.'

I abhorred all forms of intensive farming and rather liked the thought of giving some ex-battery girls a happy retirement. They were going to love clearing out the fruit cages at the end of the summer.

'What's the fox situation like here?' I asked. 'Will we need to keep them in a big run of some sort?'

I hoped not.

'I haven't seen one for a while so I don't think so. I reckon they'll stick to scratching about the yard. They'll soon settle in with the house to use as a bolt-hole should they need it.'

'Will the cat bother them?'

'She never showed any interest before, but we'll keep an ear out, just to be on the safe side. Now, eat your breakfast and then you can tell me what you came back from town thinking about yesterday, because I know there was something.'

With breakfast cleared away and a leg of lamb ready to go in the oven, Grandad and I carried on talking while we prepped the potatoes and other veg at the table.

'I hope you don't mind me inviting the Randall clan,' he said as I counted the potatoes I'd peeled ready for roasting. 'It's been a while since I've been able to have people around.'

'Of course, I don't mind,' I told him. 'They're your friends.' I was already genuinely fond of Bec and Louise. My feelings for Eliot put him in a completely different category of course, but I wasn't going to let them impact on Grandad's desire to entertain. 'And they've fast become mine too,' I therefore added. 'It will be lovely to spend the afternoon together.'

'It'll be too hot to eat in here though,' Grandad pointed out.

With the oven heating up it was almost too warm already.

'Let's eat outside then,' I suggested. 'We did that when you were poorly and it was lovely under the tree. Although we balanced the plates on our laps then. I'm not sure we'll be able to do that with a full roast dinner.'

'There's an old table in the barn,' Grandad reminisced. 'Years ago, we used to drag that out to eat in the shade.'

A memory of watching the Larkin clan from *The Darling Buds of May* on television doing something similar sprang to mind and I imagined me, Grandad and the Randall family in their place.

'Let's do that then,' I smiled. 'I'll ask Bec and Eliot to give me a hand setting it up as soon as they arrive.'

With lunch plans finalised, I took a deep breath.

'And now I'm going to tell you what happened during my trip to town yesterday, other than in the library. Thank you for talking to your friend by the way. She let me use the computer as a result.'

Distracted by Eliot's presence when I arrived back, I'd forgotten to thank Grandad for that.

'I thought she might,' he smiled. 'But that's not what's been on your mind, is it?'

'No,' I confirmed. 'I'm more preoccupied with something that could be a great opportunity for Fenview Farm.'

Grandad listened intently as I presented Jemma's idea. I made it sound as appealing as possible, which wasn't difficult given that it was such a wonderful idea, but it still didn't stop his brow furrowing as I came to the end of my enthusiastic explanation.

'But we're not a big business compared to the other places operating around here now,' he was quick to point out.

'And that's why she's so keen,' I reiterated. I'd already explained that, but he clearly hadn't grasped it. 'That's exactly why she's so interested in us. She wants seasonal, fresh and local and not too much of it. She's prepared to adapt her menu to cater for what we can offer, for as long as it lasts. She's looking to work with a smaller business now she's realised the other local farms will only supply her with massive bulk orders.'

'I see,' Grandad nodded, rubbing a hand over his stubbly chin.

'I had a proper look at the menu while I was there,' I told him, 'and on the back she's listed some of the other places she supports. Skylark honey and pork featured and I'm guessing that must be your mate Jake's farm.'

'Yes,' he said. 'That's right.'

'It would be good to see our name on there with his too, wouldn't it? This deal could be as much about raising our reputation as selling fruit.'

'Um,' he thoughtfully said.

I busied myself at the stove and let a moment of silence settle. I wanted him to have the opportunity to mull it all over, like I'd had. I very much hoped he was going to agree to what Jemma had suggested, in principle at least.

'I admit I have been concerned about what was going to happen to this year's crops,' he quietly said. 'And to be honest, I didn't think I'd be trading at all next year.'

There was a change in his tone and when I looked, I saw his bottom lip trembling. The sight of it, caused tears to prickle the backs of my eyes and a lump to form in my throat.

'Last season,' he carried on, 'Chris Dempster, who runs a stall on the market, helped me out and Jake did too, but it wasn't quite enough and we had some waste. They've both said they'll carry on selling for me, but I'd already worked out there'd be quite a surplus of strawberries again.'

'Jemma mentioned that they had stepped in,' I softly said.

'Between them they took the soft fruit and then Jake had the apples and pears for his cider and perry like he always does. The set-up worked reasonably well, but as I said, there was some waste. I had been thinking about ploughing up half the rows at the end of last year, but couldn't bring myself to do it.'

Fenview Farm really was on the cusp of scaling down and possibly even closing its trading doors and I was grateful that Mum had found it within herself to write her letter and tell me about this place, even if the details had only been brief. Had I not been made aware of this other branch of the Brown family even for just a few months longer, then I might have been visiting a very different farm to the one I was falling under the spell of now.

'Well, it's just as well you didn't get the plough out, isn't it?' I said, recovering enough to smile. 'Jemma will be buying more than the surplus and the deal could give the farm a whole new lease of life. She'll be playing up the local and fresh aspect and she's prepared to pay well too. There won't be any wasted fruit at all this year and consequently no financial loss.'

Grandad seemed to like the sound of that.

'Did she say if she had any preference about the produce being organic?' he asked.

'No,' I said. 'Not that I can recall.'

'It was something I had been thinking about before things went downhill. No one else around here is organic and I thought it might give the farm an edge. I was all set to try it, but then, like so many other things I'd dreamt up, it got set aside.'

He didn't elaborate on what the other things were.

'Well,' I said. 'I think now might be the time to pick those dreams up again. Are you interested in what Jemma is offering?'

'More than interested,' he said, his mouth breaking into the broadest smile I'd seen yet. 'If Jemma takes a good share and Chris and Jake pick up the rest then we could be properly back in business.'

I felt the tension I'd been carrying in my shoulders begin to loosen its grip.

'I think it really could be the start of an exciting new era for Fenview Farm.'

'And I can't tell you what a relief that would be, Fliss,' Grandad swallowed. 'I was convinced that I was going to be the Brown who failed after the success of so many generations who had gone before me. In spite of my recent spell of better sleep,' he admitted, 'the worry has kept me awake at night for a very long time.'

I knew that on its own, the contract with Jemma wouldn't be enough to keep the farm completely afloat, but it would provide a much-needed life raft. It would help keep our heads above water for a while and with the strawberry season about to kick off, it really couldn't have been better timed.

I was suddenly rather enamoured with Bec's lack of discretion. Perhaps folk finding out who I was might not be such a bad thing after all.

'We're not going to let the farm fail,' I said firmly, as I felt my determination to keep things going receive a hefty, potentially celestial, boost. 'It's not happening on my watch.'

Grandad beamed again.

'I'll get in touch with Jemma and invite her here so you can negotiate the contract as soon as possible.'

'I'll want you onboard for that too,' Grandad quickly said.

'I'd be honoured to help.' I told him.

'Oh Fliss,' he gasped, reaching for my hand. 'What a breath of fresh air you've brought to this place. And to me. Before you came along, I was practically resigned to selling up and moving to a boxy little bungalow to see out my days.'

'That's not going to happen either,' I said, squeezing his fingers in mine. 'I want to see this place thrive again. There's no way you're going to have to part with any of it.'

Grandad nodded, but didn't comment further.

'Now,' I said. 'Let's get this lamb in the oven, otherwise we'll be eating dinner rather than lunch!'

*

I was fanning myself with a tea-towel by the back door when the Randall clan rocked up. I was mightily amused to see Eliot squeezed into the back of the Banana-mobile and it was most entertaining to watch him prise himself out and unfurl.

It was the first time I'd seen him wearing proper going-out clothes and I tried not to stare when I noticed how good his long, toned legs looked in cargo shorts. I supposed their impressive shape was the result of gripping that powerful Ducati so tightly between his muscular thighs. Perhaps best not to think about that. Lustful thoughts about legs didn't have any place in the 'friend zone', did they?

'Felicity,' beamed Louise, pulling me into one of her trademark hugs. 'How are you settling in?'

'It's been a surprisingly wonderful few days,' I told her, quickly banishing the inappropriate thoughts about Eliot's physique and focusing instead on everything that had happened since she, Grandad and I had had our heart to heart. 'Given the circumstances.'

'I'm so pleased,' she said, kissing my hair.

The second she released me, Bec filled the space in my arms that Louise had left and gave me a squeeze that rivalled her mother's. When she eventually stepped back, I found myself facing Eliot. We hesitated for an awkward second and then he thrust a bag that clinked with bottles into my arms.

'Bill said we were having lamb so really it should have been red,' he said, looking a little rosy himself. 'But given everything that's happened, we thought champagne would be a better option, didn't we, Bec?'

'You did,' she shot back. 'I would have settled for elderflower cordial as I'm driving, but you said it should be top shelf champers to celebrate Fliss's arrival in our lives or nothing.'

'Well, thank you,' I said, feeling genuinely touched that he felt that my turning up was something worth celebrating in such style and at such expense. 'I'll put it in the fridge.'

'And just wait until you hear what Fliss has come up with for the farm,' Grandad chimed in. 'Then you'll be even more pleased that you splashed out, Eliot!'

Bec, Eliot and I carried the table out of the barn and set it down in the shade of the apple tree before adding a tablecloth which Grandad told me had been embroidered by his mother, my great-grandmother, along with a mismatched collection of crockery, cutlery, glasses and chairs.

The dinner, carried out in covered tureens that also hailed from my great-grandmother's era, was delicious, and the accompaniment of the champagne ensured we were all, other than Bec, a little drowsy by the time I served up apple pie swimming in pools of thick double cream.

I'd found the apples in the freezer and it had been a treat to make the pie using Fenview fruit. I had felt the same surge of pride as when I cooked using the Rossi produce in their Italian kitchen.

I smiled to myself as I thought of the heady pleasure I would derive from baking Nonna's highly prized cherry and almond tart using Fenview cherries. What an amalgamation that would be! The delicious taste of home would be doubly delicious then and I willed the harvest to ripen all the faster.

'That,' said Louise, licking her spoon clean, 'was another absolutely wonderful meal. Who was it who taught you to cook, Felicity? I don't think you told us before.'

'It's Fliss, Mum,' Bec pointedly said, from her end of the table.

I don't know why she still bothered trying to correct her. I was always going to be Felicity to her mum, just as she would always be Rebecca.

'I had the most amazing teacher,' I told Louise. 'I honed my skills under the tutelage of the most accomplished cook and wisest woman I've ever known.'

'Not your mother then,' Louise smiled.

'No,' I said, thinking of Mum's inability to even cook pasta. 'Not Mum.'

'You sound very fond of this person,' said Bec.

'I'm more than fond,' I told her.

'Well,' said Eliot, who sounded a little squiffy. 'I think we should raise a toast to her.'

'I agree,' I said, raising my glass and accidentally spilling some of its contents. Apparently, I was a little squiffy myself. 'To Nonna Rossi.'

'To Nonna Rossi,' they all chorused.

We drained our glasses and Eliot refilled them. He tried to bypass Bec, but thanks to the impact of the bubbles on his balance, he knocked into her and she scowled up at him, clearly unimpressed. The sight of him looking a little wobbly and her so annoyed made me want to laugh.

'So, Bill,' said Eliot, flopping heavily back into his chair, once he'd done the rounds. 'What exactly is it that Fliss has come up with? It certainly seems to have put a spring in your step.'

'I knew it,' said Bec, sitting forward in her seat, once Grandad had finished giving them the lowdown. 'When I mentioned Fliss and the farm at the café, Jemma quizzed me for *ages*.'

'She told me that until you filled her in, she'd assumed Fenview Farm had ceased trading so I suppose we should be thanking you for not keeping my arrival to yourself,' I smiled at her.

'Well, I never,' chuckled Louise. 'I never thought I'd live to see the day when my daughter's inability to keep a secret would actually do some good.'

Bec stuck out her tongue and Grandad chuckled.

'Your mum's right,' he nodded. 'But try not to keep making a habit of it, my lovely.'

'I'll do my best,' she sheepishly smiled.

'So, are you going ahead?' asked Eliot.

'Of course,' said Grandad. 'Fliss is going to invite Jemma to have a look around and then it should be all systems go.'

Eliot nodded. 'That must be a weight off your mind,' he then said, looking at me.

'Oh, it is,' I sighed. It was a really good feeling, knowing that within days of my arrival I was already playing a part in helping the farm find its feet again, even if the partnership had been Jemma's idea. 'And just in the nick of time too,' I added, smiling at Grandad and thinking of the concerns he'd mentioned earlier as well as the speedily ripening strawberries.

'Yes,' said Eliot. 'You'll be able to leave knowing this place has a chance again now, won't you?'

'What do you mean?' I frowned, my gaze snapping back to him. 'Leave for where?'

'Italy,' he said, slurring the word a little. 'Bill said you have an important job on this farm in Puglia. You won't be giving that up for good, will you?'

I hoped Grandad hadn't discussed my life in Italy with Eliot because he was worried about me disappearing like Mum had. With each new day I was feeling more and more connected to the farm, and to Grandad, and I didn't want him worrying that I was just biding my time. That wasn't the impression I'd got from him when we talked about it before, but Eliot's intoxicated comments suggested that could have been on Grandad's mind, even if they didn't confirm it.

'Well,' I said, 'we still haven't sorted out the finer details of how things will work out here in the long-term, but I have absolutely no plans to go anywhere at the moment.'

'Good,' said Eliot, raising his glass. 'I'm relieved to hear it.'

I was pleased that he was relieved, but I wasn't thrilled to think that Grandad might have been worried about me leaving. He didn't look particularly perturbed, but I'd have to talk to him about it again and the sooner the better.

'I better get these dishes cleared away,' I said, standing up and hoping the action might prompt the others to go so I could get on with it.

'I'll give you a hand,' said Bec, shooting her brother another less than loving look. 'Ignore Eliot,' she said, once we were alone in the kitchen. 'He hardly ever drinks and I don't think he meant for that comment to come out the way it did. I don't even think he's realised how it sounded. He knows full well you're not going anywhere.'

It wouldn't be the first time he'd failed to find the right words where I was concerned, so I supposed I shouldn't be feeling too put out by it.

'I hope you're right,' I said. 'Because I'm really not, however I am a bit worried now that Grandad might have said something and he's thinking I might disappear . . .'

'I don't think he's thinking that at all,' Bec quickly said. 'I reckon what just happened was more about Eliot than Bill.'

'What do you mean?'

Bec looked outside again. Eliot, Louise and Grandad were still sitting under the tree.

'I think he's got the hots for you Fliss,' she whispered. 'And he was trying to sound you out.'

'Sound me out?' I spluttered.

'Yes,' she nudged. 'But not very discreetly, thanks to the champagne. I reckon he wanted to make sure you're here for the long haul before he declares his . . .'

My cheeks blazed and I quickly began noisily scraping the plates.

'I don't think so,' I said, cutting her off. 'He wasn't about to declare anything.'

Bec shrugged but didn't say anything further and I fell to

wondering if that was what Eliot's lowered inhibitions had just exposed. Had the addition of expensive bubbles revealed the fact that he was struggling to keep his feelings for me in check? As thrilling as the thought was, it was unsettling too.

My life, as well as the day-to-day running of Fenview Farm, was going through a huge transformation and as much as I fancied Eliot, and as hard as I found it not to act on the spark that had ignited between us, I knew I was going to have to try that little bit harder because the last thing I needed, as much as I wanted it, was to throw a love affair into the mix. We had already agreed that we would stick to being friends and, tipsy or stone-cold sober, that was what we both had to commit to.

Chapter 12

The celebrations turned rather flat after Eliot's sozzled suggestion that I would soon be returning to my job in Puglia and, once he had been bundled into the back of the Bananamobile, Grandad took himself off for a nap.

Determined not to let my concern that he was worried I was going to leave fester, I resolved to address the situation the moment he got up, however he had other issues he wanted to discuss and we worked through those first.

'I want to talk to you about the farm finances, Fliss,' he said, seriously. 'There's a box file in the dining room sideboard. Would you go and fetch it, please?'

'Isn't this a private matter, Grandad?' I asked, as he opened the box and pulled out a pile of papers and bank statements.

'It's a family matter,' he told me. 'And you're family, aren't you?'

'Yes,' I agreed. 'Of course, the only family, as far as I know.'

But it still felt like an intrusion, me knowing the state of the farm affairs. That said, I soon set any awkwardness aside, because the financial affairs were in a bit of a state.

'So, to sum up,' I said, as I looked at the papers spread out on the kitchen table, 'you own Fenview Farm outright and there's no mortgage or any other loan secured on it.'

'Correct, and no credit card debts or anything like that either.'

That was a huge relief.

'But there are a number of outstanding accounts with local businesses and the overdraft is getting near its limit.'

'It is,' said Grandad, shaking his head. 'There's not enough to clear the accounts *and* live on and the bank manager has been very patient, but I know he won't extend it further.'

Grandad sounded mortified. He had explained that the family had never gone in for borrowing in a big way and living off money that didn't exist didn't sit well with him.

'My father always told me,' he said, sounding even more upset, 'that if you didn't have the money to buy something outright, then you went without it.'

'That's a wonderful ethos to live by,' I said, 'but times have changed and that's not always possible, is it? I daresay the farm earned its money differently when your father was alive, didn't it?'

'That it did,' he agreed.

'Well,' I said, shuffling the papers together and sounding more confident than I felt, 'I'd see this current situation as a minor blip, Grandad. This deal with Jemma couldn't have come at a better time and it's going to be a big help. It's not going to be the answer to everything, but you can go to the bank and tell them that you've got a lucrative new contract which will help clear the overdraft *and* a granddaughter brimming with ideas to pull the finances out of the red and back into the black.'

Grandad looked rather taken aback. 'Are you brimming with ideas?' he asked.

'No,' I said, with a smile. 'Not really. But they don't need to know that, do they? And I'm sure I will be soon. Something else will come along, I just know it, and in the meantime, I'm happy to live frugally.'

My time in Italy had taught me how to appreciate life's simple pleasures. Home-cooked food, friendship and family were what really mattered and now I had further opportunity to enjoy all three in abundance.

'And I have more than enough saved to clear these other outstanding accounts,' I added, nodding at the 'to be paid' pile.

Grandad vehemently shook his head. 'No,' he said. 'There has to be another way. In fact, there is something else, Fliss . . .'

'No,' I interrupted. 'I don't want to hear it. I'm living here now too, and I want to contribute and pay my way. I'd like to help pull Fenview Farm into the future, both by the work I can do and the little financial support I can offer. I'm going to be here for a very long time Grandad. Which,' I pushed on, 'brings me on to what Eliot said earlier.'

'Yes,' said Grandad. 'I thought that might come up.'

'You aren't worried that I'm going to disappear like Mum did, are you? I hadn't realised that you'd talked to Eliot about my life in Italy.'

'Of course, I'm not,' he said, every bit as forcefully as I had when I made my speech a moment ago. 'You might be your mother's daughter, but I know you'd never do that. I know you're here for a long time, Fliss, and I don't know what got into Eliot.'

'Too much champagne?' I suggested, relieved that he hadn't jumped to the same conclusion as Bec.

I was going to have to be extra careful when I talked about Eliot around her now. The last thing I needed was for her to work out that the feelings she'd guessed he had for me were reciprocated.

'Well, yes,' said Grandad, with a small smile. 'I think that probably was a factor. He doesn't usually drink.'

'So Bec said.'

'The bubbles definitely went to his head,' he laughed, then looked thoughtful, as if he was trying to puzzle something out.

'Well,' I quickly cut in, before he could speculate further, 'let's keep a dry house from now on, shall we?'

'Sounds good to me,' he chuckled.

As it was getting late, we decided to call it a day. I was pleased to draw a line under the conversation but relieved that I had had the opportunity to say my piece and that Grandad was convinced that I wasn't going to be rushing back to Italy. I was also pleased that I was going to be able to help Fenview Farm in a bigger way than simply flexing my muscles, even if Grandad was reluctant to let me.

And with that in mind, he was going to get in touch with

the bank and explain how things were changing and as I slipped into sleep, I hoped that Eliot's imminent hangover would act as a reminder to him that he needed to work as hard to keep the feelings we had for one another under wraps as I was. I had already resolved to embrace life at the farm without a love affair complicating things, and Eliot needed to stick to that plan too.

Andersons were as good as their word and their delivery van rolled into the yard just as I was finishing breakfast early Monday morning. It was another clear bright day and the forecast was looking good for the whole week, which was a blessing.

The sunshine would enable me to get on with my list of jobs, stop me fretting over Eliot and the fact that I still hadn't had a reply to my email to Marco. I knew that was most likely because of lack of phone signal at the farm, which meant my account wouldn't update, but there was a tiny part of me that was worried that he was upset about my decision to stay on at Fenview.

'Where do you want it all, love?' shouted the chipper Andersons delivery driver as he hopped out.

I knew it wasn't the sort of thing that usually raised the heart rate of a woman in her twenties, but what I was looking at was some of my contribution to keeping my family farm on track and, as a result, I felt my roots stretch a little deeper and hold on a little tighter to the Fenland soil beneath my feet.

'In here will be fine, thanks,' I said, pulling open the barn doors. 'If you could stack it all at the front, then I can move it as I need it.'

'What's all this lot then?' he asked eyeing the tea-chests and boxes as he ferried the things inside.

'I don't really know,' I told him, shifting a little to block his view.

I still hadn't got around to asking Grandad what the things all amounted to and why they were there, but they must have meant something to someone in my family and consequently I felt protective towards the motley assortment.

'Looks to me like you want a skip, love,' said the driver. 'You need to have a good clear-out.'

It was on the tip of my tongue to tell him that I wasn't his 'love', but settled on not tipping him instead.

'Oh, I don't know,' I tightly said. 'One man's junk and all that.'

With the chat firmly nipped in the bud and my order stored, I decided the first thing I was going to do was mend the cages. The opportunistic blackbird had been back again and I knew that if he had a nest nearby then his fledglings would be feasting on the farm profits before long.

Opening the barn might have kicked off my curiosity about the collection again, but there would be plenty of time to ask Grandad about that once the most urgent chores and tasks were ticked off my list.

And talking of Grandad . . .

'What on earth are you doing?' I called, as I lugged the

roofing felt and cage mending supplies over to the freshly scrubbed henhouse.

He was attempting to drag one of the garden chairs across to the wheelbarrow that I was going to use to ferry the other things I needed.

'You're going to repair the fruit cages, aren't you?' he asked, coming to a stop and sounding a little out of breath.

'That's right.'

'I want to come and watch you do it then,' he puffed. 'And I'll need something to sit on by the time I've walked all that way.'

It wasn't all that far, but I was pleased he knew his limits.

'Are you checking up on me?'

'Absolutely,' he grinned, his eyes sparkling. 'I've only got your word for it that you know what you're doing, after all.'

'Fine by me,' I laughed, before walking back to the kitchen for the large umbrella which was propped behind the door.

'It's not going to rain,' Grandad tutted.

'I know,' I said. 'But it's going to get hot and you don't want heatstroke, do you?'

'You'd better get some drinks as well then,' he suggested. 'We don't want to dehydrate either.'

It took a little while to reach the cages. The barrow was heavy and a bit wobbly with the stepladder balanced across it and it was the furthest Grandad had walked since his surgery.

'It's going to take us longer to get set up, than it will for you to do the job,' Grandad grumbled, sounding frustrated and fed up. 'I should have stayed inside.'

'No, you shouldn't,' I told him. 'This is a milestone for me. The first proper job I've done on the farm and I love that you're with me while I do it.'

He looked happier after that and took up his position in the chair, protected from the sun by the umbrella which featured Moto GP drivers.

'It belongs to Eliot,' said Grandad.

'Well, I didn't think it was your style.'

Was there no part of the farm that Eliot hadn't infiltrated? I was supposed to be setting my thoughts about him aside while I worked and yet, here he was again. Wherever I turned the leather clad carer popped up. I quickly turned my attention back to the task in hand.

'You've done a grand job,' Grandad proudly said, when I finally finished.

'*We've* done a grand job,' I amended, standing back to look. 'You've done just as much as me.'

There had been more holes than I first realised and he'd fixed those that were within reach, while I had mended the highs and lows, so he didn't have to bend and stretch. The blackbird had been indignantly squawking throughout, but he would have to go and find someone else's profit to pick his way through because we needed every penny of ours.

'I'm going to do some weeding,' I said, 'and then we'll stop for lunch, shall we?'

'That sounds like a grand idea,' said Grandad, sitting back down and rearranging the umbrella because the sun had shifted.

I looked over at him and smiled. Day on day he was looking better, and that morning, with the benefit of the sunshine and a task to keep him occupied, he positively glowed. It was amazing to think it was just ten days ago that I had arrived and he had been so poorly. It was also amazing to think that it was just ten days ago, full stop.

Whether it was because I was used to working on a fruit farm and familiar with the routine, or whether it was because this was my family farm and where I truly belonged, I couldn't be sure, but I felt as though I'd been at Fenview Farm for far longer. Mum's suggestion that I would be a good fit here, had turned out to be right. So far at least.

I hummed as I worked my way between the bushes, hoeing up some weeds and pulling up others, while Grandad watched from outside, chatting companionably to the still irate blackbird.

'That'll do for today,' I said, grimacing as I stretched out my aching back and checked my phone. It showed me the time, but precious little else. 'Definitely time for lunch.'

We had a scratch meal of bread, cheese, fruit and chutney and then Grandad went for a nap while I measured, cut and hammered on the new roof for the henhouse. After that, I headed back over to the barn. Throughout the morning, when I wasn't thinking about Eliot, Marco or Mum, my mind had drifted back to it and I was eager to have another look.

The cat was asleep on top of one of the tea-chests and when she realised I was going to be moving stuff about, she stretched and yawned and stalked out, no doubt resolved to find somewhere else to snooze the rest of the day away.

This time I looked properly inside the chests and pulled more things out. Some held framed photographs while others were packed with newspapers, which had turned yellow with age. A few of the photographs were of Fen skating, which matched the boots I'd seen before, and others were of wily looking eel catchers in tweed caps and grubby work clothes, a couple holding the same willow traps I'd already identified.

None of the newspapers, I realised, were being used as wrappings or to pad things out, but had been kept because they recorded particularly interesting stories and events. Most were about farming and local agricultural shows, and others recorded births, deaths and marriages in the area. I was interested to see that there were quite a few Browns listed.

A shadow fell across the doorway and I jumped. It was Grandad.

'I hope you don't mind me looking,' I swallowed, thinking that I really should have asked before I rifled through it all. 'I spotted it all the first time I came in here and again this morning when the order from Andersons arrived and my curiosity got the better of me, I'm afraid.'

'I daresay you think it's all a load of rubbish,' Grandad said.

He stepped further in and I could see he looked more uncomfortable than annoyed, but there was an air of defiance in the way he stuck out his chin.

'None of it looks like rubbish,' I quickly said.

'No?'

'No, it's fascinating. An amazing record of life around here. I've learned loads just from looking at the newspapers. Some of these should be framed and preserved like the photographs.'

Grandad looked taken aback.

'And these eel traps are incredible,' I said, picking one up. 'I had no idea they were so skilfully woven when I saw them online.'

'Why were you looking at them online?'

'I did a bit of research about the area and its history before I came here. I found out a few things, but it's not the same as seeing them first hand, is it?'

'You don't think it should all be put in a heap and burned then?'

'What? Of course not!'

'That's all your mother said it was good for,' he huskily said. 'Whenever I found something new, or someone gave me a piece for safekeeping, she'd sneer and tell me how sad I was, being stuck in the past.'

'But that's ridiculous. This is a treasure trove of local history and I can promise you Grandad, that's not what Mum would have said if she could see it all now.'

'No?'

'No,' I said. 'She would have appreciated this every bit as much as I do.'

'She obviously changed a lot over the years then, didn't she?'

'I think she must have done,' I agreed. 'Teenagers often

bear little resemblance to the adults they become, in my experience, and it's such a shame you didn't have the opportunity to know Mum once she'd got all of that angst out of her system.'

It pained me deeply to know that she'd never come back to Fenview Farm to make amends. I wished with every fibre of my being that Grandad had known the worldly, well-travelled and much-loved woman his daughter had become and that his memories weren't confined to the argumentative and sulky girl she had been.

'Some of this looks unique,' I carried on, steering the conversation back to the collection. 'It should be treasured, not torched.'

'It is,' said Grandad. 'That's why I've kept if for all these years.'

'So, what are you going to do with it?' I asked. 'What are your plans for it? I can't imagine that you've kept it all just so it can gather dust.'

'Well, no,' he said, shifting from one foot to the other. 'I had thought about finding a way to put it all on display at one time, but nothing ever came of it.'

'You should do it,' I said, picking up one of the maps. 'I'm sure people would be interested, especially if you talked to them about it too. A personal connection is a very powerful thing.'

Grandad gently took the map out of my hand and turned it up the right way. He clearly loved the collection he had so painstakingly put together and I was going to make sure it got the recognition it deserved. Shut away in a dusty old barn wasn't doing it any good or any justice at all.

'Promise me you'll think about it,' I asked him, but he didn't have a chance to answer as a car pulled into the yard.

'Are you expecting anyone?' I asked.

'Not as far as I know,' he shrugged.

I quickly put everything back where I'd found it and closed the barn again.

'Jemma,' I smiled, as she climbed out of her car. 'How lovely to see you. Grandad, this is Jemma from the Cherry Tree Café.'

'I thought I recognised you,' he said, also smiling. 'I was going to give you a call this afternoon.'

'With good news, I hope,' she said, reaching back into the car and reappearing with a large cake box. 'I hope you don't mind me just turning up out of the blue, but I was so excited after our chat, Fliss, that even though I'd said there was no rush, I couldn't wait another day to find out what you'd decided, Mr Brown.'

'In that case, you'd better call me Bill,' Grandad told her. 'I like to be on first name terms with anyone I do business with.'

'That sounds promising.' Jemma grinned. 'Bill it is then.'

In the kitchen, she handed over the box which was full of cakes, biscuits and cream-based confectionery.

'Well now,' said Grandad. 'I can see where your talent lies, my dear. These all look delicious.'

Jemma flushed prettily. 'And I know where yours lies too,'

she said back, 'and I'm hoping it's going to enhance mine all the more.'

Grandad nodded approvingly.

'Why don't you and I go and have a look around the farm?' I suggested to her. 'And then we'll have tea and cakes while we talk business.'

'That's an excellent idea,' Grandad agreed. 'I'm all walked out for today, but I can run to making a pot of tea.'

I gave Jemma the full tour, explaining what would be coming into season and when and she was enthralled with everything.

'This is just the sort of collab I'm looking for,' she said excitedly as we walked around. 'I've got a similar set-up with Jake and Amber from Skylark Farm.'

'I guessed as much from what I read on the back of the café menu,' I told her, stopping to pluck a couple of strawberries which had conveniently ripened just in time.

By the looks of it, I was going to have to start making daily checks of the rows. Mindful of Grandad's concerns, I didn't want to waste a single fruit and the straw delivery couldn't come soon enough now.

Jemma closed her eyes as she bit into the soft, sweet flesh.

'Plucked straight from the plant,' she said, chewing appreciatively. 'You can't get any better than that, can you?'

'You certainly can't,' I agreed, picking a few for Grandad. 'And I can easily get them to you within just a couple of hours of picking.'

Or at least I could if I had transport. I was really going to have to address that situation sooner rather than later, but in the meantime, perhaps Bec might be able to help me out. She certainly had the right vehicle for ferrying fruit about!

'Come and see what we've got in the cages,' I said to Jemma, determined not to let concerns about my lack of wheels jeopardise our deal. 'There's nothing ripe yet, but you'll be able to get an idea of the yields we can offer.'

An hour later, going organic had been discussed, along with apple, pear and plum varieties and the deal was done. It was all sealed over a few more strawberries and some sumptuously frosted cupcakes which felt and tasted like a wonderful way to do business to me.

'This is a lovely barn,' said Jemma, nodding over to where Grandad's Fenland collection was stored as she prepared to leave. 'I don't suppose you'd consider selling it, would you?'

'Absolutely not,' I said, before Grandad had a chance to answer.

'I didn't think so,' she laughed, 'but I thought I'd ask. Tom and I rather fancy taking on a conversion project.'

'If it had been built further away from the house then it might have been a possibility, but I don't think it would be ideal having someone living so close by, do you Grandad?'

He looked at the barn, but didn't answer.

'There'd be all sorts of issues with access too.' I pointed out. 'What with sharing the drive and everything and especially as this is a working farm.'

'That's fair enough,' said Jemma. 'Let's just stick to the fruit deal then. Tom would probably have had forty fits if I told him I'd put a deposit down on a barn, rather than a fruit harvest this afternoon!'

Once she'd gone, I indulged in a little happy dance, which made Grandad laugh.

'Now all I need to do, is sort out some transport to get the fruit to town every day,' I said, linking my arm through his, 'and we'll be all set.'

'Oh, that's no problem,' he said, pulling me closer to his side. 'By this time tomorrow you'll be up and running. You have got a driving licence, haven't you?'

I stopped and looked at him. What was he talking about?

'Yes.'

'And it's here?'

'What's going on?'

'Have you got your licence or not?'

'Yes,' I said. 'It's Italian, but I can drive on it here for a year, I think. Then I have to get it transferred to a British one.'

'Good,' he said, before mysteriously adding, 'I'll need to borrow it later.'

'Are you going to tell me why?' I asked, dancing around him again.

'No,' he laughed. 'I want it to be a surprise. Let's go and have another cake.'

I wasn't sure I needed more sugar, but I followed him back inside wondering what exactly he was going to surprise me with the next day.

Chapter 13

The following morning Grandad and I made the most of the time before his friend, Jake, was due to arrive with the straw and hens, by shifting the henhouse into position and surrounding it with a simply constructed run.

'I know I said we wouldn't bother with a run,' said Grandad, as he handed me the stakes and ties so I could hammer it into the ground, 'but I've been giving it some more thought and, as these are ex-battery girls, I reckon they'll feel a bit more secure in an enclosed space for a while.'

I had to agree and the spot we'd picked, still just in sight of the house, but in the shade of a tree, was perfect.

'It was fortunate you remembered you had this,' I said, as I hammered in the last stake. 'It's just the job.'

'It's getting on a bit,' said Grandad, giving it a shake to make sure I'd secured it properly. 'But it can still do the job.'

'A bit like you then,' I grinned up at him.

'You cheeky beggar,' he laughed.

A horn tooted in the yard.

'That'll be Jake,' he said, distracted from my mischievous comment. 'Let's go and see what he's got for us, shall we?'

I felt a bit nervous about meeting Jake Somerville. I knew he was a good friend of Grandad's and had been more than generous when it came to helping keep Fenview Farm running during the last couple of years. I smoothed down my work shirt, my heart skipping in my eagerness to make a good impression, but I needn't have worried. Jake was kindness itself and not at all how I had imagined him.

He was about twenty years younger for a start. Definitely older than me, but not by all that much. Unkempt haired with hazel flecked eyes, a ready smile and a firm handshake. He pumped my hand with something akin to relief as he said how pleased he was to meet me and that he hoped Grandad wasn't giving me too much trouble.

'He's behaving himself so far,' I said, returning his smile, 'but I'm expecting that will all change once I've found my feet.'

'Oh right,' said Grandad, talking over us. 'I can see how it's going to be. You two are going to gang up on me, aren't you?'

'Definitely,' said Jake, winking at me.

'In that case,' Grandad sniffed, 'let's have a look at these hens and then I'll go and make us a drink while you pair get on with the work.'

Jake's Kawasaki Mule and trailer were loaded up with straw bales, a bag of feed for the hens and another of grit, while the box containing the three chickens was wedged securely in the passenger footwell.

As we approached, I could hear a gentle clucking which grew all the louder when Jake jumped behind the wheel and manoeuvred the vehicle over to the run.

'This is exciting, isn't it?' said Grandad, forgetting his former scolding and honing in on exactly how I felt. 'It's going to be lovely having chickens again. Livestock and poultry make a place feel more alive.'

'And then there are all those fresh eggs,' I wistfully added. 'I've got the most amazing meringue recipe I want to make again and it will go perfectly with our fruit.'

'You'll be giving Jemma a run for her money at this rate,' Grandad chuckled.

I packed some straw into the henhouse and filled the feeder and drinker while Jake lifted the box into the run.

'We're supposed to leave them shut in, aren't we?' I asked the two men who knew far more about poultry welfare than I did.

'As a rule, they'd be in the house overnight to get their bearings,' said Jake. 'But it's going to get hot today, and as you've got a run and they can't wander off, I reckon they'll be able to come out after about an hour. What do you think, Bill?'

'Yes,' he agreed. 'That should do it. Let's get them in, shall we?'

Jake opened the box and Grandad carefully lifted the first hen out, expertly tucking her under his arm. She was the classic ginger and white Rhode Island cross-breed and in far better condition than I had been expecting.

'She doesn't look too bad,' said Grandad, as he gently stroked her back.

'I've had them a little while,' explained Jake, reaching into the box and handing me the second one. 'So, they've already had some fairly decent feather growth. They hardly had any wing feathers at all when I collected them.'

They certainly had them now. The hen I was holding gave a mighty flap and Grandad stepped forward and tucked her wings in so I could get the same grip on her, as he had on his.

'She's a feisty one, isn't she?' he laughed as Jake picked out the third, who was docile by comparison.

'She's definitely the boss,' said Jake, nodding at mine as he lifted the henhouse lid and lowered his demure bird inside.

I quickly followed suit, keen to let go of the ringleader before she flapped out of my arms. She clucked and gave me a very hard stare as Grandad deposited his. Jake carefully closed the roof and I checked the door was secure.

'That's that then,' said Grandad, looking well pleased. 'You'll have to let me know how much you want for them, Jake.'

'Nothing for the hens,' he said, brushing his hands down his trousers, 'but I'll charge you for the feed and grit.'

'Grand,' said Grandad. 'Let's have a drink before you two shift this straw, shall we?'

By the time Jake and I had finished lugging the bales about and stacking them on wooden pallets as close to the strawberry rows as we could get, I was feeling hot and ready for another drink.

'Thank goodness you had the Mule,' I puffed as we

covered the bales in a sheet of tarpaulin and secured it with a couple of bricks.

Rain wasn't forecast, but I didn't want to get caught out. Grandad had said the area was known for freak thunderstorms, so I wasn't taking any chances.

'I would have had to shift this lot individually with the wheelbarrow if you hadn't.'

'That would have been a killer,' Jake agreed, wiping the sweat from his brow. 'You could do with widening the path to get bigger vehicles down here. The farmer who owns the field next door doesn't mind the tractor coming through his gate and on to here, but it's not ideal.'

Working out how to widen the path would be another job to add to the ever-growing list.

'Thank you for supplying these,' I said, nodding to the stack of covered bales. 'Now all I have to do is get the straw down and we'll be all set. I'll make a start on that tomorrow.'

'Have you got anyone to help you?'

'No,' I said. 'It's just going to be me, but I don't mind that.'

'Bill said you know a lot about the industry already. He reckons you could run this place single-handed.'

I felt rather proud that he had such a high opinion of me and my experience.

'I know my way around,' I said as we climbed back into the Mule and headed to the yard where Grandad was waiting with three glasses of lemonade. 'And I've recently come to realise that my whole life has been leading up to me coming here. First off I've always had this slightly unusual passion for fruit farming and now I've discovered that it's the family business and embedded in my genes.'

I didn't mention how I'd found out it was the family business.

'I'm looking forward to hearing more about it,' said Jake. 'And my partner, Amber and aunt, Annie are desperate to meet you. They're hoping you'll spend the afternoon with us, if that suits you.'

'I'd love to,' I said, my sudden willingness to mingle with people I'd never met, taking me by surprise, 'but I don't want to put you out. You must be busy and it hardly seems fair that you've got to chauffeur me about.'

'Only one way,' he said. 'And I'm going back to the farm anyway.'

Immersed in the stint of hard work, I'd forgotten that Grandad had a surprise that required my driving licence.

'Bugger,' Jake laughed, clapping his hand over his mouth. 'I almost let the cat out of the bag there. Don't tell Bill. He'll have my guts for garters.'

'Your secret is safe with me,' I told him, even though I was bursting to pump him for further information.

It was no surprise that it was Little Miss Bossy who first emerged from the henhouse. She was soon followed by the other two and they stalked about, scratching at the ground and clucking over any tasty morsels they unearthed.

'It's amazing that they know what to do, isn't it?' I mused, squatting down to watch them. 'You'd think their instincts would have been squashed after that year in a cage.'

'It's nearer eighteen months they're kept like that,' Jake sadly said. 'But I've never housed one yet who hasn't got the hang of life beyond the confines of the cage.'

'That's good,' I said, standing up again. 'These look as though they've been here for ever already, don't they Grandad?'

'They do,' he agreed. 'And they're going to be worth their weight in golden eggs when it comes to helping us clear the fruit cages after harvest.'

'Oh yes,' said Jake. 'They'll love that.'

He looked at his watch.

'Crikey,' he said. 'We'd better get going. Amber and Annie are laying on lunch in your honour, Fliss. We'll skip that refill you were just about to offer us, Bill.'

Grandad rolled his eyes and took our empty glasses.

'Are you sure you don't want to come?' Jake asked him. 'I can drop Fliss off and easily come back for you.'

'No, but thank you for the offer,' Grandad said. 'I'm actually looking forward to a bit more peace and quiet.'

I wondered if Eliot might call in again and interrupt Grandad's longed-for solitude. If he did, he'd only be offered coffee to drink!

'I'll just get changed,' I said, noticing my slightly grubby straw covered vest and shorts.

'No time,' said Jake. 'Come on.'

Skylark Farm was closer than I expected, so there was no opportunity for my courage or freshly found willingness to mingle, to fail me. He explained, shouting over the noise of the engine and the wind rushing by, that Bill and Annie had known each other for ever and that she had been really worried about him until she heard that I'd shown up.

'To be honest,' said Jake, his volume lessening as he slowed down at his farm, which was easily identified by a large and smart painted sign at the gate, 'we've all been worried. Chris Dempster and I both thought the farm was going to fold and Bill was going to end up in a home or something. He was so frail and . . . well, defeated.'

'But not now?'

'God no,' he said, swinging in. 'I could hardly say anything to his face, but it was a shock seeing him today. And a good one. He looked like a changed man. You've given him a new lease of life and I hope, we all hope, that you're going to be staying for good.'

I was just about to tell him that we still had to work the finer details out, but it was certainly looking that way, when I caught sight of a very familiar Ducati parked up at the farmhouse.

'Oh,' smiled Jake. 'Eliot's here. Maybe he'll stay for lunch too. He's been popping in to sit with Annie while Amber and I are busy on the farm. Not that we'd let her think that's what he's here for. She had a fall earlier in the year but she's a stubborn cuss and wouldn't appreciate us thinking that she needs minding.'

'Has she not worked it out?' I asked.

I couldn't think of any other reason why she might think Eliot would spend time with her. Unless of course, she just liked his company. From the little I knew of him so far, it seemed like everyone else did, so that was most likely it.

'If she has, she hasn't let on,' Jake told me. 'I daresay you've already met Eliot, haven't you? What with him being such a close friend of Bill's too.'

'Yes,' I said, picking more straw off my clothes. 'Our paths have crossed.'

I spent a very happy afternoon at Skylark Farm. Amber was every inch the picture-perfect farming type in her Joules patterned wellies, and Annie, with her periwinkle eyes and sharp wit, was both shrewd and observant. She reminded me of a Fenland equivalent of Nonna Rossi. Amber and Jake had two children, but they were at school, so it was just the five of us for lunch. Six if you counted the elderly Labrador scouting for crumbs.

Eliot and I said a brief, but slightly awkward, hello and I did my utmost to steer the conversation away from talk of how long I was planning to stay at Fenview Farm. The last thing I wanted was him picking at the thread he'd started to pull at the day of too much fizz.

We ate outside, in a set-up not all that dissimilar to the one Grandad and I had established, and which largely featured delicious fare in the form of pork, honey and apples, which were all produced on the farm.

'It's a beautiful place you've got here,' I said, looking around and taking in the pretty garden, tidy yard and well-maintained farmhouse.

There was a wooden building which looked quite new

and was covered in bright hanging baskets. That, Jake told me, was where they sold their produce, along with some of the Fenview Farm fruit, direct to the public. They also had a stall at the fortnightly farmers' market in Wynbridge.

Skylark Farm made Fenview look shabby by comparison, but I knew I needed to keep my mind focused on sorting the farm finances before I dealt with the aesthetics. Helping the farm make more money had to take precedence over making it look pretty, for now at least.

'Thank you,' smiled Amber, clearly delighted with the compliment. 'We're very happy here and it all looks rather different to how it did when I arrived.'

'She's had a big hand in transforming the place,' said Annie, eyeing me beadily, 'just like you're now doing at Fenview. A little bird told me, that you're going to be supplying the Cherry Tree Café with their fruit from now on.'

My gaze flicked to Eliot and I wondered if he was the little bird in question.

'That's right,' I smiled at Annie, thinking there was no point denying it, even if I wasn't sure if Grandad, Jemma or I wanted it widely known just yet. 'And that's just the beginning,' I added for good measure, suddenly deciding to face full on the one issue I'd previously tried to avoid. 'I've got more great plans which will help secure the future of the farm *and* my role in it.'

Eliot looked at me and raised his eyebrows and I wondered what he was thinking. Had I just raised his hopes and led him to assume that I was hinting that I was staying on, partly so that we could act on our feelings for one another? I hoped not, because that hadn't been my intention. I was more interested in ensuring that Grandad heard from every possible corner about my commitment to the farm.

I felt my temperature rise as I again remembered Grandad's now imminent visit to the bank. I hoped these great plans would soon land fully formed in my lap because it was all well and good bandying the words about, but I was going to have to come good on them at some point.

'Then Bill's a very lucky chap,' Annie nodded in approval. 'It seems to me the women around here are entrepreneurial in the extreme. There's Jemma and Lizzie at the Cherry Tree and Lottie up the road with her vintage glamping, not to mention the girls with the plant nursery, and that's just off the top of my head. And now there's you too, Fliss. The area is very lucky to have you. Don't you agree, Eliot?'

'Yes,' he said, turning slightly pink. 'Of course, and for good, too.'

That sounded as if my intentions to stay were sinking in, but I hoped for all the right reasons. I briefly met his gaze and he knocked me for six with his thousand-kilowatt smile. Wishing it wouldn't, but unable to stop it, I felt my face turn far redder than his.

'It's a huge comfort to know that Bill has you with him, Fliss,' Jake joined in.

'And I couldn't agree more about us entrepreneurial women, Annie,' said Amber. 'We've all found our niche and we all work well together. We're all happy to support each other's businesses too and I think that's why we're thriving. The networking scene in and around Wynbridge is a huge help.'

'In that case,' I said, turning my attention back to the conversation and pushing aside my concerns about what Eliot was thinking, 'I'm even happier to be here.'

A little later, Amber had to go and collect the children from school and Eliot was thankfully expected elsewhere too.

'Why don't you show Fliss around properly?' Amber suggested to Jake once Eliot was no more than a speck on the horizon and I had relaxed again. 'She might get even more ideas for Fenview.'

'What do you think?' he asked me. 'Have you got to rush back?'

'I can't rush anywhere,' I reminded him, 'until you've revealed what it is that I'm going to be rushing back in.'

'That's true,' he said. 'Come on then.'

The whistle-stop tour started with the rare breed pigs, which were raised for their prime meat and after that we drove through the immaculately kept orchards which supplied the fruit for Skylark cider and perry.

'And we let the pigs graze in here too,' said Jake, as he weaved the Mule between the trees. 'They clear up in much the same way as your hens will in the fruit cages.'

'Do you think the apples the pigs eat flavours the meat?'

'Yes,' he said. 'Definitely. It's subtle, but definitely noticeable.'

There were bees too, providing honey and wax and a pretty bungalow called Meadowview, which was a holiday let decorated with a vintage twist.

'So, there you have it,' he said when we pulled back into the yard, 'that's our place.'

'It's fantastic,' I told him. 'And I think it's great that you can sell what you produce on site and I'm grateful that you've helped Grandad by selling our fruit here too.'

'Yes, selling direct has worked out well and I'm happy to keep doing it for you, Fliss. The only other thing we'd like to do is host events where we could cook and serve the food we produce to paying guests.'

'What like an annual food festival?'

'No, something more regular than that.'

'An exclusive supper club?'

I'd recently read about a couple in a magazine. They looked and sounded wonderful.

'Yes,' he said. 'Exactly that, but unfortunately, we haven't got the room here.'

The venues I'd seen online were idyllic. One was located in the old glasshouses of a former garden centre, and the menus changed for every event so that the very best of what was on offer in the area could be presented at its peak.

'Um,' I said, looking about. 'I suppose you are a bit tight for space here now, aren't you?'

'Yes,' Jake agreed, 'and the occasional waft from the pigs probably wouldn't go down all that well with discerning diners either. We've had the odd wedding here in the past, pitching a marquee in the meadow, but we decided to stop when we increased the pig numbers.'

I couldn't help thinking that if folk were dining or tying

the knot in the country then they should perhaps be expecting earthy smells, but I didn't say so.

'What you really need,' I said instead, my heart fluttering as my mind tracked back to the farm's produce and whirred with the beginnings of an idea, 'is somewhere, not too rural, that has the capacity to park a few cars and the space to serve food to enough people to make it profitable, but not so big that you lose the exclusive and intimate ambience . . .'

'Exactly,' he said, 'and as you can see, we haven't got the capability for anything like that here.'

I tucked the idea away for further thought.

'Which is a shame,' Jake carried on, 'because locals often complain about not having somewhere special to eat in the evenings.'

'Funnily enough,' I told him, 'Lizzie in the Cherry Tree Café was discussing that very thing, just last week. I'm surprised Wynbridge hasn't got more restaurants given the demand.'

'There are a couple,' he said, 'and they're lovely, but nothing out of the ordinary and then there's the pub. Once you've exhausted those three, and the takeaways, then there's nothing else for miles.'

'I see,' I said.

'I'm going to investigate further,' Jake mused. 'I know the answer is around here somewhere, I just have to find it.'

We were both lost in our thoughts for a moment and then Annie came out to join us.

'You're still here,' she smiled at me. 'Would you like some tea? I'm just making a pot for when Amber gets back.'

'Thank you, but no,' I said. 'I really should be going. I've been gone ages. I hope Grandad's all right.'

'I shouldn't worry,' she said. 'Eliot told me he was planning to pop in on his way past. I'm sure he would have let us know if anything was amiss.'

So, Grandad's peaceful afternoon had been interrupted after all. I hoped Eliot had made a point of reassuring him that I had been talking about staying on at the farm.

'Was Eliot all right?' Jake frowned. 'He seemed a bit quiet to me.'

'Lots on his mind, I expect,' said Annie, looking enquiringly at me. 'Affairs of the heart, I reckon.'

I bent to fuss the dog to avoid her eye.

'I should have warned you, Fliss,' said Jake. 'Annie can read minds as well as hearts. You have to be careful what you're thinking around her!'

I hoped he was joking. I didn't need anyone else working out that Eliot and I were trying to maintain a bit of distance.

'As if,' tutted Annie.

'Right,' said Jake, thankfully abandoning the subject. 'Let's get you moving, Fliss.'

He jogged off and reappeared not on foot, but behind the wheel of a green Land Rover. He turned off the engine, jumped out and tossed the keys to me.

'She's a Defender County,' he said, patting the bonnet affectionately, 'a two thousand plate, and Bill's pride and joy.'

'You're kidding,' I gasped, my eyes on stalks. 'She belongs to Grandad?'

'His last big investment and she's as reliable as they come.'

She was also gorgeous and would be a huge help on the farm and in getting me to and from town with fruit for the Cherry Tree.

'What's she doing here?' I asked.

'She's been with us for about a year,' said Annie. 'Once Bill's hip really started to play up, he couldn't get in and out of the cab anymore, so he asked Jake to drive her.'

'He was never going to part with her,' Jake further explained, 'so I said I'd keep her here, out of harm's way in case anyone saw her standing in the yard and took a shine to her.'

'Stole her, you mean?'

'Exactly. Rural crime's big business and I think Bill felt a bit vulnerable having her at the farm and of course, he wanted to keep her running. He's planning to drive her again himself as soon as he can comfortably get in and out, but in the meantime, she's all yours.'

'He wanted my licence to sort the insurance, didn't he?'

'He sure did.'

My hands were shaking as I climbed inside and inhaled the smell all working farm vehicles seemed to have. It was a combination of earth, oil and something indefinable.

'What do you think?' Jake asked, opening the passenger door and depositing a bag into the footwell. 'Everything look familiar?'

'Yes,' I said, checking the dials and switches. 'She's in great condition.'

'She's certainly been loved.'

He was right about that.

'What's in the bag?'

'Just a few bits,' he shrugged. 'I promised Bill a jar of honey.'

'There's more than a jar of honey in there,' I laughed.

'There's some cider,' he reeled off, 'and sausages, a few slices of bacon and a couple of chops, oh and a salve Annie's made to help Bill's scar to heal. She's a bit of a white witch on the side.'

'I can hear you Jake Somerville,' she said. 'If you have to call me anything, I think I prefer healer, if it's all the same to you.'

He looked at me and raised his eyebrows and I turned the engine over.

Having thanked them for lunch, the tour and the Skylark supplies, I set off, under my own steam at last. Grandad was waiting for me, thankfully alone, under the apple tree and his face was a picture when I gave him a blast on the horn.

'What do you think?' he asked.

'I think I'm in love,' I told him, as I jumped out. 'Isn't she a beauty and she drives like a dream.'

'I had a feeling she'd be your sort of vehicle. Jake's been very kind to keep her running and looked after.'

'It seems to me the whole Somerville clan are kind,' I said. 'Wait until you see what he's sent me back with.'

'They're good friends,' he agreed. 'But I've realised recently that as grateful to them, and everyone else who has rallied around me, as I am, there's nothing quite like your own family to look after you, is there?'

Thanks to Mum's letter, I was in a position to begin to appreciate that myself now.

'No,' I said, giving him a warm hug. 'There really isn't.'

Chapter 14

The next day I started strawing long before the sun was up. Grandad and I had let the hens out into their run together, much to the fascination of the cat who sat on the sidelines and watched, her tail swishing. None of the girls paid the slightest attention to her, so after checking I had everything I needed, and that he approved of my straw spreading technique, Grandad ambled back to the house to see to the laundry.

I tackled the task slowly and methodically, knowing there was nothing to be gained from trying to rush. I would only tire all the sooner and with dry days at my disposal there was no need to throw my back out on the first day.

That said, when faced with the field packed full of long rows of plants, it did still feel like a daunting task. I broke the straw bales into around two-kilogram biscuits and then pulled it all into place, ensuring it was deep and wide enough to do the job it was intended for.

Even though I was pacing myself, it was a back-breaking chore and some would argue unnecessary, but with the occasional skylark shooting up out of the leaves and singing overhead to distract me from their nests, I was content enough. I let my mind wander as I worked my way up and down the long, straight rows and the sun appeared over the Fenland horizon. It then rose quickly, taking the temperature with it.

I mulled over the conversation I'd had with Jake and the extremely ambitious idea which had taken hold as a result. I had been considering asking at the pub about bar work to supplement the farm income as I had some experience, or even waitressing at the Cherry Tree with Bec, but if I could get this idea to hatch then I wouldn't need to.

Grandad and I weren't too tight for money (assuming he'd let me spend some of mine) and, if I could convince him to give this project a go before we were, then we might end up far better off. I couldn't help thinking that it felt almost like an answer to a prayer. I'd been wishing for a big idea to land and now it most definitely had.

'Fliss!'

I stood and shielded my eyes from the sun to see Grandad pointing at his wrist. It was time for a break. I hopped over to the next row, which was still straw free and went to join him.

'Doesn't that look grand,' he said, smiling broadly.

I looked at the finished rows and found my smile matching his. I could see the odd bright red berry shining in the sun and knew I would have to start picking properly soon.

'Picture perfect,' I said. 'In fact, I think I'll take a picture on my phone. I want to record every aspect of my first season here on the farm.' I hoped he noted the emphasis I put on first. 'I'll take some of the hens too.'

Along with the arrival of the grand plan, I'd been thinking about setting up an Instagram account to show off the farm's seasonal highlights. If my ambitious idea did come to fruition (pun intended), then it would be good to have an already established social media presence.

'I hope you've got something delicious for elevenses,' I said, as I snapped away and my empty tummy rumbled. 'I'm starving.'

By three o'clock, I'd had enough of work and was ready for a muscle unclenching soak. Over half the field was finished, which was really good going, but I wasn't sure I'd get it all done the next day. Progress would definitely be slower after the initial effort I'd put in, and my back would be groaning when it realised it would have to go through the same exertion again.

'Put a few drops of this in your bath,' said Grandad, handing me a small brown bottle before I went up to the bathroom. 'And some Epsom salts too. They're in the bathroom cupboard. They'll see you right.'

'What is this?' I asked, unscrewing the bottle lid and taking a tentative sniff.

It was surprisingly pleasant. There were hints of lavender and peppermint and possibly some subtle chamomile too.

'It's from Annie,' said Grandad. 'I swear by it.'

'Have you tried the salve that she sent yesterday?' I asked, only just remembering.

'Oh yes,' he said. 'I'd been using it for a while, but I'd run out. It's very good. All of her tinctures and tonics are.'

With such a lofty endorsement, I willingly lowered my aching body into the warm, salt and remedy enhanced bath and let the water gently lap over me. Had it not been for the sound of voices a while later, I might have ended up staying there all night. The water was quite cool as I came to and I realised, I must have drifted off.

'Hello Felicity,' said Louise, when I went back down bare-footed, in my bathrobe and pyjamas and with my hair piled up on top of my head.

I was feeling more than a bit blissed out.

'Hello,' I yawned, before quickly covering my mouth. 'Oh, sorry. I've been strawing up the field today and I'm ready for my bed.'

'I know,' she said. 'Bill's been telling us. He said you've done a fantastic job.'

'It's going well so far, but there's still about half left to do. Fingers crossed I'll break the back of it tomorrow.'

'If it doesn't break yours first,' Louise sagely said.

'Mm,' I agreed. 'Did you say us? Have you got Bec with you?'

'Yes,' she said, 'and Eliot. Bill's taken the pair of them to meet the hens and admire your handiwork too, I shouldn't wonder.'

I sniffed the air.

'Can I smell fish and chips? Or am I hungry enough again to be hallucinating?'

It didn't seem to matter if I was in Puglia or Wynbridge, the fresh country air in both places gave me a consistently healthy appetite.

'It's fish and chips,' Louise confirmed. 'Bec came back with them when she finished at the café and as she'd got enough to feed an army, we thought it would be nice to all eat together.'

I didn't bother getting dressed again, but pushed my feet into my sandals and gave her a hand to set up outside, adding a few bottles of Skylark cider to the tray of cutlery, vinegar, salt and ketchup. Once we'd finished, I pulled the band out of my hair and ran my fingers through it, leaving it loose in the warm evening air.

'And here's my hard-working granddaughter,' Grandad proudly said.

'Crikey Fliss,' said Bec. 'You must be all in. You've gone great guns today.'

'Well,' I said, taking one of the plates Louise was handing around. 'It needed doing and as the weather's so good and there's already a bit of colour showing, I thought I'd best get on with it.'

'She was born to this life,' Grandad said, to my mind standing that little bit taller. 'Even if she was late getting here.'

'Through no fault of her own,' Louise mildly added.

'Oh, I know that,' Grandad responded, but with no rancour as he sat down.

'And thanks to her years in Italy,' Bec grinned, 'she's got some awesome culinary skills and I for one am very grateful for that. Have you heard anything from your Italian family since you've been here, Fliss?'

'Not as far as I know,' I told her. 'I sent them an email from the library a few days ago, but because my phone doesn't pick up a consistent signal here, I don't know if they've emailed back.'

It had been playing on my mind a bit and I hoped the Rossi trio weren't feeling abandoned. I had no intention of disappearing out of their lives for good, but it had been a busy few days. They'd understand that, wouldn't they? The internet in Puglia could be temperamental at times too, so I hoped they were factoring that into their thoughts about my prolonged radio silence.

'I'll try and check again next time I'm in town,' I added.

Eliot opened his mouth to say something, but Bec got in first. I was trying my best not to look at him. He needed a shave I noticed, and wore a day's worth of stubble a little too well.

'And I hear you can get there yourself now,' she nudged, taking a swig of cider. 'The services of the Banana-mobile are no longer required. By the way,' she added, addressing her brother and holding up the bottle for him to see, 'you're driving back tonight.'

'Fine by me,' he muttered.

Grandad caught my eye and winked and I had to bite my lip to stop myself from laughing out loud. I'd completely forgotten our resolve to keep a dry house. It felt good to have an inside joke.

'Oh,' said Grandad, once he'd recovered, 'and talking of your phone signal, Fliss.'

'I was just about to mention that, Bill,' said Eliot, giving Bec a look.

'What about it?' I asked, popping another delicious chip into my mouth.

'We're getting broadband,' Grandad announced. 'Here at the farm.'

'Oh really?' I spluttered, swallowing the chip before I'd properly finished chewing it.

That was music to my ears. It would make keeping in touch with the rest of the world so much easier. I'd be able to video call the Rossis from the comfort of the farm kitchen *and* introduce Grandad to Nonna like I'd thought about before. I'd also be able to keep the fledgling Instagram account updated without any fuss too.

'Yes,' Grandad continued. 'Eliot said it'll be easy enough because we already have a landline and it won't cost much either.'

'What made you change your mind?' I asked, reaching for my cider. 'I thought you were happy to manage without it as you'd never had it.'

As thrilled as I was about getting connected for my own more selfish reasons, I couldn't really see Grandad as an enthusiastic silver surfer type.

'It was my nagging,' Eliot piped up, this time managing to speak without getting cut off. 'I thought you might appreciate it Fliss and I'm going to set Bill up with his own laptop, so he can use it to order his prescriptions and make appointments and perhaps even do the farm banking. You could even get your shopping delivered straight to the farm, Bill.'

Grandad looked mightily impressed, but I wasn't quite so enamoured. What Eliot was suggesting, would make my role as the helpful granddaughter all but redundant. I hoped he wasn't still thinking I was going to leg it and was therefore setting up the internet to give Grandad a backup, because he really didn't need one.

'But I've got the Land Rover now,' I pointed out, trying not to sound peevish. 'So, I can do all those things. I want to do them. And Grandad will be driving himself about again soon, too.'

'All true,' said Eliot, 'but this will keep Bill more independent, even though he is going be driving again, which is no bad thing.'

I couldn't argue with that, I supposed. It would be good for Grandad to be able to properly sail his own ship again. He hadn't said as much, but I knew he'd found it hard relying on the help of others for so long. That said, I didn't think that included help from me.

'And like you said at Skylark, Fliss,' Eliot further added, 'you've got big ideas for this place and you're going to be busy. I reckon Fenview Farm has a bright and exciting future now you're here to steer it in a new direction, but that's going to take up a lot of time. Getting Bill online will free you up a bit and give you more hours to focus on the business.'

Stupid as it was, I felt a bit emotional as I listened to him say that. Not only was he confirming his belief that I was staying put, he was also letting me know that I was up to the job too and that his suggestion to get us online had nothing to do with sidestepping me. Tears pricked my eyes and I tried to blink them away. I don't think I'd even held him in fonder affection than I did in that moment.

There was no hint in any of what he said that I had given him hope of taking our relationship further when I spoke so passionately at Skylark Farm and I can't deny there was a pang of disappointment attached to that realisation. I should have been pleased that he was as committed to keeping us on the straight and narrow as I was, but I wasn't.

At least Grandad looked delighted.

'I'm actually looking forward to it now,' he chuckled. 'It's going to be quite an adventure, I think!'

'You'll have to give Bill a lesson in cyber safety, Eliot,' Louise laughed. 'Otherwise goodness knows where he's going to end up.'

She had a point.

'The engineer will be coming out next week,' Eliot said, turning his attention back to Grandad. 'And when we've finished at the hospital tomorrow Bill, we'll go and see about a laptop. There's a place in town where you can pick up a perfectly decent reconditioned one for a fraction of the price of something brand new.'

Grandad looked even more thrilled.

'I thought I was taking you to the hospital,' I said, quickly recovering. 'I've scheduled the time out into tomorrow's work.'

Eliot shook his head.

'That step into the Land Rover is too high,' he said, 'and then you've got to negotiate getting out at the other end.'

'There are plenty of apple crates kicking around here that we could use as an intermediary step,' I pointed out. 'It will be a darn sight easier than Grandad swinging his leg over the back of your Ducati.'

Everyone was quiet for a moment and then as one we all burst out laughing, our heads filled with an image of Grandad in bike leathers, riding pillion.

'You wouldn't get me on that thing,' he said, taking out his handkerchief to wipe his eyes, 'even without the trick hip.'

Eliot caught my eye and I started laughing again.

'So, what is happening then?' I asked.

'I'm going to lend Eliot my car,' said Bec, 'and I'll come here and help you with the strawing up. If you think I'll be able to get the hang of it, that is. I thought you might fancy a bit of company.'

She had no idea what she was letting herself in for, but she was right. A bit of company, hers especially, would be wonderful and we'd hopefully get through the work all the faster.

'All right,' I agreed. 'Just be prepared for stiff legs and an aching back at the end of the day.'

I could have quite easily taken umbrage that they'd organised things without asking me, but I was well aware that they all had Grandad's best interests at heart and I needed to remember that they had been helping him long before I came on the scene. They weren't meddling, or taking over, they were simply and kindly pulling together, just like the Rossis did in times of need and of course, many hands really did make light work.

I was awake bright and early again the next morning and, having wished Grandad luck for his post-op follow-up appointment at the hospital, I headed to the strawberry field for round two. So immersed in the task in hand, I didn't hear the Banana-mobile arrive but that was probably no bad thing.

Eliot's little speech the evening before, combined with the rugged stubble and dazzling smile he'd bestowed upon me at Skylark Farm, had cranked my feelings for him up another notch and I was really beginning to doubt my ability to keep a lid on them. All the while I'd been thinking that he was the one who needed to get a grip, but actually it turned out, I was having just as much difficulty, if not more, than him.

What I needed was a distraction, something other than the farm. Something that wasn't in any way connected to Eliot. Perhaps a dalliance with someone else would stop my traitorous heart constantly undoing all the good work my head was struggling to do and convince Eliot that I was sticking to our self-imposed rules? It was certainly food for thought.

'How's that?' puffed Bec, stepping back to admire her first attempt after I'd shown her the most efficient way to get the straw from the bale and into the rows. 'I know I'm much slower than you, but that's not too bad, is it?' she asked, pushing her sweaty curls away from her face.

It was already a sweltering day; I'd applied plenty of

sunblock and stripped down to my bikini top and shorts and Bec, with her pale skin, was turning rather pink in spite of the factor fifty. I hoped she wasn't regretting her offer to help.

'Perfect,' I told her, even though some of the straw needed thinning out a bit. 'I think you deserve a strawberry for that, possibly even two.'

She immediately plucked a succulent beauty from the row and popped it in her mouth.

'Oh wow,' she said, practically swooning in the row. 'That's so good. Fenview fruit really is the best.'

'I know,' I winked, picking a berry for myself. 'That's why we're the exclusive suppliers to the best café in Wynbridge and we've got you to thank for that.'

She gave a little curtsy and we both laughed.

'I didn't realise,' she said, looking about her, 'until Bill showed me and Eliot this field last night, just how big the strawberry plot is. How on earth are you going to manage to keep on top of it when you have everything else to do?'

'Well,' I told her, 'I'm a pretty fast picker and I'll only need to go over the rows every other day, so as long as I'm out here every day and working my way through at least half, it should be fine.'

'That's a big commitment.'

'It's life on a fruit farm,' I simply said. 'The season is relatively short, but it's intense when everything starts to come in.'

'You know, if you want an extra pair of hands, you only have to ask. I've only got three shifts a week at the café, so I can always help out here around them.'

'That's really kind, Bec,' I told her. 'But we couldn't afford to pay you.'

'I wasn't expecting you to. That's not why I asked.'

'I'm not sure Grandad would be happy about you working for nothing,' I frowned. 'And I wouldn't be either. Strawberry picking is hard work and if there's no reward at the end of it . . .'

'I'm sure we can come to some arrangement,' she cut in, eagerly loading her fork with straw. 'Perhaps you could pay me in food. That Italian feast you cooked up the other weekend was to die for. I'd pay good money for that and I bet you've got plenty of recipes to turn all this fruit into fine fare, haven't you?'

I thought of Nonna's much-anticipated cherry and almond tart, along with all the other dishes I had at my disposal thanks to her culinary education, and my mouth watered.

'That I have,' I confirmed, and another big idea landed.

The time flew by and it wasn't long before we'd got a system going and the rows were almost complete. We were both ridiculously hot, but with regular breaks and plenty of drinks and chat, we pressed on determined to get finished before Grandad and Eliot arrived.

Not only did working with my new friend make the task more bearable, her presence also stopped me worrying about how Grandad was getting on. I thought he'd made great progress, and so did he, but we weren't the professionals so our opinions didn't count for much.

'That must be them,' said Bec, when we were just half a

row short of finishing and heard a car on the drive. 'I'll keep going and you go and see how they got on. I know it's been on your mind.'

'Thanks,' I said, 'but I'm pretty sure that's not them. It didn't sound like the Banana-mobile horn to me.'

'Oh, that's a point,' Bec frowned. 'It didn't, did it?'

I was just about to walk up the row and retrieve my abandoned shirt when a man appeared around the corner, making me jump.

'Well now,' he called. 'Aren't you a sight for sore eyes?'

'Anthony,' I breathed, crossing my arms. 'Crikey, you made me jump.'

'Sorry,' he said. 'I knocked at the house first, but when there was no answer, I gave a blast on the car horn and ventured down. I hope that was okay?'

I walked towards him and sensing my discomfiture, he picked up my shirt and handed it to me.

'Thanks,' I said, shaking it out.

It was a nightmare to pull on, thanks to the layers of sunscreen and sweat and I could feel my temperature rising even higher as I struggled to force my arms into the sleeves.

'And what about me?' asked Bec, as she finished the final couple of metres of strawing up and tucked her damp curls behind her ears for what must have been the hundredth time. 'Am I a sight for sore eyes, too?'

'Absolutely,' Anthony seriously said. 'You're both a vision of the modern rural idyll.'

'That's all right then,' she smiled.

'So,' I said, giving up on the slippery shirt buttons. 'To what do I owe the pleasure? Is this a social call or are you here to scrump my strawberries?'

Bec let out an inelegant snort and I felt my face flush. Anthony raised his eyebrows and I bit my lip to stop myself from laughing.

'It is a social call,' he grinned, 'but I could go for a strawberry, if that's what's on offer.'

'Why don't you pair go to the house,' suggested Bec, digging me in the back, 'and I'll pick some and bring them around in a minute.'

Anthony and I wandered off towards the yard.

'I see you've got hens,' he said, when the run came into sight.

'Yes,' I said. 'They're new additions. They've only just arrived, but they seem to be settling in okay.'

'A bit like you then,' he said.

I ducked inside the run, lifted the lid on the nest box and found two beautiful eggs.

'Oh, well done, girls,' I said, picking the eggs up. 'That's a very good start.'

I wondered which of the trio was yet to perform. I would have put good money on it being the quiet one, who was hiding behind her larger coop mates.

'Hold these would you?' I asked, handing the eggs to Anthony so I could secure the door again.

When I took them back, I saw he had a dollop of hen poo on his hand.

'Oh god, sorry,' I said, 'you'd better come into the kitchen and wash your hands. It'll set like concrete before you know it.'

Had he been dressed like Grandad, or even Jake, he would have no doubt wiped his hand on his trousers and thought nothing more about it, but Anthony wasn't the type to go around in clothes smeared with chicken poop. His outfit probably cost more than I'd ever earned in a month.

'Can I get you a coffee or something?' I offered once he'd washed his hands and was looking happier again.

'No,' he said, handing me back the towel. 'I better get back to work.'

'Not a very long social call then.'

'Afraid not,' he said.

'I still don't know what it is that you do,' I commented. 'It seemed to take me an age just to find out your name.'

'That's sort of why I'm here.'

'To tell me it's not Anthony Judd, after all?'

'No,' he laughed. 'To speed up us getting to know each other.'

'Oh,' I said. 'And how do you propose to do that?'

'By taking you out to dinner Saturday night.'

'Oh,' I said again.

'Not in Wynbridge,' he added. 'We'll have to go a bit further afield, if we want to eat somewhere special.'

I didn't think I had the right clothes to wear to eat somewhere special, but I did wonder if dining out with Anthony, no strings attached of course, might be just the sort of distraction I had been angling for when thinking about Eliot earlier. If Eliot somehow accidentally on purpose discovered that I had been out with someone else, then that would definitely help keep his feelings for me in check, wouldn't it? And in turn, mine for him, too.

'So,' said Anthony, when I didn't answer. 'Is it a date?'

He really wasn't my type, but that wasn't the point. His timely offer of a dinner date could serve a very useful purpose. I hoped that wasn't too sly of me to think it. For all I knew, he might have been harbouring very different intentions. I would have to make sure I kept things properly platonic between us from the off.

'I'll even tell you what I do for a living and what my favourite colour is, if you like?' he temptingly added.

'What about, whether you're a cat or a dog person?' I quizzed.

'Naturally.'

'Whether you believe in ghosts?'

'Yep.'

'If you could change one thing about yourself, what it would be?'

'All that and a whole lot more,' he promised. 'So, what do you say?'

'In that case, how can I possibly resist?' I grinned. 'I'd love to have dinner with you.'

We sealed the deal by exchanging mobile numbers and then tucked into the strawberries Bec had picked and taken an age to come back with.

'I'd really better go,' he said, once he'd helped polish off the lot.

At least with Bec finally present there was no opportunity for an awkward goodbye kiss.

'What kept you?' I asked her as we waved him off.

'I wanted to give you a bit of time,' she replied, waggling her eyebrows.

'Very tactful.'

'He looked as though he was going to pass out when you sauntered up the row in that top and those low-slung shorts,' she giggled.

'I did not saunter,' I gasped. 'And these aren't low-slung,' I added, hoisting them up, 'they're just a bit too big, that's all.'

'Well, whatever,' she said. 'He *definitely* liked what he saw.'

Given that she'd hinted that her own brother had designs on me the other night, she didn't seem all that bothered about me getting on with Anthony, which was a relief. However, if she was right about Anthony's reaction to seeing me half-dressed, then I was going to have to be mindful of any misleading flirting.

I'd showered and changed by the time Eliot and Grandad got back and so had Bec. She'd borrowed an oversized T-shirt and pair of shorts and I was relieved to find that my muscles felt nowhere near as stiff as they had the day before.

Not only had Bec done more than her share of the work, I must have also been more relaxed while I did mine. Working with her had been a total tonic and I was grateful for her company.

'So,' I said to Grandad. 'How did you get on?'

'Absolutely fine,' he proudly said. 'They were thrilled with the progress I've made, weren't they Eliot?'

'They were,' his friend confirmed, that gorgeous smile that I was trying not to think about firmly in place. 'The consultant said you looked like a new man, didn't he?'

'He did,' said Grandad. 'And I feel like one too. And,' he added, 'we've just picked up this new-fangled contraption, by way of celebration.'

The contraption in question was a laptop.

'I'll come and set it up at the weekend,' said Eliot. 'If that's all right?'

'Saturday night?' Grandad suggested.

'Perfect,' said Eliot.

It was perfect too, because Eliot would find out about my dinner date. But what on earth was I going to wear?

I was already planning to pick and take the ripened strawberries to the Cherry Tree Café the next day, so I could have a look in town then. I didn't think a little retail therapy would go amiss and I'd maybe wear Mum's bangles for luck. She was always a savvy shopper. And I could ask if I could check my emails in the library too. I was certain I would have a reply from Marco waiting for me. I only hoped it was an understanding one.

Chapter 15

The next morning, there were enough ripe strawberries to fill two trays and I carefully lifted them into the back of the Land Rover with a more surging sense of pride than I'd ever experienced before. Sure, I'd helped pick and transport tonnes of fruit over the years, but none of it had been grown on my own family farm.

This was going to be a very special delivery indeed, and with that knowledge making my chest swell and the comfort of some of Mum's many bangles familiarly jangling on my wrists, I turned on my phone and took another couple of photos to record the moment for posterity.

'More pictures,' chuckled Grandad as he came to look at what I was up to. 'I'll have to make sure I'm always looking my best at this rate, in case you get me in the corner of any of your snaps.'

'I can do better than that!' I told him.

I switched the camera to selfie mode and took a few shots with us both in the frame. Then I took a couple of him on his own, holding one of the packed punnets of strawberries.

'How's that?' I asked, showing him the results.

'Really lovely,' he nodded. 'That's a very clever phone you've got there, Fliss.'

I passed it to him and he looked more closely at the images.

'Do you know,' he said, his tone a little emotional, 'you look just like your grandmother.'

'Do I?'

I took the phone back again and looked at myself with fresh eyes.

'Yes,' he said. 'You do. I've got some albums in the house somewhere. I'll have to find them when we get back and then you'll be able to see the resemblance for yourself.'

'I'd really like that,' I told him, before I realised what he'd said. 'Are you coming to town with me, then?'

He did look a bit spruced up. He'd changed out of his work gear and into the obligatory 'farmer goes to town' outfit. In my experience, it was mostly reserved for market days and meetings at the bank.

'Yes,' he said. 'I've got an appointment with my solicitor *and* the bank manager, so we'd better get a move on. The solicitor in particular is a stickler for punctuality.'

'Right,' I said. 'Fair enough. I'll just get my bag and lock up and then we'll find a way to get you in and out of the Land Rover that Eliot would approve of.'

'I rather liked your apple crate idea.'

I rather liked it too because by the time I'd finished in

the house, Grandad had fetched one and, having checked the strength of it by standing on it myself, he then easily stepped up and into his beloved Land Rover. I put the crate in the back with the fruit, so he could get out again, and we were off.

'I knew that would work,' he said, with a satisfied look and I can't deny I felt rather chuffed.

I parked in the space closest to Miller, Moffat and Matthews, the only solicitors in Wynbridge, and arranged to meet Grandad in the same spot a couple of hours later. He would have finished at the bank by then too. I had offered to attend that appointment with him, but he said he was keeping me up his sleeve for future appointments. Whatever that meant.

'If I'm finished before you,' he told me, 'I'll go and have a coffee in the pub, so don't worry about rushing.'

'All right,' I said, looking over at The Mermaid with its many floral baskets and tubs. 'I haven't been in there yet, so I might be late on purpose just so I have to come and find you.'

Grandad laughed and I crossed the road to the Cherry Tree, carefully carrying the treasured trays of fruit. Jemma spotted me through the window and quickly opened the door.

'Well,' she said, her eyes lighting up, 'this is a surprise.'

'I know you weren't expecting any yet,' I said, following her inside and handing over the trays, 'but this lot were keen to ripen and I felt sure you'd be able to rustle something up.'

It was a monumental moment and when I explained to her just how significant it was for me on a personal level, she looked quite moved. It was all I could do to stop myself from welling up too, but I managed it. Just.

'In that case,' she said, putting the trays down and giving me a hug, 'I'll definitely make the most of them.' She looked thoughtful for a moment. 'Do you know,' she mused, 'I'm going to keep it simple to kick the season off. I'm going to advertise that we've got fresh local strawberries, naming the farm of course, and I'm going to serve them with meringue pieces and vanilla cream. Give it an hour of chalking that on the board and I'll be inundated.'

I didn't doubt it. My mouth was watering and I'd already eaten my fill that morning as I was picking.

'Do you want me to pay you for them now?' she asked.

'Oh no,' I said. 'We don't want anything for these as you didn't ask for them. Consider this lot a sort of try before you buy.'

She looked at the trays filled with the perfect, plump fruit and shook her head.

'No way,' she said. 'I'll do you a deal. Are you in town for a bit?'

'A little while, yes.'

'In that case, come back later and I'll give you something sweet for the weekend in lieu of cash.'

'All right,' I agreed. 'Thank you.'

'No,' she said with emphasis. 'Thank you.'

I took a couple more snaps on my phone, this time with Jemma posing instead of Grandad, and was just about to leave when a thought occurred.

'You don't happen to know anywhere in Wynbridge where I might find a dress I could wear to go out in the evenings, do you?'

'What's the occasion?' she keenly asked.

'Nothing specific,' I fibbed, because I didn't have time to go into details.

However, I was surprised and a little disappointed that Bec hadn't shared news of my imminent dinner date. If she hadn't mentioned it to Jemma, she probably hadn't talked about it at home either. I would definitely have to make sure Grandad was on the case when Eliot came to set up his laptop.

'But I haven't got anything smart here and you never know,' I further said to Jemma.

'It doesn't hurt to be prepared, does it?'

'Exactly.'

'I'd give Bella's Boutique a try,' she suggested. 'She has all sorts of lovely stuff.'

Armed with detailed directions, I left Jemma preparing her first Fenview Farm fruit delivery and went in search of Bella's. It was tucked away in a little courtyard, along with a bookshop, music shop, jewellers and a tiny antique store. Had Jemma not told me exactly where to look, I never would have found it. I wondered if the shops ever did any business and didn't really hold out much hope for finding what I wanted.

If only Eliot had talked Grandad into getting the farm web connected sooner, I could have ordered online for next day delivery. I glanced around the courtyard again. Perhaps

I would have been better off going straight to the library and asking if I could log on to a computer again. I could quickly check my emails *and* peruse the clothing sites there.

'Good morning,' said a woman, stepping out of the boutique just as I was about to turn away.

She was in her fifties and smartly dressed in a layered linen outfit with cropped grey hair and colourful statement jewellery.

'I'll just finish putting these out,' she said, arranging some pretty planted containers and a tiny metal table and two chairs, 'and I'll be right with you.'

'Thank you,' I said, stepping around her and inside because it would have been more awkward to walk away.

The shop was far larger than I expected and packed to the gunnels. As well as outfits arranged along the rails in rainbow colour formation, there were myriad accessories, shoes and scarves. It was very lovely, but I still didn't think there would be anything for me.

'So,' said the woman, as she stepped back in and closed the door. 'Welcome to Bella's Boutique. I'm Bella and this is Princess.'

Princess was a pure West Highland White Terrier, with a pair of bright eyes and a cute button nose. She looked like a well-groomed teddy bear and had impeccable manners.

'Pleased to meet you, Bella and Princess,' I said, feeling warmed by their welcome but increasingly scruffy in my work gear.

'What a fabulous collection of bangles,' gasped Bella.

'Thank you,' I smiled, feeling warmer still. 'They were my mum's.'

'They're stunning,' she nodded. 'Your mother has impeccable taste.'

'Yes,' I agreed.

'Are you looking for something in particular?' she then asked, taking me in. 'You're a size ten, right?'

'I'm almost always a twelve,' I told her. 'Depending on the cut.'

In my early twenties I had been a consistent ten, but all the time spent eating in Nonna's kitchen had added a few lingering pounds, in spite of the physical work involved on the farm. I was grateful for the hard toil though. Had I not had the benefit of it, all those calories she loved to fill me up with would have stuck fast.

'And I need something for a dinner date,' I added. 'Somewhere special.'

'Somewhere special,' Bella repeated, sliding on her glasses which hung on a chain around her neck. 'Give me a moment, I think I have just the thing.'

I was pretty certain that she wouldn't, but I politely waited while she disappeared through a curtain into what I guessed was her stock-room.

'What about this?' she asked, dashing back and presenting a dress with a flourish. 'Isn't it perfect?'

To my surprise and delight, it was just what I was looking for. A simple, black Bardot midi dress which fit and skimmed in all the right places.

'There,' she said, standing back, once she'd zipped me into it. 'Oh, hold on.'

She went back to the till and returned with a large tortoiseshell patterned hair claw.

'I know it doesn't match, but just put your hair up so it's off your shoulders,' she urged, looking at my reflection in the mirror, 'then we'll get an even better idea.'

Lifting my hair further enhanced the vision and I was amazed to see myself looking so chic.

'Shoes,' said Bella, whizzing off again.

'Size six,' I called after her.

'Funnel heeled, platform toe with a rounded tip. I have these in black, mustard and red.'

The pair I slid my feet into were black.

'I rather like the red,' she said. 'But these are probably the more sensible choice.'

Suddenly, I didn't feel much like being sensible.

'Can I try the red?'

Finished with a small red clutch, I felt transformed. Gone was the girl with fruit juice stained hands and denim cut-offs and, in her place, stood someone elegant and sophisticated. Still with slightly pink fingers, but even so. I wasn't sure I knew who the person looking back at me was.

'A nice pair of earrings to finish it off,' Bella nodded, 'and you'll be all set. I can do you a deal if you take the dress, shoes and the bag. I'll give you a minute to think it over.'

She twitched the dressing room curtain closed and I swished this way and that before looking at the price tags.

Even with a discount, the dress was a bit out of my league. It wasn't extortionate, but as I was watching the pennies, I couldn't really justify spending quite so much on just one outfit.

Feeling disappointed, I slid off the shoes and unclipped my hair.

'So, what do you think?' Bella asked, when I emerged dressed in my everyday clothes. 'Are you going to go for it?'

'I would love to,' I sadly said. 'But I don't think I can really afford it. I'm sorry to have wasted your time.'

'I haven't told you what the discount is yet,' she warmly smiled.

'I know,' I said, 'and I really appreciate you offering me one, but I'm going to have to leave it for today.'

'All right,' she said kindly. 'But it will all be here if you change your mind.'

I appreciated that she wasn't rankled, but I left feeling rather down in the dumps and rushed over to the library where I had to wait to speak to Grandad's friend before I could log on to a computer. I wasn't going to have time to look for anything online now, so I would either have to cancel my plans with Anthony or ask if he would be willing to dial down the 'special' and replace it with a bar meal. I had a couple of cotton summer dresses that would pass muster in the pub.

Mindful of the time, once seated, I quickly logged into my email account. Just as I'd hoped, there was a reply from Puglia and I braced myself to read it. I hadn't even got through the first couple of sentences, before I realised that my fears that the Rossi relatives would feel abandoned were entirely without merit.

Marco wrote how his father and Nonna had given him a talking to after I'd gone and once he had stopped sulking and properly taken onboard the importance of me embracing my new life at Fenview Farm, he had knuckled down, got to grips with my role and thrown himself into it. The very end of the email soon set my tears flowing.

This from Papà . . .

Marco signed off and Alessandro took over.

> Darling Fliss, you will be delighted to read that Marco is completely committed and working diligently every day. I know it's early days, but so far, everything is running like clockwork and even though we miss having you here, we are managing, so it's fresh starts all round. I hope that is a comfort to you and allows you to carry on with your new life, with your family, without worrying about us.

I didn't have a tissue, so wiped away the silent tears which slid down my cheeks with the back of my hand, hoping no one would notice what a state I was in. The relief I felt was immense and I was in no way prepared for the wave of emotion it unleashed.

Again, I wished the internet had been connected at the

farm earlier so I could have sobbed in private. I sniffed hard and blinked, trying to compose myself, but I couldn't seem to stop and reading on didn't help at all.

> And before you are feeling completely redundant our dear Fliss, both Marco and I know only too well that we wouldn't be managing at all if you hadn't done such an amazing job in setting everything up. You have established something wonderful and unique for Nonna and us to carry on with and for our guests to enjoy. We will always be grateful for the wonderful legacy you have left us.

More tears fell as I clicked on the attachment and an image of Nonna, Alessandro and Marco standing together and smiling out at me filled the screen. They were in the orchard, under the very tree where I had read Mum's life-changing letter.

I wondered if Marco had remembered the significance of the spot or if it was just a coincidence. Without meaning to, I let out a little sob.

'Fliss,' said a voice behind me and a whole bundle of tissues appeared over my shoulder. 'Take these.'

I quickly grasped them and noisily blew my nose.

'Thank you,' I croaked, turning to find Eliot, of all people, standing right behind me.

'Oh Fliss,' he said again, having taken in the state of my face. 'What on earth's happened?'

He dragged over a chair and sat beside me, shielding me from the curious looks of the other library users.

'Nothing bad,' I said, shaking my head.

'Well, thank goodness for that,' he smiled. 'Although if this is how you react to good news . . .'

I found my lips curving into a smile. I supposed my reaction was a bit extreme, but I couldn't have lessened it if I'd tried.

'This is the Rossis,' I said, nodding at the screen, 'who I lived with in Puglia. My darling Nonna, her son Alessandro and grandson, Marco.'

Eliot leant further in.

'No wonder you're crying,' he tutted. 'Fancy leaving behind a hunk like that.'

'Don't be silly,' I said, beginning to feel better. 'Marco's like a brother to me. Or did you mean Alessandro?'

Eliot looked relieved that I had made a joke.

'The silver fox of course,' he grinned. 'Seriously though, don't let Bec see this. Marco is just her type.'

'Is he?' I asked, looking at the screen with fresh eyes.

'She'd fall into a dead faint if she caught sight of him.'

I mopped up the last of my tears, wiping away the final traces of mascara and shut down the email.

'Feeling better now?' Eliot asked.

'Yes,' I said. 'Sorry.'

'Don't apologise,' he said wheeling his chair closer still and putting an arm around my shoulders. 'I can't even begin to imagine how you're managing to cope so well with everything you've got going on in your life right now, Fliss.'

'It has been a bit full-on recently,' I conceded.

'A bit,' he smiled.

'All right, more than a bit.'

'And you know, I'd do anything I could to help you, don't you?'

He leant in and softly kissed my cheek and I felt my heart start to clamour. If I turned my face, just the slightest bit, our lips would be just millimetres apart. It would be stupid to do it, but I was going to. I was powerless to resist and if I leant in just a little further still . . .

'Is everything all right over here?' came a voice behind us. 'Eliot?'

'Yes,' he said, clearing his throat, backing his chair away and taking his luscious, soft lips with him. 'Thank you, Miriam. Everything's fine.'

Everything was *not* fine thanks to Miriam's interruption. I was pretty certain Grandad's friend wouldn't have ruined the moment on purpose, but then I came to and realised that Miriam had actually just saved my bacon and stopped me making a gargantuan gaffe.

'Thanks for the tissues,' I said to Eliot, reaching for my bag. 'I'll see you later.'

I didn't give him the chance to say anything further. I dashed out of the door and went straight back to Bella's. I needed that date with Anthony more than ever now and I was going to look my very best for it, whatever the cost. The shock of what I'd almost just done ensured I was dry-eyed by the time I burst back into the boutique.

'You've changed your mind,' Bella beamed, not noticing my red-rimmed eyes. 'I knew you would.'

In fact, she'd been so sure, that she'd got everything boxed, wrapped and in a bag *and* she'd applied a generous discount, along with a very pretty hair slide.

'You're going to absolutely knock their socks off,' she winked once the transaction was complete and she handed over the bags.

'I certainly hope so,' I told her, feeling determined.

Grandad was waiting next to the Land Rover when I finally got back to the market square.

'Sorry I've taken so long,' I puffed.

'You're fine,' he said. 'I haven't been finished all that long. Are you all right? You look a bit flustered.'

'I'm okay,' I insisted. 'Just a bit hot from all the rushing about, that's all.'

'Do you need more time? I didn't realise you had so much to do.'

'No, I'm sorted now. Did you get everything done that you wanted?'

'Oh yes,' he said. 'All sewn up at the solicitors and the bank manager was sympathetic too. He wouldn't extend the overdraft, but in view of the new contract, he was happy to give us until the end of the year to start making a dent in it.'

'That's wonderful news,' I practically cheered.

'He's also looking forward to finding out what your big ideas are too,' Grandad smiled. 'So, I hope you've been giving them some thought, my girl.'

'Don't worry,' I grinned. 'I have.'

'That's all right then,' he nodded. 'And I bumped into Eliot too.'

'Oh, did you?' I casually asked, as I opened the back door of the Land Rover and carefully placed my bags inside. 'I bet he wanted to know how you'd got here, didn't he?'

'He did and I told him.'

'What did he say to that?'

'After the success of the hospital appointment, he said he thought it was no bad thing that I was upping the activity and stretching a bit more and that the apple crate was just the thing.'

'Well, that's all right then,' I nodded. 'I always knew it would be.'

'And he's definitely coming to set my laptop up tomorrow night and he's offered to cook dinner too, if that's all right with you.'

'That's fine by me,' I said, 'but I won't be there, I'm afraid.'

'Won't be there?'

'No,' I said. 'I'm going out for dinner.'

'Oh,' said Grandad, sounding shocked. 'Anywhere nice?'

'I have no idea,' I told him. 'It's a surprise.'

'Who are you going with? Is it Bec?'

'No,' I secretively said. 'It's a chap I met in town the day I arrived. He's very nice and don't worry, he'll have me home before his car turns into a pumpkin.'

'I see,' said Grandad, looking slightly perplexed. 'I didn't realise you knew anyone here other than the Randalls and Somervilles.'

'And the Cherry Tree ladies,' I reminded him. 'But he's nothing to do with them either.'

'Right.'

'Now,' I said, thinking I'd given him more than enough intriguing information to let Eliot know I had intentions elsewhere, 'do you want to go to the pub?'

'Not now,' he said, wincing as he eased himself up and into the Land Rover. 'I just want to get home, if that's all right.'

He did look tired.

'Of course,' I said, picking up the crate. 'You sit tight while I run over to the Cherry Tree. Jemma's promised us something sweet for the weekend.'

'How did she like the strawberries?'

'She was thrilled with them,' I told him, with another grin. 'But then she would be, wouldn't she? You can't beat any of the fruit from Fenview Farm.'

'That you can't!' he smiled back.

Chapter 16

True to her word, Jemma sent Grandad and I back to the farm with the most delicious treat – a full afternoon tea for two, complete with local cream, some of our very own strawberries transformed by her meringues and a delectable array of both sweet and savoury treats.

We ate it all as soon as we got back, and as a result neither of us were good for any further activity and spent a lazy few hours under the apple tree in the garden. Unbidden, my mind kept wandering back to the almost kiss with Eliot in the library, but I determinedly swapped it out for thoughts of the beautiful dress hanging in my room. I was tempted to try the whole outfit on again, but didn't dare risk it with a belly full of carbs!

I woke early on Saturday and felt jittery all day. It had been a long time since I had been on a date, and never a faux one, and the fact that this one required a certain amount of preparation and smart new clothes made it all the more nerve-wracking.

I had a long run early in the day, followed by a shower and then another trip to Wynbridge where I stocked up on groceries and a new nail polish. Once back at the farm, I calmed my nerves the only way I knew how – in the kitchen.

'Is all of this for just the two of us?' asked Grandad, when he came in from cleaning out the hens.

'Pretty much,' I said, looking at the very British selection of savoury flans, sausage rolls, cheese scones and straws filling the table.

'I'll be the size of the barn by the time I've eaten my way through this lot,' he commented, pinching a still warm cheese straw. 'And the doc will be moaning about my weight again.'

He chewed for a few seconds and nodded appreciatively. 'But never mind,' he smiled. 'These are a bit different. What's in them?'

'Smoked bacon, cheddar and a little paprika,' I reeled off.

'Very moreish,' he said, leaning in for another, but I batted his hand away.

'They're supposed to be for the freezer,' I told him. 'All of it is really.'

Fresh homemade desserts were my real passion, but there was more to my current cooking marathon than taking my mind off my dinner date and satisfying my sweet tooth.

'Well,' said Grandad. 'I did wonder. Not that we couldn't eat our way through this lot in one sitting, but for a minute there I thought you'd forgotten Eliot was cooking tonight.'

How could I possibly have forgotten that?

'No,' I said, 'I haven't forgotten. This is all for when the harvest is properly in full swing. The last thing either of us will want to do then is too much cooking. This will be ready and waiting when we want it and it will fill us up too.'

'That's a very good idea,' Grandad nodded. 'In the past, it was always the wives who came out to feed the troops at mealtimes during harvest, especially on the arable farms. I suppose times have changed a bit now and the women are as likely to be driving the machines as slaving over the stove.'

'That's true,' I agreed. 'I know Mum never used to help out here, but what about Nana?'

'Oh yes, Felicity did,' said Grandad, sneaking another straw. 'We always worked together. We were equals in the farm *and* in the house. She used to work on the market in town during the winter months while I was here and then it was my responsibility to have dinner on the table and run the vacuum about.'

I was impressed.

'Although, I never got the hang of ironing,' he reminisced. 'I could do everything else, but not that. I did try many times, but I was never any good at it.'

'Me neither,' I laughed.

While I bagged and labelled everything for the freezer, cutting the flans into meal size portions so we wouldn't be defrosting them whole and then eating them for days on end, Grandad sought out the photo albums he had mentioned the day before.

By the time I needed to start getting ready, I felt as though I had been whizzed through an emotional spin cycle. There were albums going as far back as my great-grandparents and it was wonderful to have the visual blanks finally filled in.

'You're right, Grandad,' I said, picking out a photo of my namesake. 'Even I can see it, in spite of my different colouring. I do look like her, don't I?'

'Yes,' said Grandad. 'You can keep that one out if you like.'

'I'd rather have this one,' I said, swapping it for another.

It was of him and Nana on their wedding day, standing outside a church in Wynbridge flanked by their respective parents.

'Look at this one of your mother,' chuckled Grandad, as he turned a page. 'It wasn't even all that cold!'

The snap was of Mum standing in the yard I now knew so well, in the snow. She looked as though she was wrapped in a hundred layers and had the biggest scowl on her face.

'How old is she there?' I asked.

'Seven or eight I reckon,' Grandad tutted, 'and she didn't build that snowman. She just stood there looking miserable and moaning to come back indoors while I did it.'

'Given her obvious aversion to the cold, it's no wonder we only ever visited the UK in the summer. For the rest of the year she always opted for far sunnier climes.'

I helped put the albums away and felt another connecting layer adhering itself to the one I'd already established since I arrived. Fenview Farm was truly beginning to feel like my home now, the place where I was the perfect fit, even though until just a few weeks ago, I'd never even heard of it.

'You'll have to show me more of the photos on your

phone,' said Grandad, as he pulled me to my feet and I closed the sideboard door. 'Although, I daresay you haven't got any pictures of when you were little on it, have you?'

It was then I realised that Grandad had just as many blanks to fill in as I did.

'No,' I said. 'Afraid not, but I have lots of Italy. I'd love to show you those.'

Having looked at the photo Marco had sent, it felt all the more important that I should incorporate the Rossi family into my life at Fenview. In fact, the time to finally make Nonna's beloved cherry and almond tart felt so close, I could almost taste it.

Having washed my hair the night before so it would be easier to pin up, I had a bubble bath and quick manicure. The new polish went on easily enough as I'd gone for clear because I'd never been any good at painting my nails, and then I put on some make-up.

I'd never mastered the dramatic winged eyeliner technique some of the Rossi cousins favoured, but I managed a pretty enough smoky eye and enough liner to complete the look. Once I had zipped myself into the dress, I added a sweep of red lipstick, and a spritz of perfume for good measure.

I slipped on the shoes and picked up the clutch, then turned one way and then the other in front of the bedroom mirror. Once I was satisfied that I looked, and felt, the best I ever had, I stepped out on to the landing and promptly bumped straight into Grandad. He looked at me for a moment as if he couldn't quite believe his eyes.

'My goodness me,' he gasped. 'I hardly recognised you, Fliss.'

'I hardly recognise myself,' I laughed.

'You always look beautiful,' he kindly said, 'you have the Brown genes, after all, but I'm used to seeing you in your work gear.'

'I'd better give you a twirl then,' I said, turning on the spot. 'This might be the one and only time I look like this.'

'You look stunning,' he said, once I'd finished. 'But there's something missing. Come with me.'

I followed him into his room where he opened the dressing table drawer and took out a jewellery box. He set it down on the bed and beckoned me over.

'These,' he said, presenting me with a small velvet box, 'belonged to your great-grandmother. Your mum's gran, that is. They were a ruby wedding present from your great-grandfather. Felicity never wore them,' he sighed. 'She was saving them for our ruby wedding, but of course, she sadly wasn't here for that.'

I sat on the bed, took the box and carefully opened it. Nestled inside, on pale pink silk, were two round ruby studs, surrounded by diamonds.

'Oh, my goodness,' I gulped as the overhead light caught them and they sparkled, sending myriad patterns dancing around the walls. 'They're exquisite. Are they real?'

'Of course,' Grandad smiled. 'And they'll go perfectly with your outfit.'

I felt my phone suddenly vibrate in my bag which was on the bed next to me. It was a shock because it had never gone off in the house before, but in view of the conversation Grandad and I were having, I ignored it.

'They would look amazing,' I agreed, imagining the look and feel of them as I tried to hand the box back to Grandad, 'but I can't possibly wear them.'

'Of course, you can,' he insisted, putting his hands behind his back. 'Besides, they're yours now and I don't hold any truck with saving things for best, not anymore, not since I lost your grandmother and now your mum. For all we know, this right now, this very moment, might be the *best* we've been waiting for or that we'll get.'

His words caused a lump to form in my throat. I looked at the earrings again. Having lost Mum at such a young age, I sadly understood exactly what he meant. One day, I wouldn't have any more tomorrows, so what was the point in holding out? From now on, if an opportunity presented itself, I was going to take it. Or in this case, wear it.

My phone buzzed again.

'Almost everything in this box belongs to you now,' said Grandad, picking up a sophisticated looking watch. 'That, in part, was what I went to talk to my solicitor about.'

'I don't know what to say,' I swallowed.

'You don't have to say anything, but get those earrings on quick,' he urged. 'That's probably your date who keeps making your phone go off. You don't want to keep him waiting, do you?'

'No,' I said, my hands shaking as I put the earrings in.

'There,' said Grandad, looking from one ear to the other. 'Just the ticket.'

I leant forward and looked in the dressing table mirror. He was right, they did look wonderful.

'What if I lose them?' I nervously asked.

'You won't lose them,' Grandad tutted.

'Well, what about you?' I asked. 'Are you going to wear that watch?'

'Not today,' he said, turning it over. 'But at some point, I certainly intend to.'

'Is it a Rolex?' I asked.

It looked very old but in wonderful condition.

'Yes,' he said. 'Passed down from Brown father to son and worth a pretty penny, so I've been told. I know I just said we shouldn't save things for best, but you wouldn't catch me picking fruit with this on my wrist.'

'In that case, don't you think it should be somewhere a bit more secure than your dressing table drawer?'

'This is where it has always been kept,' he said. 'Now, look lively or you'll be late.'

'Are you not coming down?' I asked, picking up my bag. 'What time's Eliot getting here?'

'He'll be a little while yet.'

It was a shame he wasn't going to arrive in time to see me leave. Seeing me step out, as Nonna always said, with another man, would show him that I was every bit as capable as him at keeping my feelings in check.

'You have a lovely evening and I'll see you later,' Grandad kindly said. 'I'm going to get showered, so lock the door and put the key back through the letterbox for me would you, there's a love?'

I kissed him lightly on the cheek so as not to leave a lipstick mark.

'Thank you,' I said, touching the rubies again.

'Don't keep fiddling with them,' he scolded. 'Otherwise you will lose them.'

I locked the farmhouse door and posted the key back through as Grandad had requested and then checked my phone. There was a voicemail message from Anthony apologising that he might be a few minutes late.

I sat under the apple tree, wondering if Eliot might actually arrive first, but it was Anthony's Audi which swung into the yard. When he spotted me, he yanked off his sunglasses and jumped out of the car. For a second, he didn't say anything, but the expression on his face more than justified the amount of money I'd spent on my outfit. It was a shame he was the only guy who was going to see it.

'Wow,' he said, sounding a little dazed, before walking over and kissing my cheek. He smelt divine, but there were no fluttery tummy fireworks, like when Eliot was in such close proximity. 'You look absolutely beautiful, Fliss.'

'You don't scrub up so bad yourself,' I smiled, although of course he always looked smart so his transformation was nowhere near as surprising as mine.

'What this old thing,' he joked as we walked over to the car.

He opened the passenger door and I sat on the edge of the seat before swinging my legs in. It felt completely alien, trying to embrace a touch of elegance. I had no hope of keeping it up all evening.

'So,' I said, discreetly touching the rubies, just to make sure they were still there, 'where exactly are we going?'

The restaurant was over an hour's drive away, but Anthony promised it would be worth the journey, and the warm reception he received when we arrived suggested that he was a regular guest.

The conversation between us in the car had flowed easily – mostly small talk – but it became a little stilted once we were seated and had listened to the waiter running through the elaborate and, to my mind, extortionately expensive, menu. I knew it was expensive because my menu didn't have any prices on.

'Is this all right?' Anthony asked, looking at me in concern, once the waiter had gone. 'It was the best place I could think of. I've always got on well here before.'

He'd obviously gone to a lot of trouble to make an impression, so I could hardly tell him the restaurant felt out of my league and I was worried about using the wrong fork. I was completely out of my comfort zone but then I remembered why I had accepted his invitation, as well as the conversation we had had in the farm kitchen.

He'd promised to tell me all about himself and I knew I was up to listening to that, even if I couldn't order half the dishes because I couldn't pronounce them. I took a deep breath, phased out the upmarket ambience and focused solely on him.

'It's wonderful,' I smiled, taking a sip of the water that had been poured during the waiter's lengthy monologue. 'I'm just feeling a little impatient, that's all.'

'Impatient?'

'Yes,' I said, looking straight at him. 'We've been in each other's company for a couple of hours now and I still don't know if you're a cat or dog person, if you believe in ghosts or what your favourite colour is.'

Anthony's shoulders relaxed and he shook his head.

'Oh god,' he grinned. 'It's a disaster, isn't it?'

'Total tragedy,' I said, playing along.

'I should have at least told you what I'd like to change about myself by now, shouldn't I?'

'At the *very* least,' I pouted.

'Well, it's your fault,' he shot back. 'Had you not looked so beautiful against the backdrop of that shabby old farm, then I would have been able to stay on track, wouldn't I?'

'Hey,' I said, more than half meaning it. 'Less of the shabby, thank you very much. That's my heritage you're talking about.'

He held up his hands, half apology, half surrender.

'But I suppose you're right,' I cheekily agreed. 'I am a total vision, so it's only natural that the backdrop didn't look its best. Or,' I frowned, 'do I mean that I looked my best because the backdrop was a bit rough around the edges. That's unsettling.'

We both laughed and I felt heaps better. I wasn't even bothered by the looks our laughter attracted from the other diners.

'You were right first time,' Anthony said. 'You are a total vision.'

'Phew,' I said. 'That's all right then.'

'God,' he said, fixing me with a stare that was suddenly serious, 'you really are a breath of fresh air.'

Grandad had said that too, but he hadn't meant it in the same way Anthony did.

'You're nothing like the girls I usually go out with,' he carried on.

'Lots of them, are there?'

'You know what I mean.'

He was nothing like the guys I usually went out with either, not that there had been many, and I felt rather bad that I was out with him with an ulterior motive. I would have to tread carefully now he had showed his hand. I didn't want him feeling that I had used him, even if that was in part, what I was doing. Suddenly, I didn't feel quite so good about myself.

'And is that a compliment?' I swallowed.

'Oh yes,' he said, his gaze shifting to my lips, 'it is. A glowing commendation. Shall we have some champagne?'

'But you've got to drive back,' I reminded him.

'We'll get a taxi,' he shrugged.

I was about to say it would cost a fortune, but checked myself. Anthony didn't strike me as the type of guy who worried all that much about money.

'Champagne would be wonderful,' I therefore said instead.

The food was delicious, but there was nothing local and the portions were tiny. I didn't say as much obviously, because it was high-end fine dining, not a pie in the pub, but even so, I knew I would be making a sandwich before I went to bed.

'So,' I said, as Anthony refilled my glass from our second bottle of champagne. 'That's green for me, red for you. Dogs for you because cats are too independent and both for me. What about ghosts?'

'Bugger ghosts.'

'Excuse me.'

'I want to know more about you, Fliss.'

'Isn't that the whole point of this rapid-fire Q and A?'

'You know what I mean.'

'I thought your sources back in Wynbridge had already filled you in.'

'They don't know *everything*, obviously.'

'We haven't got time for *everything*,' I batted back, feeling a little dizzy from the conversational back and forth as well as the bubbles.

'Give me the potted history then. The bits you consider most important.'

I drank some more champagne and gave him a very brief lowdown on my childhood, life with Mum in Italy, her death and my subsequent arrival in Wynbridge. I stuck to the facts, which perhaps came across as a little cold in bullet point format, but with a belly full of fizz, I wasn't going to risk taking the emotional, and potentially tearful, route.

'Finding out about Fenview must have been a dream come true, considering your passion for fruit farming,' Anthony shrewdly said.

'It really was.'

'So, tell me more about that,' he sounded genuinely interested. 'Your eyes light up whenever you mention the place. What's going on there? Have you got plans for it?'

My fingers reached for the ruby earrings and my mind tracked back to the idea I'd had for the barn and the exciting future I envisaged for it.

I might have been feeling tipsy but my inhibitions weren't so lowered that my big idea was up for discussion. Grandad would be the first person to hear it, because he was the only person whose opinion mattered when it came to farm business.

'I have got plans,' I confirmed, 'but I'm not ready to talk about them yet.'

'Fair enough,' Anthony shrugged. 'I just hope they don't involve that big barn.'

It was the first time my heart had raced all evening.

'The barn?'

'Um,' he said. 'I noticed it when I called in before. The roof looks a little dipped, which made me wonder if the structure's sound.'

'Oh,' I swallowed.

It had seemed fine to me, but I'd have to check it out properly now.

'But never mind about that,' Anthony carried on. 'Tell

me about Eliot Randall. Have you factored him into your grand scheme?'

'Eliot?' I asked, puzzled. I hadn't even realised he would know who Eliot was. 'No, should I have done?'

Anthony sat back in his chair and let out a long breath, then sat forward again and steepled his hands. His change of demeanour didn't strike confidence and I wondered what on earth he was going to say.

'Given the circumstances,' he said, 'I think you probably should.'

'What circumstances?' I frowned.

I hoped he wasn't someone else who had got wind of mine and Eliot's mutual attraction. Surely, he would have realised that if I felt something for Eliot then I wouldn't be sitting opposite him in the swankiest restaurant in the county. That said, that was exactly what I was doing, wasn't it? However, that wasn't what he was getting at. At all.

'You have heard the rumours about him, haven't you?' Anthony asked, with something akin to relish, and I felt the colour drain out of my world.

Chapter 17

Seeing the look on my face, Anthony apologised immediately and said it really wasn't his place to say anything, but I couldn't possibly let him get away with that.

'It's probably all bullshit,' he backtracked, looking flustered. 'Idle town gossip.'

'That's as maybe,' I said, sitting up straighter, 'but tell me what it is, and then I can decide for myself.'

The abundance of bubbles was suddenly making me feel nauseous rather than relaxed and I set my glass down and pushed it away. As far as I was concerned, Eliot Randall was the perfect man, and I knew Grandad felt the same way too. Not for the same reasons, obviously, but he was the best friend and closest confidant my grandfather had.

'All right,' Anthony eventually caved. He didn't look anything like as happy as he had before. 'I'll tell you, but you have to promise to remember that this is all hearsay, okay. Promise?'

'I promise,' I said, remembering one of Nonna's favourite maxims – *There's no smoke without fire.*

That saying was never far from her lips, usually when word had reached her that Marco had been up to mischief with the neighbouring farmer's daughter in the olive grove (again) and he was hotly denying it. I hoped I wasn't about to find myself capable of applying the same aphorism to Eliot.

Anthony ran a hand through his hair which fell neatly back into place and I immediately thought of Eliot's hair which never laid right when he'd been on his bike and how he didn't care at all. I would have been hard pushed to find two more different men anywhere on the planet.

'Okay,' Anthony began. 'Well, it was the arrival of the bike that first got folk talking.'

'The Ducati?'

'Yes. How much would you say a bike like that would set you back?'

I puffed out my cheeks and thought about the catalogues and price lists Marco used to leave lying about. I did a quick mental calculation, exchanging euros for pound sterling.

'Depending on the model, but brand new, somewhere between fifteen and thirty-five thousand, I would think.'

Anthony whistled under his breath. 'Thirty-five thousand. Jeez.'

'That's top of the range,' I pointed out. 'I don't know where the bike that Eliot rides fits on that scale.'

'How do you know about the prices though?' Anthony asked. 'I wouldn't have had a clue.'

'I have a Ducati obsessed friend,' I said. 'Besides Eliot, I mean.'

'Fair enough.'

'I don't see how Eliot buying a motorbike could be cause for gossip.' I shrugged.

Anthony leant further forward. 'You don't think it's a bit strange that a guy who still lives at home with his mother and sister and who cares for old folk for a living, could afford a machine like that?'

'Not really,' I said. 'Plenty of people have finance. He's probably making payments. Living with Louise must be cheaper than living alone so he could afford to do that.'

'But what if it's all paid for?'

'How do you know it is?'

'I don't,' Anthony admitted, sitting back again. 'But let's pretend we do and it is.'

'Okay,' I said. 'Well maybe he had a win on the lottery.'

'Not likely.'

'Inherited some money then?'

'Bingo,' said Anthony. 'That's more like it. Well, sort of.'

'How can you *sort of* inherit some money?'

'If an elderly woman you're looking after dies and she leaves you a lump sum in her will.'

'Well, there's no law against that, is there?' I snapped, not at all liking the libellous insinuation this obviously nasty rumour was gearing up to infer.

'If the person named in the will had undue influence over the person who died, then there most likely is.' Anthony expanded. 'If the person in the position of trust made themselves indispensable and made the other person feel beholden to them . . .'

'So, that's what this rumour amounts to, is it?' I interrupted, narrowing my eyes. 'That Eliot looked after this woman with a view to getting his hands on her estate?'

Who on earth could possibly think that? Certainly, none of the people I'd come across in Wynbridge or the surrounding countryside. Granted, my social circle might have been somewhat limited, but it didn't alter the fact that what Anthony was saying was absurd.

'From what I've heard, yes,' he confirmed.

I shook my head, rolled my eyes and reached for my glass again. The look on Anthony's face suggested that wasn't the reaction he had been expecting.

'You're not at all concerned about that?' he asked. 'Given this guy's closeness to your grandad. You're not at all troubled?'

'You just told me,' I swiftly reminded him, 'to promise you that I would remember that this is just a rumour. Idle town gossip and hearsay, were your exact words.'

'But even so . . .'

'No,' I said, cutting him off. 'This is ridiculous, Anthony. Eliot's loved by absolutely everyone.' I felt my face flush a little when I said that. 'I might not have been in the area long, but I've never heard or seen anything to back this nastiness up.'

We sat in silence for a minute or two then. I finished my champagne and Anthony ground his teeth. He looked more than a little put out that I had dismissed him so adamantly.

'I only mentioned it out of concern for your grandfather,' he eventually said.

'I'm sure you had the best of intentions,' I responded, although actually I wasn't all that convinced he had.

'It's just that Eliot's always had an eye for things that don't belong to him,' he then carried on, encouraged by my comment. 'He was cautioned for shoplifting when we were at school and, having heard the rumour, I've been wondering if he might have moved on to bigger things than aftershave and PlayStation games.'

'Are you suggesting that he's got his eye on inheriting Fenview Farm?' I snapped. 'Because that's preposterous!'

'I'm not suggesting anything,' Anthony recoiled, but he clearly was.

The date wasn't going how I had expected it to at all. I might have agreed to it to make Eliot think I wasn't still harbouring feelings for him, but after our heated moment in the library and the way I had just defended him to Anthony, I wasn't sure it was worth it. Perhaps denial was futile.

'Are you all right?' Anthony asked. 'You look a bit peaky.'

'I'm fine,' I told him. 'But I would like to go home now, if that's all right with you?'

'I've ruined the evening, haven't I?' he said, with a hangdog expression.

'Yes,' I truthfully said. 'You have.'

We were both quiet on the taxi journey home and my head was spinning. I knew what Anthony had told me was total rubbish, but now it was stuck in my head and I resented him for that. I briefly wondered if I should mention it all to

Eliot, but knowing it would upset him, I resolved to try and forget about it. Easier said than done of course.

I noticed the stars were shining as the taxi reached the drove road which led to the farm. There wasn't a single bit of cloud cover. Had the meal gone better, it would have been a romantic end to the evening. Not that I had romantic feelings towards Anthony. Far from them now.

'I'm sorry I've messed up,' he said.

'It's fine,' I replied, although it wasn't. 'You don't really believe it though, do you? The rumour about the woman's will, I mean?'

He hesitated before answering. 'Well, no.'

'You're a rubbish liar,' I accusingly, said.

'Had I not known about what happened when we were at school,' he shrugged, 'I most likely wouldn't have given it a second thought.'

I was sure that brief anti-social interlude would have been part of what Louise had talked about when she told me about her husband, Eliot and Bec's father, dying. It was little surprise that Eliot had had a moment of angry rebellion at some point when he was growing up, was it? And it in no way meant that he'd moved on to bigger things now he was an adult, as Anthony had implied.

'It's all completely wrong,' I firmly said.

'I sincerely hope so,' Anthony nodded.

'Can you stop here, please?' I asked the taxi driver.

We were a little way away from the farm, but it was later than I had been expecting to get back and I guessed Grandad would be in bed. I didn't want the sound of a car on the drive disturbing him.

Anthony and I both climbed out and I thanked him for the meal. He didn't make any attempt to kiss me and I was relieved about that.

'I'm going to call you,' he said, leaving me at the top of the drive. 'Very soon and we're going to go out again, and I'm going to make amends for the balls up I've made of tonight.'

'Right,' I said, refusing to say anything which might salve his conscience. 'Goodnight, Anthony.'

As I reached the back door, aided by the torch on my phone I heard the taxi pull away and realised that I had no way of getting in. I had posted the house key through the letterbox before I left. I took a step back, checking to see if there were any lights on, but the house was in darkness and I was just about to try and ring Anthony and ask him to come back, when the floodlight in the yard came on and the back door opened.

'Eliot,' I gasped.

'Come in quick,' he said, 'and I'll turn the light off again.'

I hadn't noticed the bike anywhere, so he was the last person I expected to see. I had assumed he would have been long gone and I would have had the chance to shrug what Anthony had said off before we talked again. At least now he got to see me all dressed up for my date though. That said, all of a sudden and in the grand scheme of things, it didn't matter anywhere near as much as it had before.

'Why are you still here?' I whispered. 'Is everything all right with Grandad? I thought you'd be gone by now.'

'He's in bed,' Eliot quietly said. 'He was shattered so I said I'd wait for you, as you hadn't got a key.'

'Thank you,' I said. 'I'm going to get some more cut so this won't happen again.'

'Are you likely to stay out this late again then?' he asked, his brow furrowed.

'I might,' I said, biting my lip.

'Well,' he said, taking me in. 'I'm not surprised your date was a success, you look gorgeous. Completely different to how you usually look.'

'Thanks.'

'Not that you don't usually look good,' he said, running a hand through his hair. 'But whoever had the pleasure of your company tonight, was very lucky indeed.'

He sounded a bit put out and I should have been pleased that he'd got the message that I'd moved on. My masterplan was bearing fruit, but the taste it left in my mouth was surprisingly bitter.

'Thank you,' I said again, turning away to take a glass out of the cupboard.

I just wanted the evening to be over now. My feet were throbbing and my body wanted to be free of the confines of the dress and back in its familiar, and much looser, loungewear.

'Oh, and before I forget,' Eliot then said, 'Miriam from the library asked me to give you these.'

I really didn't want to be reminded of the library.

'What are they?'

'A couple of leaflets about opening times and clubs and things, I think.'

He held them out and I felt my face flush as I took them.

'You left in such a rush that she didn't get the chance to give them to you herself,' he unnecessarily pointed out.

'I didn't want to keep Grandad waiting,' I told him, putting the leaflets on the table and draining the glass I'd filled to avoid having to look at him, 'and I still had things to do.'

I rinsed the glass out and put it on the drainer.

'I'll get off then,' Eliot said.

'All right,' I said, moving to open the door. 'Thanks for waiting for me to get back. I didn't much fancy having to sleep in the barn with the cat.'

Now I knew he was leaving, it was easier to talk.

'I'll see you later,' he smiled, looking a little sad.

For a moment, I thought he was going to say something else, but he didn't.

'Night,' I brightly called after him. 'See you soon.'

I quickly locked the door and leaned back against it, gratefully slipping off my shoes and wishing that I really did have as tight a control of my feelings for him as I had just convinced him I had.

Chapter 18

I had quite a hangover the next morning, but it wasn't the ordinary, average, run of the mill effort. This descended, not only as a result of the two bottles of champagne Anthony and I had emptied, but also because of the emotional wringer that I'd been squeezed through before, during and after drinking them.

A morning spent baking in a hot kitchen was tiring enough, but then there had been the photograph albums, the gift of the beautiful earrings from Grandad, the ulterior motive surrounding my first date in ages, the indigestible rumour about Eliot *and* the awkward exchange with the man himself which topped the twenty-four hours off. It was no wonder I was feeling below par. It had been one hell of a day.

I had my fingers crossed that my plans for Sunday would buck me up a bit. If they went according to plan, they should totally restore my zip and zeal and give Grandad a hefty dollop too.

'Afternoon,' smiled Grandad when I ventured down to the kitchen just after eight. 'Good night, was it?'

'It was interesting,' I told him, as I rifled through the medicine cupboard for painkillers. 'It didn't end quite how I thought it might, but it was okay.'

Grandad narrowed his eyes. 'I don't like the sound of that,' he frowned. 'You got home all right, didn't you?'

'Oh yes,' I said, quickly quashing his concern. 'All safe and sound.'

'That's all right then,' he said, sounding relieved. 'Are you ready for a bit of breakfast? I was just about to scramble some eggs.'

'That would be lovely,' I gingerly nodded. 'But first, I want to give you these back.' I put the box containing the ruby earrings on the table. 'I don't mean for ever, just for safekeeping. I'd feel better if they were with the other pieces in your room, with the watch and everything, where they've always been. I haven't got anywhere like that to keep them.'

Mum's bangles were consigned to a jangling, and comfortingly familiar, pile on the nightstand.

'That's a good idea,' Grandad agreed. 'Did you enjoy wearing them?'

'I did, but it took me ages to stop checking them. They're beautiful, and the family history makes them even more precious, so I was terrified of losing them.'

Grandad smiled and I wished the farm had a safe or something, somewhere we could keep the contents of the box properly locked away.

'I can understand that,' he said. 'I feel the same about the watch.'

'But you did tell me yesterday that we shouldn't save things for best,' I reminded him. 'Don't you ever wear it?'

'I haven't been anywhere in a long time that's warranted putting it on.'

That didn't surprise me. As he'd already said, it wasn't an appropriate timepiece to wear while picking fruit or convalescing and from what I understood, he hadn't recently done much else.

'Be a love,' he said. 'You go and put the earrings away while I get on with the eggs. It would save me having to negotiate the stairs again.'

'I thought you were supposed to be moving a bit more,' I pointed out.

'I've been moving all morning,' he tutted. 'I had to walk across the yard to let the hens out and collect the eggs because you were in bed, sleeping the day away.'

Given that it was still much nearer eight than half past I thought that was slightly unfair but when you were used to getting up with the sun in the summer, I supposed my later than usual appearance did appear a bit lackadaisical.

After breakfast, during which we agreed that next time I was in town I should get another couple of sets of farm keys cut, I got ready to head outside. Grandad was full of enthusiasm for his laptop and planning to fire it up and get to know his way around it a bit better. Eliot had suggested it would be a good idea ahead of the internet being connected the following week.

'That way I can hit the ground running,' Grandad

beamed, clearly looking forward to the delights of discovering life online.

'That's an excellent idea,' I said, pulling on a pair of wellies.

It was too warm for them really. I would have to add a short pair, like the ones Amber at Skylark Farm favoured, to my shopping list. Though not designer ones. A functional Dunlop duo would be good enough for me.

'What are you up to today?' Grandad asked. 'I had a look at the strawberry rows and there's nothing that'll need picking before tomorrow. The cloud cover yesterday seems to have halted putting the paint on them a bit.'

I was pleased about that because I did have something specific in mind to get on with, and it didn't involve being bent over the strawberry rows. With the main fruit harvest beginning to peep over the horizon, I knew that my time was soon going to be limited so I intended to grasp the nettle while I could.

'It's a secret for now,' I mysteriously said.

Grandad looked at me over the top of his glasses. With the laptop in front of him, he looked almost studious.

'All will be revealed later,' I told him. 'In the meantime, if you can just stay inside until I come and get you it would be much appreciated. I'll only be about an hour.'

'All right,' he agreed, looking at the screen again.

'We aren't expecting company, are we?'

Given what I had in mind, I didn't want any interruptions, from anyone. This was strictly going to be for Grandad's eyes only.

'Not as far as I know,' he answered.

'That's all right then. Now, you stay in here and I'll see you in a bit.'

I walked down to the barn and took a proper look at the roof. It didn't look in the slightest bit dipped to me, and the walls were sound and the doors were hanging straight, so I dismissed Anthony's concerns about its safety and ducked inside.

It didn't take me long to realise that having everything ready in an hour was an extremely optimistic target. Even within two hours, I still wouldn't be able to have things *exactly* how I wanted them, but I would hopefully be able to make a decent enough presentation to convince Grandad to agree to what I had in mind.

Rather than launching straight in, I spent a few minutes, taking stock and getting a feel for the space before deciding how best to arrange it. Next, I pushed, dragged and carried everything I wouldn't need to the far end, which left me with a large central area and space along the back wall.

Lugging the bales about kicked up a fair amount of dust, but eventually, I had things set as well as I could get them, and I stood back to admire my handiwork. In my mind's eye, I could see it all properly finished – clean and welcoming, with twinkling fairy lights and Grandad's much-treasured Fenland collection adding that all important USP.

I could hear the chatter of happy voices, the sound of glasses being raised in a toast, cutlery going to work and music playing quietly in the background. If I could pull my big idea off, our barn could have the potential to not only secure the future of the farm, but also help a few other people pursue their own dreams, and I hoped Grandad had enough imagination to conjure the vision as I could see it.

I knew I was getting carried away, and that the project wouldn't come together overnight, but what was the point in having dreams if you never pursued them? The contract to supply the Cherry Tree Café was a good one, it meant that there was still value in growing fruit at Fenview Farm. However that, along with supplying Chris on the market and Jake at Skylark Farm, wasn't enough to guarantee a secure future, but what I imagined creating inside the barn might be. It could be more than enough to keep the bank manager off our backs and the farm in the black.

It was time to take action, just like I had in Puglia when Alessandro told us that there was a hole to plug in the farm's finances. I had got my thinking cap on then and, inspired by Mum's meandering across the globe, struck on the ideal opportunity to assist the Rossis. Hopefully what I had in mind for Fenview Farm would be every bit as much of a triumph.

I went back outside, remembering another job which had been playing on my mind. I quickly straightened and washed the grime off the roadside farm sign, then went back to the house feeling content with my morning's work. I was a bit grubby, but happy, and my hangover was completely forgotten as was everything that Anthony had told me about Eliot.

'I was just about to ring the gong,' said Grandad, who had

packed away his laptop and was busy at the cooker. 'It's well after twelve. You said you'd only be an hour.'

'I know,' I said, as I pulled off my boots. 'I got carried away.'

'For a change,' Grandad grinned.

'What's for lunch?' I asked. 'It smells great.'

'A lovely bit of brisket and I'm just about to put the Yorkshire puddings in.'

'Fantastic,' I said, my tum rumbling in true Pooh Bear fashion. 'I'm famished.'

Grandad turned from the oven to look at me properly and his face dropped.

'Oh Fliss,' he tutted. 'What have you been doing? You're filthy.'

I tried to run a hand through my hair but it felt clogged with dust and my arms and legs were covered in a cloying layer. I hadn't realised I was in such a state.

'Don't answer that,' said Grandad, scolding me as if I was a child who had been making mud pies and stirring puddles with sticks. 'Just go and get showered.'

'But what about the puddings?'

'They'll be a few minutes yet. You can get done in that time, can't you?'

With the promise of a fully laden roast, I was washed, dressed in clean clothes and back downstairs in no time. Grandad piled our plates high and as it was a little cooler, we ate inside, but with the back door open.

'How did you get on with the laptop?' I asked Grandad

as I spooned more broad beans and white sauce on to my plate.

'Fine,' he said. 'I think. I wrote a letter using the Word thingy, just for practice, but I'm not sure if I saved it or not.'

'I didn't know you could type.'

I realised there were a lot of things I didn't know about him. I could most likely spend the rest of my life at Fenview Farm and still discover something new every day. It was an exciting, rather than demoralising thought and made me more determined than ever to squeeze the most out of each and every day. I had almost thirty years to make up for, after all.

'I can't,' Grandad laughed. 'It was a very short letter.'

As he'd prepped and cooked, I cleared, washed and put away. It didn't take all that long but every extra minute in the house gave the dust more opportunity to settle in the barn. As we'd eaten, I'd had another idea I wanted to complete before the grand reveal, so I mentally rescheduled showing it all to Grandad until teatime.

'What are you doing this afternoon?' I asked him, as I threw the damp tea-towel into the washing machine.

'Finding out what you've been up to this morning, I hope,' he said.

'I could just do with a few more minutes, if that's all right?'

'In that case,' he said, 'I'll shift snoozing in my chair to top of the agenda. I want to be properly rested to help with the harvest. Last year was a disaster for my mental health, having to watch Jake and Chris do all the donkey work, but this year with the new contract and the new hip, I'm feeling more like my old self and looking forward to getting stuck in again.'

'Oh right,' I said, pretending to huff, 'and there was me thinking that my arrival was the reason behind the upturn in your wellbeing.'

Grandad shook his head. 'You know full well the huge part you've already played in that,' he chuckled. 'Don't go fishing for compliments.'

'Fair enough,' I grinned.

I hoped the revelation of my big idea was going to send his spirits soaring even higher. If he was onboard, and if he agreed to let me invest my savings in the project, then the farm could be facing a dazzlingly bright future and his mental health would be fully restored. It was a thrilling prospect.

With Grandad softly snoring and the television babbling in the background, I got together everything I needed to complete my presentation.

Just as I had hoped, the dust had settled and with the addition of a cloth on the makeshift table, rugs and cushions on the bales, and fresh flowers in rinsed out jars, the barn looked a treat. I set out the crockery and cutlery, but left the food for our afternoon tea in the cool box, just in case the cat took a fancy to it, and then went back to the house.

'Time for a cuppa?' I asked Grandad, who had just woken up.

'Is it that time already?'

'It's gone half four.'

'It never is!'

'It is,' I laughed at his outraged tone. 'You had a dig at me for getting up late this morning, but you've practically slept the entire afternoon away.'

'I only meant to have half an hour or so. I'll get the kettle on.'

'The tea's made,' I told him. 'But we're not having it in the house. Come with me.'

My heart was solidly thudding as we walked to the barn and Grandad looked completely confused because he'd assumed we were heading for the apple tree. I'd left the barn doors wide open, a bale holding each back and the light streamed in picking out the few motes which still refused to settle.

'What's all this?' Grandad frowned.

His gaze tracked from the pretty improvised eating area to the makeshift display of some of his collection.

'What have you been up to, Fliss?'

I led him to his garden chair, which I'd carried inside because I wasn't sure how he'd cope with perching on a bale, but he didn't want to sit down.

'I've never seen it all arranged like this before,' he huskily said, looking over the few bits and pieces from his collection that I'd gathered together. 'There's a lot more than I thought. There didn't look to be anything like this amount when it was all still in boxes.'

'And this is nowhere near half of it,' I said, pointing out the rest tucked to one side. 'There's all that lot, too.'

While he looked at everything, I set out the food and poured the tea. The occupation stopped me getting ahead of myself and blurting out what it was I had in mind. I knew that if I let my enthusiasm get the better of me, I would forget things, or get in a muddle, and I wanted to give this idea the best possible shot.

'There's tea here, Grandad.'

He reluctantly left the collection and sat down, and I handed him a plate filled with finger sandwiches, mini scotch eggs, a slice of quiche and a couple of sausage rolls. It was a technique I'd seen Nonna adopt in the past and to great effect.

Whenever she wanted to speak without interruption, she gave the person who was going to be on the receiving end mountains of food and made sure they'd tucked in before launching forth, and that was what I planned to do.

I waited with bated breath, but Grandad didn't fall for my cunning plan and simply balanced the plate on his lap. He was supposed to be chewing before I said anything further, but I was out of luck.

'Come on then,' he said, his mouth still empty. 'Out with it. I know you haven't gone to all this bother just to bring me down here and stuff me full of tea.'

Had I met my match? Nonna would have been mightily amused that Grandad had seen through her ruse, but I felt my fragile confidence and courage crumble a little. Not only had Grandad seen through Nonna's psychology, but his tone had a defensive edge to it too. I would have much preferred an amused one, something malleable that I could readily bend to my will.

'Well,' I said, knowing I would just have to go for it, whether he was chewing or not, 'I've been thinking about the farm and its future and as wonderful as the new Cherry Tree contract is, I don't think it's enough. I think we need to have other irons in the fire, beyond Jemma and Chris and Jake, if we want to see the place really thriving again.'

'I agree,' said Grandad.

His acquiescence made my heart skip as did watching him finally take a bite of the quiche.

'Has this got bacon from Skylark Farm in it?' he asked, once he'd swallowed his first mouthful.

'Yes, it's their streaky smoked.'

'Go on then,' he said, taking another bite.

I swallowed hard and stood up straighter.

'And I've been listening to what people have been saying about having nowhere local to eat in the evenings.'

'There's the pub.'

'And a couple of restaurants, but nothing else. People want a new local experience and, having listened to Jake too, I think there's an opportunity for not only offering a different venue, but a rather different dining experience as well.'

Grandad's eyes roved around the barn.

'Jemma said she's not prepared to open in the evenings and Jake mentioned that he would love to sell dishes showcasing the food he can create with the produce he and Amber have perfected at the farm, but they haven't got the room.'

Grandad's eyes tracked back to me.

'What I'm thinking,' I said, walking over to his collection, 'is that we could open the barn up as an exclusive supper club. We could invite different growers, farmers, and producers to come and serve dishes here, featuring their own produce. We could keep it local, seasonal, fresh and exciting. We could even have pudding evenings, highlighting the fruit that we grow here.'

Grandad didn't say anything so I carried on.

'All the food, other than ours, could be prepared offsite to begin with.' I had plans to install a catering kitchen in one of the adjoining outhouses if the idea took off, as well as cloakrooms and a wood burner to keep the barn cosy in the winter, but I didn't want to get into all of that too soon.

'And it wouldn't take much to create an authentic rustic ambience which the guests would love because the setting already is rustic. Some twinkling fairy lights, lots of greenery for decoration and to top it all off, your collection, would be more than enough. I thought we could change your things to match the seasons. There's certainly enough of it to do that. The collection could be a real draw and a fantastic USP to give the enterprise a unique edge.'

I watched as Grandad put the last bit of quiche back on the plate.

'There's parking for a dozen cars if we reorganised the yard a bit,' I carried on. 'And I think a monthly or twice monthly event would be more than enough to keep it exclusive and create demand. We could charge for venue hire and decoration along with a share of the ticket price.'

Grandad opened his mouth to say something.

'Oh,' I said, clapping my hands together, 'and I thought we could have some space,' I added, pointing to the back wall, 'to highlight a local artist. Like Bec for example and we could have all your papers and things properly framed for display.' I finally stopped to draw breath and looked around. 'I think that's it. So, what do you think?'

It took me a moment to get my breath back and my rapid heart rate steadied. I hoped I'd done the idea justice. I'd ended up getting a bit gushy and carried away, just as I'd known I would, but that was only because I was so excited. Fingers crossed my enthusiasm for the project was highly contagious and Grandad had caught a dose too.

'Well,' he eventually said, looking around again. 'You've clearly given it a lot of thought.'

'I have,' I cut in, 'and I know there's definitely some demand but I'm going to look further into exactly how much . . . sorry.'

'And in theory,' he carried on.

I felt my shoulders drop.

'In theory, it sounds amazing, but to do it properly would cost a fortune, Fliss.'

'Only a relatively small one,' I insisted. 'And we could easily get going without the kitchen and loos. We could get a few quotes in for the work that needs doing and do loads more planning before making a bigger financial investment.'

'But we haven't got the funds to make a bigger financial investment, Fliss or even a small one come to that.'

'But I have,' I said. 'I have more than enough saved to get us going and,' I quickly added to gloss over the suggestion that I would be putting in all of my own money, 'I could do all the prep myself. I can do rustic and simple standing on my head. I could start everything off and then . . .'

'But I wouldn't want you to risk putting your own money in,' Grandad said, focusing on the one thing I'd tried to rush over. 'And as you know, I haven't got a spare bean.'

He sounded upset rather than excited and that was the last thing I wanted.

'Please don't say no,' I pleaded, crossing my fingers. 'And don't worry about the money. We've got to speculate to accumulate.'

I was pretty certain that if I went to the bank with a bona fide business plan we'd be approved for a loan, but I didn't suggest that. Not given the Brown attitude to borrowing. And besides, I really did have enough to cover it sitting in my savings account.

'I'm sorry, my love,' Grandad said, shaking his head. 'It's a grand idea, it really is, but it's not just about the money.'

'What then?' I shot back. 'What else is it about?'

'It's just out of the question.'

That wasn't a proper answer.

'Why?' I demanded, frustrated that he wouldn't explain. 'Why is it out of the question?'

He refused to tell me and I inwardly cursed that I'd got carried away and suggested it before I'd done further research. I should have at least got Jake onside before I said anything. I should have got him and Amber fired up and then we could have presented the proposal together.

'If it is the money that you're worried about, but you're pretending it isn't . . .'

'It's not that,' Grandad snappily said.

I walked over and reached for his hand.

'What then?' I asked again. 'I thought you'd love this. I thought you wanted to move the farm forward and this idea will do that, in a really exciting way.'

Grandad shook his head.

'It's got to be better than Jemma's idea of selling the barn for conversion,' I joked.

My ears picked up a rumble on the road which heralded the approach of a certain Ducati. I let go of Grandad's hand and, resigned, sat back on the bales. Discussion time was over. Not that I felt we'd had a discussion, not a proper one anyway. I would have needed to know why Grandad was objecting to the idea in order to have properly thrashed it all out.

'What's all this then?' Eliot asked as he wandered in a few seconds later, his bike helmet tucked under his arm.

'Nothing important,' I shrugged, feeling decidedly lacklustre.

Originally, I hadn't wanted anyone else to see it all, not even Eliot, but it didn't matter now. So much for the plan to restore my pep. Not even the sight of Eliot looking lovely in full leathers could breathe life into my sagging spirits.

'Oh,' he said. 'Right. Well, it all looks great.'

I shot Grandad a loaded look, but he purposefully wasn't looking at me.

'See?' I wanted to say to him. 'It will work.' But I didn't.

'I think I'll go back up to the house,' he huskily said, standing up and handing me his plate. 'Do you want to come with me, Eliot?'

'Can do,' he said, checking his watch. 'I only stopped because I spotted the barn was open and wanted to make sure everything was all right, but I've got a few minutes before I need to get to Walter's place. Are you coming, Fliss?'

'No,' I tightly said. 'I need to tidy this lot away.'

'Want a hand?'

'No thanks.'

I knew I sounded sulky and I didn't mean to take my disappointment at Grandad's reluctance to climb aboard the good ship supper club out on him, but I couldn't seem to help myself.

'Bec was moaning earlier that she's tried ringing your mobile, but it's switched off.'

'There's no point having it on,' I told him. 'There's not enough signal to warrant wasting the battery. Is she all right?'

'Yes,' he said. 'She's fine.' Then his tone changed. 'I think she wanted to ask how you got on last night.'

I pasted on a smile thinking that as everything else had been such a flop, I might as well make the most of this opportunity.

'Can you tell her it was wonderful,' I dreamily sighed,

hopefully implying that I was reliving a very happy memory, 'and that I'll fill her in next week?'

'Will do,' he glumly said. 'Come on then, Bill.'

I knew I would have to give Bec a dramatically doctored retelling of how the evening had gone because I could hardly tell her that her brother had been the hot topic, and not in a good way, could I?

'Thank you,' I said to his and Grandad's retreating backs.

I watched them walk away and along with them went my hopes and dreams for the farm's new venture. I had no idea why Grandad was so set against my seasonal supper club plans and, as he obviously had no intention of telling me, that was the end of that.

Chapter 19

Later that evening, after Eliot had gone, I couldn't resist asking Grandad again why he was so against the diversification idea, but he refused to expand on what he'd already said. We didn't argue about it, but this back and forth continued into the following week and by then, our newly-formed relationship was beginning to feel the strain.

It felt obvious to me that his main concern centred around me making a personal financial commitment – even though he insisted it wasn't – but I couldn't shake off the feeling that there was something else too. Something it was proving impossible for me to prise out of him.

We were talking a little less and left to my own devices, by the end of the week, I'd established a routine of picking the quickly ripening strawberries from early morning until lunchtime, then taking the fruit to town, dropping most at the café and the remainder to the market and Skylark Farm, before driving back and working through my share of the household chores and any other farm business.

When I had first arrived, it was the sort of settled lifestyle I had imagined, but suddenly it wasn't enough. I was determined that Fenview Farm, and the part I had to play in securing its future, would equate to more than just going through the seasonal motions. Selling the fruit was all well and good, but with such a magnificent barn at our disposal, it felt frustrating to not be utilising it, especially now I had struck upon the perfect idea.

As keen as I was, I hadn't talked to Jake to find out what he thought about it all because with Grandad so set against it, it would have been a waste of time and of course, I didn't want to aggravate him further by going behind his back when he'd already, unwaveringly, said no.

'Anyone home?'

It was my first trip to the Randall residence, and having knocked on the cottage door and got no answer, I'd ventured around the side of the house, through the gate and into the slightly overgrown garden. I knew Bec was home because the Banana-mobile was parked on the drive and the sound of music led me to her shed/studio. I knocked hard on the door, hoping I wouldn't make her jump or disturb her artistic flow if she was in the zone.

There was a momentary lull in the music and I knocked again.

'It's open!' she shouted, and I yanked at the door to find her standing in the middle of what looked like colour splattered chaos, a huge smile lighting up her face.

She skipped over to a workbench overflowing with pots

of brushes, tubes of paint and piles of sketchbooks and turned the music off.

'I'm not disturbing you, am I?' I asked, the smell of paint filling my nostrils and making me feel a little lightheaded.

She really could have done with cracking a window or keeping the door propped open. No wonder she was smiling like a loon.

'Where have you been?' she demanded, pulling off her saffron and cerulean smattered smock and throwing it over the back of an equally paint embellished chair. 'I've missed you every day when you've dropped the strawberries off at the café and your phone's never on. I was beginning to think you were avoiding me!'

I felt a bit bad about that and now I'd come to the cottage because I had an ulterior motive which, given her obvious excitement to see me, made me feel a bit mean.

'You go out with the best-looking guy in town and then . . . nothing. I'm supposed to be your new BFF, remember? I want *details*! And,' she added, 'you were supposed to give me a shout about when I could come and give you a hand with the strawberry picking.'

Preoccupied with certain *details* as well as daydreams about what the barn could look like if I had my way, I'd completely forgotten about her generous offer. And she seemed to have forgotten that she'd hinted that her brother had been about to declare something to me the day of too much champagne. Was she so scatter-brained that she'd misplaced that particular observation – I hoped so – or had she observed him further and changed her mind about what she'd said?

'I'm sorry,' I apologised. 'I've been preoccupied.'

'That good was it?' she speculated. 'Have you had round two yet? Is that why I've been abandoned?'

Anthony had called about 'round two' as Bec put it, one day when I was in Wynbridge and happened to have my phone turned on. He'd said he was sorry for not ringing sooner but he was currently swamped with work. He then ruined the apology by asking if Eliot had shown any signs of being the swindler, the town gossips had labelled him as, and I ended up getting a bit cross. He insisted he was joking, but personally I didn't think it was anything to joke about and the call had ended coolly, from my end at least and without us arranging a second date.

However, Anthony's aggravating reminder had put Eliot firmly back at the forefront of my mind, not that he'd ever been all that far from it, and I realised that he was exactly the person I needed to enlist to get Grandad onside about the supper club. If anyone would be able to help, it was Eliot. Hence my trip to the cottage.

'You haven't been abandoned,' I said to Bec. 'I've just been busy establishing a routine and if the offer still stands, I really would appreciate some help soon.' The ripening was definitely picking up pace now the days were consistently warmer. 'And as far as the date's concerned . . .'

'Stop,' she interrupted. 'Let's get a drink first and find somewhere comfy. I've been looking forward to this!'

We sat with a pitcher of lemonade in the garden and I injected as much enthusiasm into my retelling of the evening as I could. After all, I still wanted Eliot to think that I really had set my feelings for him to one side and started something up elsewhere, with someone who was nothing like him, and hearing it from his sister was bound to help that cause.

Consequently, I told Bec all about the outfit I'd found in Bella's, the swanky dinner in the far away restaurant, the champagne and the hugely expensive taxi ride, along with what Anthony's favourite colour was. She'd already guessed red, but given her artistic calling, that was no surprise.

'But he didn't kiss you goodnight?' she asked, wrinkling her nose and sounding unimpressed.

'No,' I said. 'With the taxi waiting, it would have been a bit awkward, but I could tell he wanted to.'

'Well, I suppose that cranks the anticipation up a bit, doesn't it?' she sighed. 'You'll be panting to get your hands on him next time, won't you? And vice versa.'

'Absolutely,' I fibbed. 'And I still don't know what he does for a living, so we'll have plenty to talk about in-between all the kissing.'

'Um,' Bec wistfully sighed. 'And there was me thinking you and Eliot . . .'

'There was you thinking me and Eliot what?' I asked, the sound of rushing blood filling my head as my heart pounded and I realised she hadn't forgotten after all.

'Well,' she said. 'I really thought he liked you and I was beginning to think that you liked him . . . but I suppose you wouldn't have gone out with Anthony if that was the case, would you? And he is gorgeous, so if he's more your type . . .'

'Oh, he is,' I cut in. 'Definitely more my type and I do like Eliot, how could I not, but only as a friend.'

In view of the fact that Anthony was so easy on the eye and that I'd already been on a date with him, she seemed to accept that and I hoped I'd said enough to clear everything up and put it all nicely in its place.

'With regard to Anthony's job,' Bec smiled, getting back on track. 'I know what he does. Well, I sort of know. He's something to do with the building trade.'

I found that rather amusing, but it did go some way to explaining his observation about the barn. I was certain there was no merit in what he'd said, but knowing he was in the trade, I would have another look. Just to be on the safe side.

'Really?' I said, thinking of his impeccable hands. 'He doesn't look like a brickie.'

'That's what I thought,' Bec giggled. 'I daresay he's in management. More suited to telling the brickies what to do.'

That, I agreed sounded far more like it, then thoughts of Anthony's hands led me to imagining the touch of Eliot's.

'I don't suppose your brother's around, is he?' I casually asked, attempting to suppress the sudden glow. Hopefully Bec would think it was down to talk of Anthony, rather than the conversational switch to her big brother.

'No. He's at work. Why?'

'I wanted to ask a favour.'

'Does it have to be from him?'

'Afraid so. It's to do with Grandad.'

'Oh well, yes then,' Bec nodded. 'It's definitely Eliot you want. You can leave him a note if you like.'

With Bec acting as intermediary because Eliot was so busy, arrangements were made for us to meet in The Mermaid Friday night. I felt shockingly nervous. There was a lot riding on how the evening went, and I didn't want to mess it up.

'He'll meet you there about seven,' Bec told me, when I dropped the strawberries at the café. 'He said he's sorry he can't be more specific. It will all depend on how his last visit goes but if you have your phone on when you get to town, he'll let you know if he's running late. He's been rushed off his feet this week, picking up extra shifts left, right and centre.'

It was the first time I was going to see him alone and away from the farm, other than at the library of course, when I'd cried all over him so that didn't really count, and without either Grandad, Louise or Bec around. I rather hoped he was going to turn up looking exhausted from his working week. That might temper my attraction to him a bit. Either that or it would make me fall even harder because he'd be heroically wearing the hours he'd been putting in looking after the elderly and infirm of Wynbridge! I was doomed.

'What can I get for you, love?' asked the pub landlady who introduced herself as Evelyn that Friday evening.

'A Coke please,' I said, looking back towards the door.

'Lemon and ice?'

'Yes, please.'

I found a table with a good view of the door and didn't have to wait many minutes before the throaty rumble of the Ducati rolled into the market square. It was as if Eliot had his own early warning system and I wasn't the only person who'd heard it.

He was barely over the threshold before he was besieged. First by a couple of young women who went into full hair tossing and eyelash batting mode and then by a middle-aged woman who, from what I could make out, insisted on buying his drink.

Once he had said a word to practically everyone in the place, he looked around, spotted me, and came over.

'Hi,' he said, putting down his drink.

Was it my imagination or did he look as edgy as I felt?

'Hey,' I said, budging along the bench to make room for him.

The chairs which went with the table had been carried off to accommodate a large group who were sitting next to the piano, so we had no choice but to squeeze in together. The group were noisily enjoying the end of the working week and no doubt the prospect of the weekend ahead.

'I'm sorry I'm late,' Eliot apologised, putting his helmet and gloves on the table before pulling off a leather jacket I hadn't seen him wearing before.

'You're not really,' I said. It was only a couple of minutes after our designated time. 'Bec said you would have to be flexible because of your last call, so I knew you might not be here bang on seven.'

He nodded and took a long drink. 'Crikey, I needed that,' he said, once he'd finished. 'It's still hot out there.'

'And it must be hot on the bike,' I said. This wasn't the way we usually talked to each other, so the situation was clearly getting to both of us. 'Although you aren't in your leathers today,' I inanely added. 'Apart from the jacket.'

'These are Draggin jeans,' he said, slapping the top of his leg.

'Draggin jeans?'

'Basically, they look like jeans, but they're made from Kevlar and as tough as old boots. They cost a fortune, but they're worth it.'

'I see,' I said. 'Safety first.'

'Always,' he smiled back.

Once we'd exhausted the health and safety merits of his outfit, someone else came over, which thankfully ended the small talk. It was a guy this time and he put two drinks on the table.

'Evelyn said what you were drinking,' he said to me. 'Coke, right?'

'Yes,' I said. 'Thanks.'

'This is just a thank you for sorting Mum out,' he then nodded at Eliot.

'Cass has already said thank you,' said Eliot, holding up his almost empty glass.

'And I'm saying it again,' insisted the guy. 'She'd have been in real trouble if you hadn't stayed with her.'

Eliot shook his head. 'It was no bother, John. I was just doing my job, so let's say no more about it. But thanks for the drinks.'

'Yes,' I said. 'Thanks.'

I emptied my first and picked up the second, taking a sideways glance at Eliot who was looking a bit flushed. Clearly, he'd again gone above and beyond, earning himself the gratitude of yet another local family. Whoever had spread the rumour about him definitely had the wrong Eliot, because the one sitting next to me was much loved and very highly thought of.

I almost wished Anthony was with us to witness it in action. That would have soon crushed his suspicions. Eliot's only motive was to provide the best possible care for those he looked after, with Grandad being right at the top of the list, not take their life savings.

Along with wishing Anthony had just been within earshot, I also wished I'd known that the Eliot fan club was going to be in such enthusiastic attendance. I would have suggested meeting somewhere else because having his kind, considerate and caring nature highlighted at every turn was doing nothing to help stave off my feelings.

'A bit weird this, isn't it?' he said. 'Being in the pub rather than at the farm.'

'Yes,' I agreed. 'It is. I was thinking the very same thing before you arrived. This is the first time we've been in each other's company beyond the farm boundary.'

'Don't forget the library,' he reminded me, then turned

bright red. 'Although you probably rather would, wouldn't you? Sorry.'

'It's all right,' I said, taking another swig from my glass which prompted him to do the same.

'Bec said you had a favour to ask.'

'Oh, yes,' I said, pulling myself together. 'That's actually why I wanted us to meet away from the farm.'

'Well, ask away.'

'Although it is to do with the farm.'

'Oh?'

I'd really hoped to keep the planning stage between just me and Grandad but as he was so determined not to let me even give it a try and I was equally determined to give convincing him one last shot, I knew talking to Eliot was my only hope.

'I've had this idea about how to utilise the barn,' I began.

'Is that why you were in there on Sunday serving up afternoon tea?'

'Yes,' I nodded. 'I thought if I set it all up, using some of Grandad's collection, then I might have a better chance of explaining to him what it was that I had in mind.'

'What collection?' Eliot frowned.

I was completely taken aback that Eliot didn't know anything about Grandad's hobby of collecting anything and everything connected to the history of the Fens. And I was sad too. Mum's cutting teenage remarks had really left their mark all those years ago if Grandad hadn't shared his passion with his closest friend. Thank goodness he hadn't done as Mum suggested and trashed the lot.

I took a deep breath and enlightened Eliot about both the collection and my plans for it and the farm.

'Crikey,' he said, once I had shared everything. 'Wow.'

I gave him a minute to let it all sink in. His initial reaction sounded far more promising than Grandad's, but I wasn't counting my chickens.

'So,' I said. 'What do you think?'

'I think it all sounds amazing,' he beamed. 'Definitely a long-term enterprise that will see the farm way into the future.'

'Well,' I said, thinking back to the night of our champagne fuelled fish and chip supper, 'like I've said before, I am planning to be here long-term.'

For the briefest moment our eyes met, but it was plenty long enough to remind me that living at Fenview Farm for ever and not letting my feelings for Eliot get the better of me was going to be the hardest project of all.

Even though I had drafted in audacious Anthony to help with operation 'I Don't Fancy You Anymore', it was going to be an every day struggle to keep my hands off the man currently sitting next to me. I wondered if he was thinking the same thing . . .

His gaze flicked to my lips and he jumped up.

'I'll get us another drink,' he said, making for the bar before I'd had a chance to tell him what the favour I wanted to ask of him was.

He was still in the queue when Anthony walked in. I must have conjured him up, but now I wished I hadn't.

'Fliss,' he smiled, rushing over when he spotted me trying to make myself invisible. Clearly ineffectively. 'This is a surprise.'

'I wasn't expecting to see you either,' I said, my eyes on Eliot's back.

I know I'd wanted him to see how loved Eliot was by the locals, but I hadn't really expected him to walk in. I didn't have him down as The Mermaid type. He would have looked more at home in a nice wine bar or relaxing on a rooftop terrace. Not that there were either in Wynbridge.

'Let me get you a drink.'

'No,' I quickly said. 'You're all right, but thanks. I'm with someone and they're about to get served.'

He looked at the helmet and gloves on the table, then turned and scanned the people standing at the bar. Eliot was deep in conversation with the customer standing next to him.

'You're not here with Eliot, by any chance, are you?' Anthony frowned, turning back to me.

'Yes,' I said, feeling guilty, but with no idea why.

His expression quickly changed. 'Ah right,' he said, tapping the side of his nose. 'Sussing him out a bit and keeping him in plain sight. Great idea.'

'No ...' I began, thinking what a misinformed idiot he was, but there was no chance to set him straight because Eliot was on his way back.

'I'll leave you to it,' Anthony whispered, with a theatrical wink.

I could have thumped him.

'Crikey, it's rammed in here tonight,' Eliot said, once he'd weaved his way through everyone not lucky enough to secure a seat. 'Sorry I took so long.'

'No worries,' I told him. 'I had no idea the place was so popular.'

He shifted a little closer and leant in to make himself heard as the level of chatter escalated.

'I have to say I absolutely love your idea for the barn,' he restated, his soft breath caressing my neck and making my spine tingle. 'The farm is the perfect setting and the old building is ideal. Just the right size and with everything you need to adapt and convert right within reach. It's going to be amazing.'

'Well,' I said, 'it would be amazing if Grandad felt the same way as you.'

'What do you mean?' he asked, pulling back a little to look at my face.

Our heads were very close together.

'He's said no,' I swallowed.

'Oh.'

'He won't even entertain the idea, let alone let me put any of my own money into getting it up and running.'

'Well,' he said, leaning in again, 'knowing him as well as I do, I can understand that he would be reluctant about that, but it's such a brilliant idea. Has he given you a reason, other than him not wanting you to spend your money, I mean?'

'No,' I said, 'and that's the most frustrating thing. If he would only explain then I might be able to accept his refusal, but as it is, I just can't let it go. I can picture it all in my head and I know there's the demand for something like it around here.'

'It would be lovely to have somewhere special to go in the evenings that's not too far afield.' Eliot pondered, further confirming what others had already said.

'Precisely.'

'And it would be even lovelier to see local food showcased by the folk who grow it.'

'My point exactly.'

'Having access to food from all over the world at any time of year is wonderful in its way, but personally, I don't think you can beat seasonal eating and local food. There's nothing better than a bit of rare breed pork from Skylark Farm, served with their apple sauce and cider or any of the fruit from your farm, Fliss, picked and eaten within the day.'

'Quite,' I agreed, swooning a little as I realised that he was as passionate about local food as I was and that he'd grasped exactly what I wanted the supper club to represent.

'Would you like me to talk to Bill?' he then offered, tipping me completely over the edge. 'Do you think he'll mind that you've talked to me about what you have in mind?'

'That was actually the favour I was going to ask,' I said, resisting the urge to throw my arms around him. 'And to be honest, I think he'll be delighted that I've talked to you. He trusts you more than anyone and he truly values your opinion.'

'He does?' Eliot asked, fixing me with his dark eyes.

I wondered if my pupils were as dilated as his.

'Yes,' I said. 'He does.'

'I'll talk to him tomorrow then,' Eliot beamed.

'Thank you,' I said, finally looking away.

With plans arranged, we left the pub together and I followed his bike out of town. When we reached the yard, he slowed down, looked over his shoulder and waved and then accelerated away. I tried to push away the pang of disappointment that struck as I watched him become a speck on the horizon and I was denied the opportunity to say a more intimate goodnight, but it refused to budge.

Chapter 20

I barely slept that night. My head was buzzing worse than it had been after any of the champagne I had drunk since my arrival at Fenview Farm. A heady cocktail of thoughts played on a dizzying merry-go-round until it became impossible to separate them.

It was more than obvious, although hopefully only to me, that I hadn't got my feelings for Eliot anywhere near as under control as I'd hoped. The close proximity of him in the pub, the way my body reacted to the caress of his breath and my disappointment when he hadn't stopped at the farm gate, were all proof beyond any doubt, not that I really needed it, that I was smitten. Given the effort I'd gone to to try not to be, even going out with Anthony to prove otherwise, it was most frustrating.

And then of course, there was Anthony. I had felt really rather disgruntled that he had assumed I was only out with Eliot to 'suss him out'. He had implied I had a motive which was guilt inducing, as any motives I did have were entangled in going out with him!

I was going to have to give him up and find a way to set him straight about Eliot and the sooner the better. Dating him hadn't helped at all so I wouldn't do it again, even if Bec was going to be denied the delicious details. Not that there would have been any because I felt no desire to kiss Anthony at all.

My simple new life at Fenview Farm was getting far too complicated and I needed to pare it back and focus on the things that mattered most.

I was in the fruit cage, checking the red and blackcurrants when I heard the Ducati the next morning. Both currant varieties looked as though they were going to come in a little earlier than expected, thanks to the continuing good weather, but knowing Eliot was in the vicinity completely threw my calculations on trying to work out when, so I closed and secured the cage and headed back to the house.

He was in the kitchen by the time I had collected the eggs and topped up the hens' water and, at the mere sight of him, my traitorous heart leapt and clattered about my ribcage with all the intensity of a bucking mule.

'Morning, Fliss,' he smiled, sending my BPM even higher.

'Morning,' I said, my voice catching as I deposited the eggs into the basket and washed my hands at the sink.

'Would you like tea, my love?' Grandad asked. 'I'm just about to make another pot.'

'No,' I said. 'Thank you. I'm going to get changed and go for a run before it gets too hot.'

Given the sleepless night, I wasn't really in the mood to run, but I wanted to make myself scarce while the pair of them talked. If I put a mile or two between me and the kitchen door I wouldn't be tempted to eavesdrop or interrupt, so it wasn't the worst idea I'd ever had.

'There aren't enough strawberries to warrant picking today,' I added. 'But I reckon there'll probably be a few currants by the end of next week.'

'Mmm,' groaned Eliot, making the most sensuous yummy noise imaginable. 'My favourite.'

'Are they?' I swallowed.

'Absolutely,' he said, torturing me further. 'Picked fresh from the bush and eaten there and then. I love the way they pop in your mouth and you get that exquisite explosion of flavour. They look so delicate and yet they pack a powerful punch.'

I felt my cheeks start to blaze.

'Yes,' I said, as I hastily left the room. 'They are good, aren't they?'

Neither he nor Grandad were inside when I went back down and I set off along the drove, trying not to think about the sensations and tastes Eliot had described and focused instead on sending positive vibes to the conversation he was hopefully now embarking upon about my plans.

The Ducati was still there when I returned, so I ducked into the barn to work through my cool down stretches and send a few more encouraging thoughts. As I bent and stretched, I sized the place up again. I imagined it completely transformed, with the catering kitchen next door, the wood burner casting soft shadows around the mellow walls and the sound of contented chat and more yummy noises than even Eliot could muster.

A sound behind me made me jump and I spun round to find him standing there, still with his leathers pushed down to his waist and his T-shirt stretched tight across his broad chest. It was a look that definitely suited him and he wore it extremely well. Even his tousled, uncontrollable hair had a stylish charm. I wondered if it would feel soft to the touch if I ran my fingers through it. The thought sent my heart rate, which had only just steadied after my run, sprinting again.

'Eliot,' I gasped, my tone hopefully full of optimism, rather than longing. 'How did you get on? What did he say?'

His face broke into the broadest smile.

'Yes,' he beamed. 'He said yes. He told me he'd changed his mind and was planning to tell you himself, so you didn't actually need my help at all.'

'I don't believe it!'

'Well,' Eliot laughed, 'you'd better. Bill told me he's given it more thought and now he's happy for you to investigate further and go ahead. He said he was taken aback before because it was all so unexpected, and even though he's still worried about your savings, he knows you're determined to make it happen, so . . .'

'Oh, Eliot.'

Within two strides I was across the barn and had flung myself at him. With his muscular arms wrapped tight around me, I kissed him hard and he kissed me back. The deep groan which escaped him was loaded with lust and I pressed my body tighter against him as my libido leapt even higher in response.

As one we stumbled, and my back made contact with the bales. Effortlessly Eliot lifted me up on to the stack. I ran my fingers across his chest while his hands held my face and he moved his body closer again, this time filling the space between my legs. Our kisses were rough, and arousing and my back arched in response. I wrapped my legs tight around his waist and urgently pulled him closer in. His leathers felt hard between us, at least I think it was his leathers.

Just for the briefest moment he pulled away again and our eyes met. I loosened my grip a little and he smiled, his breath every bit as hard and fast as mine. For those few seconds we'd let our guard down and released the safety valve. We'd given in to something we'd both been trying so hard to suppress. Had he not broken away, I know I wouldn't have been able to stop, but he had . . .

'Oh my god, Eliot,' I gasped, the words escaping in a rush on the out breath. 'I'm so sorry. That was terrible!'

He released me and I jumped down from the bale, my face aflame with a heady mix of desire, shock and shame.

'And there was me,' he said, shaking his head, 'thinking it felt absolutely perfect.'

He was right. It was perfect, but given that we'd vowed to not let it happen, it was also forbidden which in turn made it terrible.

'You know what I mean,' I said, my heart racing far faster than it had been during and after my run. 'I shouldn't have done that. I don't know what came over me.'

He looked at me and cocked his head. 'Well,' he said, smiling as he readjusted his suit, 'it was most likely one of two things. Either my ridiculously rugged good looks finally wore you down and you gave in to temptation, or it was sheer relief that your amazing idea has been given the go-ahead.'

I couldn't stifle the laugh which bubbled up as much out of relief that he was able to make light of what I'd done, as anything else.

'Or possibly both,' he carried on, as if he was mulling over some complicated scientific theory on the laws of attraction. 'I don't mind whichever it was, it was still a bloody brilliant kiss.'

'Yes,' I huskily agreed. 'It was rather, wasn't it?'

It was even better than I'd imagined it would be and, since I'd arrived in Wynbridge, I'd imagined it a lot.

'But,' he added, 'we probably shouldn't let it happen again . . .'

As devastating as that was, I knew he was right.

'Absolutely,' I agreed. 'It was just a one-off momentary lapse of the agreement we made to keep our feelings firmly under control.'

'A lapse on your part,' he teasingly pointed out. 'I was just standing here when you . . .'

'Well,' I butted in, 'you did reciprocate.'

'It would have been rude not to.'

This wasn't putting any distance between us and what had just happened at all. It was far too flirty.

'Well, whatever,' I carried on, attempting to draw a line. 'As you said, it was a spontaneous reaction to the supper club idea getting the go-ahead.'

'Yes, that was most likely it.'

We stood in silence for a moment and then he took a step towards me again.

'But the thing is,' he began, 'I've been thinking about our agreement, and I'm not sure . . .'

'Fliss?' came Grandad's voice from the yard and we sprang apart.

'Yes,' I called back. My voice sounded surprisingly normal given what had just happened. 'I'm here. I'm coming.'

Eliot grinned and I knew exactly what he was thinking.

'I better get going,' he said, heading for the barn door. 'I'm expected at work, but I was pleased to be of some use this morning.'

I wondered whether he was referring to his, as it turned out unnecessary, role as mediator or the more unusual one of willing recipient of my passionate kisses. I was also curious to know what it was about our agreement that he suddenly wasn't so sure about.

'Has he told you?' Grandad asked, stepping into the barn. 'Has he told you that I've changed my mind?'

'He has, Grandad,' I said, rushing to give him a hug. 'And I'm so excited. This project is really going to put Fenview Farm on the map.'

He hugged me tightly back and I felt a surge of happiness course through me.

'I'm still not sure about you putting in your own money though,' he said, looking worried when we broke apart.

'Let's go back to the house,' I suggested, 'and we can talk it all through properly.'

'I'll see you both later,' said Eliot. 'And not that it's anything to do with me, but I think you've made the right decision, Bill. Fliss is one very passionate and ambitious woman. She's going to make a success of this.'

'You're right my lad,' Grandad agreed.

'She's like those currants I love.' Eliot winked, as he pulled on his gloves. 'Delicate on the outside but inside she packs one heck of a punch.'

By the end of the day, the secret supper club (as we had taken to unofficially calling it) had Grandad's unconditional blessing and I had drafted up an action plan which suited us both. Grandad was insistent that I shouldn't rush headlong into the venture and, even though I was keen to forge ahead I understood his concerns and I also appreciated the value of thorough market research and careful financial planning. I would only get one shot at this project and was willing to do everything in my power, and by the book, to ensure the SSC was an unmitigated success.

Therefore, between that fateful Saturday in May and the end of the year, it was decided that I was going to be managing the harvest while sounding out local demand – both from producers and potential club members as well as getting in quotes for the kitchen and cloakroom installations and finding out what building regulations we would need to comply with as well as what permission from the local authorities.

It wasn't going to be a speedy process, but given that just a few weeks ago, I had no idea that Grandad and Fenview Farm even existed, I didn't think that a slow burn would be such a bad idea. After all, the total transformation of both our lives was proving to be a steep learning curve, so pacing ourselves would make it all far more manageable.

For the rest of that day, I forced myself (not always successfully) not to think about what had happened with Eliot in the barn, or speculate on what he had been going to say before Grandad found us.

It was exasperating to think that just as I had vowed to pare back my life, I'd completely lost control of my emotions, along with all common sense, and succumbed to my feelings. Both my body and my brain had taken full advantage of the unguarded situation and I'd foolishly allowed another complication in. I couldn't deny it was an utterly seductive few seconds, but I hoped I'd be able to keep myself in check from then on in.

Mum's presence felt very strong that afternoon and I knew she would have been mightily impressed that I had done something so spontaneous, that I'd let my heart rule my head without a thought for the consequences. But then that was her all over. She'd always been an act first, think later, type of woman and with mixed degrees of success. As a rule, I stuck to the rational and sensible path and that was where I was firmly planting my feet again.

Grandad and I had just finished clearing away after dinner that evening when the Banana-mobile arrived.

'Evening, Bec,' said Grandad, as he took in her smiling face. 'You're looking happy tonight, my love.'

'I'm in a good mood and I'm off to the pub,' she beamed. 'I wondered if you might fancy it, Fliss?'

'Oh yes,' said Grandad, before I had even opened my mouth. 'You should go, you've got plenty to celebrate.'

'So have you,' I pointed out. 'Why don't you come with us?'

'Yes, do,' said Bec. 'The more the merrier. What are we celebrating?'

'I don't think I could keep pace with you, young things,' he chuckled. 'But you should definitely go Fliss. Spread the word about our plans.'

'What plans are these?' Bec asked again.

'Or alternatively,' he said, noticing Bec's inquisitive expression, 'just tell Bec here and let her do the rest for you.'

'Hey,' she protested. 'I'm not that bad.'

'I know plenty of folk who would beg to differ,' Grandad good naturedly pointed out.

'Is it anything to do with my brother by any chance?' she guessed, not bothering to further defend her inability to keep a secret.

'Sort of,' Grandad and I said together.

'I knew something was up,' she mused. 'He came home

in a really weird mood earlier. It wouldn't have anything to do with you and him, would it, Fliss?'

'No,' I said, blushing so hotly, that I had to turn away. 'Of course not.'

Struggling again to push the memory and resultant tingling sensations aside, I gave myself a shake and almost made myself laugh out loud by mentally vowing that there would be no more pouncing on the hot biker.

I turned back to find Grandad and Bec exchanging what I could only describe as a loaded look, which nudged my determination to behave up another notch.

'Go and get changed then,' Bec urged, with a somewhat unsettling smile. 'The pub will be closing at this rate.'

Chapter 21

Grandad left it to me to tell Bec what it was that I had in mind for the farm. She was as excited about it all as I was but in no way satisfied that it was entirely responsible for Eliot's weird mood. However, knowing it would be a huge mistake to fess up, I kept the real reason for his Tiggerish behaviour to myself.

'Oh look,' she said as she swung the Banana-mobile into the market square, 'that's Anthony's car, isn't it?'

'Anthony,' I said, quickly jumping out the second Bec had applied the handbrake. 'Are you heading to the pub by any chance?'

I hoped he was. It would be the perfect opportunity to take him to one side and set him straight about Eliot *and* tell him that I hadn't been with him in The Mermaid the other night with a view to sussing him out at all.

It wasn't until I got closer however, that I realised Anthony didn't look in a particularly happy frame of mind. In fact, he had a face like thunder.

'Afraid not,' he tightly said in response to my question. 'I was just about to ring and ask if you fancied a run over to this wine bar I know in Peterborough, but something's come up and I've got to work.'

'What, now?' I frowned.

'Yes,' he said, chewing his lip and looking riled.

'Oh,' I said, 'that's a shame.'

I meant about him having to work in the evening, not about me missing out on the trip to the wine bar. The Mermaid was definitely more my scene.

'Well, not to worry,' he said, climbing in and starting his car. 'We'll do it another time. You've obviously got plans anyway.'

He sounded as narky about that as he did about having to work.

'Come on,' said Bec, as he sped away, 'otherwise we'll never get served.'

Luck was with me in the pub, not only because it was date night for Jemma and Lizzie and their respective partners, but also because Jake and Amber were enjoying a rare evening away from Skylark Farm too.

'Just the folk I was hoping to see,' I said to Bec, as I took a deep breath and plucked up the courage to approach them.

'I'll get us a drink,' she kindly offered. 'I'm on the lemonade because I'm driving, but you can have a drink, drink. In fact, I think you should. You've got more cause than ever to be celebrating tonight.'

'You're right,' I said. 'Thank you. I'll have a G and T, please. Something fruity if they've got it.'

I didn't have time to get too nervous about talking to the group as Amber spotted me and beckoned me over and Jake went in search of another chair.

'I'm with someone,' I told him, when I realised what he was doing.

'In that case,' he smiled, 'I'll nab two.'

'But we don't want to intrude,' I gabbled, 'I just want a quick word with you all really.'

Jemma wafted my words away.

'Don't be silly,' she said. 'It's a free for all in here tonight. There's going to be some music later. Come and meet my other half.'

Once I'd been introduced to her husband Tom and then Lizzie's partner, Ben, and Bec had got served at the bar, we all sat, sardine-like around the table.

'This is delicious,' I said, taking a sip of the very pink gin. 'Thank you, Bec.'

'It's blackberry,' she told me. 'From the Brambles distillery on the far side of town.'

'I didn't know there was a distillery in town,' I said, taking another flavoursome sip.

'Oh yes,' she said, 'it's a fairly new venture. You might want to think about asking them to come onboard with your plans.'

I knew that locally sourced drinks would be just as important as the food and I'd already factored the Skylark Farm cider into my ideas. Brambles gin would be a most welcome addition too and I wondered if there was perhaps a micro-brewery producing beer somewhere about.

'What plans are these?' Jemma asked.

'Oh sorry,' Bec winced. 'Me and my big mouth.'

'No,' I reassured her, 'it's fine.'

This was it. This was the moment I'd been hoping for, when I could float the idea to some of the people who had the potential to really help it take off.

'My plans for a diversification project at Fenview,' I said with as much confidence as I could muster. 'It's down to some of you that I've come up with it actually.'

I had everyone's attention and they all listened intently as I explained how Jake had told me about his desire to do more with the Skylark Farm produce than simply sell it, along with Lizzie's long-held wish for somewhere local and exciting to eat out in the evenings.

'So,' I recapped, having gone through it all in as much detail as I currently had, 'Grandad and I plan to open up the barn to local businesses to serve their produce at exclusive supper club events which will run on at least a monthly basis, possibly fortnightly, depending on the season and the demand.'

Jemma nodded encouragingly and looked every bit as enthusiastic as she had when she told me of her desire to collaborate with the farm and buy our fruit.

'I'm going to manage the club and the venue, and it will be up to the producers to come up with the menu. We're also going to invite local chefs and cooks too,' I added, 'as long as they use locally grown and sourced ingredients.'

'In that case, I'm in,' said Jemma, without a moment's hesitation.

I could have kissed her.

'And what about Fenview Farm fruit?' Lizzie asked. 'Will you be having your own evenings where you serve up dishes made with that?'

'Definitely,' I said. 'I have more than enough recipes and if I can pair the desserts with a wine merchant or distillery like the one that produced this delicious gin,' I held up my glass, 'then we'll be in for an amazing evening.'

Just as I said the last word, I looked over at the bar and spotted Eliot. He'd already seen me but looked away when our eyes met.

'That could be the perfect partnership,' nudged Bec.

'Yes,' I stammered, hoping she hadn't spotted the look that had passed between me and her brother and was referring instead to my desserts and Brambles distillery. 'Exactly.'

'I love it,' said Lizzie, sounding every bit as excited as Jemma.

'It sounds amazing,' Amber agreed, looking at Jake who I then realised, hadn't said a word. 'Is it going to be possible to prep the food on-site?'

'Eventually,' I said. 'But to begin with it will have to be prepared in advance. We need to make sure the idea has got legs before we invest in putting in kitchens and cloakrooms.'

'I don't think you'll have a problem with planning permission,' said Jemma's husband, Tom, who worked for the local council.

'And there's going to be something else too,' I mysteriously added. 'Something really special and very unusual, but I'm not going to share the details of that just yet.'

Grandad's fascinating Fenland collection was going to be the perfect extra element to embed that all-important sense of setting and place into the supper club evenings. I wanted everyone who came to the barn to know the captivating history of the area as well as the provenance of what they were eating and drinking.

'Now I'm even more intrigued,' said Jemma.

'Good,' I laughed. 'That was my intention.'

'And what about a name?' chimed in Lizzie. 'Are you going to call it the secret supper club?'

'I'm not sure,' I frowned. 'At the moment that's what's stuck, and more by accident than design, but it might change.'

'I like it,' said Lizzie's partner, Ben. 'It sounds exclusive and I love that the menu will always be changing too.'

'I'm so pleased,' I smiled. I had wondered if that might be a sticking point, but everyone seemed to understand what it was I was hoping to achieve. 'I want the ethos of the events to be seasonal, local and fresh. That's really important, so some dishes might only be available for a very short while. Our currants for example,' I said, doing my utmost to banish the image of a redcurrant popping on Eliot's tongue, 'are going to be ready next week.'

'Oh goodie,' said Jemma.

'But might be over earlier than usual, which is down to the weather,' I carried on, 'and obviously other growers will be impacted by that too and therefore, the menus will reflect the current season and how it's playing out.'

'It sounds amazing, doesn't it, Tom?' Jemma asked her husband.

'I think it sounds great,' he nodded, 'and I'm really pleased Bill's found a better use for the barn.'

'Than what?' I asked.

Jemma answered for him.

'He's just relieved I didn't talk Bill into selling it so we could convert it, aren't you?' she giggled, planting a kiss on his cheek. 'We've gone off the idea now.'

'I'm not surprised,' said Bec. 'It seems to me that you've already got more than enough on your plate.'

'Oh Bec, don't say that,' I whispered, loud enough for everyone to hear, 'she might change her mind about signing up for a Cherry Tree evening at the barn.'

'No chance,' said Jemma. 'I'm already planning it in my head.'

Bec looked at me and raised her eyebrows.

'Sounds like you're on to a winner,' she smiled.

It felt like it too. Or it would if Jake would only say something.

'What do you think, Jake?' I asked. 'Is this the sort of thing you had in mind when we talked at Skylark Farm?'

He shifted in his seat.

'Exactly the sort of thing,' he confirmed, but he didn't look very happy about it.

'Oh good,' I smiled and Amber looked away.

'But the thing is, Fliss,' he then carried on. 'I was so buoyed up after that conversation we had that I started looking for other potential venues straightaway.'

'Oh,' I said, my heart sinking, 'I see.'

'And I found somewhere willing to offer us an exclusive contract to serve our food every few weeks.'

I felt winded.

'Meaning that if you have Skylark produce events there,' I asked, 'you can't have them anywhere else?'

'Exactly,' he said. 'Committing to them would mean we couldn't be a part of the Fenview Farm venture. If only I'd known before what you'd been thinking, I wouldn't have looked elsewhere.'

It was a blow and I swallowed down the bitter knowledge that had it not been for Grandad's initial reluctance he would have known. Had I talked to Jake before Grandad, as I wished I had when Grandad initially said no, then he would have been in the loop from the start. The pork and apple products from Skylark Farm were such a major draw, I had imagined their events being some of the most popular by far.

'Is this going to affect our contract, Jake?' Jemma asked.

'No,' he told her. 'Don't worry about that. It's just our finished dishes this place is interested in, not the raw produce. We'll still be able to supply you and carry on selling direct on the farm and at the market too.'

Amber looked at me and back to Jake.

'But we haven't actually signed the contract yet, have we?' she reminded him, offering me a glimmer of hope. 'Nothing's been made official.'

'No,' he said, 'I was all set to next week, but having listened to what you're planning Fliss, I'm not so sure now. I'd far rather support you and Bill than this other place which was a compromise really and nothing out of the ordinary, but I'd need to see what exactly you have in mind before I commit.'

'Is that going to be possible?' Amber encouragingly asked me. 'When's your first event going to be?'

'Oh yes,' said Jemma. 'You need a trial run, Fliss. That way you can tempt Jake away from this other venue and let us see exactly what you have in mind. You could serve up some fruity desserts, couldn't you?'

I puffed out my cheeks, aware that they were all looking at me. This was all happening far faster than I had expected and I had no idea what Grandad would say, but I couldn't risk losing potential Skylark Farm supper evenings, could I?

'How about next Saturday night?' I said, embracing Mum's act first, think later philosophy. On this occasion I thought it more important than my slow and steady approach to things. 'Are you all free?'

The answer was a resounding yes and I gulped down more of my gin. It was mad to think that I would be able to pull it off in just a week, especially with everything else that needed doing on the farm, but I didn't have much choice.

'It will only be a taster of what I have in mind,' I told them all as they chattered excitedly away and Jake looked at me and smiled. 'So you can get a sense of what the space is like, and we'll be sitting on straw bales until I can source tables and chairs so you'll need to bring blankets and rugs because they're a bit scratchy.'

'What about glasses and cutlery?' someone asked. 'Shall we bring our own?'

'No,' I said, 'I can manage those, and crockery, but my budget won't run to alcohol so please bring whatever you want to drink.'

There was so much to think about. I needed to start making some serious lists.

'Will that be enough do you think?' I asked Jake. 'To tempt you away from this other place, as Jemma put it?'

'I'll answer that next week,' he said, with a smile. 'If that's all right with you?'

That was fair enough. Grandad might have been a good friend, but this was business we were talking about.

'Of course,' I said, feeling more determined than ever to make it all work.

'Here's to the secret supper club,' said Jemma, drawing everyone's attention again. 'A brand-new venture for Fenview Farm!'

We all raised our glasses in a toast and then Ben and Tom headed off to help get the music started and I went to the bar for more delicious gin and another lemonade for Bec.

'I take it explaining your plans for the farm went well?' said Eliot, who suddenly appeared beside me.

His breath was another gentle caress as he had to lean in to make himself heard and just like before, I felt my skin tingle in response, only this time more intently.

'Quite well,' I managed to shout back, over the opening

bars of a rousing Mumford & Sons tune. 'Not quite as perfectly as I'd hoped, but . . .'

'What?' Eliot mouthed.

'I said . . . Oh never mind.' I shook my head, knowing it would be impossible to explain now everyone was joining in with the lyrics.

'Dance with me!' Eliot yelled, as a few people filled the tiny space in front of the piano and began moving with abandon.

Before I could object, he took my hand, twirled me around and pulled me close. Without a care for the tune, he then enthusiastically joined in with the singing and I didn't have time to feel self-conscious, but then, looking at his happy face and shining eyes, I found I wasn't. I just wanted to dance and sing and sway and stay in his arms as we all laughed, danced and drank the night away.

We weren't quite the last to spill out into the square, but we were somewhere among the stragglers. The Cherry Tree and Skylark crews had left with cries of how much they were looking forward to the supper club and I was so relaxed I didn't feel panicked about it at all.

'I'll follow you back,' said Eliot, turning his bike around as I grappled with the seatbelt in the Banana-mobile.

'That was a great night,' I said to Bec. 'Thank you for inviting me along.'

I'd really felt a part of the community and I appreciated Bec including me. I hadn't felt that sense of belonging among a crowd in a while and it was wonderful to feel welcome both at the farm alone with Grandad and further afield among the friendly Wynbridge folk.

'I'm pleased you had a good time,' she laughed, coming to my rescue because I couldn't seem to make the belt fit into the holder.

It turned out I was trying to shove it into the seat.

'That was a typical Saturday night in town, so you'll have to get used it because you're one of us now.'

I rather liked the sound of that.

'And I have to say,' she impishly added, 'you and Eliot looked really good dancing together.'

'He danced with everyone,' I pointed out.

'But he kept coming back to you,' she quickly batted back.

I couldn't deny that because he had.

'I'll give you a hand next week, getting everything ready,' she kindly offered. 'I know there's only so much you'll be able to do, given the time limit, but I'll do whatever you ask of me so you'll have the hours to make it look as close to what you're imagining as possible.'

'I'd really appreciate that,' I told her, feeling suddenly more sober again. 'I'm going to start making some lists tomorrow and working out what to prioritise. Even though this is just a trial run, I need it to go well if I want to get Jake and Amber onboard.'

We were soon back at the farm and I clambered out and waved her off, but unlike the other night, Eliot stopped.

'I bet you've forgotten your key, haven't you?' he said, once he'd pulled his helmet off and climbed off the bike.

'Oh bugger,' I said, clapping my hand against my forehead. 'I have. I didn't give it a thought.'

The house was in darkness, so I didn't think Grandad had realised or waited up just in case.

'Lucky I've got mine then, isn't it?' said Eliot, pulling a chain out of the neck of his T-shirt.

'What else have you got tucked down there?' I giggled.

'Never you mind,' he said. 'Come on.'

I'd only taken a couple of steps towards the house when I happened to look up.

'Oh wow,' I gasped, tugging at his arm, 'look at the stars.'

It was a completely cloud free night and the moon was little more than a crescent so we could easily pick out the constellations. It looked very much like the sky I used to spend my evenings gazing at in Puglia. There was no light pollution there either. It didn't cross my mind then, that stargazing with Eliot felt far more romantic than me noticing the pinpricks of light when Anthony took me home after our meal. I'd been aware of the illuminated night sky then, but not in the same way.

'It's a beautiful night,' Eliot whispered. 'That's Venus, isn't it?'

I looked to where he was pointing.

'Yes,' I said. 'I think so.'

'Associated with beauty and love and . . .'

'Desire,' I swallowed and then, for the second time that day, I found my lips on his, only this time, he was the one who kicked the kiss off.

'I was going to say prosperity,' he whispered, when we finally broke apart.

'I'm sorry,' I whispered back.

'What are you apologising for?' he grinned.

'For interrupting,' I smiled back.

'Not for kissing me?'

'No,' I squeaked. 'That was definitely you this time.'

'Well,' he said, holding my gaze. 'I wanted to level things up a bit, so you didn't feel quite so guilty about earlier.'

'Was that the only reason?'

He shook his head and, still smiling, leant around me, unlocked the kitchen door and gently pushed me inside. Then he turned and left without another word.

Chapter 22

The next few days were a whirlwind of frenetic activity. Together, Bec and I picked the fruit early in the day and then she kindly took it with her to town as she was working in the café. After she'd gone, I would carry on making lists, giving the barn its basic makeover and devising a simple menu, incorporating the succulent Fenview Farm strawberries, to give a flavour of the potential supper club events to come.

There was also the added excitement of getting the internet sorted and knowing Fenview Farm's connection to the world wide web was imminent. I couldn't wait to have my first video call with Marco, Alessandro and Nonna. As wonderful as my new life was, I missed being able to include them in it and I was looking forward to combining my two fabulous families. I just knew Grandad and Nonna were going to get along.

However, even with the hectic schedule, I was never quite busy enough to stop thinking about what had happened between me and Eliot after our evening in the pub. He might have said that he had kissed me with a view to alleviating the guilt I felt for throwing myself at him first, but his impish actions served to confirm that I wanted to kiss him and I wanted him to kiss me back, again and again. And again.

'How's it all going?'

I was indulgently mulling over thoughts of kissing Eliot as I was giving the barn one last sweep ahead of arranging the seating and working out how best to incorporate some of Grandad's collection, however the sound of Louise's voice hastily pulled me out of my fantasising reverie and put a bit more colour in my cheeks too.

'Hey Louise,' I blushed, as I leant the broom against a straw bale and shifted focus from her son to her. 'So far, so good, but there's a long way to go and I'm still struggling to get rid of the dust.'

With her hands planted on her hips, she took the space in.

'You probably won't until you've properly sealed the walls and floor,' she practically pointed out. 'If I were you, I'd stop sweeping and brushing until you can do that, otherwise you'll just keep kicking it up.'

'I think you're right,' I agreed. 'I'm never going to banish it with a broom, am I? I can't wait until the internet's up and running and then I can start getting prices for things like sealant online.'

Banishing the motes was going to be quite an undertaking, but one I was very much looking forward to.

'And you do know about the auction sales in town, don't you?' asked Louise, stepping further in and looking up at the ceiling and around the walls.

I had done the same myself when addressing Anthony's concern about the soundness of the building, but I hadn't found any of the problems he'd hinted at. It all seemed fine to me. Had it not, I would never have suggested having the trial run. I would have been inviting a structural surveyor around instead.

'No,' I said. 'What auctions are these?'

'Oh, they'll be just the thing for you,' she keenly said. 'They're at the town hall once a month and they sell anything and everything. It'll be ideal place to go for bits and pieces for here. You can pick up tables and chairs for practically nothing and there's always a good range of household items like cutlery and crocks.'

'Oh wow,' I said, thinking of the ever-growing list of things I was going to need once the events – hopefully – took off. 'That does sound perfect.'

'I'll let you know when the next one is, but bear in mind it's a bit of a mishmash. You probably won't get complete sets of anything.'

It sounded more appealing by the minute. I wanted the supper club experience to be eclectic and unique, with a vintage twist, so mismatched would be ideal and most likely cost less. I knew I was getting a bit ahead of myself, thinking about décor and design, but now I had Grandad's blessing and the idea had met with such enthusiastic approval from my Cherry Tree friends, there was no harm in dreaming, was there? Thinking big would hopefully help me convince Jake and Amber that Fenview Farm was the right place to serve their fabulous Skylark produce.

'That's fine by me,' I smiled, already imagining the bargains I would be able to pick up. 'Perfect in fact.'

'I had a feeling it might be,' said Louise, looking well pleased. 'Do you happen to know where Bill is?' she then asked. 'He wanted me to come and give him a hand with something.'

'I'm here,' he said, briskly announcing himself in the doorway and making us both jump. 'And Fliss doesn't need to be bothered with details, Louise. She's got more than enough going on.'

'You scared me half to death,' Louise tutted, fanning herself with her hand. 'My temperature's gone right through the roof. You can't do that to a woman of my age without inducing a hot flush. You'll have to wait for me to cool down now.'

'No time for that,' he said, walking out again. 'Come on.'

I was intrigued to know what they were up to, but Grandad was right, I did have my hands full. I watched them walk away then turned my attention back to the barn and forgot all about the clandestine conversation happening in the house.

'Oh, my goodness,' drawled Bec as I ran her through the proposed list of taster desserts for Saturday night while we were picking the conveniently ripened plump and juicy red and blackcurrants. 'Can't you just make them all?'

'Yes,' I said, thinking of the delicious Anglo-Italian combos I'd come up with, 'I certainly could.'

I was going for a fusion menu. The finest Fenview Farm fruit incorporated into my Italian favourites. I had briefly wondered about including Nonna's tart, but the farm cherries weren't ready and I really did want my first taste of it away from Puglia to be a more private experience and made with Fenview fruit.

'Great,' Bec smiled. 'Because the semifreddo and sorbet both sound divine.'

'But I'm not going to,' I told her.

'Why not?' she pouted.

'Because if I do, I'll have nothing left to serve later in the season, will I, you clot.'

That was assuming the first evening was enough of a success to warrant thoughts of doing it again. Bec gave my pronouncement further thought, while I fretted on the whys and wherefores of the evening to come.

I was excited about the prospect of creating and managing the club, but as Saturday drew nearer, I was also increasingly worried that I wouldn't be able to make it the total triumph I needed it to be. Without thinking, I began to twist and turn the selection of Mum's bangles I had taken to wearing.

'That's fair enough,' Bec finally agreed, before checking her watch. 'I suppose you're right. Crikey, I better get going.'

'Oh blast,' I said, when she showed me the time, 'me too. It's later than I thought and I've got to head to town. I need to pick up some stuff.'

I was planning to create a cosy ambient setting in the barn and with just two electric sockets installed, I was investing in an abundance of twinkling fairy lights to help set the scene. The longest strands were going to be powered by electric, while the others, which I could twine around the place settings and bales, were battery operated. They were something I would be using when and if the business properly launched so I wasn't worried about the money I would be parting with to buy them. It was all part of my, speculate to accumulate and fingers firmly crossed, plan.

On Grandad's recommendation, I'd called the hardware store in Wynbridge and they were only too happy to oblige me with the lights as they had a few boxes left over from their festive stock. I'd also ordered the batteries from them and added a couple of wallpaper pasting tables to the list as they were cheap and relatively sturdy.

I might not have been able to have everything in the barn *exactly* how I wanted it, but I was determined to get it looking and feeling as good as possible. I hoped everyone, but especially Jake and Amber, would understand that the evening was a work in progress. I was planning to make notes on what everyone thought had worked, along with anything that hadn't. Hopefully there wouldn't be too much to scribble on that page.

I didn't linger in town, calling only at the café, the hardware store, and the deli for a few extra ingredients. When I got back to the farm, I was surprised to find Anthony's car parked on the drive. He wasn't in it, but the low murmur of voices led me to the kitchen where I found him talking to Grandad.

'Hi,' I said, walking in and dropping my bag from the deli on the table.

I'd left everything else in the Land Rover, ready to unload straight into the barn.

'Fuck,' Anthony swore, as he spun round to face me. 'Where did you spring from?'

Grandad looked equally as shocked.

'Town,' I frowned. 'I've just got back. What's going on?'

'Nothing,' they said together.

'I'm sorry I swore,' Anthony apologised. 'But you really made me jump.'

'No worries,' I said, my gaze flicking between the two of them. 'I'm guessing you were looking for me, Anthony?'

'What?'

'That's right,' said Grandad. 'I said you wouldn't be long so he might as well wait. You were quicker than I thought though.'

For some reason, I got the feeling that was problematic rather than pleasing.

'Do you two know each other?' I asked.

'Yes,' said Grandad.

'No,' said Anthony.

'Well, you either do or you don't,' I pointed out, struggling to read the atmosphere.

It might have been strained because I had made them jump, but then again it could have been something else entirely.

'Sort of,' Anthony conceded. 'A bit. Not well.'

'Right,' I said, still none the wiser.

'Mr Brown has just been telling me about your plans for the barn,' Anthony carried on. 'You've certainly got some big ideas, Fliss. Have you had the building checked out, like I suggested?'

'There's nothing wrong with it,' I told him, feeling annoyed that Grandad had mentioned what I had in mind. 'I've had a good look over it and it's fine.'

'In that case,' Anthony smiled, 'I hope I'm invited to the launch this weekend?'

'It's not a launch,' I told him. 'Just a few friends getting together to talk about the idea and have a look at the venue.'

'Oh, well that's even better,' he said, shoving his hands in his pockets and rocking back on his heels. 'Just my area of expertise. I'll be happy to come along and offer an opinion.'

'Right,' I uncertainly said.

If it was his opinion about the barn's safety, then I didn't want it.

'I'm a friend after all, aren't I?' he laughed.

Suddenly I wasn't so sure what category I'd put him in, and Grandad's expression suggested he wasn't either. What with his banging on about the barn and his repugnant rumour about Eliot, I was rapidly beginning to regret my decision to have dinner with him in an attempt to throw the man I really wanted to be with a curveball.

'Of course,' I swallowed.

'I'll see you Saturday then,' he brightly said.

My stomach churned at the thought of him and Eliot being in the barn together. I knew Eliot wouldn't do anything to jeopardise the smooth running of things, and besides, he surely couldn't know what Anthony had said he'd heard about him, but

I wasn't sure Anthony would be able to resist making mischief. I didn't want Eliot knowing it was Anthony I'd been out with now, but their coming together was beginning to feel inevitable.

Watching Anthony in the farm kitchen and noticing Grandad's reaction to him, I realised, I didn't really know him very well at all and in the last few minutes my brain had shifted him from convenient smokescreen to explosive loose cannon. It did nothing to settle my nerves.

'What time are you kicking things off?' he asked.

'Seven,' I said. 'Or just after.'

'Well, I'll see you then. I better get going. Bye, Mr Brown.'

Grandad didn't answer.

'I'll see you off,' I said, moving to follow him out. 'I was hoping to have a quick word.'

I wouldn't get a better, or more private, opportunity to make my feelings about what he had told me about Eliot more forcefully known. There was no way I could risk him coming Saturday night thinking I was in two minds about the integrity and motives of Grandad's dearest friend. Now was the time to nip all that in the bud.

'No time,' he said. 'I'm in a rush.'

'Just two minutes.'

'We'll catch up on Saturday,' he nodded and was gone.

Now I'd have to call him instead, which was far from ideal. And as well as repressing the rumour, I'd have to ask him what it was he had come to the farm for too. He'd acknowledged that he'd come to see me, but he hadn't said why before he'd shot off again.

'I didn't know it was him that you'd been seeing,' Grandad gruffly said as the Audi shot out of the yard.

He didn't sound impressed.

'We've only been out once,' I pointed out. 'The night you gave me the ruby earrings.'

'I know when it was.'

I didn't know why but he clearly didn't approve of my choice of dinner date and neither did I now. Going out with Anthony had been a huge mistake and it hadn't stopped Eliot and I falling further for each other either. Truth be told, I didn't think there was anything that could.

I woke to rain on Friday which was no bad thing because it stopped me splitting my focus even further. Unable to pick any fruit, I could justifiably divide my time between dressing the barn and prepping dishes.

Even with Bec's help, I still had a mountain of jobs to get through, pretty much all of the most important ones, and time was running out. Marco had always teased me about being a control freak and I was beginning to wonder if he was right. Maybe I should try delegating a little more.

'Commis chef, porter and general dogsbody reporting for duty,' grinned Eliot as his face appeared around the kitchen door.

'What?' I snapped, looking up from my lists.

I didn't have time for messing about, and to be honest, whatever guise Eliot had turned up in, I didn't have time to spare for mooning about over him either. More than anything I needed to remain calm and collected and the reaction of my head and my heart to his sudden appearance rendered me incapable of either.

'Sorry,' he said, sensing the tone and dialling it down. 'Not the time?'

'Definitely not the time,' I agreed.

'In that case,' he said, turning around, 'let me try that again. I was only clinging to humour to make our first meeting after the snog-gate part deux debacle less excruciating, but I read it wrong. Hold on. Wait there. Don't move.'

He walked back out and I shook my head.

'I really don't have time for this,' I called after him, but I was smiling as I said it.

A few seconds passed.

'Hi,' he said, walking back in and looking a little damper than he had been before. 'I had a feeling that you might be busy today so, as it's my day off, I thought I'd come over and see if I could lend you a hand.'

'Idiot,' I muttered, but I was still smiling.

'I'm going to sort the internet,' he carried on, 'but then I'm at your disposal to chop fruit, arrange tables and carry boxes.'

'The ideal dogsbody.'

'Exactly. And I absolutely promise not to kiss you or even mention what happened before because that would make it awkward again . . .'

I raised my eyebrows and bit my lip.

'Bugger,' he groaned. 'I almost had it, didn't I? Hold on.'

He went to walk back out again.

'Enough,' I said, holding up my hands in a gesture of

surrender. 'You've worn me down. You've got the job because the last thing I need are more damp footprints trailing in and out of my kitchen.'

'Excellent,' he grinned. 'And just as well because I've got no way of getting home until Bec picks me up.'

'No bike today?'

So preoccupied with my plans I hadn't noticed he was wearing civvies.

'Not in this weather. I'm not a fair-weather biker, but it's been a while since it rained and the roads are pretty greasy. So, what can I do?'

While he faffed and fiddled setting up the internet and swore a bit at Grandad's laptop in the dining room, I settled to making the strawberry semifreddo which was going to be the following evening's star turn. I also baked half a dozen small strawberry loaves and prepped three trays of meringues. They would take ages in the oven so could be left to their own devices while we dressed the barn.

'This is driving me crazy,' said Eliot, coming back into the kitchen and washing his hands.

'Can't you get it to work?'

'What?'

'The internet.'

I hoped he could because I really wanted to talk to the Rossis before the main event.

'Not that,' he said. 'That's all sorted. You're up and running.'

'Oh, yay!' I beamed, resisting the urge to cover him in kisses. 'What's driving you crazy then?'

'The fabulous smells coming from this kitchen, of course,' he drawled. 'You probably can't smell them because you've been in here all morning, but they are divine.'

'Just as well I made an extra strawberry loaf for lunch then, isn't it?' I grinned. 'Although, this one has no glaze. I'll be doing that tomorrow along with dipping some strawberries in chocolate.'

Eliot licked his lips and I hastily looked away. I wondered what redcurrants dipped in chocolate would taste like.

'In case you hadn't worked it out,' I said, piling the used pots and bowls together and gladly focusing on a different fruit, 'tomorrow's theme is strawberries.'

'Very apt,' he grinned. 'The perfect fruit to kick your new business off.'

Hearing someone else say it, and so close to the event, made it all feel very real and my heart gave a little flutter.

'Shall we get this lot washed up before we eat?' Eliot suggested, reaching for the washing up liquid.

'No,' I said, feeling wobbly. 'Let's eat first. I'm famished.'

As soon as we'd eaten our fill, which took ages because Eliot and Grandad were determined to demolish the entire loaf *and* sing the praises of every mouthful, not that I objected to their praise because it was just the confidence boost I needed, we tidied away. Then I went to finish setting up the barn, and Eliot followed on a few minutes later.

Grandad was in charge of keeping an eye on the meringues, but I'd set a timer on my phone, just in case he got distracted. He hadn't seemed quite himself since Louise's visit and Anthony had left something behind in the ether which affected the atmosphere too. After Saturday I would try and get to the bottom of it all, but for the moment I had to stay on task.

Eliot and I were soon immersed in things and it felt like no time at all before Grandad was calling from the house and my phone alarm buzzed in my pocket.

'I'll be back in a sec,' I said to Eliot, before rushing off to rescue the meringues.

When I walked back into the barn, I realised just how much I, along with Bec and Eliot, had achieved since that very first day when I pulled open the doors and found Grandad's collection of Fenland paraphernalia all piled up, along with the cat's preferred sleeping spot.

'What do you think?' Eliot asked, looking around.

'I love it,' I swallowed, feeling a little wobbly again. 'It's nothing short of a miracle.'

Eliot nodded, but didn't look quite as entranced by the vision as I would have liked. It was only then that I realised he'd been rather quiet since he'd joined me after lunch. What was going on there, I wondered?

'And with all the lights on,' I added, 'it will look even prettier.'

Rather than try and fill the whole barn, we'd concentrated on setting up one area instead. There were only going to be a small group of us on Saturday, and I wanted to create a cosy pocket, rather than spread us about. When the club was properly up and running the entire space could be filled in the same way, but for the first foray into entertaining, the intimate area we'd put together would be perfect.

'It's a shame there's only limited power though,' I said, casting my eyes over the pasting tables and at the ceiling above, where we'd draped the strings of lights.

The tables were covered with plain white sheets and embellished with hessian runners which I'd made from strips cut from a roll I had spotted in Lizzie's crafting corner in the café. I'd ended up buying a few other things from her too, including some bunting made out of strawberry patterned fabric. It was those little details which made the biggest difference.

Grandad hadn't looked impressed when he spotted the hessian or when I told him I was going to glue strips of it around rinsed out jars to make tea light holders. Looking at them lined up though, the hessian further embellished on some with sage green raffia bows and on others with string, I thought they looked perfect. And they'd only cost pennies which was a real bonus.

'That won't matter for tomorrow,' said Eliot. 'You've got so many candles as well as these battery-operated lights, that you'll get away with it and Mum's got a dozen or so Mason jar solar lights which she said you can borrow.'

'They'll be great.' I nodded. 'Fingers crossed the sun will be shining brightly enough to charge them.'

'And I can supply the music,' Eliot carried on. 'Unless you'd got other ideas for that?'

'Music,' I said, pulling a face. 'I hadn't even thought of it.'

'Leave that to me then. I'll set up a playlist. Nothing too rousing,' he added. 'Just chilled out background stuff.'

'Thanks,' I said, adding music to my list and writing his name next to it. 'I'll cut the flowers and greenery fresh for the other jars in the morning and Grandad has already helped me to put together a box of glasses, cutlery and crocks that we can use.'

It was a motley collection, garnered from odd things he'd hung on to for years and I loved it all the more for that. When the club properly launched, I wouldn't be using it because it was too precious, but using family pieces for the trial run felt perfect. I knew Nonna would approve of that. In fact, she was going to love everything about the club. Bringing people together to enjoy good food was her favourite thing in all the world.

'Fliss?'

'Mm?'

'Are you all right?'

'Yes,' I said, clearing my throat and blinking away the tears the thoughts of Nonna evoked. 'Sorry, what did you say?'

Eliot walked over and tentatively put his arm around my shoulders. I leant against him and put my arm around his waist then rested my head on his chest. We didn't say anything, but we didn't need to. I wondered if he was suppressing the same urges as I was. To me, those few seconds felt more intimate than either of the kisses we'd shared.

'What was it you were saying before?' I eventually asked, looking up at him.

He cleared his throat. 'I was asking about what you'll do for crockery and stuff when more people come.'

'Your mum mentioned the sales in town,' I told him. 'They sound like the ideal place to pick things up.'

'That's what I was going to suggest too,' he said, looking down at me.

I felt my heart start to flutter again so gently extricated myself from his comfortable embrace.

'There's just Grandad's collection to think about now,' I said, indicating the corner of the barn where everything was stacked. 'I don't want to give away too much about it tomorrow night, just enough to strike up a conversation and create some interest.'

'I'm interested already,' he said, picking up the pair of skates. 'What is all this stuff?'

I gave him a quick rundown on what Grandad had been hoarding, even explaining what some of it was because he didn't know and by the time I'd finished, Eliot was as enthusiastic about incorporating it into the barn as I was.

'This is the perfect USP,' he said, sounding entranced as he turned one of the eel traps over in his hands. 'You could even get Bill to tell a few tales at some of the events and explain to the guests a little about the history of the Fens. He's got enough anecdotes to keep everyone entertained for hours.'

'That's a brilliant idea,' I agreed. 'Why hadn't I thought of that?'

'Not on your Nellie!' said Grandad, who had slipped inside without either of us noticing.

'You don't fancy it, Bill?' Eliot laughed.

'No chance,' he said. 'By all means, put my collection on show, but I won't be talking about it.'

Eliot and I exchanged a conspiratorial smile.

'And you needn't look like that, the pair of you,' Grandad said, shaking his head as he came further in. 'I won't change my mind.'

'Maybe you could tell Fliss and she could do it,' Eliot suggested.

'No dice,' I quickly said and the two of them laughed to have turned the tables on me.

Grandad spent a few minutes taking everything in and by the time he'd finished, he looked a little tearful himself.

'You'd never think it was the same place,' he sniffed. 'And I can see what you had in mind for that old sacking now,' he added. 'It doesn't look too bad, does it?'

I went to say something, but spotted him wink at Eliot so knew he was teasing.

'You've done a grand job,' he then said. 'I never would have believed it could look like this.'

'And this is just one corner,' I pointed out. 'Think how it'll look when it's full.'

Grandad nodded and looked around again.

'I've made tea,' he said huskily, 'so come up to the house when you're ready.'

Eliot and I gave him a few minutes to recover. We both knew the significance of what I was trying to achieve and what a difference it could make to the future of the farm. We finished checking everything was as perfect as possible and then pulled the doors shut.

'I know Bec still wants to help,' I smiled at Eliot as I made sure they were bolted tight, 'but I don't want her seeing it until tomorrow night now.'

'I don't blame you,' he agreed. 'Otherwise the whole town will know what it looks like before you've even started.'

'There is that,' I laughed, though I'd been thinking more of watching her reaction to seeing it all set up for the first time.

'She's helping out in the evening though, isn't she?' Eliot asked. 'With the serving and stuff.'

'Yes,' I said. 'Between the two of us we should be able to manage.'

'Three,' he said. 'I'll be helping too, don't forget.'

'You don't have to,' I told him. 'I know you've got a full-on workday, so I wasn't expecting you to.'

'I know you weren't,' he said. 'But I want to. If that's all right? This is a huge deal for the farm and I want to be a part of it. That is okay, isn't it?' he frowned.

'Of course,' I swallowed. 'I just didn't want you feeling you had to when you'd been on the go all day. I'm more than happy for you to find a seat and let the food come to you.'

'Are you sure about that?' he asked, one eyebrow cocked. 'You're not trying to keep me out of the way, are you?'

'What?' I frowned. 'No, of course not.'

There was no way I could explain to him that I wanted him in one corner, this guy Anthony, who I'd been out with and who was bad-mouthing him, in the other and never the twain should meet, without revealing the mess I'd made of things. Far better to feign ignorance instead.

'You're not worried about me bumping into your boyfriend?' Eliot then shockingly asked.

'Who?' I blustered.

'Bill happened to mention after lunch, that the chap you went out to dinner with the other week is going to be here.'

I wondered if that accounted for Eliot's change of mood. I was rather annoyed that Grandad had said anything.

'Oh,' I said. 'Right. Yes, he is, but he's not my boyfriend. I only went out with him to . . .'

The words had rushed into my mouth before I could stop them, but I forced them back down.

'Yes?'

'Oh,' I said. 'It doesn't matter now.'

'Well, I'm relieved he's not your boyfriend,' Eliot smiled. 'Because I don't go around kissing women who are already spoken for. I was worried I'd broken the unwritten rule.'

'You haven't,' I huskily said. 'You didn't.'

'That's all right then,' he said back.

'Perfectly all right,' I agreed.

But of course it wasn't all right, and I was already spoken for, because my heart unreservedly now belonged to him.

Chapter 23

I lost count of the number of times I snuck out to try and call Anthony that evening. Either my phone signal dropped out before the call had connected or he didn't answer when it did. In the end I gave up and resigned myself to hoping that I would be able to grab a few minutes with him prior to everyone else arriving. It wasn't ideal, but it was the best I could do.

'So,' said Grandad, peering at the laptop screen as I prepared to make my first call to Puglia, 'are you sure you know how this works?'

'Yes,' I told him. 'It's ever so easy. Sit here next to me and I'll introduce you to everyone.'

If possible, my heart was hammering even faster than it had been when I'd locked lips with Eliot in the barn. It felt like for ever since I'd seen my Italian family and I couldn't wait to fill them in on everything that had been happening. A written email was all well and good, but actually seeing them was going to be wonderful.

'No, no,' said Grandad, hastily backing towards the kitchen door. 'You say your hellos first and I'll come back in after I've checked the hens.'

He sounded nervous, and truth be told, I was a bit jittery myself. Once he'd gone, I wiped my hands down my jeans, took a deep breath and pressed the button to connect the two farms. I kept my fingers crossed, hoping that Marco would pick up and I didn't have to wait many seconds before he did.

'*Ciao* Fliss!'

'Marco!' I beamed as his familiar face and the backdrop of the comfortable Rossi kitchen filled the screen.

My nerves disappeared in less time than it took my heart to beat again.

'Papà!' he shouted over his shoulder. '*Vieni qui*, papà! Nonna! *Come stai*, Fliss?'

'I'm well,' I smiled back. 'Really well. How are you all?'

'Fliss!' shouted Alessandro, appearing suddenly in shot and looking a little red in the face. 'This is a surprise. How are things?'

'*Il mio bambino*!' I heard Nonna call out before she also appeared. 'What has taken you so long?'

Once they were seated so they could all see the screen, I explained that the farm had finally been connected to the internet and how from then on, I would be able to keep in touch on a regular basis.

'Finally,' Nonna smiled in approval.

'And how is life on the farm?' Alessandro asked. 'How is your *nonno*?'

'Grandad is very well,' I said. 'He'll be here in a minute so I can introduce you, and we have exciting new plans for the farm.'

I told them all about the secret supper club idea and how the following evening was going to be a trial run. Nonna wanted to hear all about the menu I'd devised and whether her cherry and almond tart was going to be the main attraction.

'I haven't made it yet,' I told her.

'What, no taste of home?' she tutted.

'I'm waiting until our cherries are ripe,' I told her. 'I want it to be a proper Rossi-Brown amalgamation.'

She willingly accepted my reasoning and agreed that would make it all the more special. She also gave her blessing to the dishes I'd decided upon, which went some way to settling my jangling nerves. If they were good enough for my nonna, they'd be good enough for our first guests.

'You've settled in well, Fliss,' Alessandro smiled, once I'd told them more about the place and what I'd been doing.

'You look healthy,' Nonna observed.

'No wonder you've abandoned us for so long,' Marco quipped, and his father nudged him so hard he nearly fell off his chair.

'By the way, Marco,' I said, just to get my own back. 'I have a friend with a Ducati.'

Marco looked enraged, Nonna shook her head and Alessandro groaned.

'Thank you for that,' he tutted. 'He's not talked about bikes in weeks!'

'I'm not really teasing you Marco,' I giggled. 'I just thought it might encourage you to come and visit me once the olive harvest is finished there and you need a break from trying to fill my shoes. I have another friend I think you might like too.'

I told him all about Bec and by the time I'd finished he was ready to book his ticket to come and meet her. We chatted a little longer and I was just about to give up on Grandad when he finally crept back into the kitchen.

'Come and say hello,' I insisted, budging my chair along and pulling out another for him.

He sat down, looking awkward.

'*Ciao*,' he then shocked me by saying. '*Piacere di conoscerti*.'

'Nice to meet you!' I gasped as the Rossis all laughed at my obvious surprise. 'I didn't know you spoke Italian, Grandad!'

'I don't,' he said. 'But I thought I should learn a few phrases now we're all connected.'

I was more touched than he probably realised. With introductions made, Nonna and Grandad fell to chatting as if they'd known each other for ever and when talk turned to Mum, Alessandro, Marco and I said our goodbyes and left them to it.

I could still hear them talking long after I'd had my shower and climbed into bed. It felt wonderful to finally have my two lives running on the same track but, as comforting as it was, it didn't help me sleep.

Throughout the night, my thoughts ran rampant, flitting from how seductive it had felt to kiss Eliot, to then wondering what Grandad and Louise were scheming, and on to whether Anthony was going to say something indiscreet during the supper club.

When Saturday finally dawned it was soft, bright and thanks to the rain, refreshed. Which was more than could be said for me.

'No arguments,' said Grandad when I winced at the sight of the cooked breakfast he'd prepared. 'It's going to be all hands to the pumps today and you'll need your strength. Did your mother never tell you that breakfast is the most important meal of the day?'

'Funnily enough, she didn't,' I said with a wry smile. 'But Nonna did.'

'What a woman,' he wistfully said.

'I heard you talking late last night.'

'I hope we didn't keep you awake?'

'No,' I said. 'You didn't.'

If anything, the sound of their voices drifting up the stairs had been a comfort. Much like when I was little and used to listen to the Rossi babble from below in the kitchen, not that the murmur had helped me nod off last night, but then nothing would.

'She told me so much about your mother,' Grandad carried on, sounding a little choked. 'And the woman she became.'

I daresay Nonna could tell him things that not even I knew.

'It was all rather a surprise,' he said, with a watery smile, 'but a good one.'

'I told you she was different to the tempestuous teen you had to try and cope with, didn't I?'

'That you did,' he said, turning back to the stove. 'And Marta and I are going to keep in touch, so I daresay I'll hear more about her soon.'

'I'm sure you will,' I smiled, thinking how wonderful it was to hear Nonna's name on Grandad's lips, even with his Fenland accent.

Rather than pile my plate high, he added only a little of everything to tempt me and as I slowly worked my way through it, I began to feel better.

'So,' said Grandad, tucking into a succulent Skylark sausage, 'what's on the itinerary ahead of the grand launch?'

I had told Grandad of Jake's plans to sign a contract with another venue and he had apologised for not agreeing to my idea straightaway and giving me the chance to get in first. Consequently, he was now as mindful as I was as to how much was riding on the evening's success.

'Actually,' I said, looking down my list which hadn't been more than a couple inches from my side all week, 'thanks to Eliot's help yesterday, there's nowhere near as much to do now as I had expected. It's all finishing touches in the barn and simple makes in the kitchen.'

The few tasks still to be completed, such as dipping the strawberries in chocolate, were thankfully stress free and repetitive, real nerve soothers.

'He's a good lad,' nodded Grandad. 'And it was a pleasure to see you both getting on so well yesterday, even if you did gang up on me a bit. I had a feeling the pair of you would shake down well.'

We might have shaken down even better if he hadn't mentioned Anthony, but there was no point dwelling on that now. Eliot and I were still trying to keep a lid on things, so it was most likely for the best that he thought I'd got romantic ambitions elsewhere, even if I had denied them when he'd asked.

'So,' said Grandad, pushing away his empty plate, 'what do you want me to do this morning? Stay out of the way or get stuck in?'

'You can help me make the chocolate dipped strawberries if you like.'

'They sound wonderful.'

'And they taste amazing,' I proudly said. 'I'm going to go and pick the biggest and the best and then we'll get started.'

I'd found excellent quality bars of milk, white and plain chocolate in the Wynbridge deli and I made each sauce separately, letting the glossy, melted mixture cool a little so it thickened slightly before we dipped the strawberries.

'Oh no,' Grandad tutted, on more than one occasion, quickly popping the chocolate heavy berry into his mouth before I had time to check it. 'That one was dipped too deep.'

'I'm really not sure you should be in charge of quality control,' I told him, looking at his chocolate stained lips.

Between us we decided the dark ones were our favourite. The bitterness of the chocolate balanced the sweetness of the strawberries perfectly, but the ones I'd added a light sprinkling of sea salt to were very good too.

Once they had all completely cooled, I applied a drizzle

and put them in the fridge. The dark and milk chocolate berries had a white drizzle and the white ones a milk or dark. It took a while but I was delighted with the results, and the additional smears of chocolate across Grandad's face were proof enough that he was happy too.

'I'm not sure they count as one of your five a day,' he said, taking the sheet of damp kitchen towel I offered him, 'but they should.'

'They're not exactly cutting edge in cooking either,' I pointed out, 'but they are delicious and I think they'll be a nice way to end the evening.'

'Definitely,' he agreed. 'Perhaps with a lovely glass of champagne.'

I'd rather gone off champagne. My last two experiences with it hadn't been much cause for celebration.

'Maybe,' I said, wondering if third time really might be a charm.

After lunch, I cut the flowers – a mix of Nanna's roses, peonies and frothy Alchemilla mollis – and arranged them in the glass jars along the hessian runners. With a tea light in a jar in-between, and the simple place settings laid out, the tables looked lovely. Simple and rustic but with an elegant twist. No one would ever need know there were cheap and basic pasting tables underneath. They weren't going to be a long-term solution, but for kicking things off, they were ideal.

'Mason jars as promised,' said Louise when she turned up a little later. 'And hopefully they'll be fully charged by the end of the day, thanks to the upturn in the weather.'

As well as the jars, she also had two large terracotta tubs filled with bedding plants in the back of her car. They were a riot of bright orange and purple petunias, red geraniums and frothy blue lobelia which trailed artfully over the sides.

'I saw them for sale on the market and thought they might look nice either side of the door,' she said, as I helped her manoeuvre them into place. 'Consider them my contribution to the evening.'

'They're beautiful,' I said, giving her the hug she usually managed to get in first. 'They're the perfect welcome to the barn. Thank you so much.'

'You're more than welcome,' she said. She looked well pleased by my reaction. 'And I'll be back later to help carry the food from the house.'

Once she'd gone, I thought about the logistics of using the farm kitchen as a holding area for future events. It would be fine in the short-term, as would letting people pop into the house to use the loo, but the sooner we got the building work done the better. Assuming the club proved popular of course.

If it was all systems go by the end of the year, I hoped the money I had squirrelled away would be enough to cover what needed doing. My 'saving for things as I went along' philosophy was much like my Brown ancestors', but then, if what I had wasn't enough and borrowing was the only way to move things forward then needs must.

Chapter 24

'I can hear a car!' Grandad called from his room to mine, when I was getting changed.

My fingers fumbled to do up the final button on the floral-patterned tea dress which, out of the few things I had in my wardrobe, seemed to fit the evening best. Teamed with my old but comfy Converse All Star plimsolls, the ensemble felt pretty but practical.

'But it's too early!' I called back as I swept my hair into a ponytail.

'I know, do you want me to go and see who it is?'

'No,' I said, taking one last look in the mirror, 'I'm dressed, so I'll go. Given the time, I'm pretty certain it won't be any of the guests.'

But it was.

'Anthony,' I said, rushing into the kitchen and finding him already there. 'You're very early.'

The sight of him caused a rush of both relief and exasperation. Relief because I would now have the chance to set him straight about Eliot, but exasperation because it really was ridiculously early.

'I know,' he said, moving away from the dresser and presenting me with a huge bouquet which he had somehow hidden behind his back, 'but I wanted to give you these and wish you luck before everyone else arrived.'

'They're lovely,' I said, taking the cellophane-wrapped bunch. 'Thank you so much. I'll pop them in a jug for now and unwrap them later, when I've got a bit more time.'

'I knew you'd like them,' he said, pulling out a chair and making himself at home.

'I do,' I said, trying to sound grateful, even though the gaudy, tortured bunch wasn't my cup of tea at all, 'and actually I'm pleased you're early, because although I haven't got time to sit with you, I do want to talk to you. Just give me a minute.'

I ran back upstairs to tell Grandad who had arrived and that we were going for a walk. He looked about as impressed as he had the day he found out it was Anthony who had taken me out to dinner.

'Have you got time for a walk?' he frowned, looking at the clock next to his bed. 'I know Judd's early but you still have things to do.'

'It'll be fine,' I reassured him. 'It will help settle my nerves.'

I didn't specify what the nerves were about and just let him assume the obvious.

'All right,' he said. 'I'll listen out for anyone else.'

I quickly kissed him on the cheek and went back downstairs to whisk Anthony away.

'It's about Eliot,' I said, the second we were out of earshot of the house.

'Oh yes,' he keenly said, linking his arm through mine. 'What have you found out?'

'Nothing,' I said, disentangling myself and turning to face him. 'Absolutely nothing.'

'I can't say I'm all that surprised,' he sighed. 'He's probably too clever to leave any hint . . .'

'No,' I said, cutting him off. 'I don't think it's because he's too clever to be the sneak you're suggesting, it's because there's nothing to find. You did warn me, that what you'd heard was all supposition, didn't you?'

'I did,' he hesitantly agreed.

'And that's exactly what it is,' I forthrightly said.

The look Anthony gave me as he shook his head was extremely patronising.

'He's done quite a job on you, hasn't he?' he mockingly said.

'What's that supposed to mean?' I flushed, instantly riled.

'Never mind.'

'Look,' I said. 'Whoever was spreading those rumours has got things completely wrong. Eliot's no conman, in fact he's probably the best friend Grandad's got and even if he did go off the rails when he was younger, he's certainly made amends for it since.'

'You seem very keen on the senior citizens' saviour all of a sudden,' Anthony laughed.

'Not in the way that you're insinuating.'

'Well, that's all right then.'

I didn't ask why.

'Eliot's a friend,' I said, meeting Anthony's gaze and hoping the truth wasn't written all over my face. 'A good one and a trusted one.'

I knew beyond any reasonable doubt that I was in love with Eliot but I wasn't going to admit it, especially not to Anthony. All I was interested in achieving, was getting through the evening without him mucking things up.

'Well,' Anthony said, letting out a long breath. 'I'm relieved to be proved wrong and if I hear any more about it, I'll be sure to set the gossip-monger straight.'

I wasn't sure I believed he would, because I was beginning to think that the only person spreading the gossip, that I hadn't even heard so much of a hint of, was him. That said, I supposed, as long as he kept his mouth shut that would be the end of it.

'Fliss!' I heard Grandad call. 'Come on. It's almost time!'

I hoped Anthony really was going to suit his actions to his words and I rushed back to the barn to make the final few adjustments. Our early arrival spent the whole time getting under my feet and didn't offer to help once.

'Why don't you move your car?' Grandad suggested when he realised I was getting wound up. 'In fact, I'll show you where you need to park it, Anthony and then you can stand at the gate and direct everyone else as they arrive.'

The look of disapproval on Anthony's face soon restored my humour.

'That's a great idea, Grandad,' I grinned as he took Anthony off.

There was an influx of cars just before seven and everyone congregated on the drive. I wanted to let them all into the barn at the same time so I could gauge their collective response. The only people missing were Eliot and Bec. Louise explained that Eliot had finished work and the pair had just had to rush off somewhere.

'They won't be long,' she reassured me. 'They'll definitely be here before you want to start serving the food, but I'm here to help if needs be so don't worry.'

I felt rather disappointed, because I'd wanted to have the pair of them with me when I opened the doors, but I couldn't leave everyone standing about. So, before my nerves got the better of me, I took in the eager faces of my new friends, noting that they'd all dressed up for the occasion and were carrying bags bulging with bottles and blankets.

'Evening everyone,' I said, pulling in a breath. 'Thank you all so much for coming tonight. I know that you were as keen as I was when I explained about the secret supper club plans in the pub last week.'

'Hear, hear!' quipped Jemma and everyone laughed.

'But,' I said, trying not to look at Amber and Jake, 'what I want to find out is whether that was alcohol fuelled enthusiasm,' everyone laughed again, 'or if you really think I'm on to something.'

The group quietened.

'What you'll experience inside the barn tonight is just a

small taste, no pun intended, of what I envisage the whole could eventually be and I'd really appreciate any feedback you'd be willing to offer. I want to hear the good and the bad, but more than that, I want you to enjoy your evening.'

With that, I pulled open the doors and led everyone inside. The collective gasp and excited chatter which followed me in released the air I'd been holding in my lungs, and I just knew that I'd made an impression and a good one. Whatever the Skylark duo decided, I'd given it my best shot.

'Sorry,' said Bec, as she rushed in a few minutes later. 'We missed it didn't we? Your opening speech. Oh wow!' she then added, stopping in her tracks and looking around. 'This is *amazing*.'

I was delighted that she thought so.

'That seems to be the general consensus,' I agreed, happily looking around as my guests acquainted themselves with the space, admired the decorations and listened to Grandad waxing lyrical about his collection. 'And don't worry, I didn't really give a speech.'

'So much for Bill not wanting to make an announcement of his own,' said Eliot, who smelt incredible and looked gorgeous in an open necked dark shirt and jeans.

'I know, right?' I laughed, glancing over to where he had Jake, Ben and Lizzie hanging on his every word as they passed around an eel trap.

'Oh god,' Eliot then muttered. 'Is that Anthony Judd?'

Bec followed his gaze and I looked too. Anthony and Jemma's husband Tom, were deep in conversation at the back of the barn next to the table which was laden down with the drinks everyone had brought along.

'What's he doing here?' Eliot frowned. 'He was a total prick at school and rumour has it, he's not changed much.'

More rumours, although I had to admit this one had the potential to carry more merit than the alleged one about Eliot ever had.

'That's who Fliss went out to dinner with,' Bec informed him. 'He's Mr Helpful. I didn't realise you knew him and I certainly don't remember him from your year at school.'

'What?' Eliot gasped. 'He's the boyfriend Bill told me about?'

Grandad obviously hadn't provided a name.

'He's not my boyfriend,' I said again. 'And we only went out once.'

'Have I put my foot in it?' asked Bec.

'No,' Eliot and I said together.

'I'll go and get the music sorted,' he then added, striding off.

Bec tried to stop him, but he was out of reach before she'd realised he was going.

I left Eliot to it and while Bec and Louise lit the many tea lights, I played the hostess and gratefully soaked up the abundant praise and enthusiasm. I did my best to shrug off Eliot's reaction to finding Anthony ensconced and tried not to hone in on Jake and Amber. Undue pressure wouldn't help the supper club's cause and besides, left to their own devices, they looked happy enough.

'Have you got a sec?' Eliot asked, once he'd set the music

playing and had apparently recovered his temper. Outwardly, at least. 'Bec has something for you.'

His words reminded me that I had something for her too. I would have to tell her about Marco as soon as I got the chance.

'This is why we were late,' she said, presenting me with a bottle of pink coloured liquid. It was quite small and it didn't have a label. 'It's from the owner of Brambles,' she added, eyeing it greedily. 'One of a very limited trial run. Eliot told him about your plans for this place and he wanted to give you this.'

'We had to go and pick it up.'

'So, it's more a gift from both of you,' I began to say, but Eliot cut me off.

Now he knew I'd been out with Anthony, he didn't seem to want to give me anything.

'It's strawberry gin,' he said. 'Their first ever batch. Jack wanted to call in himself, but he's running a private tasting session tonight. He asked us to tell you that he'd like to talk to you about a potential collaboration event, combining Fenview fruit with his drinks.'

'Oh wow,' I gasped. 'That's amazing. Thank you both so much.'

Bec was smiling, clearly delighted to have found me more business, but Eliot looked down in the dumps. I didn't know what to say to make him feel better. With the evening in full swing it was hardly the time or the place to come clean and explain properly about what I'd been up to. I had thought I was going to get away without revealing any of it, but apparently not. It would just have to wait for now and in the meantime, I'd try and keep him and Anthony apart.

'I'll go and put this on the drinks table,' I told the pair. 'But right at the back, so no one opens it.'

'I wouldn't if I were you,' said Anthony, who had silently sidled up. 'What sort of table have you set up for the drinks, Fliss? It looks to me like it's beginning to sag in the middle.'

'Oh bugger,' I said. 'I thought it would be okay, but there's a lot of weight on that one. I hope the rest are going to be all right.'

I looked around and found everyone had taken their seats. The rest of the tables looked fine but then they didn't have the same number of filled bottles on them.

'I need to rejig it,' I flapped, feeling increasingly hot, 'but it's time to start serving the food. I don't want to keep everyone waiting.'

'We can deal with the drinks table, can't we?' Eliot briskly said to Anthony. 'And Bec and Mum can bring the food from the house while you talk everyone through the menu, Fliss. Sorted. Yes?'

'Yes,' I agreed. 'All right.'

So much for keeping the pair of them on opposite sides of the barn.

'Right,' said Bec, 'let's get this show on the road.'

Talking through the dessert dishes and watching everyone tuck in, while Eliot helpfully topped up their glasses was the easiest part of the whole event. Everything tasted delicious and the cool evening temperature meant there was no melted chocolate or warm drinks.

'That semifreddo,' said Jemma, closing her eyes, 'was the best I've ever had. Where did you get the recipe and more to the point, do you want a job in the café? I could do with an extra member of staff who can whip up dishes like that.'

I felt myself flush under her praise.

'My nonna in Italy taught me how to make it,' I explained to her and Amber who was also listening. 'I've got a whole head full of her recipes, so if the supper club doesn't work out Jemma, I might take you up on that offer.'

'Oh, there's no chance of you taking her on then, Jem,' Amber smiled. 'This place is going to be a hit. Jake and I are already planning winter supper dishes we could serve here.'

'Are you?' I gasped.

Amber nodded.

'We are,' Jake chimed in, 'and we want you to add a wood burner to your list,'

'It's already on there,' I said, feeling slightly dazed. 'Are you *really* going to pick Fenview Farm over your other venue?'

'There's no contest,' he told me. 'The barn is beautiful and the added attraction of Bill's collection is the ultimate cherry on the cake.'

My head began to spin and I'd barely had a sip to drink.

'And Bill took me to look at the washhouse and other outbuildings earlier,' said Tom, joining in, 'and I can't imagine there would be any objection to you putting in a kitchen and cloakroom. There's more than enough space for both.'

I didn't know what to say. I'd always had faith in the idea, but listening to everyone else's approval made it suddenly feel very real. The Fenview Farm supper club was going to happen. I couldn't wait to tell Grandad what everyone was saying. And the Rossis. Nonna would be cock-a-hoop to know how fast her semifreddo had vanished.

The limited money in my savings account sprang to mind again and I hoped I would be able to find a way to make the vision I, and everyone else, imagined the place could be, a reality. Tears then filled my eyes as I wondered what Mum would have made of it all. She had been delighted by what I'd done for the Rossis and I wondered if she would have felt even more proud here because Fenview was our very own family farm.

'And you know we'll help,' said Bec, cranking my emotion up another notch. 'Won't we, Eliot?'

'Of course,' he nodded, leaning in to refill Jemma's glass. 'I can wield a sledgehammer as well as the next man.'

'I'm not sure we'll need anything knocking down,' I quickly said, but nonetheless felt extremely grateful they were both so willing to get stuck in.

'Well, a paintbrush then,' he smiled.

'Hey,' said Bec, swatting his arm. 'That's my line.'

We were all in fine spirits by then and it was a relief to see Eliot smiling again. I was just about to tell Bec my plans to offer wall space to local artists when Anthony announced he had to leave but couldn't get his car out because of how everyone was parked. Considering he'd been put in charge of parking, I felt a bit miffed about that, but at least his early departure put paid to him saying anything untoward to Eliot.

'I was hoping we would have more time to chat,' he said, when I saw him out.

'Well, I did tell you it was going to be a busy research evening, didn't I?' I reminded him.

'You can get your car out now,' said Eliot, who had untangled the mess Anthony had made of arranging the vehicles.

Anthony didn't acknowledge him, but pulled me into his arms and kissed me firmly on the lips. I was furious and rigidly unresponsive.

'I'll call you tomorrow,' he said, releasing me. 'We'll go to that wine bar and talk all this through. I'll give you the benefit of my business knowledge.'

I didn't want the benefit of his business knowledge and I hadn't wanted that kiss either. He had no right to go around pressing his lips where they weren't wanted. I took out a tissue and wiped my mouth.

'So much for him not being your boyfriend,' Eliot glowered.

'He's not,' I said. 'He's really not.'

'Well, you better tell him that then hadn't you,' he said walking away, 'because that kiss suggested otherwise and so did what he said to me earlier.'

'What are you talking about?'

'When we were taking those bottles off the table,' he said spinning round to face me, 'which, by the way, there was absolutely nothing wrong with, Anthony made it very clear that you and he were an item and that if I'd got any romantic feelings for you, then I should forget about them as soon as possible.'

Chapter 25

I tried not to dwell on what else Anthony might have said to Eliot in the brief time they had been thrown together and, as no one else was in a rush to leave, turned the music up a little before going around with my notebook to talk over how the evening had gone. It turned out that Eliot wasn't the only person Anthony had had a quiet word with and my resolve not to get distracted by his comments was soon tested to its limit.

By all accounts the evening was a huge success and both Jemma and Jake were going to be among the first to book events, much to mine and Grandad's delight and relief, but they did have a couple of issues for me to iron out. As did practically everyone else.

Thankfully, all of the problems were easily solved, minor things which were simple to address and the largest, the safety of the barn itself, was soon dismissed by Tom and Jake. However, the one thing practically all of the issues had in common was that they had been flagged up by Anthony.

As I made my way around, I realised that he'd had a word in everyone's ear, and he seemed to have contributed little that was positive to balance out his gripes. That, added to what he'd said to Eliot about steering clear of me and his gaslighting over the strength of the drinks table, combined to leave me with a bitter taste in my mouth. Considering the sweetness of the menu, that was quite an accomplishment.

Once the last of the guests had left, Grandad and I cheerfully talked about the success the evening had been, along with what we should plan to do next, and then he left me and the Randalls to tidy away. I didn't mention Anthony's antics and as I watched him walk back to the house, I knew one of us was guaranteed sweet dreams.

'So,' said Bec, when we'd almost finished. 'Have you talked to the Rossis yet? Eliot said you've finally got the broadband connected now.'

'Yes,' I smiled, 'thanks to your brother we have and yes, I have talked to them.'

As we gathered the last few glasses and dishes together, I gave her a description of Marco, explaining how I thought she and him would be the perfect match and she was enthralled. Even more so when Eliot asked if he was the hunk he'd seen on the photo in the library. Bec was someone else who wouldn't be having nightmares. I on the other hand . . .

I fell into bed feeling exhausted but I hardly slept. Earlier in the day, I had imagined I would be too excited to sleep and would lay until dawn mulling over how well things had gone, but instead I was wondering why Anthony had gone out of his way to try and sabotage everything.

First thing the following morning, I used the house phone to call him and made arrangements to meet.

'This is a pleasant surprise,' he said, when I arrived in town. 'I thought you'd be too busy clearing up to even think of me.' Given his interference, I'd thought of little else. 'Does this mean you'll have time for the wine bar later?' he hopefully added.

'We tidied and sorted last night,' I brusquely told him, 'but none the more for that, I won't be going to the wine bar with you. Is there somewhere we can talk?'

It was bank holiday Sunday and still early, and as the town was having some sort of event in the park the next day, it looked like everyone was making the most of the day of rest. There was no sign of life anywhere other than the newsagents and that was hardly the spot to have the kind of conversation I had in mind.

'Actually,' I said, climbing back into the Land Rover, 'we can talk here. At least saying it behind closed doors will keep it private.'

Anthony looked rather taken aback.

'We could drive on to Peterborough,' he suggested. 'There's bound to be a coffee shop open there.'

'No,' I said. 'I haven't got time for that.'

'Sit in my car, then,' he tried. 'I can put the air con on.'

'No thanks,' I said, wanting to keep the conversation on my turf. 'We can open the windows. It's not that hot and don't worry, the seats are clean. You won't mess up your trousers.'

Sensing that I meant business, he got in and I cracked the windows open a little further. His aftershave was rather overpowering for so early in the day but then he was always dressed for business and smelt ready for action whatever the hour. He never had a loose thread or a hair out of place, unlike Eliot who constantly had mussed up hair thanks to his bike helmet and clothes full of comfortable creases to match.

'So,' Anthony said, when I didn't say anything.

'So,' I echoed back, pushing thoughts of Eliot's hair and wardrobe aside.

I'd rehearsed what I was going to say a hundred times between asking him to meet me and arriving in the market square, but now it seemed rather dramatic. In the cold light of day and faced with the fact that he clearly had no idea why I had summoned him, I began to wonder if I'd got his words and actions a little out of proportion.

But then I reminded myself how he'd made a point of talking to *everyone*, including Eliot, and not only about the supper club, and I knew that if I didn't have it out with him, I'd always wonder.

'About last night,' I began.

'A roaring success,' he beamed. 'I don't think it could have gone any better, could it?'

I turned to face him.

'Or not?' he questioned, taking me in. 'Did something happen after I left? I'm sorry I had to duck out just as it was getting going and I know I messed up with the parking. That sort of thing really isn't my forte, I'm afraid. I did try and tell your grandad. I hope it didn't cause too much of a rumpus.'

'No,' I said. 'It didn't.'

'Thank goodness for that,' he sounded genuinely relieved. 'So, what is it then? You don't look like someone who's just successfully unveiled a business idea, Fliss.'

'The thing is,' I said, launching before I lost the nerve, 'when I went around, after you'd gone, and asked everyone about the venue and how they felt the evening was going, they all had a bit of a niggle.'

'Right.'

'Nothing major and all easily addressed.'

'So that was good then, wasn't it?'

'Well, yes,' I said. 'But the thing was . . .'

'The thing was what?' he asked when I faltered.

'The thing was,' I said, taking a deep breath, 'that all of the problems I had to address had been pointed out by you.'

He looked at me and blinked.

'And what I want to know,' I said, my voice getting louder, 'is why? Why did you put those doubts in everyone's heads, when you knew how desperately I wanted the evening to be a success? You know how much I want the supper club to work and yet you went around disrupting it.'

There, I'd said it.

'I'm sorry, what?' Anthony asked, shaking his head.

'I want to know why you tried to mess it up?'

'Mess it up,' he repeated, sounding perplexed. 'Fliss, you

told me the evening was supposed to be a fact-finding event, didn't you? Or have I misremembered that?'

'No,' I said, 'you're right. I did say that. That was the point of having a trial run.'

'Okay, so the focus of the evening was to iron out and address any problems before you invested any money, right?'

'Right,' I swallowed.

'You put the event on, not only with the intention of showing everyone how great your idea could be and what a good cook you are, but also to find out if you had missed any issues in your planning that might later trip you up, yes?'

'Yes,' I squeaked.

'You didn't really want everyone to just tell you how clever you were and not look beyond the pretty flowers, delicious food and twinkly lights, did you?'

I mulled that over for a moment.

'No,' I then huskily answered. 'Of course not.'

Anthony lifted his hands and let them drop in his lap.

'And yet you're accusing me of messing things up when all I really did was take an objective look at the situation and talk to your guests in the hope that you might take the opportunity to resolve any issues that those exchanges flagged up.'

I chewed my lip and looked out of the window. At the pub, Jim was watering the colourful flower baskets and Evelyn was putting out the chalkboard.

'I thought I was being helpful,' Anthony said, sounding hurt and I realised I could hardly blame him.

As far as highlighting any potential problems was

concerned, he'd achieved that. I was the one actually at fault because I'd got caught up looking at everything through rose-tinted specs.

'But what about what you said to Eliot?' I pointed out, remembering that Anthony's comments hadn't been *all* business. 'He said you warned him off me.'

'I think *warned him off* is a bit strong,' Anthony tutted. 'I just let him know I'm looking out for you. I know you said that I'd got him all wrong, but watching the pair of you last night, showed me how he's wormed his way into your affections and I'm sorry, but I still don't trust him. I know that will make you angry, but it's the truth.'

I hadn't realised he'd been watching us.

'And I suppose, although it pains me to admit it,' Anthony carried on when I didn't comment, 'I was a bit jealous.'

'Jealous?'

'Yes,' he said. 'I'd give anything for you to look at me the way you look at him.'

'Oh.'

I hadn't realised I did look at Eliot in a certain way. I hoped no one else had noticed whatever expression I had on my face when our eyes met.

'But that,' Anthony added, 'had nothing to do with any of what I said to everyone else. I didn't have some sort of ulterior motive, even though you've just suggested otherwise.'

Now it was his turn to stare out of the window.

'Oh Anthony,' I said. 'I'm sorry.'

Even though we weren't on the same page about the heroic

carer, I did now feel bad for using him in my failed attempt to make Eliot think that I'd moved on. Not that I was about to reveal that. Now I knew Anthony harboured genuinely romantic feelings for me, coming clean would only make him feel even worse, and me even more guilty.

'It doesn't matter,' he shrugged, but his tone implied it did. 'Your response to my kiss last night was a clear enough indication that you don't feel the same way about me, and as far as the other stuff's concerned, it was just my business head talking. I'm so driven, I do come across a bit strong because I don't know how to switch off. I never should have said anything. I'm the one who's sorry.'

'No,' I said, 'you don't have to apologise, I do. I'm pleased you said what you did. You made sure the evening fulfilled its purpose. I learnt loads and I have a much clearer understanding of how I can make it all happen now. I'm grateful to you, I really am.'

Although I still wasn't grateful about what he'd said to Eliot of course.

'Well, that's good then,' he sighed. 'Even if you don't fancy me.'

'I'm sorry about that too.' I further apologised.

I reached over to squeeze his hand and as he moved his fingers to grasp mine, the cuff of his shirt slipped back. Before I could take another breath, my mouth had gone dry, my heart had missed a beat and my shoulders were back up around my ears.

'Where did you get that watch?' I gasped, completely distracted from what I had planned to say next.

He, however, wasn't at all perturbed by the sudden subject change. It was like he'd flicked some sort of internal switch.

'Isn't it a beauty?' he commented, twisting his wrist so I could see it properly. 'I found it yesterday in the jewellers in the courtyard. Second hand obviously, which isn't something I usually go for, but it isn't every day that you find one of these.'

'No,' I said, trying to lubricate my painfully dry throat by swallowing hard. 'I don't imagine it is.'

'I paid a pretty penny for it, but it was worth it. To be honest, to begin with, I couldn't believe that something like this would turn up in a town like Wynbridge. It's vintage, rare and in immaculate condition. It was even boxed. Can you believe it?'

'No,' I said. 'I can't.'

Back at the farm, I was both surprised and frustrated to find Grandad was still in bed. With him asleep in the room, there was no opportunity to satisfy my suspicions and I flitted from one task to another, achieving little and settling to nothing properly.

Eventually, feeling desperate for distraction, I turned on his laptop and set about creating the Fenview Farm Instagram account. I would eventually use it to promote the supper club so establishing a bit of a following before it launched would be a great help.

I put the finishing touches on a sunny image I'd taken of the strawberry field with the hens in the foreground, adding as many hashtags as I could think of, then logged off just as the throaty rumble of Eliot's bike met my ears.

'Morning,' he said as he wandered in, leather clad, dishevelled and looking lovely.

'Hi.'

'How are you feeling?'

For the briefest moment, sitting in the Land Rover with Anthony, safe in the knowledge that I'd read him wrong, and in spite of the fact that he had romantic feelings for me and had caught me looking at Eliot all doe-eyed, I'd felt good, but the sight of that watch had been a huge shock and now I just felt bilious.

'All right,' I nodded. 'Lots to think about though.'

'Mm,' Eliot agreed.

'Look,' I began, 'about what Anthony said.'

'Do we have to talk about that?'

'We don't have to, but . . .'

'Good,' he cut in, before hauling himself out of his leathers. 'Is Bill about?'

It was only then that I realised I hadn't heard a peep out of Grandad. There had been no squeaking floorboards to prompt me to fill the kettle.

'Do you know,' I said, forgetting everything else, 'he's still in bed.'

Eliot looked at me and raised his eyebrows.

'I had to pop into town earlier and he was still asleep when I got back.'

'I was a bit worried about him yesterday,' Eliot frowned. 'I think he's taking on too much.'

'No, he isn't,' I snapped. 'I haven't let him.'

'But with all the changes ...'

'I'm dealing with those,' I told him. 'I haven't dumped anything on him, if that's what you're suggesting.'

'Of course, it isn't,' he said, looking surprised. 'What's got into you, Fliss? I thought you'd be walking on air.'

I heard a creaking overhead.

'There,' I huffed. 'You've woken him up.'

'I'll go and check on him then, shall I?'

I felt bad when they eventually came down because Grandad did look a bit peaky, even though he insisted he was fine.

'Just not used to sleeping for so long,' he said, when I commented that he looked pale. 'I'm all out of kilter, but I'll be right enough when I've had a cuppa.'

'I'll leave you to it then,' said Eliot, addressing Grandad. 'I'm sure you'll be right as rain again tomorrow, but I'll ring anyway, just to check.'

'Fuss over nothing,' Grandad smiled as Eliot thrust his legs back into his suit. 'But it's been a pleasure to see you again today, my lad.'

'At least someone thinks so,' Eliot grumbled, as he zipped up and walked out.

'Have you two fallen out?' Grandad asked as we heard the bike start up.

'Of course not,' I said. 'We're right as rain too.'

Chapter 26

Worryingly, Grandad wasn't as right as rain the next day and took to his bed for the whole day. We had planned to drive to town to take part in the bank holiday celebrations, but instead he quietly rested and I caught up with the fruit picking, cleaned out the hens and carried on writing up my supper club plans.

I briefly checked in with Marco again, giving him the good news that Saturday had been a success and Nonna's semifreddo a total triumph. I also passed on Bec's email address and mobile number at her request, and later researched ideas on how best to convert the barn and what official permission we would need in order to get the project underway.

In spite of my best efforts to keep my mind occupied it was still filled with the image of the watch I had seen Anthony proudly wearing. With no way of sneaking unseen into Grandad's room to check, my thoughts were dominated by a cocktail of upset and fear and the tiniest chaser of hope that it was all just an unsettling coincidence and

Anthony's new watch wasn't the treasured Brown family timepiece at all.

Tuesday dawned with a palpable air of relief because Grandad, although a little pale, was seemingly back to his old self and once out of bed, only slightly later than usual, I offered to air his bedroom and change the sheets.

'Oh, yes please,' he said, enthusiastically taking up my offer and subsequently triggering a pang of guilt. 'That would be much appreciated.'

As soon as I could see he was settled in his chair under the apple tree with the newspaper, I abandoned the bed, went to the dressing table and took out the jewellery box. My hands were shaking as I lifted the lid. Everything was still neatly arranged, but on the bottom layer there was the Rolex box shaped gap I had dreaded, but known deep down, that I would see.

My stomach churned and my hands felt clammy as I returned the depleted box to the drawer. There was no doubting it now. Anthony was wearing my great-grandfather's watch, but why had Grandad parted with it? He had told me it was precious, that it held many special family memories, so why had he let it go?

Was this what he and Louise had been secretly talking about? Selling his prized family heirloom and, if it was, then why did Grandad need that sort of money? My guts lurched again as I wondered if at some point in the not too distant future, he was going to surprise me with a supper club set-up fund. Was selling the watch a decision he'd made after he'd originally dismissed the club idea and before he told Eliot to give me the go-ahead?

I sincerely hoped not because I genuinely wanted to use my savings to get the business up and running. I could easily work to replace the cash, but no amount of filled punnets and boxes of apples would be able to replace the watch.

I re-made the bed and rushed downstairs remembering that Anthony had said he'd found the watch in the jewellers in the courtyard. I would go there and quiz the staff before talking to Grandad. Anything to put off having to face the potentially unpalatable truth – that he had parted with his treasure to help fulfil my vision.

He walked back into the kitchen just as I arrived in it and I quickly scooped up my bag along with the Land Rover keys.

'How are you feeling?' I asked.

If he wasn't able to convince me that he was at least ninety-five per cent better then my quest would have to wait.

'I'm fine,' he said, waving my concern away. 'Don't fuss.'

His impatient dismissal was good enough for me. If he was well enough to object to my coddling then he was well enough to be left alone for an hour or so.

'But I'm a bit worried about the weather,' he added.

'The weather?'

'Yes,' he said, 'I reckon there's a storm brewing and that won't be good news for our fruit.'

The sky I could see through the window was blue for as far as my eyes could see.

'I'm sure it will be fine,' I said, thinking he was fretting over nothing.

'You haven't experienced a Wynbridge storm yet, have you?' he pointed out. 'Where are you off to all of a sudden?'

'I need to pop to town,' I told him. 'I won't be long. Do you need anything picking up?'

'No,' he said, looking outside again. 'I don't think so, but you better hang on a minute, there's someone just pulled on to the drive.'

I felt my frustration grow as I looked out the door and saw a man dressed in a suit climb out of his car, reach back inside for a clipboard and then stride over to the barn. Before I'd had a chance to take a step, he'd slipped inside.

'The cheeky bugger,' said Grandad, clearly irritated, as was I.

'I'll go,' I firmly said.

The last thing I needed was for him to get riled up.

'Why don't you put the kettle on?' I suggested. 'Whoever he is, he's bound to expect tea. Everyone around here does.'

'I don't think so,' Grandad muttered, but he filled the kettle anyway.

'Can I help you?' I demanded, as I marched into the barn and found the man sticking his rather beaky nose into the boxes which held some of Grandad's collection. 'That's private property, as is this barn. What do you think you're doing?'

He turned to look at me, in his own time which was irritatingly much slower than mine, then consulted the clipboard in his hand.

'Felicity Brown?' he questioned.

He both looked and sounded annoyingly smug.

'Yes,' I said, standing straighter. 'That's me. What do you want and who are you?'

'My name is Peter Pagett, I'm from the council.'

'Right,' I said, raising my eyebrows in the hope that it might encourage him to elaborate.

He took his time looking around. Beadily taking everything in before he spoke again.

'I'm here to discuss an event which occurred here at the weekend.'

'You'd better come into the house then,' I said, attempting to usher him out.

I had no idea as to what there could possibly be to discuss, but I didn't like seeing him in the barn any more than I had liked watching him poke his nose into Grandad's things.

'Mr Pagett,' I bluntly said to Grandad when we went into the house. 'From the council, here to discuss Saturday night.'

Grandad looked as clueless as I felt.

'Tea?' he offered.

'No thank you,' Peter Pagett said, again checking something on his clipboard. 'Was this the kitchen where the food that was served on Saturday was prepared?'

'Yes,' I frowned.

He pulled a pen out of his top pocket and put a tick next to something I couldn't read because it was upside down and too far away. I gripped the back of a chair. My frustration with being held up was already on a slow rolling boil and I could feel it bubbling faster with every second.

'And,' he said, glancing up from the sheet, 'the barn that wc were just in was where the food was served, was it?'

'Yes,' I said again, raising my eyebrows in Grandad's direction. 'But I'm guessing you already know that.'

'I just need you to confirm it, Miss Brown,' he said with a nauseating smile.

'Have you got some sort of ID?' Grandad asked. 'What's with all the questions?'

'It has come to my department's attention,' Mr Pagett explained in a monotone and as if he was reading straight from a manual, 'that you have been preparing food for public consumption in a kitchen that has not been council approved. As far as I am aware, you have no food business registration, no food safety qualifications and there has been no visit from the environmental health team. Is that all correct?'

'Yes,' I shrugged, 'but . . .'

'And furthermore,' he continued, 'you have also been using the barn outside as a venue in which to serve the food that has been prepared here in this kitchen. That is correct, isn't it?'

Grandad and I exchanged another look.

'Where are the conveniences for your paying guests?' he continued, having consulted his list and piped up again before either of us could answer.

'Conveniences,' Grandad repeated, sounding nonplussed. 'Paying guests?'

'Look,' I said, holding up my hands. 'Just hang on a minute. The kitchen hasn't been approved and the barn hasn't been registered because the business isn't up and running yet. It won't be launched until the conversion work has been carried out.'

'And yet you had a function here Saturday evening?'

'What we had,' Grandad furiously said, 'were a few local friends visiting to try out some of my granddaughter's wonderful food. No money changed hands and anyone who needed the loo nipped into the house.'

'Our get together Saturday night,' I exasperatedly told Mr Peter Pagett, 'was nothing more than a dinner party for friends.'

'I see,' he said.

'I am going to be converting the barn and setting it up as a venue for hosting supper club evenings featuring different local producers in the future, but right now we're miles away from that. Right at the beginning of the journey in fact, but if I have to deal with people like you to reach the destination, then . . .'

'Fliss,' Grandad cut in.

'It was a dinner party,' I restated, amending my tone. 'For friends. Nothing more.'

'May I ask who suggested otherwise?' Grandad asked.

That was a very good question.

'You may,' said Mr Pagett. 'But I am not at liberty to tell you.'

'Some snake in the grass,' I said to Grandad, 'looking to scupper our plans before we've even started. It certainly wouldn't have been anyone who was here on Saturday.'

'Of course, it wasn't,' he agreed.

'I'm sure they reported what was going on with the best of intentions,' said Mr Pagett. 'Their motivation would no doubt have been a concern for public health and safety.'

I had to laugh at that.

'There was absolutely no risk to public health and safety . . .' I started.

'I'll see you out,' Grandad cut in, sensing that my temper was about to get the better of me.

'I can see myself out,' said Mr Pagett, thankfully doing just that.

'Don't worry about the apology for wasting our time,' I called after him, 'or taxpayers' money.'

'Fliss!' Grandad scolded. 'Pipe down.'

'Well,' I scowled.

'Well nothing,' he said. 'If he's the fella we end up having to deal with, then we'll need to keep him onside.'

'We won't have to keep anyone *onside*,' I told him, 'because this place is going to be perfect by the time we want to register it and launch the business. I'm going to make sure that neither he nor anyone else can find fault with a single thing, but first I want to find out who reported us. What a ridiculously petty thing to do and what a waste of time!'

'My reckoning is that no one did,' Grandad mildly said. 'Tom works for the council, doesn't he? He most likely mentioned what a lovely weekend he'd had to his colleagues in his office and that jobsworth, Pagett overheard and made it his business to come and rap our knuckles before he'd got the full story.'

I couldn't believe he could be so calm about it.

'Do you really think that?'

'I do,' he said. 'The council is full of chaps like him. They're always desperate to use the little bit of authority their job titles give them. Now, are you still going to town?'

'Yes,' I said, my temper dissipating as I thought of what I was going to do next. 'Is that all right?'

'Of course,' he nodded. 'Just make sure you're back before this storm hits.'

I looked out at the still clear blue sky and sunshine.

'It's definitely coming,' he said, spotting my doubtful expression. 'I can feel it in my bones.'

The town was quiet after what I imagined were the excesses of the bank holiday celebrations and therefore, I split the delivery of fruit between Jemma and Chris Dempster so neither would be left with produce they couldn't sell. Both Jemma and Lizzie were still full of enthusiasm for Saturday night and I knew neither they nor Jake and Amber would have played a part in reporting us to the council.

'I wouldn't be too long before you head back to the farm,' said Lizzie, following me to the café door and looking out. 'There's a storm coming.'

'Not you as well,' I tutted. 'Everyone's obsessed with the weather today, and look at it. A perfect summer's day.'

'Not according to Annie, who was here earlier,' she darkly said before disappearing back inside.

Bella and Princess were sitting outside the boutique when I walked around to the courtyard.

'Hello my love,' Bella warmly smiled. 'Are you coming to see me?'

'Not today I'm afraid,' I said, reluctantly turning towards the jewellers.

I hesitated, taking in the peeling signage and gloomy interior. The little shop would have been a perfect addition to Diagon Alley and when I stepped over the threshold, I discovered that the proprietor could have been mistaken for Mr Ollivander himself.

'Hello my dear,' he smiled. 'Can I help you with anything, or would you prefer to browse?'

'I do need some help actually,' I swallowed, knowing there was nothing to be gained from prolonging the agony. 'I want to ask you about something that I believe you had for sale here recently.'

'Ask away,' the shopkeeper obligingly said. 'I'll willingly help if I can.'

'It was a watch,' I said, my voice catching, 'a gent's Rolex.'

'The nineteen forties rose gold square,' he beamed.

He sounded utterly besotted.

'That's the one,' I nodded.

'Came in and out as quick as a flash,' he said, sounding regretful. 'If I'd have known, I wouldn't have put it out so soon. I would have liked a bit longer in its company. The arrowhead shaped batons and exquisite movement,' he dreamily added, clasping his hands together. 'Such a rarity and in such wonderful condition.'

There was no doubting it was Grandad's watch he was

describing, but of course I'd known it would be, what with the Rolex-shaped gap in the jewellery box back at the farm. Coming out of his reverie the shopkeeper looked at me and narrowed his eyes.

'There wasn't a problem with it, was there? The person who sold it had more than the usual provenance and I paid handsomely for it.'

'Oh no,' I said. 'No problem at all. I'd just like to know if you can remember anything about the person who came in with it.'

'Oh, well . . .' he began, taking a step back, 'I'm not sure . . .'

'Please,' I pleaded. 'It's very important.'

He tussled with his conscience for a moment or two.

'It was a woman,' he eventually said. 'Middle-aged, curly grey hair. I can't recall her name but she's local. I'm sure I've seen her about the town.'

I muttered a hurried thank you, left the shop and walked back to the square where I stood and rested my head on the Land Rover door while I thought about what to do next. The only conclusion I could come to was that Grandad *had* sold the watch to fund the club and I felt sorely disappointed in Louise for not talking him out of it. I bet if Eliot had known what was going on, he'd have put a stop to it and told me to boot.

A sharp gust of wind tugged at the bottom of my T-shirt and I noticed it felt much cooler than before. I looked up and found the sun had all but disappeared behind a sky loaded with dark clouds. The anticipated storm was coming. It was the perfect portent and I shivered with more than the chill.

'Fliss,' said a voice close by, 'are you all right?'

'Oh Anthony,' I said, feeling dazed and, for the moment, unguarded, 'no, not really. I've just had a bit of bad news. I think I need to sit down.'

'Come on,' he said. 'Let's go over to the pub.'

He steered me into a seat next to the door and then went to the bar.

'Here,' he said, when he came back. 'Drink this straight down.'

I gulped down the contents of the glass in one and spluttered as the heat of the amber liquid burned my throat.

'What was that?' I gasped.

'Brandy.'

'I can't drink brandy,' I told him, still coughing. 'I'm driving.'

'It was only a small one.'

He walked back to the bar and returned with two glasses of Coke packed full of ice. As he sat down, I couldn't help noticing that he was wearing the watch again. The sight of it undid most of the good the brandy had just done.

'What's going on?' he asked, a deep frown etched across his forehead. 'You looked as though you were either about to throw up or keel over out there.'

'I've just had a bit of a shock,' I said, as I took a sip of the sweet chilled Coke and began to feel a little more in control.

'Oh no,' he said. 'What is it? Trouble at mill?'

He said it with an awful Yorkshire accent, no doubt trying to raise a smile, but he hadn't got a chance of that.

'No. Trouble at the farm, of course,' I snapped.

Grandad's worrying bout of tiredness, Mr Pagett's unsettling visit and the sadness of the lost Rolex, all wrapped up in something else I couldn't quite grasp, swam around my head in a kind of cloying and gloopy soup that I couldn't wade through.

'What's going on?' Anthony asked, leaning closer and giving me another glimpse of the watch. 'It's nothing to do with our crossed wires after Saturday night, is it?'

'No,' I said, wishing he'd pick up the glass with his other hand. 'Nothing to do with that.'

Or was it?

'What then?'

I drank more of the Coke and then described Mr Pagett's unsavoury visit, playing for time as I tried to reach whatever it was that was still just beyond my fingertips.

'Grandad thinks it was just a misunderstanding,' I finished up with a shrug, 'but it was unsettling nonetheless.'

Anthony mulled it all over.

'I can imagine,' he said. 'And it does make you think, doesn't it?'

'Think what?'

'That this whole supper club idea might be more trouble than it's worth.'

'What?' I blinked.

'Well, it's already causing upset and you haven't even started yet,' he pointed out.

'Only because of someone else's meddling,' I frowned. 'I thought you thought the idea was a good one.'

His words seemed to have oiled some cogs in my brain that had previously been stuck fast.

'Anyway,' I carried on, 'that visit's the least of my troubles really.'

'There's something else?'

'Yes,' I said, 'there is.'

I reached for his hand and pushed back the cuff of his shirt.

'This watch,' I said with a sigh, 'belonged to my Grandad.'

'What?'

'It's true,' I said. 'It was his most treasured piece of family history, aside from the farm of course, and last week Louise sold it and I'm still trying to . . .'

He didn't give me the chance to explain that she and Grandad had been scheming over it together.

'There,' he loudly and triumphantly announced. 'What have I been telling you all along? The whole bloody family are at it!'

'No,' I began, but he talked right over me.

'Louise and the watch, Eliot and his undue influence and Rebecca with her bout of teenage shoplifting. The whole Randall family's rotten to the core. You should be thanking me, Fliss.'

I looked at him aghast.

'Well, I'm sorry,' he frowned. 'I know you want to think the best of Eliot . . .'

'No,' I said, this time interrupting him. 'You said it was *Eliot* who was caught shoplifting, not Bec. You said he'd pinched stuff and that now he'd moved on to bigger things, such as old ladies' savings.'

'Did I?' he shrugged, as if it didn't matter at all. 'Well, it was one of them and with a mother like that, it's little wonder, is it? Bill's going to be absolutely devastated. If I were you,' he said, his tone softening as he turned to look at me, 'I'd forget all about your plans for the business and focus on making sure this blow doesn't finish the old fella off. I mean, there are bound to be quicker ways to make money out of that barn, you know.'

Everyone in the bar let out a collective screech as lightning suddenly lit the pub up. It was a blinding flash and in the second it struck, everything I had been trying to work out fell into place.

'Oh my god,' I gasped, as a deep and menacing rumble of thunder rolled overhead.

'Am I right, or am I right?' Anthony nodded, looking smug.

I couldn't believe I had been so blind to what had been in front of me all along.

'This is all about you, isn't it?' I shot at him. 'You want the barn, don't you? That's what this has all been about. I thought I was using you as a smokescreen to hide my feelings for Eliot, but actually you were using your bullshit about him as camouflage to try and distract me.'

'What are you talking about, Fliss?' Anthony scowled, but I knew I was right.

There was no point in him denying it because I'd finally worked it out.

'The only rumour you've heard about Eliot is the one you made up,' I started, 'anything wrong with the safety of the barn is all in your head, you didn't put all those questions in everyone's heads Saturday night with the best of intentions *and* you were the one who reported us to the council . . .'

'Now wait a minute . . .'

'No,' I said, raising my voice, 'you wait a minute. I know that Grandad and Louise cooked up that plan to sell the watch together and you've just implied that Louise stole it. You've rather shot yourself in the foot, haven't you?'

He wasn't looking quite so smug anymore and I felt like Angela Lansbury on a roll.

'Does Grandad know you want the barn?' I demanded. 'Is that why you were really at the farm the day I came home and found you in the kitchen?'

'Of course, he bloody knows,' Anthony nastily said. 'He was the one who approached me with a view to selling it! I offered him a good price and he'd accepted it just before he went into hospital and then you turned up with your bouncy personality and your great plans to save Fenview and it all went belly up.'

Grandad had told me about his fears that he was going to end up in a bungalow somewhere, but he'd never mentioned his vain attempt to put off the inevitable. What was his plan, to sell the farm off piece by piece as it got harder for him to manage until he was just left with the house? I was furious he hadn't told me, but also sickened and sad to think that he had thought this was his only option.

'Has Grandad signed anything?' I choked. 'Is there anything official to say he's selling it to you?'

Anthony looked appalled.

'Do you really think I would have been wasting time messing about with you and making up all this bullshit if there was?'

I could hardly believe it and yet as everything fell sickeningly into place, I knew it was true.

'So, you don't wish I looked at you in the same way I look at Eliot then?' I peevishly said.

I felt such a fool and I could feel tears gathering, but I refused to let them fall. I didn't care in the slightest that Anthony's overtures to me had all been fake, but I did care that I had been so preoccupied with pretending my feelings for Eliot didn't exist, that I hadn't realised what Anthony was up to sooner.

'You really have been trying to sabotage everything, haven't you?' I demanded, meeting his gaze. 'You've been trying to mess it all up with a view to putting me off my plans in the hope that you'll still get your hands on the barn.'

Now I'd said it aloud it was as plain as the nose on my face. What a fool I'd been. I thought I'd had the upper hand when actually, Anthony had all along.

'I've got a buyer for that barn,' he loudly said, drawing the attention of the people closest. 'I've invested thousands in plans and fees already and I'm not giving it up. I refuse to be left out of pocket.'

'Oh my god,' I gasped, as further recognition dawned, 'that's why Grandad sold the watch! He wasn't going to offer the money to me, he was going to use it to pay you off. You're blackmailing him, aren't you?'

Anthony smirked at my distress. He actually smirked. I'd never wanted to do someone a physical harm more.

'And now I get the money and the watch,' he said, turning smug again.

'Take it off!' I snarled.

'What?'

'You're not having it!' I shouted. 'Take it off.'

'You must be joking! It's mine. I paid good money for it.'

'Everything all right?' asked Jim, stepping out from behind the bar and rushing over.

When I looked up, I realised our exchange had drawn quite a bit of attention. Another flash of lightning struck and another rumble of thunder roared as the customers eyed us curiously.

'Take it off and give it to me,' I said to Anthony, feeling even braver now I knew I had the attention of The Mermaid regulars, 'before I tell everyone in this pub, and the police, that you've been blackmailing my Grandad.'

'I haven't blackmailed anyone,' he snarled.

'What's going on?' Jim demanded.

I looked Anthony straight in the eye, determined that he

would see that I wasn't going to back down and that I wasn't going anywhere until I had Grandad's watch back in my possession either.

'Bill was going to give me the money that was rightfully mine,' Anthony spat, finally noticing the interested onlookers as he grappled to undo the watch strap.

'The police won't see it that way,' I told him. 'Grandad has signed nothing and therefore you're entitled to nothing. It would be your word against his. You're the conman, Anthony Judd, not Eliot.'

'Hey,' said Jim, sounding gruff. 'What have you been saying about our boy?'

'Here then,' said Anthony, tossing me the watch and standing up. 'Take the fucking thing, it's more trouble than it's worth.'

'Right,' said Jim, lunging for Anthony's arm. 'I think we've heard enough out of you for one day.'

'One day?!' Anthony bellowed as Jim propelled him towards the street. 'You won't be seeing me in here again.'

'Fine by me,' said Jim, slamming the door behind him.

My hands were shaking as I zipped the watch into the pocket of my bag.

'Are you all right, love?' Evelyn asked, as everyone turned back to their own conversations. I'd have bet good money on knowing what they were discussing.

I nodded and stood up. My legs felt worryingly wobbly.

'Looks like you need another brandy,' commented Jim.

'Better not,' I shakily said. 'I need to get back to the farm before this storm really hits.'

'Bit late for that love,' Jim chuckled.

But of course, I wasn't talking about the weather.

Chapter 27

I had hoped, that on the drive back to the farm I would have the opportunity to think everything through, perhaps even run through what I was going to say to Grandad before I returned the watch to its rightful place, but the conditions didn't allow for me to focus on anything other than driving.

Clearly, Grandad's lifetime of living in the Fens ensured he knew a whole lot more about the local weather than I did. He had been right to worry about the harvest. If the rain carried on falling at the same rate there'd be no fruit left. It would be pulp before I had a chance to pick it.

My heart leapt into my mouth when I finally reached the farm gate and saw Eliot coming towards me on the Ducati. He was taking it very slowly, but with the conditions so treacherous coming out on two wheels was a ludicrous thing to do.

'What the hell are you doing?' I shouted as I climbed out of the Land Rover and he wheeled the bike into the wash-house next to the barn. 'Are you completely mad?'

We made a dash for it into the house. I was soaked in seconds and Eliot looked like a drowned rat. I tried to peel my T-shirt away from my body but it was sodden and melded to me like a second skin.

'Never mind me,' Eliot demanded, pulling off his helmet, his hair sticking up on end. 'Where have you been?'

'I had to go into town. Why? What's happened?'

Grandad wasn't in the kitchen, scolding us for leaving damp trails and soggy footprints, and I felt a growing sense of unease.

'Nothing I hope,' Eliot gruffly said. 'But I've been ringing the house for ages and got no reply and your phone's not turned on. Bec and Mum are both at work so I had to come out on the bike. Bill!' he shouted, making me jump.

I quickly checked both floors, but Grandad wasn't anywhere in the house and we knew he wasn't in the barn because the door was bolted from the outside.

'He was worried about the storm,' I gulped, wringing my hands. 'Before I left, he said there was a storm coming, but the weather was so bright and sunny I didn't believe him. You don't think he's out in it, do you? I didn't ask him to do anything while I was gone,' I hastily added.

'Well, if he's not in here and he's not in the barn, then he must be,' Eliot agitatedly said. 'I'll go and look.'

'I'll come with you,' I said, not bothering with a coat or umbrella as we rushed back out into the deluge.

The rain was falling so hard it made it difficult to see, but when we were close enough, I spotted the hen run was empty. It could have been because the hens had shown some common sense for once and sought refuge in their coop, but the reaction in my gut suggested otherwise.

'Grandad!' I shouted.

The word came out as more of a sob and I felt increasingly panicked as the storm raged and roared overhead.

'Bill!' Eliot bawled next to me.

The noise of the rain coupled with the thunder made it impossible to hear and even if Grandad had shouted back, we wouldn't have heard him.

'There!' pointed Eliot, what felt like for ever, but what was probably less than a minute, later. 'Over there. Look!'

We rushed over to the fruit cage, both of us skidding because the baked soil, unable to absorb the volume of water, had turned into a lethal slip and slide.

'Oh Grandad,' I said, rushing to his side and falling on my knees next to him.

'I'm fine,' he said, as I threw my arms around him. 'I'm fine.'

He was holding one of the hens under his arm and I didn't need to look too closely to work out which one.

'Take her, would you?' he said, thrusting her into my hands. 'And let's get inside before we all freeze to death or drown.'

I rushed to deposit the shocked hen into the coop where the other two were snuggled down and bone dry, while Eliot gave Grandad a quick examination and then the three of us walked carefully back to the house.

'I slipped,' Grandad said, between rumbles of thunder, 'trying to catch that stupid bird which had somehow got out under the run, and when I got up, my hip felt a bit sore so I thought I'd best wait for the cavalry rather than risk the slippery path back and going down again.'

'You did the right thing,' Eliot sensibly said. 'If you had fallen you could have done untold damage and set your recovery back months.'

I wondered if a mild bout of hypothermia was preferable as tears sprang to my eyes.

'I shouldn't have gone into town,' I sobbed, my voice catching. 'I should have been the one rounding up the hens and checking the gates. You said there was a storm coming.'

'It's all right,' said Grandad, trying to reassure me. 'I didn't go down with a bang, so there's no harm done.'

'We'll let the professionals be the judge of that,' Eliot firmly said. 'But first we need to get you dry and warm.'

It had almost stopped raining and the thunder had headed north by the time Doctor Clarke arrived and Eliot and I found ourselves alone in the kitchen. He had helped Grandad out of his wet clothes while I had found dry ones and towels, filled hot water bottles and made tea.

We had barely talked throughout the unfolding drama and it was only as my heart rate started to settle that I remembered the watch in my bag which I'd abandoned on the chair. The thought of it caused another palpitation. There were so many things I wanted to say and sort out, but for now they would have to wait.

'Will they be all right, do you think?' I asked, nodding to Eliot's mud streaked leathers which hung limply over the door.

'They'll need a bit of TLC,' he said. 'But I think they'll be okay.'

'Let's hope the doctor says the same about Grandad.' I choked, my vision misting again. 'I really wasn't gone long you know, and it was an important trip. I wouldn't have gone at all if I'd known something like this was going to happen.'

'Of course, you wouldn't,' Eliot kindly said, which made me feel all the worse.

Given that I had previously snapped at him when he suggested that Grandad had taken on too much, he could have used what had happened to prove his point, but that wasn't in Eliot's nature. He was kindness personified, not that Anthony would have let me believe it.

'No damage done,' announced Doctor Clarke as she strode back into the kitchen and made both me and Eliot wilt with relief. 'He's had a bit of a knock, but he'll be okay.'

'Are you absolutely sure?' I couldn't stop myself from asking.

'If I had even the slightest concern, I'd be whipping him straight back into hospital, whether he objected or not,' she told me. We all knew he would refuse. 'Thankfully, all he really needs is a warm bath, his own bed and some time to rest.'

'We can provide all of that,' said Eliot.

'In abundance,' I added.

'Good,' she said. 'He's just been filling me on a few things. What a tempestuous few months you and that man have lived through, Fliss. Here's hoping for calmer times ahead.'

Right on cue, the sun broke through the clouds and the resident robin began to sing.

'That would be most welcome,' I told her.

She nodded and smiled. 'I'll see myself out,' she said, briefly laying her hand on my arm as she passed by.

With the doctor's words ringing in my ears, I knew the last thing Grandad needed was the stress of me telling him that I had discovered he'd sold the watch and why, and that I'd got it back again. That was one conversation that would have to wait.

One thing I did want to do however, was return the treasured timepiece to its rightful spot in the jewellery box. Grandad wouldn't go looking for it because he wasn't expecting it to be there and I would feel better knowing it was where it was supposed to be.

A little later, when I was certain Grandad was asleep, I left Eliot brushing down his drying leathers, then crept upstairs and into the bedroom.

'What are you doing?' came Grandad's sleepy voice in response to the dresser drawer squealing like a stuck pig as I pulled it open.

In an instant, Eliot's feet were on the stairs and my clandestine quest had flown out the window.

'What's wrong?' he frowned. 'I thought you were asleep, Bill. Are you in pain?'

'No,' Grandad said, pulling himself further up the bed. 'The noise came from the dresser drawer, not me. What are you up to, Fliss?'

'Nothing,' I lied, as my neck and face flushed red. 'I didn't mean to disturb you. I'm sorry. Go back to sleep.'

He snuggled back down and I walked to the door to find Eliot blocking my way.

'What were you doing?' he whispered, looking down at me.

'Let's go downstairs,' I whispered back, as Grandad turned over in the bed, 'and I'll tell you.'

I supposed there would be no harm in filling him in on what I'd discovered before I told Grandad, although I might have to censor some of the details, such as Anthony's slanderous story about him. No good would come from repeating any of that.

'Fliss,' Grandad then gasped, halting me in my tracks. 'Where did you get that?'

Putting my hand behind my back had kept the watch out of sight from Eliot but had given Grandad, who had turned over in the bed again, the perfect view.

'Where did you get that watch?' came his voice again as Eliot frowned in confusion.

With a deep breath and a heavy heart, I turned back into the room, sat on the bed and carefully laid the watch on the eiderdown.

'That's your watch isn't it, Bill?' Eliot frowned. 'What are you doing with it, Fliss?'

I took a moment before answering. I might not have wanted to burden Grandad with what I'd found out so soon, but with the much-loved evidence now arranged on the eiderdown, I didn't have much choice.

'I got it from someone's wrist,' I said, answering Grandad's question first, 'and I was trying to put it back in the jewellery box,' I added, addressing Eliot's.

'But who was wearing it?' asked Eliot, sounding more confused than ever.

'Do you want to explain it all, Grandad? Or shall I?'

He looked pale as he leant back against the pillows with a weary sigh and as frustrated as I was that he'd never told me what was going on between him and Anthony, my heart went out to him. It didn't enter my head at that point that he didn't know it was Anthony who had ended up with the watch.

'As you've obviously worked it all out, you can,' he said. 'I haven't got the energy.'

As succinctly as I could, I ran through what had occurred between Anthony and Grandad prior to my arrival at Fenview Farm, along with the details of what had developed since.

'Was this why you initially objected to the supper club idea, Bill?' said Eliot. 'Because Judd had you over a barrel about the barn?'

'Yes,' he wearily said. 'I thought I was too far in to back out and then Anthony mentioned money and I thought I could pay him off. I thought that if I could raise enough to cover what he'd spent on the fees and plans he kept on about, then you'd never need know what I'd done, Fliss. I didn't want anything to ruin your arrival and settling in.'

'I hate that you've been carrying it all and not said a word,' I said, shaking my head. 'You should have told me and we could have found a way out of it together. You know me well enough . . .'

My words trailed off as I realised, he didn't really know me all that well at all. We'd only been aware of each other's existence for a few weeks and in that time, he'd been grieving the loss of his daughter and I was adapting to life without my mum. Doctor Clarke had been right, we'd both had a tempestuous time recently so it was little wonder things hadn't gone completely smoothly.

'Well,' I carried on, 'there's no real harm done. The watch is back where it belongs, Anthony's not getting his hands on the barn and that horrible Mr Pagett won't be bothering us again because he was only here at Anthony's bidding.'

'But I still haven't paid him,' Grandad said. 'I still haven't given Anthony his money.'

'What money?' I shrugged. 'You don't owe him anything. You'd signed nothing and it was his choice to push ahead, not that I really think he has shelled out as much as he's tried to make out and besides, I've told him I'll go to the police if he makes a fuss and report him for blackmail. Your agreement wasn't legally binding, Grandad. There's nothing you need to give him. Not even the time of day.'

'Are you sure?'

'One hundred per cent,' I confirmed. 'And our little show-down happened in the packed pub, so I don't think he'll be showing his face around town again for a while. Jim got the gist of it all, so Anthony's reputation is going to be more than tarnished, even without getting the police involved. But at least I got the watch off him before Jim threw him out.'

It was only then I remembered that wasn't the only thing The Mermaid landlord had overheard. Should I perhaps mention that Anthony had been bad-mouthing Eliot before he heard talk of it in town?

'Hang on,' Eliot then said. 'Are you telling me that it was Anthony who was wearing the watch?'

'Oh yes,' I said, 'that's the best part. He spotted it in the jewellers in town and paid a fortune for it.'

'So, now he's out of pocket for getting ahead of himself over the barn sale *and* he hasn't got the watch he paid thousands for?'

'Yep,' I grinned.

Given the mischief he'd caused, I didn't think he deserved anything less.

'Crikey,' said Eliot, 'he's not having a very good day, is he?'

'No,' I said, reaching across the bed and handing Grandad the watch. 'But we are and you've got a nice little nest egg out of his deception, Grandad.'

'I can't believe,' he sighed, wrapping the watch around his wrist, 'that out of all the men around here, you went out with him, Fliss.'

'Me neither,' tutted Eliot.

'Well,' I said, throwing caution to the wind, 'had we not been trying to hide our feelings for one another, Eliot, then I might not have done.'

'What's this?' Grandad asked.

Eliot looked at me and grinned.

'I've been trying to hide it, Bill,' he laughed. 'But the truth is, I'm in love with your granddaughter.'

'I see,' chuckled Grandad. 'And by the look on her face, I reckon she might be in love with you too, my boy!'

Chapter 28

Six weeks later

The weeks that followed were filled with halcyon days. There were no more storms – meteorological or otherwise – and the harvest was, according to Grandad's farm records, set to be one of the best ever. There was a constant supply of strawberries, red and blackcurrants, gooseberries, raspberries and, most longed for of all, cherries.

The fabulous Fenview Farm crops kept the café, market stall and Jake well supplied, as well as the farm kitchen and, with life finally settled, we had gone all out planning a wonderful summer party to celebrate everything Mum's final words had gifted us.

With my laptop set up on the kitchen worktop, I'd finally baked my first cherry and almond tart, using Fenview cherries of course, and with Nonna watching in the background and offering occasional words of advice and encouragement. We'd said *ciao* after it was safely in the oven and as the room filled with the delicious scent, I knew I'd carried out her instructions with aplomb.

My mouth watered for that first exquisite mouthful as I took it out of the oven, but I was going to resist tasting it until the timing was just right.

'Everything all set?' Eliot asked, as he wandered into the kitchen the day of the party and slid his hands around my waist.

'I think so,' I said, twisting around to face him. 'I've pretty much made double of everything, just to be on the safe side.'

He kissed me deeply and for the longest time, making my temperature soar even higher than the stuffy kitchen had managed, and my pulse raced to match it.

I had eventually told him what Anthony had said about him and just as I knew he would, he shrugged it off. Had I been in his shoes, I would have wanted to bop Anthony on the nose, but that wasn't Eliot's style. Also, as I had predicted, no one had seen Anthony since our showdown in the pub and that was also fine by me. Life at Fenview Farm was all the sweeter without him popping up in it.

'I'm not sure the man from the council would approve of these shenanigans in a food preparation area,' I sighed, when we finally broke apart.

'Just as well this is an invitation-only party then, isn't it?' Eliot beamed, pulling me back in for another lingering kiss.

'Yes,' I smiled back. 'And he's definitely not invited.'

Practically everyone else was though and that was why I'd

spent so long in the kitchen throughout what had been the hottest week of the year.

'Sorry to interrupt all your hard work in here,' Grandad laughed, as he caught us mid kiss, 'but I don't suppose there's any chance of a cup of tea?'

'Of course, there is,' I told him. 'I'll cover this last batch of muffins and then I'll get the kettle on.'

I swatted Eliot away and sent him off to deliver the day's harvest. He was using his belated summer holiday to help me and Bec – who was spending hours on FaceTime to Marco – on the farm, which was wonderful because it meant we got to spend every day together. Neither Bec nor Louise had been at all surprised when Eliot and I made our feelings official. Bec reckoned she'd long since worked out that Anthony was just a distraction, but she hadn't deciphered what he'd been up to.

Eliot arrived back from delivering the fruit at the same time his sister arrived with Louise bringing yet more decorations for the barn. Rather than set up just a small corner of it again, Grandad had insisted that we filled the whole space.

It had been another cost-effective makeover but every bit as pretty as the last one and I was very much looking forward to welcoming more people to the farm to see it. Combined with the dishes I had spent so long preparing, the superb setting was hopefully going to guarantee yet another truly memorable evening.

'I'm not sure you should be driving in that state, Bec,' Eliot worriedly said as they walked into the kitchen.

'What's up?' I asked. 'What state?'

'Nothing,' Bec dreamily said. 'I'm fine.'

She did look a bit wistful. Definitely vaguer than usual.

'She's just got off the phone from Marco,' said Louise, rolling her eyes. 'Again.'

It had taken me a little while to get over the part Louise had played in selling Grandad's watch, but because Grandad hadn't realised he wasn't legally bound to the deal with Anthony, he'd unwittingly led Louise to believe that he really had no choice, so I could understand why she'd gone along with it. I still wished she'd said something to me, but the ear bashing she'd got from Eliot stopped me from holding a grudge.

'So,' I said to Bec. 'Have you booked your flight yet?'

I'd thought she and Marco would be a good match, but the depth of their attachment had taken us all by surprise. My departure from Puglia, and the job vacancy I'd left behind, had really made Marco grow up fast and he was as genuinely taken with Bec as she was besotted with him.

'I have,' she sighed. 'This time next week I'll be painting in Puglia.'

'More like getting passionate in Puglia,' Grandad put in as he joined us and we all laughed.

'As long as there's no life drawing, sis,' Eliot teased.

'Oh, I don't know,' I winked at Bec. 'Marco would make a wonderful subject.'

'Hey,' Eliot pouted. 'That's enough of that.'

'Don't worry, big brother,' Bec batted straight back at him. 'Fliss only has eyes for you.'

'I should think so too,' he said, holding my hand and kissing the back of it.

'Were the Cherry Tree team looking forward to tonight?' Grandad asked him.

'*Everyone's* looking forward to tonight,' he said, shaking his head. 'How many people have you invited, Bill?'

'The whole town, I reckon,' Grandad chuckled. 'The list just seems to keep growing!'

'It's going to be great promo for the supper club,' I said. 'I just hope I've made enough of everything.' I looked nervously at the table and worktops which were groaning under the weight of all the fruity treats and desserts.

'There's going to be more than enough,' Eliot reassured me.

'We'd best get the car unloaded,' said Bec, taking Louise with her.

'And I'm going to quickly check my emails,' said Grandad. 'Marta was going to write today.'

Alone again, Eliot kissed me softly on the lips and I felt goose bumps prickle my skin, in spite of the still hot temperature. I responded by gently dipping my tongue into his mouth which made us both even warmer, and I wondered how we'd managed to keep our feelings for each other under wraps for so long.

By early evening, the finishing touches were complete and the barn was totally transformed. All that was left for me to do was fuss over the food and then get myself ready to welcome our guests.

'You're looking very dapper,' I said to Grandad who I noticed was wearing a new shirt. 'And is that . . .'

'Yes,' he said, pulling his sleeve further back, 'it is. I thought it deserved a decent airing considering everything it's been through these last few weeks.'

'It suits you,' I told him.

The Rolex watch sat well on his wrist and it was wonderful to see him wearing it.

'And you're looking very pretty too,' he smiled. 'That dress was quite a find.'

Yet again, Bella had come up trumps, this time with a simple fifties inspired sundress. The denim blue cotton chambray had a strawberry motif stamped on it and I had been so thrilled to find it, that I had invited her and Princess along to the party. I wasn't sure how the cat was going to react to having her space invaded by a posh pooch, but we'd soon find out.

'Thank you,' I said, giving Grandad a twirl. 'I'm really pleased with it and I think you'll like the lady who sold it to me. She's very much looking forward to meeting you.'

'In that case,' said Grandad, 'we better get down to the barn so we're ready to welcome everyone, hadn't we?'

It was thankfully much cooler than it had been during the day and we weren't waiting many minutes before the first guests arrived, although they weren't guests at all.

'You look divine,' said Eliot, slipping his hand into mine as Bec and Louise admired Grandad's new shirt. 'That colour really suits you.'

He kissed me lightly on the collarbone, making my tummy tingle.

'Thank you,' I swallowed. 'And I have to say, it's a pleasure to see your legs again.'

'Well,' he said, with a cheeky smile, 'it was really too warm for leathers tonight.'

With more cars arriving there was no time to get hot and flustered by thoughts of Eliot's legs encased in his bike leathers. I kissed him quickly and went to greet everyone while he turned on the twinkling fairy lights and Bec and Louise poured the drinks.

As well as Bella and the Cherry Tree and Skylark Farm contingent, there were also many of Grandad's farming neighbours, the owner of Brambles, another couple who ran a glamping site and a whole gang from the local grand country house, which was called Wynthorpe Hall. I had thought I'd been doing well getting to know everyone during the last few weeks, but apparently my small circle of new friends was about to be rapidly expanded.

With the party in full swing, I slipped unseen back to the house and uncovered the precious cherry and almond tart I had kept out of sight. I was determined that this particular sweet treat was going to be just for me. Well, the first slice had my name on it anyway.

The tart looked perfect and the smell of it sent my heart straight back to Nonna's kitchen, but how was it going to taste? With a not quite steady hand, I cut myself a generous slice and carried it down to the orchard, along with Mum's letter.

I sat under a tree, not all that dissimilar to the one in Puglia and took my first bite of the tart. It was perfect. The sweet combination of cherry and almond danced on my taste-buds and as I ate another forkful and then carefully took Mum's letter out of its envelope, I felt two tears roll down my cheeks. I did nothing to stem them or those that soon followed as I read the words she had written not all that long ago.

I think you might be a better fit for the family farm than I was too. I think your roots should be there, Fliss, buried in the British Fenland soil, not planted here in Italy where I put them.

I know I'm not in a position to make demands, but I think you should go to the farm and see it for yourself. It's called Fenview, and it's near a town called Wynbridge. Go and find it before you finally settle on your place in the world.

'Well, I did it, Mum,' I whispered, holding my fork aloft. 'I found the farm and you were right; I do fit here. As much as I love Puglia, my roots really do belong in the Fenland soil.'

I took a moment to let my tears dry and had almost finished savouring the last mouthful of Nonna's taste of home, when I heard someone approaching.

'Fliss!' Eliot called out, in much the same way that Marco had that night in Puglia.

'I'm here!' I called back, watching as the light from his phone sought me out.

'Are you all right?' he asked, pulling me to my feet.

'Yes,' I nodded, slipping Mum's envelope back into my dress pocket. 'I'm more than all right.'

I wrapped my arms around him and laid my head against his chest.

'Everyone's waiting for you,' he told me after a minute had passed. 'Bill wants you to say a few words about the farm and your plans for the supper club. Is that okay?'

'Yes,' I said, turning to kiss him. 'I had a feeling he might.'

'Come on then,' he smiled, kissing me again, before picking up the plate and fork and guiding me back through the orchard.

A warm pool of light spilled from the barn into the yard and as we stepped inside, everyone turned to look at us. Eliot gave my hand a squeeze before releasing it and my eyes came to rest on Grandad, Bec and Louise who were all standing together next to the table laden with fruit picked from the farm.

I felt a ripple of warmth flow through me, which had nothing to do with the balmy evening, and a satisfying contentment came to settle deep inside my heart. Mum had been right to tell me about Fenview Farm, but coming here hadn't been solely about finding family. Here in the Fenland countryside I had fallen in love and made friends for life and I was very much looking forward to embracing a future which combined them all.

Acknowledgements

Thank you so much for joining me on this summer trip to Wynbridge. I very much hope you have enjoyed getting to know Fliss, Bill and Eliot. Having not been to Wynbridge in the sunshine for such a long time, I was thrilled to return and loved picking strawberries in the Fenland countryside, which is how I spent many of my own school holidays.

As always, I have so many wonderful people to thank for helping me put this book together. 2020 was not the easiest year in which to be either creative or productive, so knowing I had these fabulous folk behind me made all the difference when it came to sitting down to write.

Thank you to my wonderful agent, Amanda Preston. Your kindness and words of encouragement have kept me on track and smiling.

Thank you Clare Hey, Judith Long, Harriett Collins, Sara-Jade Virtue, Pip Watkins and every other member of the Books and The City team who has supported me throughout both this write and many others.

Huge and heartfelt thanks to my author chums – Jenni Keer, Clare Marchant, Rosie Hendry, Ian Wilfred and Laura Bambrey – to name a few, for always being there with kind words, solid advice and virtual hugs.

Massive thanks as always to the innumerable book bloggers who work so tirelessly on all social media platforms to share the love for my books. Your wonderful reviews, images and blog posts are always appreciated as is the incredible amount of time you put into perfecting your posts and sharing them.

A huge hug to all the fabulous Swainettes out there, who have become firm friends as well as readers. Here's hoping that very soon we'll all be able to meet in person to celebrate all things bookish!

Thank you to everyone working in our wonderful libraries. You have faced the challenges of the last year and enabled books, in all formats, to provide an essential refuge and escape from the trials and tribulations we are enduring.

I would also like to thank Fiona Jenkins and Sue Baker who have set up and now run the Heidi Swain Facebook Book Club. The club has gone from strength to strength throughout the last few months and, as well as being a place to talk books, it is also somewhere to find friendship, companionship and above all, lots of love. I know it is cherished by every member and we all appreciate the effort put into running it.

And last, but by no means least, thank you! Thank you, dear reader, for picking up this book and giving me the opportunity to carry on doing the job I love so much. All that remains for me to say is that I wish you all a wonderful summer and may your bookshelves – be they virtual or real – always be filled with fabulous fiction.

With love,
H x

If you're looking for festive fiction, then be sure to read Heidi Swain's previous novel . . .

The Winter Garden

Freya Fuller is living her dream, working as a live-in gardener on a beautiful Suffolk estate. But when the owner dies, Freya finds herself forced out of her job and her home with nowhere to go. However, with luck on her side, she's soon moving to Nightingale Square and helping to create a beautiful winter garden that will be open to the public in time for Christmas.

There's a warm welcome from all in Nightingale Square, except from local artist Finn. No matter how hard the pair try, they just can't get along, and working together to bring the winter garden to life quickly becomes a struggle for them both.

Will Freya and Finn be able to put their differences aside in time for Christmas? Or will the arrival of a face from Freya's past send them all spiralling?

AVAILABLE IN PAPERBACK AND EBOOK NOW